BOUND TO THE FAE KING

MEGAN VAN DYKE

Published by Megan Van Dyke

www.authormeganvandyke.com

Editing: Jeni Chappelle of Jeni Chappelle Editorial

Cover and Interior Design: Megan Van Dyke

All images licensed appropriately.

Print Edition ISBN: 978-1-955532-20-4

Digital Edition ISBN: 978-1-955532-19-8

Author's Note

Bound to the Fae King is an fae fantasy romance aimed at adults, and contains material that some readers may find distressing or objectionable including: violence and blood, adult language, drinking, consensual sex, tornado damage and loss, armed robbery, death of a parent (off page/remembered), and parental abandonment (off page/remembered).

To my grandmothers.
Two strong and incredible women who've been an inspiration
throughout my life.

CHAPTER 1

M Y DAYS FOLLOW A steady rhythm: take care of Gran, work at the bar, sleep, repeat. It's fine. Mostly. At least it keeps me from dwelling on the fact that I've never been far from the small town I grew up in and my dreams of travel are on a semi-permanent backburner.

Gran's soft chuckle slips down the hall, barely audible over the background audience laughter from the show she's watching, *The Golden Girls*. I mouth Sophia's next lines and finish tying my hair back in a ponytail. It's Gran's favorite and, if I'm telling the truth, mine too. We've seen every episode so many times now that I know half of them by heart.

Light from the television—the only halfway new thing in our entire house—illuminates the living room. It wouldn't have to if she'd just open the curtains, but she can't stand the glare when watching her shows. Gran turns my way, a pleasant smile pulling at the wrinkles around her mouth. Her glasses, which she really should be wearing, sit atop her white perm, and she wrings a mug of hot tea between her hands.

"I'll be home late," I say, grabbing my purse—an old midlist designer tote I snagged on a deep discount—from its home on the dining table. "Closing tonight."

"That late already?" She deposits the tea on the side table and starts to rise.

I wave her off. "Sit. Sit. I'm almost out the door. You have meatloaf in the fridge, just need to microwave it."

She settles back into her navy-blue recliner with a deep sigh. It's a sound I'm all too familiar with. That mild disappointment she wants me to ask about. And darn if I can't help but fall for it every time. I shove my feet into my cowboy boots, savoring how my soles sink against the padded supports. When you're on your feet as much as I am, comfort is a must. But looking cute means better tips, and these beauties always snag me a few extra bucks.

The TV has Gran's full attention as I shuffle back across the thick carpet to her recliner. Her hands fold and unfold in her lap. She doesn't laugh at Sophia's joke—one of the better ones in this episode. My brows wrinkle as I place a kiss atop her head, savoring a hint of her knockoff Chanel perfume. It's our routine. Easy as breathing.

"Love you," I whisper. That, though...that's different. Oh, I say it every time but usually silently. Otherwise, Gran will cluck her tongue and swat me away.

But I do. I love her more than anyone.

After all, she raised me once my parents died years ago, and now I do the best I can to care for her as she did me.

The playful swat I expect doesn't come. Instead, she's still staring toward the screen. Her hands are the only thing moving.

My stomach drops. "What is it?" Another second passes, and I can't stand the silence. "There's one of those baked chickens from the grocery in there too." I was totally saving that for lunch tomorrow, but... "You could heat it up or—"

She beams up at me. "Meatloaf is fine, dear. I was just...just hoping to talk to you is all."

"Okay, now you're worrying me." My hand finds a home on my hip as I force a smile, trying to hide the fear from my face. We talk all the time. We live together, for crying out loud. And no way did she forget I had work tonight.

The old chair creaks as she shifts her thin frame.

"Well..." She clears her throat. "I've been thinking, and then I ran into Ms. Martingale the other day. She said that applications open up at State soon and—"

Tension flees my shoulders. I barely hold in my sigh as the rest of what Gran has to say slips in one ear and right out the other. Another summer, another lecture about trying to enroll in college. Should have figured. It might be nice—someday. But State's too far away from our podunk little town to commute, and living near campus would mean leaving Gran. Not an option. No way. No matter what she says, Gran's too old and frail to be on her own. I'd never forgive myself if she got hurt because I wasn't here to care for her.

"Thanks, Gran. I'll think about it. Really," I say, the first chance I get to jump into the conversation. And I will. Not that it'll change my mind. "I'm off tomorrow, so let's talk more about it then?"

"Sure. All right, dear." The stiffness I hadn't noticed till now slips from her shoulders as she relaxes back into the chair with a smile. "Any those boys get too flirtatious, and they're gonna have to answer to me."

I barely stifle a laugh. Most of our regulars this time of year are over fifty and know better than to try their luck with me.

The chair rocks subtly back and forth as she reclaims her mug and focuses back on the TV. This time, she's actually watching her show.

The crowd at Jolene's is light for a Saturday. A few locals—mostly men—occupy the barstools. A few families dot the tables in the dining area. The pool tables stand racked and vacant, waiting for someone to hustle a game. It won't be this way in a few weeks, not once college football starts up again. Then I'll be praying for nights like this where I'm not asleep on my feet at the end of my shift.

"Wren," Derrick nods my way as I take my place behind the bar. He's short on words—probably why he hired me to tend the bar—but he runs a solid business. He's fair, pays well, and treats his employees kindly. I couldn't ask for more, really. "I'll leave these gentlemen to you."

"Thanks, Derrick." I flash him a smile as he wanders off toward the dining area, probably to help Molly.

The tray she's carrying across the room looks heavier than her. Families flood in around dinner time for our staple food offering, a traditional southern meat and three. The sides are always the same, but the main course rotates throughout the week. But in another hour, they'll dwindle out, and it'll be just the small crowd at the bar with Derrick and me left to tend them until closing time.

"So," I say as I scan the line of half-full drinks sitting in front of patrons along the counter. "What are we having tonight? The usual?"

Smiles and nods greet me before the men focus their attention back on the news where it plays on the TV above my head. The *boys* Gran worried about would be more likely to score with her than with me. Not a one of them under sixty today. They've been regulars all three years that I've tended bar here, and honestly, their good-natured compliments make a bad day brighter some-times. It helps that they don't get their feathers ruffled when I return their volleys with little jabs of my own. It's one of the reasons I love this job. Friendly faces make any day easier.

"Looks like they found them kids," Mr. Murdock says, pointing at the screen with a weathered hand.

"Oh?" I look over my shoulder just enough to see a new reporter talking about something, but the speakers are playing country music instead of the broadcast, and Derrick left a sink full of dishes that need my attention more than some news story.

"Thank goodness." He sips his pale ale. "Don't like when kids go missing."

A hard knot settles in my chest. "Me neither."

Mr. Murdock adjusts his jean jacket, one he rarely wears, and I catch a flash of his biker patch. I fumble the glass in my hand, nearly dropping it to the floor. I'd almost forgotten he was in the same motorcycle club as my parents...before that terrible tornado outbreak that took them away.

"Nice catch," he says.

"Don't tell anyone." I add a wink to my grin. I've gotten good it, grinning through the pain. It's been years, but sometimes it just loves to sneak up and bite me like a dang mosquito.

"You know," he says. "One of them girls was almost your age."

"Oh?"

"Earlier twenties or something?" He shrugs. "Guess I should stop calling 'em kids," he says with a chuckle.

Beyond him, the way-too-heavy old door groans open. My cousin Tabitha fills its frame. Her youngest is propped on one hip, and her massive bag hangs from the other shoulder. Her other three kids don't wait for her to enter before they slip around her and make a beeline for the small cluster of arcade machines in the far corner. Derrick installed them two years ago, the product of a late-night closing chat after one too many of the old timers complained about children screaming during their game. If you give them something to do while they wait on their food, you get a lot less fussin'.

"Wren!" She practically yells across the place, giving me a far too exuberant wave.

Always smiling and upbeat, that one. But I guess she has to be to wrangle all those kids all the time, especially with her husband always out of town traveling for one construction job or another. Though, his work schedule might be a good thing. As Gran once said, all he has to do is look at her to get her pregnant, and they've already got their hands full.

I return her wave as she hustles my way, no doubt here to pick up a take-out order. Just like I have my regular crew at the bar, we have regulars for take-out too. But for Tabitha, this is a treat. Jolene's prices are reasonable, but budgets only stretch so far.

"Order for Tabitha!" I call to the kitchen window.

"You will never guess what news I have," Tabitha gushes as she cozies up the bar, baby Abigail still propped on her hip.

I lean against my side, the glassware forgotten. It can wait. "Hit me with it."

"Matt is coming home on leave soon!"

"Really?" I bounce in my boots.

Her older brother has been deployed for months. We get letters and have the rare video call, but boy, will it be nice to see him again. Though, it'd be a lie to say I didn't envy him traveling the world, seeing new people, and new places. It's all I've wanted for so long. But he was the oldest, first out, and by the time I graduated high school, Tabitha was already pregnant with her first and still deep in depression after her dad vanished. She couldn't look after Gran, and I couldn't leave either of them. Travel could wait. They couldn't.

"Yes! And he's going to stay for a while. It'll be so nice to have his help with the kids." She bounces Abigail and leans in closer. "I was thinking about a little getaway with just the hubs, maybe a long weekend somewhere."

"You could always ask me, you know. I could take a few days."

Tabitha rolls her eyes. "You got your hands full, Wren. Ain' giving Gran a heart attack having y'all watch after these hoodlums. Paul!" She snaps at her oldest.

Whatever he did, I missed it, but she doesn't miss a thing. And she's right. I love her and the kids, but they're a wild bunch. I can't help offering though. It feels wrong not to. But every time she turns me down, there's an internal sigh of relief I can't deny. Of course, the kids are the same reason I can't ask for her help with Gran. She's got her hands full too.

"I know he can't wait to see you and Gran too," Tabitha says, sliding back to our conversation as if she hadn't just chewed her oldest out across the room.

"Your mom's gotta be pleased too."

"Well..." She glances away, over to where her kids smash the Pac-Man buttons. "You know Mom."

"Yeah." I give a weak, forced smile, the mirror of hers.

Aunt Virginia's exploits would put Blanche Devereaux to shame. She's slept with at least half the town, single and married, and many of those were before her husband, Uncle Mark, up and left seven years ago. Rumor around town is that he got fed up with her and hung himself, but that's not true, at least not as much as we know. He just left. Never came back. I keep waiting for the day when Aunt Virginia will finally wake up and stop living for someone other than herself. Tabitha and I both do. Gran is Uncle Mark's mom, not hers, so I can almost reason why she never helps us out, but she could at least spend time with her grandkids once in a while.

"Order up!" The call from the kitchen breaks the awkward silence that descended over the mention of Aunt Virginia. I should have known better than to bring her up, but if anyone could get that woman together, it'd be her son.

"So." I slide over to the register. "Let's see, three meat and threes?"

"Of course." Tabitha fishes in her bag and hands over a bent credit card. "You know how the kids just love that fried chicken and mac and cheese. Mmm mmm."

I stifle a giggle and run the card. Leave it to my family to order mac and cheese as a vegetable. The stuff is darn good though.

Tabitha leaves with her kids as quickly as she came. The rest of the night goes smoothly. No complaints. No over-served customers who need a ride. When Derrick says he has to leave early to help his wife Jolene, who he named the bar after, I don't blink an eye. Apparently, a fox got in the chicken coop again, and she's distraught. I've closed down the bar a hundred times. Count the cash. Close out the register. Wipe everything down. Easy peasy. Half of it's done by the time Mr. Murdock finishes his last beer and shuffles off to his car mumbling something about the Saints upcoming season.

I've just locked up the safe in the office when the familiar whiny creak of the backdoor echoes down the hall. With the kitchen closed down and the country music off, I could hear a mouse squeak. Thankfully, we haven't had any of those this year.

"Derrick?" I call.

He must have forgotten something. Or he got his wife settled and came back to make sure I didn't forget a step. I dust my hands off on my shorts. It might be 2 a.m., but my mind is still sharp as a razor. Mostly. Well, it would be if I didn't agree to that shot with that younger guy who'd come in. It'd been a while since I'd seen a new, cute face around here, and I couldn't help myself.

When no one answers, I round the corner out of the office.

"Derrick—" The question breaks off into a gasp.

My legs freeze. A scream lodges in my throat. All the world narrows down to the two masked men standing in the hall, guns pointed in my direction.

CHAPTER 2

"**D**ON'T SCREAM." THE SLIGHTLY shorter one says in a whiskey voice thick with a southern drawl.

The bigger man, and I do mean bigger in every sense of the word, closes in next to him, filling the hallway. "Don' even think ta' run."

I swallow the silent scream aching to break free, but it won't budge. Air grows thin. Spots fill my vision, and for one horrible moment, I think I might faint. My fingers brush the wall as I sway on my feet.

"Don't ya dare." The big guy steps closer, leveling his gun at my face.

Something about the overhead bulb's shine on the gun metal douses me in ice water. Every bit of me is alert and heightened all at once. My heart pounds in my ears. The scent of Clorox I could have missed moments ago is so strong I might as well have bathed in it.

"Open the safe. Now." The shorter man gestures with his gun to the room to my right—our little back-office.

With mechanical movements, I manage to enter the room. My purse occupies a corner of the desk, but there's no way I can grab it without them noticing, much less get to my phone. There's an old baseball bat behind the door. Old Woody has settled many a fight without being swung, but it'd be a gamble to get it—more likely get me shot instead.

The men fill the space, literally and figuratively. Sweat beads on my neck, despite the air conditioning still pumping through the vents. The shorter guy's hands shake a little around the gun. He doesn't want to use it. Not really.

Give them the cash, and they'll go. Derrick's words from long ago echo in my head. *You're more important than a few hundred bucks.*

Never thought I'd have to use that bit of advice.

"The safe, Daisy Duke." Big Guy shoves me toward the black box occupying the corner.

A flash of indignance heats my cheeks as I kneel and pound in the code to the keypad. Daisy Duke... The nerve. I may have her blond hair, but my shorts are *not* that short.

"Told ya she wouldn't be a problem." The shorter man's words hit me like a jolt of lightning.

That voice. I've heard it tonight already.

It was the same one coercing me into that shot of Jose Cuervo.

My body shakes as I swing the safe door wide and back up. The big guy nearly knocks me down as he swoops in with a bag I hadn't even noticed before and starts filling it with cash. There's not much, even for a Saturday.

While he works, I risk a glance at the other man. Around his mask, I can just make out the stubble near his lips. The soft, brown hair checks out.

I checked his ID. What was his name?

As I file through my memories, our eyes catch, and he knows. He sees the knowledge I can't hide. I'm not the dumb, tipsy bartender he thought I was. The blond waves and cowboy boots might have fooled him earlier in the night, but not now, not when I desperately need them to.

The young man stiffens, all the softness I'd admired vanishing from him in a second. My stomach drops, and it's all I can do to keep my dinner of mac and cheese from coming back up.

"We got a problem." He glances at the other man.

And I've got a bigger one. He's been made. He won't be taking the cash and fleeing out the back door when I can give the cops his name.

"Yeah, we do," the guy at the safe says. "This ain' half so much as ya said."

The younger guy rolls his eyes at his companion, and I know it's my chance, my only one. They're focused on each other. My fist closes around the pot handle behind my back. I've been meaning to throw the rusty old thing away. For once, procrastination may pay.

"Not that, you idiot. She—" He flicks his gun my way, and I strike.

He roars as the rusty pot crashes into his wrist. The gun goes off—a sound louder than a cannon. I scream. They might too. It's hard to tell over the painful ringing in my ears, but that doesn't matter.

I bolt through the door, bounce off the wall, and sprint for the exit.

A strange truck is parked next to my Mazda. I race for her.

Yells reach me over the buzzing in my ears.

Shit. No keys. Adrenaline zips through my veins as my gaze darts around in the dark. *Have to run.*

The forest stretches out behind Jolene's, and I sprint for it. The back door crashes open. I zag right just past the dumpster, letting it be a last barricade between the men and me.

Another shot rings into the night. Sweet baby Jesus!

My heart skips a beat as I hunch in on myself, but the pain doesn't come. My boots kick up gravel until I reach the leaf-strewn forest floor. Tree limbs catch at my face and arms. My boots slip and my ankle twists painfully, but I keep going. Another shot strikes a tree, showering me with bits of bark.

Tears blur my vision, not that I can see a darn thing in the dark.

The heavy crunch of leaves and shouts chase me. Each breath burns my lungs. My ankle screams with each step, but I can't stop. They can't catch me. I can't die this way. Gran needs me.

Please, sweet Jesus, save me, take me away from here.

Rain pelts my face out of nowhere, one stinging drop after another.

Of course I'd die like a wet rat in the woods. It's pouring like someone broke a dam in heaven, even though it was dry as a bone moments ago.

I look back over one shoulder, but I can't see anything. I don't hear them anymore either, nothing but the rain beating in time with my thundering heart.

My boot slips. A scream breaks from my throat as I hurtle toward the ground. The impact knocks the air from my lungs. My teeth bang together. Something hard smashes into my arm as I roll down a slope.

Everything hurts. Everything is wet. Sobs rack my body. Tears mingle with the rain.

I try to push to my feet, but a bolt of white-hot pain sears my ankle, and I drop back into a wet heap on the forest floor. It's probably broken. I can't get up. Can't run. I—

"Evelyn."

My breath hitches, and I go utterly still.

A shadowed form steps between two trees. My heart lurches up my throat. They've found me. I close my eyes and give one last, silent prayer for mercy.

The rain stops. The scent of pine swarms my senses.

"Eve—"

My eyes snap open, and I forget to breathe. A man—he has to be male—looms just in front of me. Bright blue eyes seem to glow in the night. Distantly, part of me screams at the oddity. He shelters me from the rain with something dark I can't see.

I can't look away from his gaze. It's searing, searching, as if it can see into my very soul.

"You're here." His words are an awed, breathless whisper. Still, they hold all the intensity of an impassioned sermon. Whiskey over silk. Fire and ice.

Whiskey. Just like another voice I'd heard that night.

A shiver racks my form, reality crashing over me like the pounding rain.

"They're after me." I shove at his chest, urging him up, away. "I have to go. Now!"

"Who?" He grabs my arm, gentle but firm, helping me rise.

But I don't have time for gentle. "We have to—"

I put weight on my ankle and scream. A sob heaves from me as I lean heavily on the mystery man.

"Evelyn, you—"

"I'm not." That's not my name, not that it matters. "I can't walk. Help m—"

The words aren't even out before he scoops me into his arms, one arm under my knees, the other around my back. The tarp, poncho, or whatever he'd held over me retracts, only to come around me again. My breath hitches. It's not fabric.

Feathers brush my bare arm.

Wings. He has wings.

An angel? I really must be dying. I shove against his chest. He's hard as stone and just as immovable.

Panic swarms what's left of my senses. I can't die. I can't leave Gran. "Let me go. Please!"

"Shh," he croons, like I'm a wounded animal. To him, I might be.

"No. I can't die. Not yet." I thrash harder, but his grip tightens, holding me firm. "Please!"

"Die?" An eerie, blue glow emanates from his eyes. "They won't have you. Never again."

He hugs me further into his chest as if I weigh nothing at all. Sharp claws glint off his hand near my face. This is it. I can't help but watch my own doom. Everything is suddenly cold and hot at once.

Silent tears stream down my face. *Gran, I'm so sorry.*

The claws dig into his palm, drawing crimson that runs down his arm. Light swells from it, illuminating our little bubble.

My eyes widen. "What—"

He latches onto my wrist. I gasp at the contact, the heat and friction over the deep scrape that I hadn't noticed with all my other worries. My arms are smattered with mud and blood that must be mine.

The world around me swirls, and I'd swear I'm falling, despite him clutching me close.

The glow pulses. Heat rushes under my skin where we touch. It's too much. Something tingles up my arm, racing under my skin and raising gooseflesh in its wake.

"Please..." My plea is distant, like a dull echo.

"You're safe, my love."

My love? His words are far away. The world blurs. My skin isn't warm anymore. Nor cold. I'm not sure *I* am anymore.

"No one will take you from me now."

My eyes droop closed.

Gran...

Her smiling face looks back at me from the darkness before everything goes black.

Chapter 3

The sweetest dreams linger as I come to. In them, a man smelling of pine and citrus carried me through a starry night in his arms. We didn't walk; we flew. I can't see his face no matter how tightly I close my eyes and will myself to remember. He's just out of reach, a shadow in the corner of my eye that I can't quite make out. Shivers race across my skin. But I remember the gentle breeze, the lightness in my heart, and the lack of fear as he cradled me close, far above the forest floor.

I sigh, stretching my arms above my head. Every inch of me feels great—loose, limber, rested. When did my bed become so comfortable?

The light nearly blinds me as I crack open my eyes. I groan, squeezing my lids shut, and curl up on my side. I must have left the curtains open again. It's probably noon by now, but the urge to sink back down in the covers is far too strong.

I reach for my quilt to tug it over my head, and my fingers graze fur.

I suck in a breath and go utterly still. The night before crashes back over me, memories slamming into my chest with enough force that I gasp for air.

Closing up at Jolene's. The robbery.

My breaths come short and quick.

Gunfire. Running through the woods. Falling.

A stranger with wings.

My stomach clenches. I really must be dead. Otherwise, I'd be a mess of wet clothes, bruises, scrapes, and who knows what else.

My legs slide against sheets far too smooth and soft to be mine. I roll my ankle, waiting for pain that doesn't come. My clothes... Hesitantly, I touch my stomach, my hip. A nightgown, maybe? Underwear, similar to my style, but so soft I nearly sigh. At least heaven comes with clothes. I reach for the necklace around my neck, one that's rarely left it since my parents died over a decade ago. I find the little silver bird, a wren, just like my name. It was one of the last gifts they gave me before they died. Thank goodness it came with me to wherever this is.

I crack my eyes and take in the view as they adjust to the blinding light. Polished, gray stone walls greet me. A ball of light literally hovers on a sconce built into the wall. No wires. No bulb. No flickering flame. I suck in a deep breath.

Holy, sweet baby Jesus. I've never thought much about what the afterlife would look like, but it doesn't disappoint. An ornate wooden side table sits next to the bed, bedecked in crystal glasses. The ceiling, or lack thereof, catches my attention at the edge of my vision. No wonder it's so bright. A blue sky looms above. Spots of something mar what must be a clear glass roof many feet above.

"Wow." There's no other word for it.

"I'm glad you like it."

I scream and bolt upright in the bed.

A man lounges in a chair near the foot of the bed. Thin, white curtains float behind him, separating the room from a sweeping balcony beyond. Dark hair frames a strong face that somehow manages to be sharp and smooth all at once. His attire is a few shades darker than the walls, accented with silver and blue. Sinful lips quirk up in one corner as he lowers the glass of cut crystal he'd been sipping from. His grin grows as he swirls a splash of dark liquid—maybe whiskey—around in the glass.

If this is heaven, he might as well be a devil for the way he lounges as a dark spot in the bright room.

His sharp gaze dips to my chest. Heat floods my face as I grab at the heavy fur and pull it up to my neck. Pervert.

"Where am I?" This cannot be the afterlife. Unless I'm somewhere in between, being tempted by my vices: alcohol and seductive men. He's certainly that. I frown. The last time I admired pretty eyes, I nearly got shot. Or maybe I did.

"This is my home." He takes another slow, careful sip.

"Right, well, it's peachy, but who the heck are you?" Sitting under these heavy furs, I should be sweltering. The softest breeze ruffles the sheer curtains, making it all too obvious that one side of the room is wide open to the elements. But the air is light and crisp, lacking all the soup-like humidity that fills southern summers.

"Peachy?" He raises one brow.

My fingertips dig into the fur. "I'm dead, aren't I? Just rip the Band-Aid off and tell me."

"Dead? Certainly not. My master healer saw to your wounds herself."

Master healer. I mouth the words, my brows wrinkling. Like a doctor? A heavy weight settles into my stomach. I hit my head when I fell. That's it. I'm probably lying in the wet woods unconscious somewhere, and this is a dream. At some point, I'll wake up sore and miserable but alive and...normal.

A light thump sounds as he sets the glass on the table at his side—a white and willowy thing that doesn't look like it should be able to stand, much less hold anything. "You seem doubtful."

A small, humorless laugh bubbles from my lips. "I wonder why. Well," I start as I slide down into the sheets, "good night." I squeeze my eyes shut and curl up on my side. If I sleep in this dream, I can wake up, right?

Let me out, let me out, let me out.

The mattress dips behind me.

I twist around and gasp. He looms over me, one hand flat against the pillow near my head. I never heard him move. But his nearness isn't what causes my breath to catch in my throat. This close, the scents of pine and citrus tease my nose. Stunning blue eyes shine from his pale face.

"You're the man from the woods."

His slow smile nearly stops my heart. "You were terrified. Fleeing someone or something. I... I had to protect you." He looks away. "Keep you safe this time."

This time? My brows draw together.

Long fingers stretch toward me as if he might run their backs along my cheek. "You look so much like her, and yet—"

I flinch, and he pulls his hand away.

"Who?" I ask.

A flash of something, maybe pain, crosses his face. "Does it matter?"

"I..." It might, but the only thing I'm certain of right now is that he doesn't want to talk about it. "Thank you for saving me."

The words rush out. I'm still dubious. Seriously, what kind of bonkers house is this? But whether he did help me or not, the words might earn me some favor. Or help this dream wrap up sooner.

"Who were you running from?" His tone turns hard. I'd swear the temperature in the room drops as a sudden gust sends the curtains flapping out onto the balcony.

What can it hurt to tell him? I manage to sit up against the mountain of pillows, bringing the fur up with me. "Well, I was closing up at Jolene's. Derrick left early because of some debacle with his wife and the chickens." His brows rise, but I ignore him, focusing instead on the silver birds embroidered on the lapels of the jacket buttoned up to his neck. Weird fashion, but whatever. "Anyhow, I heard the door open and thought he came back to help me close, but it was two men in masks instead. They held me at gunpoint and forced me to open the safe."

"They threatened you?" he asks, as if that wasn't obvious from my story.

I purse my lips and dare a glance at his face. Mistake. My chest grows warm even as my mouth goes dry. "Yes. Pay attention." I stare out to the balcony instead. It's far less distracting. "I recognized one of the men, and he realized that too. Thankfully, he got distracted for a moment, so I hit him and ran."

"You fought back." Not a question this time, but the awe in his voice stirs up something way too visceral for a dream.

I clear my throat and continue. "Anyhow, I didn't have my car keys, so I ran toward the woods to get away. They shot at me, but I kept going." My lungs hurt just thinking about it. "It started to rain, and I fell. Then you..."

Hesitantly, I glance back at the man. He's leaned in, hanging on my every word.

My tongue is suddenly thick in my mouth, but I continue. "Well, you were there."

And had wings, I thought. But he surely doesn't now. It must have been something else. And the glow...

Well, who knows. I reach for my necklace and rub the smooth metal between my fingers. "Then I passed out."

"Humans." He taps a finger on his cheek, drawing my eye. "You were running from humans."

"Uh... Yeah?" Who else?

"And you chose to flee to Faery?"

"Yes, to—" I lurch up from the sheets. "Wait, no. Where?" My voice cracks at the end. I've had some pretty trippy dreams before, but fairy? That's a thing, a myth, not a place.

"Faery. You must have run straight through a door," he says, almost to himself. "But then how—"

"A door? No, I never saw a door." Honestly, I couldn't see much of anything in the dark, much less the rain, but surely I'd have noticed that.

This strange man inches closer, leaning over me. A lock of his dark hair slides down his face to reveal a pointed ear.

Pointed. Like freaking Spock but longer, more angular, like a...

"Fairy." My body goes numb. The fur slips away, and I can't even figure out how to pull it back.

Tingles race across my skin as he takes my hand in his. I'd swear the world spins as he raises it to his lips and places a kiss on the back. It's a more gentlemanly act than I've ever received, but the look in his eyes—all fire and mirth with a sheen of intoxication I know all too well—is anything but.

"Sigurd," he says. "King of Air."

A blink is all I can manage. A king?

Laughter shakes my chest. I choke on it, trying to hold it in, and fail. My head falls back on a fluffy pillow as hysterical laughter fills the room.

"So much like her and yet so different," he mutters as I try to rein in my emotions.

"Who?" I ask, wiping a tear of laughter from the corner of my eye.

Evelyn. The name reaches out from my memories. He'd called me Evelyn.

His fingers trail down my cheek. Holy moly. A shiver races across my skin. Laughter dries up into a plume of steam in my chest.

"You don't even know you're gifted." He edges closer on the bed, and my stomach clenches. "You must have wished to be here at just the right moment. I felt you come through. You were so close to me."

Gifted? He *felt* me? What the heck?

I can't look away from his all-consuming face as he continues, "It was just like that night so long ago."

The back of his hand caresses my skin. I should pull away. Something yells at me to, but if this is a dream—and it has to be, right—why not enjoy his attentions?

"Fate brought you to Faery. To me." His breath heats my face.

It's all I can do to keep breathing. "You're a dream."

The tip of a pink tongue slides across his lips. "Am I?"

Temptation wins, and I reach for his face in return. "Yes."

Electricity zips between us when my fingers graze his chin and the slight bit of dark stubble there. His eyes flutter closed. I can't help tracing his strong jaw up to the curve of his ear or letting his soft hair slide between my fingers.

"I mean no, I'm dreaming," I say. "This isn't real."

But the feelings churning within me feel anything but dream-like. No wet dream has ever been so intense, so real. And his face, his hair, his smell...

I gasp as his weight leans onto me, pushing me into the mattress. His other arm plants on the sheets, caging me in. When his eyes snap open, they gaze into mine, full of a longing desire that steals my breath.

"This isn't a dream," he says. "It's very real."

Not a...

He leans in, his lips aiming for mine.

Not a dream?

"Evelyn..." The name is a breathless whisper sliding over my skin.

The little bird on my necklace is suddenly heavy and cold. That's not my name. I'm Wren. I'm real, and this...

Holy sweet baby Jesus, this is real.

CHAPTER 4

I SHOVE AGAINST THE man's chest with all my might. "Get off!"

He leaps back as if burned.

Sigurd, he said his name is Sigurd. If he's real, I need to remember it.

"What—" Sigurd shakes his head, the sheen of lust and intoxication gone from his eyes.

I sit upright, pulling the furs around me. My body shakes. "You're real. This is real."

"I already told you that." He crosses his arms.

"Yeah, but..." The room takes on a whole new light. It's still beautiful and enchanting but real, very real. The air grows thin. My breaths come short and quick. "Fairies don't exist. I'm not this Evelyn you keep talking about."

"You don't even know what you are." He shakes his head, the hint of a smile on his lips. "Incredible."

My lips purse. "I'm Wren. Wren Dawson."

Something flashes across his face and is gone before I can process it. "Named for a bird."

He better not make fun of my name. Nope, nope, nope. "It's not—"

"Beautiful."

Oh, well... The heat flushing my face takes on a new form, and I can no longer meet his gaze. "I appreciate all you've done for me. Saving me. Healing me. Really, it's incredible. I'll find a way to pay you back," I ramble on, unable to glance at him for fear that the look on his face might convince me to linger. "But I really need to go home. My grandmother will be so worried. I have to get back to her and let her know I'm fine. Oh, and my boss, he's going to be so upset that—"

"No."

I snap my head toward him. All the tenderness on his face has vanished. "What do you mean, 'no'?"

"You can't leave."

Umm... "If you can bring me here, you can take me home, right?" Shoot, it must have been expensive to heal me or whatever. "I'll pay you back, I swear."

Gran has to be out of her mind that I didn't show up at home, not to mention the robbery. If she has a heart attack worrying about me when I've been sitting here flirting with this idiot, I'll never forgive myself. I slide from the bed, not caring that I'm in some silky nightgown that barely reaches halfway down my thighs. The cool floor tickles my feet as my cheeks flame. Oh, good Lord, did he undress me? Can't think about that. Doesn't matter.

Sigurd stalks toward the bed. Before I have time to process his actions, he grabs my arm, raising it before my face.

A pattern of navy wings circles my wrist in a strange tattoo. What the heck?

"You're bound to the Court of Air, Wren. To me."

The way he says my name has my heart stuttering.

A dull crash echoes from outside the room.

"Sigurd!" The furious female voice makes every inch of him go rigid.

Sigurd's hand tightens on my wrist, almost painfully, before dropping it like a soiled rag. His name still rings in the air as he turns and stalks toward the door.

"Stay here," he grates.

A lover? My stomach drops. If so, it'll be terrible if she finds me here. She'd think that we... And oh gosh, we almost...

I shake myself, but the tattoo draws my attention like a magnet. I've always wanted some ink, but Gran thought it was a terrible idea, so I caved to her wishes and avoided the tattoo parlor. This though... Ugh, I would never have picked this.

Another door looms on the other side of the bed. A closet? Somewhere to hide? I step toward it as another screech reaches my ears. "You nearly got the King of the Forest killed!"

Every part of me freezes. I glance back in disbelief. That was so not what I expected their fight to be about.

Sigurd responds, but I can't make out his words.

"Well, they're blaming you!" the woman yells back.

Public arguments at the bar aren't that uncommon. Get a little alcohol in people, and oh boy howdy, do you hear some *interesting* things. Affairs. Unpaid alimony. Family secrets. Squabbles over dating someone's sister. I've heard it all. Literally. Oh, I pretend not to eavesdrop. Every good bartender does. But some glasses get extra clean as I wash them over and over while listening to the juicy details. I've even been known to make drinks a little stronger to get some more details flowing. I just can't help it as I slink toward the door Sigurd vanished through.

"And you were where? Just flying around out there?" the woman asks, fury laden in her words.

Flying. I shiver. That's right. If this is real, if he's real, he had wings before. A fairy with wings, but ones like a bird, not the little glittering things in fairytales. I lean against the door, hoping to hear more, and it swings wide.

I screech. My footing slips. I brace to slam against the stone floor.

Strong arms catch me. Pine and citrus hug me like a firm pillow. Sigurd.

His name clamors over and over in my head as he helps me to stand. "I've got you," he whispers like I'm a wounded animal rather than a woman grappling with wild truths. "Are you all right?"

"Sigurd." The woman's voice holds a slight quaver. "Who is that?"

My stomach bottoms out. Great, just great. This is where I get yelled at for being a two-faced little floozy. It's a fight I've seen way too many times but thankfully never been the center of.

Sigurd steadies me on my feet and begins to turn me toward the mystery woman. His arm is firmly around my shoulders, clutching me like I might run at any moment.

And oh boy, I might.

She's anything but what I pictured. Tall and lean. The skintight shirt and pants duo she wears hugs her like a second skin, revealing sculpted limbs and abs a supermodel would die for. Her black hair is pulled back in a severe ponytail that highlights pale, pointed ears. The ponytail fades to crimson at the end, where it drapes down her chest. Obsidian dripped in blood. She gapes at me, her face almost ashen.

This woman could kick my butt in a heartbeat.

"Moria, this is—"

"This isn't what it looks like," I blurt, cutting him off. "I'm not... We're not"—I gesture between us—"a thing. I promise. I was hurt. He saved me. That's all. Nothing else. He's just about to take me home."

All at once, her shock vanishes. Moria, if that's her name, throws her head back, roaring with laughter. "You think I'm—"

She manages before doubling over.

Sigurd's hand flexes on my shoulder. I spare a glance out of the corner of my eye only to catch his stiff jaw and pinched look.

"Moria," he accentuates her name with pointed sharpness toward the woman, "is my cousin."

Cousin. Oh. Oh boy.

Moria slaps her leg. "Wow," she says, reining in her laughter. "I needed that." All trace of humor vanishes as quickly as it came. "For a moment there, I thought she was..." She trails off.

"Evelyn?" I supply.

Sigurd stiffens. Moria's attention snaps back to me. "You can't be—"

"No," Sigurd snaps before heaving a heavy sigh. "She is not. As I was saying, this is Wren."

It would be great if someone would actually tell me who Evelyn is. Someone I look like, obviously. Someone Sigurd desires. He made that much clear when he tried to kiss me. He wasn't that intoxicated—I couldn't even smell it on his breath. But dang, did he smell good all on his own.

"Interesting." She flicks her hair behind her. "And do you have something to do with why my cousin has basically started a war and then disappeared on me? For days!" She jabs an accusing finger at him.

"Moria..." he warned.

"Days?" I step away, pulling against his hold. "No? It's been days?" My voice cracks. My legs twitch, aching to run, to get home.

She sucks in a hissed breath. "You..."

Her wide-eyed stare shows more horror than when I fell into the room.

I pull my arms over my chest on instinct. Did I just flash her? I glance down at my chest. This nightgown isn't exactly full coverage, but frankly, it's less revealing than her tight clothes.

"You bound her!" She screeches like nails on a chalkboard, and I can't help but wince. "You bound a human?" She blinks at him before her lips thin into a hard line. "First, you pretty much start a war. Then you disappear. Now I find out you've been binding a human with that wretched spell. How did you even learn it? It's so... so..." She shivers. "I know you're your father's son, but I never believed—"

Sigurd snarls.

I gasp as a sharp gust of wind comes from nowhere and knocks her to the ground.

Holy crap on a cracker. I sway on my feet. He made that, from nowhere.

Moria twists before she's even finished her slide across the floor and leaps to her feet. Claws—yep, those are definitely claws—curl toward her palms before she swipes her arm back in our direction with a cry of her own.

Faster than I can blink, Sigurd leaps in front of me. Arms wrap around my back as he pulls me into his rock-hard chest. Everything is warm pine for the briefest second. I don't have time to move before the wind tears at me, trying to rip me apart like that horrible night my life changed. I scream, my nails digging into the fabric of his shirt as I hold on for dear life, memories slicing me up more than whatever she did ever could.

"Stop!" Sigurd's command carries through the room with volume and resonance far too loud for the man it came from. The wind dies in an instant, but I'm still shaking, the memory of the tornado pulling apart our house and my life with it, as fresh as the night it happened. He releases me to whirl on his cousin. "You dare..."

My legs wobble, and I lean against Sigurd's back out of desperation.

Silence hangs so heavy between them that I ache to break it, anything to knock me out of my grief.

"She doesn't even know she's gifted," Moria says. "Does she?"

Talking about me like I'm not even here. The nerve. It bugs me enough to find my balance and glance around Sigurd to see Moria standing with her arms crossed and a hard look on her face.

"No," he replies. "She knows nothing."

Douchebag. I cut a sideways glance his way. A hot douchebag, but still. At the moment, he's just as arrogant and aloof as the king he says he is.

Sigurd stares across the room—a large, open sitting room with ridiculously fancy furniture and far too few walls. We might as well be floating in some spaceship because all I see beyond the open wall across from us is sky.

"What were you thinking?" Moria flings her crossed arms out with a huff. Her hands fist and un-fist, those pointed claws extending and retracting.

"I wasn't." He rakes a hand through his hair. It sticks up, wild as the look in his eyes before it falls back into place. He sucks in a breath, and the look is gone. "I felt a human come through a door, shifted there, and when I saw her on the ground, I..."

He turns to stare at me, the silence so heavy all I can do is stare right back.

A human. Right, because they're not. Just peachy. Words I don't understand hang in the bubble of quiet.

"She said she was being chased," he continues, looking back to his cousin. "I didn't think. I just bound her so no one could take her away."

A thick lump forms in my throat so that I can barely swallow.

Moria whistles. "Not like you to lose your calm."

"No. It isn't." The emotion of moments ago vanishes in what can only be his typical veil of seriousness.

"Well." She looks between us. "You can tell me more later, but now, we need to discuss your *incident* with the Court of the Forest." Her fingers—definitely no claws now—drum on her hip.

Their shared fury has vanished as quickly as it came, almost like they fight like that all the time. Maybe they do. I shudder.

Sigurd gives me a once-over with cold, clinical detachment so unlike his attentions from minutes ago. "Don't try to leave. For your own good."

Both of them turn on their heel and head toward a set of large double doors at the far end of the room.

Oh no. Like heck if I'm going to be stuck in this strange place. "You can't just leave me here!"

Moria stops and turns. Sigurd keeps walking as if I never spoke. My nails dig into my palms.

"You have to take me home," I say. "Please! My grandmother is old, ill. I care for her. She needs me."

Moria has the decency to wince.

Finally, Sigurd stops. He glances back over one shoulder. "I can't. You're bound to me."

He points to his wrist and the circle of wings there, a matching tattoo to mine. Memories of the night before flash to mind. The rain. The glow of his eyes. His bloody palm around my wrist—the same one that bears this tattoo.

"Remove it." I hold up my arm, rushing toward him.

"I can't."

The statement stops me in my tracks. "What!" My shriek is even more shrill and grating than Moria's. "You're lying. Of course you can."

Moria shakes her head. "Fae can't lie."

Sigurd won't even look at me.

Hysterical laughter creeps up my throat. "I can't." Tears burn at the corners of my eyes. "I can't be stuck here forever."

If I am, I might as well be dead. For all anyone knows, I am.

"Not forever," he says, so quiet I almost miss it over the ringing in my ears.

"A day? A week?" I step toward them, pleading with all my soul for them to tell me I can go home.

Moria closes the distance between us and takes my wrist in hers. "It depends upon the strength with which the bond was placed. This..." Her thumb rubs over the tattoo.

The frown on her lips tells me everything I need to know. My knees wobble as she lets me go.

"My cousin bound you." She glances at him. "Quite strongly."

Sigurd doesn't even look at me, just strides to the doors that seem to open all on their own and leaves me standing there.

"I'll speak with him," Moria says.

Or at least I think she does. I can barely hear over the silent scream inside my head.

No sooner have the doors closed behind them than I collapse into a heap on the floor.

CHAPTER 5

I T'S NOT A SPACESHIP, this place I'm stuck in. It might as well be, though, for how far we are off the ground. One look at the snow-capped mountains in the distance and the horrible reality of my situation settles into my chest like a lead weight. This surely isn't home or anywhere near it. We don't have mountains in Mississippi, not like this anyway. Rolling hills? Sure. Forests? Oh yeah, plenty of those. But this...

I gaze out at the scene from the balcony off the main room.

This is some crazy Lord of the Rings nonsense. Snowy peaks surround a lush valley spotted with farmland and various structures. This...castle—yeah, I'll call it a castle—rises from the crest of a mountain, best I can tell anyway, and I'm stuck at the top of it. It's so far from the valley floor that I can hardly make out anything. You could tell me that cows walk upright here, and I'd believe it.

I pull my arms around myself where I sit on the polished marble floor, feet from the railing. It should be cold this high up, but it's not. Somehow its pleasantly perfect, but that does not to fix the ache in my chest.

That no-good king stuck me here. The temptation to shout every cuss word I've ever heard is almost too much to contain. But pretty girls don't have ugly mouths. At least, that's what Gran always told me growing up.

Gran. My heart clenches. Tabitha is probably with her if Gran hasn't ended up in the hospital from a heart attack. Maybe Aunt Virginia will finally get her stuff together and decide to help out for a change. One can only hope, right?

Please. I pray, for the millionth time in the last however many hours I've been stuck alone in here.

The main sitting room is like an open floorplan mansion with a massive sitting area, dining table, bookshelves, and all manner of things, though it's in no way cramped. The room is too big for that. One whole wall is covered with nothing but gauzy curtains like the ones in the bedroom, with a few support pillars keeping the roof intact. Much of said roof is glass. It must be strong stuff, too, because some freaking huge birds have roosted up there, sitting in nests that provide odd spots of shade to the room.

The doors Sigurd and Moria left through are locked. Figures. As are the large doors on the opposite side too. There are a few other small bedrooms like the one I woke up in. Four in total. Relatively modern-looking bathrooms sit between each pair. Actually, bathroom is an understatement. Each could be a fancy spa—not that I've had much experience with those—and smell like the cleanest pool imaginable.

While I was checking them out, someone must have come in because I found my clothes—cleaned—and sitting on the table along with a platter of fruit, bread, cheese, and wine. Basically the best foods ever. And boy, was I hungry. I didn't even notice until my mouth started to water and my stomach growled louder than thunder.

But the food turned ashen after a few bites. How could I enjoy it when I'd left everyone who mattered behind, probably thinking me dead? I couldn't. So, I'd left it in favor of stewing in my misery.

I hang my head in my hands. Derrick is going to feel so guilty. This will wreck him. It's not his fault some horrible dudes decided to rob his bar and then I got abducted by a fairy, of all things. He'll put the blame on himself though. He's always been that kind of guy, taking everything on himself and feeling it deeply. Even if he doesn't say so, I've always been able to see it.

The main doors groan open and sound rushes in with them. Two voices I recognize immediately: Sigurd and Moria.

About freaking time.

I'm on my feet in an instant. Cool air tickles my stomach before I tug my shirt down to my jean shorts. Back in my own clothes, I finally feel more like myself.

I savor the way my boots click across the marble. Boots, or rather, heels in general, always make me feel good. Oh, sometimes they hurt my feet like all get out, but just sliding my feet down into the soles and giving myself those precious few extra inches makes me feel powerful. I can take on the world in heels, and I need them now more than ever.

"Great, you've figured out how to get me home!" I beam with the best false smile I can manage. It's my "oh honey, sweetheart" smile I've used on many a drunk customer when I really want to deck them, but of course, I can't.

Conversation halts. A third man walks with them. Long, brown hair hangs down to his shoulders, framing a sharp, angular face.

"Most interesting." The newcomer's head tilts to the side as he takes me in.

"Wren, this is Hawke." Sigurd gestures between us, his voice flat. "Hawke, Wren."

His name is fitting, given his prominent, hooked nose. Either a nickname or his parents had excellent foresight.

"My brother." Moria slaps him on the back—hard.

Now that earns a raised brow. The similarities between them end with their tall and lean builds. He probably even has a few inches on Moria and Sigurd's six-foot-plus heights.

"Care to join us for dinner?" Sigurd asks me as he tilts his head toward the large table occupying one side of the room. It has chairs for ten, but there are far fewer of us. The platters brought in earlier still occupy one end, the chair I'd used half pulled out.

We were supposed to share that? A touch of warmth rises to my cheeks. Whoops. Not polite to start before others, but it wasn't like they'd been great hosts.

Just as I open my mouth, the main doors open, and people—no, fae—dressed in grays and light blues carry in various trays, pitchers, and all manner of things. My stomach lets out another growl as I catch a whiff of roasted meat.

"So..." I ball my fists on my hips and stare Sigurd down. "We're just going to ignore the fact that you *trapped* me here?"

"Wren..." he starts.

The servants don't even look my way. Figures.

Various emotions flicker across his face before he continues. "I cannot reverse the bond. You'll have a room here in my quarters. Food. New clothes. Any comfort you desire." He sweeps a hand around the room in an oddly regal gesture.

"My freedom?"

His jaw shifts back and forth like he grinds his teeth behind his pressed lips. "That, I cannot give."

A bonfire has less smolder than me. If only I had magic like his and Moria's and could knock his backside to the ground. Oh, what I wouldn't give for that. "So, I'm just to sit in this room forever? Or jump off that balcony and see if I can fly?"

His eyes go wide. A moment later, he's right in front of me. I never even saw him move. A gust of wind shudders through the room. "You wouldn't."

I notch my chin higher. No, he's right—I wouldn't. But at least I got his attention. I shove against his chest with all my might, but he doesn't budge. "Then what do you expect me to do?"

"Right now?" One brow arcs toward the ceiling. He gestures to the table being laid with plates and platters. "Sit. Eat."

Of all the horrible timing, my stomach gives another rumble. The corner of his lips twitch.

Infuriating man.

"Fine," I ground out before stomping my way to the table and claiming a seat at the far end. Hopefully it's his, if just to piss him off.

The servants leave as quickly as they came. Sigurd, Moria, and Hawke claim seats together at the other end of the table from me. Their impeccable table manners set my teeth on edge. I'm not one of those high-class southern belles brought up preparing for cotilion, but I'm no pig either. I might as well be compared to them though. Eating is a dance, and I'm falling all over my feet. The food is good though, even if half of it looks strange and unfamiliar.

Conversation floats across the other end of the table between Sigurd, Moria, and Hawke, despite the sharp daggers I stare their way. Mostly, they discuss all the people Sigurd seems to have pissed off lately. Apparently, it's not just me. Moria is the hot-headed one, railing him up and down about how he's endangered their whole court—their kingdom? Hawke is more levelheaded, saying little, though every sentence is as crafted and refined as his table manners. Sigurd mostly just grumbles through it all. I can almost picture a little dark cloud hovering over his too-sexy-to-be-such-a-pain self. It would be fitting.

"We'll have to postpone the games," Hawke says. He's finished his meal and sits with his fingers steepled over the table edge. His voice is grave, as if he's just announced there will be no football this season or something.

"It might be too soon for that," Moria says before depositing another forkful of something in her mouth.

He leans back in his chair. "You'd rather them be halted if things worsen?"

"We're not canceling the games." Sigurd folds his napkin and sets it on the table. "They're too important to our people."

Sounds a lot like my people. We had an outage during a playoff game last year, and I thought a fight was going to break out in the bar. I force down another bite of food, my foot tapping with impatience as it has been the whole meal. The nerve of them to carry on as if everything is normal.

"I know their importance," Hawke bites out. "My husband reminded me of it just this morning."

"And where is he today? I thought he would join us," Moria asks, probably in an attempt to break the building tension.

"He should be." He half glances over his shoulder. "Soon, I'd expect."

Sigurd ignores them. "The cauldron is almost ready. It will keep the court focused on happier things. It better."

"Cauldron?" I blurt.

Three fae heads turn my way. Whoops. I hadn't meant for the question to slip out, but there it went.

Sigurd leans over his edge of the table and stares down at me near the other end. He had taken the head of the table. Of course. "You might as well know." He gives a little half shrug. "Games are held twice a year. It's something the residents of my court look forward to. Anyone may enter in an attempt to vie for the grand prize and the honor of becoming champion."

Now that is interesting. "What kind of games?"

"It varies, and it's different every time. To keep it interesting. And fair, of course."

"There are multiple rounds," Moria says, jumping into the conversation. Her eyes glitter with anticipation as she speaks. "Some are tests of strength or intelligence, others specific skills, and some are just luck." She flips her palms toward the sky. "I've found quite a few talented warriors for my squadrons through past games."

At my questioning look, she leans in and gives a little wink. "I'm Captain of the Guard."

"Oh." Well, that's...fitting.

Sigurd had picked up his fork at some point, and now he twirls it around his fingers. His gaze is locked on me when suddenly his mouth quirks up in a grin. "It might be well received if you accompanied me to the ceremonies."

I paste on a fake grin in return. "Your people would like to see the little human you've trapped here?"

The fork tumbles to the floor with a clatter. His countenance darkens like a storm cloud. Moria turns away from him, barely hiding the laughter threatening to break across her face.

"It is rather a complicated matter," Hawke begins. "Simply, humans can aid our magic, and having you near our king in this troubling time would be seen advantageously."

"So that's why you did this?" I raise my arm, showing off the offending tattoo. Suddenly, his actions make nauseating sense.

"No," Sigurd says. "I told you it was to keep you safe."

"Uh huh. Right." I nod, not really looking at him as I push food around on my plate. "I'm sure the magic had nothing to do with it."

"I told you, fae can't lie," he grumbles.

Right. Whatever. Even if it was an accident, the fact that it benefits him makes it all too clear why he's not interested in helping me remove the blasted thing and get home.

I need a different topic. Anything to keep me from sinking into the misery of worrying about Gran and being stuck here for God knows how long. "Okay." I let out a deep breath. "What does the champion get, anyway?"

Sigurd rolls his shoulders before responding, "The champion gets to drink from the cauldron."

"That's it?" What a lame reward.

"The cauldron," Hawke says, "grants a wish to one who drinks from it. It's how my husband became fae."

Became... Fae... I blink, trying to take it in. Instead of what?

"And poor Hawke hasn't been able to beat me in a duel since," Moria laughs.

I all but ignore them, the cogs in my mind turning. If this cauldron can change someone into a fae, maybe it can do other powerful things too.

CHAPTER 6

I RUB AT THE tattoo around my wrist, pondering the magic of this cauldron and whether it would be enough to free me of my bond to Sigurd. The other members of the table carry on, oblivious to my rising hope.

"A worthwhile sacrifice." Hawke gives an uncharacteristic smile.

Moria rolls her eyes. "I suppose extra magic from your marked human is nothing to remorse over compared to love."

"If I were to drink from the cauldron," I interject, "would it remove the magic binding me here?"

The table goes eerily silent. Sigurd stares me down as if I've just asked for the moon.

Hawke swallows. "I believe it wou—"

"You're not entering the games." Sigurd slams his palms on the table, rattling the platters, and rises to his feet.

The hardness of his command has me sliding back in the chair, struggling to get as far away from him as possible. My spine stiffens against the backboard. "Why not?"

"It can be dangerous. What if you got hurt?"

"You could heal me like you did last night."

His lips thin. "It's not the same. You, out there—"

I shove to my feet, matching his stance as I lean over the table. "Then let me drink from the cauldron now. You got me stuck here, so get me unstuck."

His eyes slam shut as he pinches the bridge of his nose. "It's not that simple."

"The cauldron can only grant one wish before it has to recharge for quite some time," Hawke says with even calm. "Even my husband had to win his chance."

I cross my arms. "Seems like you'll need to cancel those games after all then."

Sigurd's lips twitch. "Things are too precarious to risk canceling the games for such a favor."

"Especially with all the mess you've gotten us into..." Moria trails off as she sips at her glass, ignoring the daggers Sigurd stares her way.

"Then you owe me the chance to try." I slap my palm on the table for emphasis. If he doesn't have the decency to undo this mess, then he sure as heck won't stop me from trying.

A muscle ticks in Sigurd's jaw. He opens his mouth to reply when the main doors groan open, drawing all of our attention.

"Ah, there he is." Hawke's tone fills with warmth.

His husband. But the man walking toward us is nothing like what I'd pictured. Hawke said he'd won the games before, so my mind painted him as a young, tall figure with bulging muscles, fitted clothes ready for a sparring match—like Moria's. Maybe a goatee. Instead, this man is only an inch or two taller me, with heavily graying-brown hair and more than a little extra girth around his midsection. He'd be more likely to conquer a tax return than win some sporting match.

"Sorry I'm late." His voice carries across to us and strikes something deep in my chest. The world tilts.

It can't be. It's not possible.

But as he nears, I can make out the angle of his face and the familiar dimples of his cheeks. His gaze slides my way as I collapse onto the chair.

"Who's our guest?" he asks without the slightest recognition.

"Uncle Mark?" The words crack from me in a shriek as my heart thunders in my ears. My nails dig into the armrests of the chair as I hold on for dear life.

Sigurd mumbles some curse I don't understand. Something clatters on the table, but I can't look away from this man who looks like he just stepped out of the photograph on grandma's mantle. His head tilts to the side, and his brows draw together, the mirror image of my memories. It has to be him.

Unless I hit my head harder than I thought.

Hawke stands and brushes the arm of the man who might be Mark. His gaze slides to me, his pupils widening as they emanate a strange glow. "You once mentioned a niece named Wren. Your brother's daughter?"

"Could it be?" Moria asked in barely a whisper.

The hairs on my arms stand on end. It shouldn't be possible, but there's no other explanation.

"Uncle Mark, you remember me, right?" Tears well up out of nowhere.

This man's ears are pointed, sticking out of his hair. His skin doesn't have the wrinkles it should, and his eyes are a little too bright. He's the image of the man who left years ago when I was still a teenager but different all the same.

"Your name sounded familiar," Hawke says. "But I never thought..."

"Wren." Lines furrow across Mark's slightly wrinkled forehead. "Wren..." Then, like a curtain has been pulled back from his mind, his gaze snaps to me. "Wren! Of course, Tim's daughter."

I nod, unable to form words. Something hard is lodged in my throat that I can't quite swallow down. My chest tightens painfully as he takes a step my way.

"You're here." He shakes his head. "I can hardly believe it. And you've grown so much." His congenial smile is the same as it always was, but it hits me like a slap to the face.

Here he is, all happy, fine, and calm like we're meeting at some weird family reunion, as if he didn't straight up vanish on us all years ago. And apparently, he got remarried. And became a...a fae? He dumped his old life, his old family—heck, his old self—and traded up for this magical life.

"It's so good to see you." He steps closer, and I flinch back into the chair.

Oh no. He's not going to act like this is all fine and peachy.

"You left us and came here? You abandoned your kids. Your wife. Your mom. Me." All the buried hurt digs its way to the surface. Here he sits, among royals if everything is to be believed, and he couldn't bother to let us know he was alive? Help us out? "God, you don't even know you have grandkids!"

Moria whistles and looks away.

I run my hands down my face, trying to scrub away this moment. I stand, unable to be still, and pace in front of my seat. What's already a nightmare has become even more twisted.

"Wren, I can explain." Mark reaches for me.

I twist away from him. "I don't want to hear it."

It's too much. All of it. Breaths come short and fast. My face feels like it's on fire. Fae are real. I'm trapped here. My uncle is alive. He abandoned us to become fae and marry some royal, when all this time we feared he might be dead.

A rogue tear leaks down my face.

I can't be here. I'd give anything to wake up from this nightmare right now.

My fingers dig into my arms, where I hug them about myself. I don't wake up, no matter how deep my nails cut.

"Wren." Sigurd's voice slices through the cloudy haze of panic rising within me.

Only then do I realize the humorless laughter floating from my lips.

"Sit," he says. "We'll—"

"No!" I fling my hands wide. "I'm done with this. I'm done with all of you. Leave me alone!"

I stumble from the table, knocking over the chair and banging my thigh in the worst way. It doesn't matter. It can't possibly make this any worse. My face flames as tears run unchecked down my face. I sprint for the bedroom, the one place I can flee to.

They call after me.

But I don't care. I don't stop.

When I finally slam the door behind me, I sink onto the floor, letting all the pain and shock of the day flood from me in racking sobs.

CHAPTER 7

I SLEEP. I SHOWER. I'm still stuck in this place when the sun rises the next day.

It's a gorgeous sunrise, painting the mountains in brilliant shades of pink and orange. White, puffy clouds dot the lightening sky. On this side of the castle, I can't see the valley below, only a stretch of mountains spearing toward the sky. A slight chill hangs in the air, but from the snow coating the peaks, it really should be colder than it is. This view could be the Rockies or the Alps, not that I've been to either. But if everything I've witnessed over the past day is to be believed, this is Faery. Another world entirely.

For years I'd dreamed of traveling. Getting out of my small town. Seeing the world. But this... I sigh. "This wasn't how it was supposed to happen."

The giant bird sitting on the balcony with me stretches its wings and gives a little squawk. Its gray-and-brown head turns my way before it blinks at me. The darn thing nearly gave me a heart attack when it flew into my room last night. I screamed and threw a pillow at it, which it dodged with expert precision. But it kept its distance and became an unlikely companion, as did the two smaller ones that joined it late into the night.

Who knew the nicest people here were the birds? Other birds linger on the glass roof, some in their massive nests. I give a half smile to my eagle—at least, I think that's what it is—companion. I guess he was brave enough to find out who this new person was staying below their roost.

I hold out my hand toward the eagle. He hops closer, stretching his neck until I graze the feathers of his head. So soft.

A knock sounds at the door, causing us both to jump. The eagle squawks and flies out over to the railing.

I purse my lips and stare at the source of the offending sound when it comes again. "Who is it?"

"Sigurd."

My stomach does a weird flip-flop.

"Do I want to talk to him?" I whisper to the eagle where he's returned to perch on the balcony railing.

It tilts its head back and forth before giving what looks eerily like a nod. Goosebumps race up my arms.

"Weird bird," I mutter.

"Come in." It is his place after all, and the door doesn't exactly have a lock, at least none I could figure out. His knock is a courtesy.

I stand with my arms crossed just inside the sheer curtains when he enters. Warmth settles low in my stomach as the door swings wide, and it's everything I can do to stand still. Why, oh why, does he affect me so? It's not like I haven't seen my share of handsome men...on TV anyway. Standing here before me, those icy blue eyes and dark locks do things to a girl.

He leans against a wall, mirroring my stance with his crossed arms. Silence hangs between us, and I refuse to break it.

"That was"—his lips purse and twist as he searches for a word—"quite an exit yesterday."

Heat prickles my cheeks. "Come to make fun of me?" I huff and turn toward the balcony. "So nice of you."

The warmth grows and seeps down to my chest when he doesn't respond. Maybe he left. That'd be fine. Great, actually.

"No."

I screech and jump at the voice just behind me. When I twist around, he's right there, barely a foot away. How on earth does he move so quietly?

"I came to check on you. To make sure you're okay."

Morning light catches on the planes of his face, softening his look. My lips part in silent wonder. His attire is more casual today. The cool grays and blues of his trousers and loose shirt soften all his hard edges.

I brush my hair behind my ear and catch part of the tattoo on my wrist from the corner of my eye. The warmth in my chest turns cold and sinks like lead. "Oh, I'm great. Just peachy."

His brows pinch. "Peachy?"

I roll my eyes. "I'm still stuck here. Oh, and my uncle, who totally turned his back on his family, is just hanging out here all happy. Wealthy too, I'm guessing." I gesture to the castle around us. "He couldn't even bother to recognize me, his own niece, who he saw almost every week for forever."

Sigurd winces. With his mild frown and downcast eyes, he looks almost sorry. "There's a reason for that."

"Oh really?"

He steps closer with one hand raised then drops it. "Faery makes it hard for humans to remember their world once they are here for a while."

He stares at me, hard.

Knowledge settles around my neck like a chain. Oh God. Oh no. My hand clamps over my mouth.

"Wren, you won't forget. I won't let you." He grabs my bare upper arm. His touch is warm and comforting, an anchor keeping me on my feet. "It's not quick. It can take years, and your uncle has been here for several of them and a fae for much of that time."

Years. I suck in a deep breath. *It can take years.*

"Your uncle... I'll let him explain. But I won't let you forget, not if you don't want to."

"He truly didn't remember me." I gape.

Sigurd's thumb rubs across my skin. "He does now. Memories outside of Faery drift away. They slide into a deep pool within the mind, but your presence surfaced them for him. Would you speak with him?"

"I..." I blink at him, at this man, this king trying to explain things that barely make sense. He may have bound me here, but he's been kind since. "Okay."

His fingertips trail down my arm, raising shivers in their wake until he takes my hand and raises it to his lips. The way they press against the back of my hand steals my breath.

"If you need me..." His gaze holds mine, holding more words than I can possibly make out.

So many thoughts race through my head, but none of them form on my tongue before he leaves me standing there, gaping at his retreating form.

Moments later, another familiar face fills the doorway.

"Wren." Mark's voice wipes away all the wonder of moments before.

The cold I expected this morning finally rushes in to wrap around me.

"Uncle Mark." I don't keep the edge from my voice. My eagle friend hops back onto the balcony, not a foot from my leg, as if it's there to offer me support. *Thanks, little buddy.*

Mark rubs the back of his neck and glances toward the door he shut behind him.

I raise my brows. Preparing to run? That'd be fitting.

"I have grandkids?" he finally says.

So that did get his attention. "Four of them, actually. All Tabitha's. She's married, you know. Matt walked her down the aisle since you weren't there."

He winces, and his eyes turn glassy. "They're okay, Matt and Tabitha?"

My traitorous heart twists.

"Peachy. Matt is still in the military, stationed overseas but coming home soon. Tabitha loves being a mother, or so she says. Her husband travels for work a lot, so she's got her hands full. She married Robbie. Maybe you remember him? Or you will?" They'd been together since freshman year of high school, before Uncle Mark left.

He nods. His throat bobs. He wants to ask about Gran. I can see it written all over his face in his darting gaze and the way the toe of his shoe taps on the floor. But he's scared. He ought to be.

"I still live with Gran." *Thanks for asking.*

His eyes snap to me and hold. "She's..."

"Alive? Was when I left, though my disappearance may have given her a heart attack." Just the thought sends me pacing across the floor.

"King Sigurd said you were being chased?"

The hint of reverence in his voice causes a humorless laugh to slip from me. The eagle gives a squawk.

"You—" He shakes his head just the way he used to when scolding us for making a mess. I think he's talking to me until he starts shooing my eagle away.

"Hey!" I protest.

He backs it out onto the balcony railing. "This is family conversation."

The eagle takes wing, and my heart drops. "It's just a bird."

"No, it's—" He shakes his head.

An eagle. Yeah... I shake my head. Uncle Mark leads me back inside and tugs on a set of heavy, navy curtains that had previously been pulled to the side, until the room is dark, save a few weird, flickering lights—some kind of magic from what I can tell—and closed off from the world beyond.

"Well, you've gotten your update and kicked out my bird," I say. "Done yet?"

A pained expression flashes across his face as his shoulders drop. "Wren, I..."

I cross my arms and stare him down. Did he expect this to be a happy conversation?

"I can explain. I want to..."

The tap, tap, tap of my cowboy boot on the floor echoes through the room.

"You're not ready to listen yet, are you?"

I swallow the lump in my throat. I won't cry in front of him. Nope, nope, nope.

"I'm sorry, Wren." His voice cracks. "Really, give me a chance."

"You want a chance?" I suck in another breath, letting the air calm me. "Get me out of here." I hold up my tattooed wrist. "That's the best thing you can do for Gran and your kids."

His gaze drops to the floor, that foot still tapping, just like mine. I force my feet still. "I can't, Wren. No one can break that bond."

Same old song.

"Then *you* go back. Go *home* and tell everyone what happened to me. And you."

He stumbles back and sits heavily in a chair. He sighs. "You don't know. Fae can't live in the human world." He stares up at me. "We...fade away."

We fade. Just remind me that you're not human, why don't you? I thump down onto the end of the bed. "Fading is bad?"

He nods.

"Instant?" I push.

"No, it can take a little time to—"

I clap my hands once, cutting him off. "Then just go tell them and come right back. Can't be too hard, right?"

He looks away again. His throat bobs once, twice, before he finally looks at me. "I've been back, Wren."

Now that nearly knocks me over.

"I went to Ma's house not long after I became fae," he hurries on. "Planned to tell her everything. She was sittin' on the front porch in her chair. I came all the way to the bottom of the front steps, but she couldn't see me—looked right through me like I wasn't even there. She just stood up and went inside without a word."

"What?" That doesn't sound anything like the Gran I know.

"Not everyone can see fae, Wren. Some of us can and can come here. Me. You."

Something heavy sits against my ribs. "But not Gran?"

He shakes his head.

"Tabitha? Matt?" I ask, dreading the answer.

He hangs his head. "I couldn't bear to try. It runs in bloodlines, whatever makes this possible. But even then, not everyone gets it. Especially if it hasn't been cultivated, or so Hawke told me."

Cultivated. As if we're plants. I push the thought away. They may not see Mark or anyone else, but I'm still human.

"Then I have to go back, or they'll really think we're both gone for good." An idea strikes me, and I jolt upright. "You want to help me?"

"If I could—"

"Then get me in that tournament."

He blinks at me. "The—"

"The games or whatever."

His expression hardens. "Wren, that's—"

"Dangerous? Don't care. You did it, didn't you?"

"I did. Won on dumb luck, really. Entered three times, which is why I know the risks it could expose you to."

"I still don't care. It's that or... What? Sit here for months, years, until this darn thing goes away?"

He smooths his hands down his pants. "It is nice here. You might come to like it."

"Ugh," I groan and smash my fist into the covers. "Look, you said you'd help. Get me into that tournament."

"Sigurd will be—"

"I don't care what he thinks." I shove to my feet, pacing again.

"He saved you."

"He *trapped* me here!"

"Wren," he scolds me like I'm a kid again.

Maybe I'm acting like one, but I don't care. With all that's happened, that's the least of my worries. "You're his cousin's husband. Surely that gives you some authority."

Cogs are turning behind his eyes. His lips pinch. "Yes, some."

So, he is part of the royal family. It's a far cry from what our family is back at home, that's for sure. Lordy, what would Gran think of all this if she knew? We'd always thought Uncle Mark ran away with some woman, but to find out instead that it was a man, a royal, who isn't even human. Air escapes between my lips. Maybe it is best that Gran doesn't know.

"But I wish you'd hear me out first, Wren." He rubs the back of his neck. "I…"

His voice tugs at me. Somehow, I have to make him see reason.

"Uncle Mark." I smooth out my voice, filling it with the southern drawl, and kneel next to his chair.

This close, I can see the few faint lines of age that no transformation to fae or otherwise can quite hide. He's different but… My chest tightens as I catch a whiff of peppermint. All at once, I'm hanging out at his house as a child, playing on the thick, brown carpet with Tabitha.

"I want to hear your story. I want to know why you left." My voice cracks over the word. "But, please, help me with this first. Show me you're the loving uncle I remember and not just the one who turned his back on us." His worn hand is so solid and real under my fingers as I give it a squeeze. "Then, I promise, I'll listen to whatever you have to say."

For the briefest moment, I forget why I'm so angry with him, why I have been for years. I want to hug him, regale him with stories from home, and tell him everything about his kids and grandkids.

But he left.

He didn't get stuck here like me, as far as I know. He chose to leave.

A heavy sigh fills the space between us. "I'll see what I can do."

Some of the weight on my chest lifts.

"Thank you." I hold his gaze as I squeeze his hand again.

He cups my cheek. A glassy sheen fills his eyes. "I never thought I'd—"

"I know." This smile isn't forced. "Me too."

CHAPTER 8

Uncle Mark didn't come back during all of yesterday or this morning. My eagle companion is mysteriously absent as well. If he scared him off for good, we're going to have words.

My stomach keeps turning over on itself, and I can barely sit still. Yesterday, in the five minutes I saw him, Sigurd asked me to accompany him to the opening ceremony of the games to be held this morning. I jumped at the chance. His brows pinched as his head cocked to the side while he tried to figure out why I was so eager to join him after my abject refusal the day before.

"I need out of these rooms," I told him.

Not entirely false. I couldn't remember the last time I spent an entire day cooped up inside, much less two. I'm still not sure how it doesn't drive Gran crazy being inside as much as she is. Maybe, when I get back, I can get her to go out more, even if it's just to sit on the porch in her rocker.

First, I've got to get there, and this competition is my chance.

If Uncle Mark failed, maybe someone there will make me a last-minute addition. It won't work if I'm stuck here though. Sigurd, the cocky bastard, wanting to parade me around to help his image works in my favor.

Moria took it upon herself to be my fashion consultant for the event. She decided it might raise too many questions if I looked like I had just stepped through a door and into Faery. Which, of course, I did, but the people don't have to know that. Better that I appear like I actually planned to be here and attend the event.

"How about this one?" I say, stepping from the bathroom.

Half the outfits she brought were too revealing. Too much cleavage. Too high of a slit up the sides. Too little...everything. Maybe they would work if I was just to sit there and look pretty, which is no doubt what Sigurd has in mind, but if I'm going to win this competition, I have to be prepared for anything. Flashing half their kingdom via wardrobe malfunction is so not on my to-do list.

This outfit, though, might just work. Tight, flexible pants—seriously, they move better than some of my yoga pants—are tucked down into ankle boots with an airy tunic shirt in silvery gray.

"A little plain." Moria taps a finger on her cheek. "Good colors though. Sigurd will like them." She winks. "Let's add a few accessories."

I fight the urge to squirm as Moria layers me up with jewelry. A long, silver necklace with a blue gem—gotta be glass, no way that's a sapphire—that hangs between my breasts. Equally stunning earrings dangle at my jawline. A few silver bangles are stacked around one wrist.

"You seem to like jewelry for someone who doesn't wear any," I say as she sorts through clips for my hair.

She frowns at a gaudy mess of silver and sets it away. Thank God. "It's pretty, but I prefer my accessories to be a little more practical." She pulls at a silver decoration on her thigh, revealing a thin blade I would never have guessed to be tucked away there. She shoves it back into place and shrugs. "Most days anyway."

Content with my appearance, we venture to the main sitting room.

Sigurd waits, standing near the edge of the large balcony. Light catches in his dark hair and on the silver accents of his outfit. He exudes casual elegance. There are no crowns for this king, no capes, nor is he decked in jewels and furs like the pictures of some kings from our human history books.

Even so, the confidence in his stance and the way he carries himself speak volumes on their own. "You chose my colors."

A flush spreads across my cheeks. His colors, huh? No wonder Moria said he'd like them. I spear her with a hard look, but she doesn't notice. Instead, I focus back on the man inspecting me way too intently. "Do I need to pay you a fee to wear them?"

His lips twitch. "Seeing you in them is payment enough."

Warmth buries itself in my chest, and I have to look away. Shameless flirt. He must really like the woman I resemble. Enough to bind me with magic in haste and still flirt with me, even though I'm obviously not who he thought I was.

I wonder why he can't have her. I peek at him from the corner of my eye. He's attractive enough. Powerful. Wealthy. Surely most women would appreciate at least some of that.

"Take my hand." The one he holds out to me is gloved. Thank God. He's stirred up enough of a mess in me. No need to add to it.

Keep your head in the game, girl.

No sooner do I take it than Moria grabs my other and Sigurd says, "Hold on."

"To—" *What.*

That's what I mean to say. But the word turns into a screech as the world shifts and bends around me. The air becomes heavy and thick, closing in like a rubber band. Everything in me feels shaken like a martini, and if they weren't holding my hands, I'd definitely fall.

As quickly as it began, the band of air pops, and the world solidifies. Only, the scene around us is different. A lower, solid ceiling hangs overhead. Actual solid walls surround us on three sides, forming a small room. The furnishings here are different too—gaudy chaise lounges and tables draped with heavy linens. Tapestries hang on the walls depicting various scenes of peo-ple—or rather, fae—doing battle. My boots shift on carpets of deep blue.

Sigurd flexes his hand. Only then do I realize I'm squeezing it, and Moria's, in a death grip.

"What the fu...dge was that?" I ask, only barely holding back the curse.

"Fudge?" Moria asks, but I ignore her and release her hand.

Sigurd, however, doesn't quite let me go.

"Shifting?" he says. "It's a way to move quickly from one place to another."

Magical fae transportation. Freaking handy.

"You can all do it?" I look between him and Moria, the only other person in the room.

"No." He shifts his grip, tugging me closer as he claims my attention. Strands of dark hair curl around his ear, and I have to fight the urge to tuck them back. Why do I want to touch him so? Sigurd's lips curve up as his chin notches higher. "Only the strongest of us can."

I roll my eyes. Of course. One moment I'm wondering what his hair would feel like between my fingers, and then he has to go and remind me of his less attractive side.

Cheers and chatter echo into the room, and not the voices of a small group. A roar like that only comes from thousands, and I've seen enough football games to know.

"Shall we?" He gives my hand a squeeze, and for the briefest moment, he almost seems nervous.

A king, nervous? Surely not.

Me, on the other hand? I am not ready. It takes everything I have to put one foot in front of the other as we travel down a long hallway to the ever-rising tide of sound. It crashes over us, building in intensity and twisting my insides into a knot as sunlight spills into the hallway, nearly blinding me.

I'm Maximus in *Gladiator* as we walk out the end of the tunnel into a massive stadium. My mouth drops open, and I blink against the light, taking in the unfurling sight. If this were a football stadium, we'd be halfway up the lower bowl in a box of sorts. It's similar enough in shape that it may have been modeled after one. Or...

A lump forms in my throat. Maybe humans borrowed the idea from the fae.

Fae—at least I think they're fae—crowd the stands. There are no team colors here, not that I can tell. The rainbow of color filling the stands looks like someone dumped a massive amount of confetti everywhere. Confetti that moves and cheers. Pennants of blue bearing a gray bird poke up from the crowd all around the stands and flutter in a light breeze.

But they're not cheering for their king, who just made his entrance. Or me, thank goodness. Instead, they're focused on the figures standing in the large, grassy oval in the center of the stadium.

The competitors? I lean forward, aiming for a better look.

"You're late," Hawke says.

The comment snaps my attention away from the crowd. Hawke and Uncle Mark occupy one side of the box. I'd been so preoccupied with the scene before us I hadn't even noticed them.

"Can I be late when I'm the one who starts the ceremony?" Sigurd asks.

I hear Hawke's sigh, but his annoyance is the least of my worries. Instead, I stare Uncle Mark down, begging for the slightest hint. *Did you get me in the tournament? Should I be down there? Help me.*

He gives a slight nod. Acknowledgment or just a friendly greeting?

Sigurd drops my hand. My fingers twitch, aching to reach for his. Not because I want him. No, of course not. But holy moly, I am unprepared for this. Either I'm about to piss off a king, or my shortcut home is gone. And handling either of those is going to be a disaster. My knees wobble, and I reach for a nearby chair to cling to its back.

"Let's get started, shall we?" Sigurd's jovial tone makes my stomach drop further.

Moria slips her arm through mine. "Exciting, isn't it?"

I nearly laugh. "That's one word for it."

She shows me to my chair. Of course, it's smashed right between hers and Sigurd's. The implication of that seating, closer even than his Captain of the Guard, isn't lost on me. Or the crowd as they start to focus our way. What is that idiot thinking? I sink down into the plush armchair, begging it to swallow me whole.

A strong gust of wind rolls across the stadium, fluttering clothes and pennants before silencing the crowd. Yet, not a hair on my head is displaced. Chills race across my skin in response to what must be magic. Sigurd stands at the edge of the box, looking out at the crowd. That wind came from him. It had to have.

All eyes turn to the king. His squared shoulders and broad grin are mesmerizing.

"Begin." His voice echoes with resonance across the assembled, so much louder than it should be yet somehow not offensive to my ears at all.

Horns blare. Sigurd's gaze roams over me as he crosses the box to take his seat at my side. The lump in my throat is hard as ever, and I can't help it when my shoulders hunch in further.

Below, a fae male speaks into a large horn that projects his voice through the stadium, a fae loudspeaker of sorts. He drones on and on about the great history of the games and the honor to be bestowed upon the champion.

"The winner receives the opportunity to drink from the cauldron created by the ancient queen Áine." The announcer pauses, giving the crowd the chance to react with a chorus of cheers. "The cauldron shall grant the winner the desires of their heart if their wish should be honest and true."

"Honest and true?" I ask.

"Áine created the cauldron as a gift for her children," Sigurd says, just loud enough for me to hear him. "She didn't want them to use it for ill, so she bound part of her will to it so that it can't be used to wreak abject destruction."

"No plagues. No wishing for someone to die," Moria interjects. "Things like that."

I nod. That's fine. My wish is honest, right?

The announcer continues to summarize the games, but it's obvious from the shifting of the crowd that they already know this part. It's new to me though.

There are five rounds. Competitors will be eliminated in each one until a winner is announced after the final game. A winner that won't be me, clearly. The competitors are down there, waiting to be introduced, and I'm stuck up here.

A heavy sigh slips out before I can stop it.

Sigurd glances my way, a question on his face, but I ignore it. He probably just thinks I'm bored, which I might be, if depression didn't already crush my chest like a dropped barbell.

The announcer begins introducing the competitors. Each steps forward as their name is called to receive cheers of encouragement from the crowd. There are no boos, no jeers, until a prince from the Court of Fire—another fae kingdom?—is introduced.

Sigurd leans forward in his chair, suddenly straight and stiff. The tension swarming around him is almost tangible. "That *boy* comes to my court to compete in my games and doesn't even bother to introduce himself to me?"

"You have been a little absent," Moria says with a wince.

The air stirs up around us. "Who approved his entry?"

"I did," Hawke says.

Attention snaps to him. Hawke, as always, looks completely bored and unfazed by Sigurd's irritation.

"With all that's happened with the Court of the Forest, the Unseelie," Sigurd snaps in a harsh whisper. That last word coils down into my chest, all inky and wrong. "You thought it a good time to grant an outsider from a rival court free entry here?"

"I didn't know about such...complications when I approved his request," Hawke says.

Sigurd drums his fingers on the arm of his chair, his jaw set. Another name is announced to thunderous cheers.

"His presence could be a good signal to the people," Hawke says. "Perhaps it will make them feel that all is well."

His careful words aren't lost on me. Make them *feel* that all is well, not that all *is* well. Without the ability to lie, he can't say that, can he?

Sigurd's jaw twitches, and he leans back in his chair. "You have a point."

Hawke nods, and the air settles. I slide back into my own chair and try to focus on the announcements. But the uneasiness, the potential war Moria mentioned, prod me like sticks. If I am stuck here, and there's a war, it doesn't bode well for me getting home, even once this stupid bond is gone.

"Wren Dawson," the announcer calls.

My stomach bottoms out. A strong hand latches onto my forearm, squeezing so tight as to wrench a yip from my lips. The air around me moves, tightening. Suddenly, I'm lightheaded.

"You," Sigurd all but snarls.

The air steadies, and I suck in a breath of air gone thin. He leans over my chair, so close I catch a whiff of citrusy pine. My skin flushes at his nearness, at the crowd as their cheers fade into breathless silence.

I turn, blinking at the furious king still clenching my arm.

A sharp prick grazes my skin, and I catch a flash of claws before they recede.

The announcer calls my name again, a question in his voice. *I'm not there. They're looking for me.*

Sigurd's feral expression, the blue glow of his eyes—*oh my God, they're actually glowing*—dims and evens out.

Then all at once, he's the smiling king. He lifts my arm, drawing me to stand with him, and guides me to the edge of the box. But the grin stretching across his face can't mask the fury simmering behind his eyes as he turns to me.

"Wren Dawson," he says loud enough for the crowd to hear and raises my hand high.

His words are for them, for the second round of cheers that nearly shakes the stone below my feet. But that look, it's all for me, and it's a promise: we'll talk about this later.

It's sure to be an unpleasant discussion.

"I'll see her to the field." My uncle stands behind Sigurd, his hand outstretched and waiting for mine.

In a show of gentlemanly courtesy, Sigurd passes my hand into my uncle's waiting one.

This is so much worse than I ever imagined.

CHAPTER 9

EVERYONE WE PASS, LITERALLY everyone, stops and stares. Whispered words—and some way too loud—chase after us. The worst reaction of them all was Sigurd's.

"He's pissed," I whisper as we make our way down flights of stairs.

"Yeah." Uncle Mark coughs. "Yes, he is."

My heart thunders, growing more insistent as we near the field. I'm doing this. This is happening. It's what I wanted, but oh my God, now that it's here, I can barely put one foot in front of the other.

We reach the edge of the field, and my uncle gives my hand a little pat.

"Good luck," he says.

I'm going to need it. My pulse beats in my throat as I clasp his hand in mine. "Thank you. So much. Even if nothing comes of it. If I lose today..."

I drop his hand and stare at my boots.

Sigurd will be pissed once he figures out how I got into this contest. Hawke probably will be too. And Moria, who strangely didn't even say a word. I might have alienated Uncle Mark from his whole fae family, and he still did it for me.

"I believe in you, Wren. If I can do it, you can." He grasps my shoulder, giving it a firm shake. His eyes shine with something. Pride?

My nod is shaky. "Thank you. Whenever you're ready to talk, I—"

"Soon." He glances back toward the field. "But now you have a competition to win. The first game starts in minutes."

Right. No pressure. "I'll, uh, see you later then."

Sweat breaks out on my neck as I stride across the field. It's not hot or humid—the temperature is pretty darn perfect, actually, but it might as well be a steamy day in August under a blazing noon sun.

Everyone stares at me. My boots are suddenly clunky. The earrings pull at my ears. All I want to do is run back to the edge of the stadium and find somewhere to hide.

But then I'll lose my shot, my way home to Gran.

I straighten my spine and look straight ahead at my competition.

I can do this. For her.

"The king's little human? Don't think that gives you an advantage," one woman taunts as I pass.

A few others glare my way. One bares pointed fangs.

Oh peachy, just peachy. As if I wasn't at a disadvantage already being human, my competition hates me.

I could stand near the outside of the group and face the crowd, but somehow that would be so much worse. The fae are all taller than me. If I can get to the center, maybe I can fade from view. I glance back over one shoulder, judging the distance, and smack right into somebody.

The impact knocks the wind from my lungs, and I stumble back, arms flailing as I try to keep my balance.

The man grabs my hand to steady me. "Careful."

"I'm sorry. So sorry. I didn't mean to bump into you like that." The words spill out of me. "Really, I thought the way was clear. I looked back, then bam! Right into you and—"

"It's fine. You're small enough that you bounced right off." His lips twitch as if he's holding back a laugh.

"Right, well." I brush stray hairs behind my ear. I hold out my hand to shake. "Anyhow, I'm Wren."

He stares at it.

Shoot. Probably not a fae greeting. I'm about to drop it when he grabs my hand and gives it a little shake.

"I know." Warm brown eyes twinkle with mirth.

A flush creeps across my cheeks. Of course, I bet they all do after that announcement and Sigurd showing me off to the crowd.

"I'm Galen," he says.

"Nice to meet you, Galen."

He's built like a warrior but with more lean muscle than the body-builder type. Brown hair—not as long as many of the fae, male or female—curls around tanned ears in a balanced face that's more boy next door than football star but still handsome.

I stick close to him as the announcer gives another grand, sweeping history of the games, most of which is drowned out by the steady thump of my pulse in my ears.

"And now," the announcer says, "we shall begin the first game of this season's competition, where no less than half of our competitors will be eliminated."

I suck in a breath. Half? Already?

A murmur runs through the fae around me. Competitors shift on their feet and nudge one another. The heel of my boot slides across the ground. I'm not ready. Whatever this is—

"Fate," the announcer begins, his deep voice carrying over us all, "always plays a hand in shaping our destinies and guiding our great court. It is only appropriate that it plays a role in our first challenge as well. Competitors, if fate is on your side, you shall advance. If not..."

I can't see him. Even so, I can picture his shrug as the crowd responds in chuckles and indistinct commentary.

"A game of luck?" I ask.

Galen glances over at me. "Sounds like it."

"Each competitor shall advance and select one gem from within this bag," the announcer says. Above the heads of the fae around me, I can just make out the top of a blue sack as it's raised in the air.

Competitors jostle toward the announcer. A few take off at a run, aiming to be first. One at a time, each reaches into the bag and pulls forth a glittering gemstone so big the potential value of it has me swaying on my feet. The blue stone hanging against my chest is suddenly heavy. It's not real, is it? I glance toward the box, where Sigurd and the others sit in the shadows under an awning. My fingers slide over cold, hard stone. It's so different than the little bird that sits just below my collarbone. I insisted on keeping my own necklace, even if it doesn't fit perfectly with the rest of the outfit.

One by one, stones are drawn.

Rubies. Emeralds. Diamonds. Sapphires. The sapphires earn the loudest cheers. They are blue after all, the same color as the pennants. Sigurd's color. Once each person has a stone, they stand with others of the same type. The implication is clear. Some will be lucky, others not.

It's the most boring game ever and possibly the most nerve-racking.

The line dwindles. Galen advances and pulls forth a stone.

"Emerald!" The announcer calls to the crowd.

Galen pales as he stares at the stone.

Is it bad? Does he know?

"Next, next," the announcer says, shooing him away. Galen gives himself a little shake and goes to join the others.

It's my turn.

The announcer's face is dusted with glittering silver. Long feathers are strung through his hair and drape down his back to look like the crest of a great bird. His attire is no less fanciful, all sparkle and feathers like a showgirl—or rather showman. Silver rings curl along his fingers to look like long, metal claws, which clutch at the bag.

With a little shake, I step across the stage-like area and shove my hand into the bag. My fingertips trail across the various stones. Some are smooth, others sharp. It's impossible to tell what any of them are, not that'd I know which one to pick if I could. Only a few are left, probably just enough for the remaining competitors.

I suck in a deep breath and grab a stone.

"Another emerald!" the announcer calls as I turn over the stone in my hand as the others had done.

Good or bad?

A gust of breeze teases my hair, and I glance toward the box. Sigurd stands at the edge, his palms on the railing. His expression is impossible to guess from here.

I join Galen with the other emeralds. "I guess we're in this together."

He gives me a tight smile that doesn't meet his eyes. "Looks like it."

I can barely stand still as the rest of the stones are drawn, and the competitors take their places. The emerald, twice the size of my thumbnail, is like a hot potato in my hands. This little stone holds my fate. Whether I continue is completely out of my hands now. Or rather, in them, but I have no control. I snort.

Maybe they intend such cruel irony.

"Now, now, the moment you have all been waiting for," the announcer says. "Competitors with the following gemstones shall advance. All others will be eliminated."

Bile crawls up my throat. The roar of the crowd becomes one continual buzz.

"Ruby."

Cheers erupt. My fist tightens around the stone.

"Amethyst."

My throat tightens.

"Diamond."

The buzz of the crowd grows. How many stones were there? How many colors?

"And emerald."

I gasp for breath. My fist unfurls, and I stare at the circular stone and the imprint it left upon my skin where I clutched it for dear life.

A strong hand clamps on my shoulder. I gaze up into Galen's smiling face. He says something, but it's lost in the roar of the crowd and the hysterical breaths I suck in one after another.

We made it to the next round.

CHAPTER 10

U NCLE MARK AND HAWKE met me on the field shortly after the first game concluded and took me back to Sigurd's quarters via that horrible teleportation thing they do.

"The future rounds will not be so easy," Hawke told me.

Easy? Okay, I didn't actually have to do anything, but I'd rather have my fate in my own hands than left up to chance. I said as much.

"You'll have to be careful," Uncle Mark said. "Some games can be dangerous. If there's a duel or, worse, a test of magic…" He shook his head.

Yeah, I'd be screwed. "You don't know what they are?"

They looked at one another.

"The games must be fair to all," Hawke said. So, they did know or at least had some idea, and neither looked optimistic.

Just peachy.

That's how I ended up raiding what I can only describe as the liquor cabinet once they left me alone. I could be miserable, stewing in the adrenaline that barely lets me sit still and the racing thoughts that make me want to vomit off the balcony, or I could drink and hope it calms something.

I sip at a crystal glass containing a smooth whiskey that practically begged me to drink it the moment I took the cap off.

Stored in fancy crystal bottles marked with swirls I can't begin to make out, I have no idea what kind it is or the age—some fae vintage, no doubt—but it would impress the socks off anyone who stepped into Jolene's.

My bare feet dangle off the edge of the sofa as I watch the light fade and the sun sink further behind the mountains. The eagle who'd kept me company returned the moment I sat down. At least, I think it's him. He's been sitting here listening to the worries that started to slip out after my first sip of whiskey. The only person I've seen since Mark and Hawke left was a skinny fae woman with a dinner tray, and she had little to say.

"Feed the human but don't talk to her," I say to the eagle. "She might give you bad luck or confuse you with her simple, human ways."

The main doors groan open, and I jolt in the seat, nearly spilling my glass.

Sigurd marches in, still dressed in the same clothes he wore earlier today. Where he's been, I can only guess. But, oh wait, that's right, I don't care.

Except, maybe I do. Darn it.

His step falters for the briefest moment when he spies me on the couch. His gaze darkens, and I sip my whiskey, waiting for storm clouds to manifest around his head.

They don't. But my eagle friend swoops across the room to perch on his outstretched arm. My lips purse. Traitor.

Every step Sigurd takes toward me, my back stiffens one piece of my spine at a time. When he finally stops a foot away, we lock into a staring contest that I refuse to lose.

"You entered the games," he says.

I blink. "Obviously."

"How—" He bares his teeth before wrinkling his nose and looking away. "Never mind. I think I know."

And the win goes to me. My body relaxes as I cross my legs and sink into the cushions. "Why should it bother you if I enter the games or not?"

"It could be dangerous," he bites out.

"And you care?"

He opens his mouth, closes it, then finally speaks. "I might."

I swirl the remnants of my drink in the glass. "Worried it'll hurt your reputation if your poor little captive human gets hurt in a game?"

Sigurd visibly bristles before throwing himself down on the other end of the sofa from me. "It's not just the games themselves that can be dangerous. Your competition will be fierce. They saw you at my side. They may think you have an advantage through me, though I would not defile the games by showing such obvious bias."

My fingers press hard into the glass. Of course he wouldn't. Why help me now? "I get it," I snap. "Wouldn't want to damage your spotless reputation any further."

"This isn't about me, Wren," he says with a sudden calm that only makes me more furious. "This is about you putting yourself in danger after I forbid it."

"Oh, fuck you!" The retort springs free before I can stop it. I clamp my hand over my mouth, the shock of what I've said cooling some of the anger his comment inspired.

Sigurd's lips twitch as he stares me down. "If you'd like."

My face burns hotter than a torch, and I scoot away until the arm of the sofa bites into my side. Dang my whiskey-loosened tongue, saying something so foolish. "You don't even know me."

"Perhaps I'd like to." His arm drapes across the back of the sofa, as if he suddenly decided to settle down and stay a while.

I roll my eyes. Fine, if he wants to play... "Hi, I'm Wren Dawson, and I'm a bartender."

"A what?"

"Bartender."

He only blinks at me.

I cock my head to the side. "You don't have bartenders here?" I shift in my seat. What kind of backward place is this? "I make drinks for people." I swirl the last drops of liquid in my glass for emphasis. "It's my job. What I do. How I make money."

"You make drinks for people," he echoes, as if he must have heard me wrong.

"Yep." I paste on my best blinding smile.

"I see you found my collection." He eyes my glass, one dark brow lifting. "Make me a drink?"

Why not? I need a refill anyway. I don't ask what he wants. He's going to get whatever I serve him, king or not. His fault for not being specific.

I bring him a glass, the twin of mine.

"Whiskey. Neat," I say as I pass him the drink with a curtsy that almost has me falling on my backside.

"You just poured it into a glass."

The whiskey sloshes dangerously close to the edge of my glass as I plop onto the sofa. "Yep. Not my fault you didn't say what you wanted."

His head falls back against the cushion as laughter booms into the quiet space. It's deep and rich, the kind that sinks into the soul like dark chocolate and makes you beg for more. I bite my lip, holding in the grin trying to break free.

Sigurd reins in his humor and sips at the drink. All I can think of is what it would be like to taste the whiskey on his lips.

"Humans pay you to do this?" he asks.

The fluttering feeling in my chest stops instantly. "Yes, in fact, they do." I notch my chin higher. "Some people love a simple, well-aged drink all on its own. Many more, though, prefer a beer in a chilled mug with just the right amount of foam." I measure the height with my fingers. "Or an old fashioned with the perfect little twirl of orange peel. I'm pretty darn good at those, if I do say so myself. And of course, there's the conversation. Having a drink alone is...well, lonely. No one wants that. Half the time, people come just for someone to talk to."

He sips his drink again and leans in. "And do you scowl at them all too?"

My lips press thin. "I do not."

I gasp as he tips up my chin, his thumb brushing across my skin. His lips quirk up in one corner. "Just me then."

"Yes." It's a throaty whisper. "You deserve it."

"I suppose I do." I shiver and pull away from his touch. He settles back onto his side, though he still seems far too close. "So, Wren the bartender who was drinking alone, you must be lonely and in want of company?"

A pleasant burn settles in my throat with the whiskey. *Lonely, I—*

"You said you care for your grandmother?" he asks.

Gran. My chest squeezes.

"Yes." I find the little bird around my neck and give it a squeeze. "She..." I look away and shake my head. All these years later, and it still makes me choke up to talk about it. No time to get emotional. A deep, steadying breath fills my lungs. "A tornado hit our house when I was a kid. I made it out. My parents didn't."

"A construct of wind," Sigurd says, almost absently.

The irony of it isn't lost on me. My life has changed drastically twice in my life. Once by a powerful twister made of wind and now another time being bound by a king of air.

"Anyhow," I continue, trying to force the hard memories away, "Gran raised me after that. Then, by the time I was old enough to care for myself, her health had gotten worse, and I couldn't leave her alone. After all she'd done for me, how could I? So, I stayed and cared for her." At some point, my gaze had slid far away, out to the darkening night. I shift it back to him. "Until you trapped me here."

His hand flexes on his glass, the only tell that my words hit their target.

"You thought I was someone else. Ev—"

"Don't," he snarls.

I straighten. "Don't?" A glimpse of sharp teeth between his pulled-back lips should have me running, but curiosity pulls me closer. "Don't what?"

"We're not talking about her," he says before downing the rest of his glass in one go.

Whoa. Way to make me want to ask about her even more. Whoever she is, he cares. A lot. Enough that jealousy's dark head rears itself within me. It's not over him, of course not, but to have someone care so passionately... It's a dream so far out of reach I can't help but yearn for it.

"Fine," I huff.

"Ask me about something else. Anything else."

Anything, huh? I fight the devious grin trying to break free. "Is it true you started a war with the Court of the Forest?"

His eyes go wide.

I blink innocently. "You said anything."

"Ugh." He runs a hand down his face. "I haven't had enough to drink for this."

"Oh." I set my glass aside and stand. "Well, I can fix that." I pluck the glass from him and head for the liquor cabinet before he can protest.

I gasp as he appears directly in front of me, and I wobble on my tipsy feet. The empty glass tumbles from my fingers.

Faster than I can blink, Sigurd catches the glass just before it shatters across the stone floor. His other palm rests on the back of my thigh, steading my wobble and stirring up a whole mess of butterflies within me. Heat spreads through my chest as I stare down at him, unable to breathe, much less move.

His fingers trail ever so lightly up the back of my thigh as he rises. His gaze never leaves mine. Tingling chills race across my skin.

"Let's play a game, shall we?" His voice is rich as the beverage we drank and warms me even more. "For each question one of us answers, the other takes a drink."

I nearly laugh as I slide by him to grab the bottle we've been using. "Are you sure you want to play a drinking game with a bartender?"

Sigurd smirks. "Oh, I think so."

CHAPTER 11

W E START OUT EASY with our game of questions and sips. Favorite color. Favorite food. Sigurd asks more questions than I do, and I'm happy to let him drink his fill. The world already blurs a little at the edge, and the last time I thought about standing up... Well, I didn't.

"So," I drawl as I empty the last of the bottle into his glass. "Back to my original question. Did you start a war?"

He glowers then heaves a sigh. "Maybe."

"Maybe?" I scoot closer. My leg brushes his. When did we get so close? "What kind of answer is that?"

"They have not formally declared war upon us, but they've moved troops near the border. Cut off all outsiders entering."

"What do you have to do with that?"

His gaze dips to the glass in my hand.

"Nuh, uh." I wag my finger at him. "This counts as the same question." The last word slurs, and the flush clinging to my cheeks burns hotter.

"Well." He stretches his arms over his head. "I might have almost gotten their king killed."

"What!" Whiskey sloshes over the rim of my cup and runs down my fingers. *Blast it all.* I set the cup on the table.

Sigurd moves with too much grace for all he's consumed and takes my hand in his. "Shame to waste something so fine."

He raises my hand toward his lips.

My heart stops. My eyes fly wide as my lips part. He's going to lick it off me, use that wicked tongue to—

Instead, he wipes my hand with his sleeve. Quite un-king-like. Intimate. Casual. Something too much like what I would do. My heart beats again. I remember to breathe, but everything I'd planned to say has vanished from my head.

"All better," he says.

"Y-yes." I drop my hands to my lap, twisting them there, unable to hold still, especially with him so close. Our legs touch. His scent tangles around me, mixing with the whiskey on my breath.

"But yes," he says, leaning back against the cushions as if nothing just happened. "What occurred was unintended. I planned to pay him back for an offense from long ago. I thought if I got some measure of revenge, I'd feel better. Or maybe he would realize the pain he caused me."

"Do you?"

"Hm?"

"Feel better?"

He sighs through his nose. "No, nor did I get my revenge exactly. There was a complication with the Unseelie, and his human woman was much more..." His brows pinch before the hint of a grin stretches his lips. "Not what I expected."

Inky, slimy feelings curl within me.

"Who are the Unseelie?" I ask, shifting the topic away from some girl I've never met and totally can't be jealous of. I reach for my drink and make sure to slide my hand down his thigh as I settle myself against him again.

It's the whiskey. It has to be.

Sigurd coughs into his fist. A sudden breeze stirs my hair and encourages me to nestle closer. Could be the whiskey, but I'd swear he shivers.

"The Unseelie are dark fae. We were all one people once, many ages ago, but the Unseelie were dissatisfied with our ways. They corrupted our magic and preferred to live differently—apart. And so, they split from us. The ages have changed them even further, creating them into the monsters they are now."

The hard edge in his voice makes me shudder. I sip at my drink, savoring the warm burn that smooths away the goosebumps on my arms.

"They were of your kingdom? People of air?"

"This was before the Court of Air existed." His eyes shine a little brighter. "Fae history is long." He brushes a strand of hair behind my ear. "Complicated."

"And fascinating." I lean in.

"You think so?" His arm slides around my shoulder, pulling me closer.

"If the Unseelie wanted to be separate, why do they bother you now?"

"So many questions, so few drinks." He winks.

I raise my glass, but he places his hand atop it.

"If you have any more, you may not remember a word I say." He plucks the drink from my hand and sets it on the side table with his own.

"This game was your idea." I poke him in the chest.

"And a lovely game it's turned out to be." That look in his eyes...

I could melt and slide right off this sofa. I could drown in it. It'd be so easy. The whiskey almost has me brave enough.

Almost.

"Um..." I start.

He leans in, but the bird around my neck is suddenly cool on my skin.

I pull back ever so slightly, and the small action snaps the cord of tension between us.

"The Unseelie?" My voice is a hoarse whisper.

"Their king died long ago without an heir or close relations. So, their land has slowly died as well."

My brows pinch. My whiskey brain can't follow it. But one part catches like a loose nail and settles heavily in my chest. "Do you have an heir?"

A soft rumble echoes in his chest as his arm flexes around me. "No. But Hawke and Moria are close enough relations that the magic would pass to them. Not that either of them want to rule. Moria once claimed she'd seek out a way to curse me beyond death if I died without a direct heir and the magic settled on her."

Without thinking, I trail a hand down his shirt, letting the soft material tease my skin. "Did you want to be king?"

He stiffens and looks away.

I press my hand against his chest, feeling the quick thump of his chest.

"No," he replies at length. The soft smile that crosses his face pulls at my heart. It simmers with sincerity, possibly the first true smile I've seen. "What about you? Did you always wish to be a bartender?"

Now it's my turn to laugh. "No. I wanted to travel. See the world. Maybe be a flight attendant or a travel writer." I shrug. "Something."

"Why didn't you?"

"Gran." I sigh and nestle against his side. "She needed me. *Needs* me. I couldn't leave her." A heavy yawn escapes from nowhere.

"You gave up your dreams for her."

"Not forever. Just..." I attempt a shrug and fail. "She cared for me for years. How could I leave her?"

"You're so much like her and yet not at all."

"Like Gran?" My brows scrunch. How would he know?

"No." He cups my cheek, a sad look in his eyes. "Someone from long ago." His sorrow settles over me like a blanket, tempting me to give in to the shadows closing in at the corners of my vision.

"What happened to your wings?" I ask, stifling another yawn.

"Ah. Would you like to see them again?"

"Yes." My lids drift closed.

He pulls me closer, and I snuggle into his warmth. "Then you'll have to fly with me, Wren."

The way he says my name stirs up butterflies in my chest. It holds so much more than just a few letters. He makes it full, vibrant, wonderous—so different from the plain little bird I'm named for.

Long fingers slide through my hair, and it's the best feeling in the world. So soothing. So calming. Tender. I sigh.

"Let me show you the world as you long for," he says.

"That would be nice," I whisper. Or I mean to. I'm not sure if the words make it out. Something soft brushes my forehead before the comforting darkness claims me.

CHAPTER 12

I LURCH AWAKE. EVERYTHING spins. A headache pounds behind my eyes as I squint into the blinding light. My gut does somersaults within me, and for a horrible moment, I have no idea where I am.

Faery. I groan and pull the covers over my head. The movement sends my stomach lurching.

I barely process the heavy weight on the bed next to me before I stumble out of the sheets and race for the bathroom, bare feet slapping across the stone. My knees crash to the floor seconds before I hurl my guts out into the fae version of a toilet.

Everything spins. The acrid scent burns my nostrils.

Why oh why did I drink so much? My cheek lands on the toilet seat—it's pleasantly warm. I'm still not sure how they do that when there's no electricity. Some fae magic? A blessing for sure.

Another wave hits me, and I barely pull my hair out of the way in time.

It takes almost all my strength and rational thought to find the handle and flush. These toilets work a little differently than human ones. The first time I used one, it took me an embarrassingly long time to find the stone on the wall that releases a stream of water to wash everything away. Thank God for plumbing though. It takes the mess away and somehow leaves a clean and clear scent behind that soothes a little of my headache.

"You sound wretched." Sigurd leans against the doorframe—the one leading to my borrowed bedroom—in nothing but loose-fitting pants that hang about his waist.

Warmth races across my cheeks and down to my chest. Good God.

How the fu-reak is he so normal? So... sexy. Dang it. I scrub my arm across my mouth and picture myself from his perspective—still in yesterday's clothes, hair a mess, and vomiting into the toilet. Oh yes, I'm sure I look just peachy.

He, on the other hand, doesn't seem bothered by the whiskey at all, if his perfectly sleep-tousled hair and easy expression are any indication. Pale scars accent the sculpted, lean muscle of his chest and abs, drawing my attention. My mouth dries.

The scars, yes, that's all. A particularly wicked-looking one curves down into the waistband of his pants.

"Your fault," I mumble. How dare he be fine when I'm so not.

Sigurd leans his head back on the doorframe. "Is it?"

I shiver on the floor and glance back at him. "Yes, you— Oh my God." The doorway he stands in is the same one I fled in here through. "You, you—"

"Yes?"

"You were in my bed."

He grins. "I was."

I sputter like a fish. Suddenly, I'm dizzy for a whole new reason. A quick scan confirms all my clothes are in place. Thank everything holy for that.

Sigurd kneels beside me. "What kind of gentlemen would I be if I left you after you passed out on me?"

The closeness is overwhelming. His presence, his scent. I turn back to the bowl and dry heave. Sigurd smooths the hair back from my face, holding it behind my head in a move so tender it would wreck me if I wasn't already a mess.

"This may be my fault," he whispers. "I forgot how much stronger our drinks can be than your human ones. Haven't had much contact with humans lately, except your uncle. Well, when he was human. He's not much of a drinker though."

No. He never was.

"You don't have your own room?" I accuse.

"The king's suite is through the doors near the dining table."

"The king's, not yours?"

He glances away then back. "I don't prefer those rooms."

Interesting. There's more there, but I'm in no shape to ask about it.

Sigurd finally releases my hair. I gasp as a cool rag touches my face.

"Here, let me," he says. My flush deepens as he wipes my face. "It's a good thing the next event isn't until tomorrow. I wouldn't want you to blame me if you got disqualified for failing to appear."

I frown and swat at him, but it's all for show. "What time is it?"

"Almost noon."

So late. I'll be lucky if I'm fit enough for anything tomorrow at this rate. "Ugh, this is miserable."

"I have something that may help. Wait here."

A shiver rolls across my skin as he vanishes into thin air.

"Sigurd?" I call, but he's well and truly gone.

Seconds tick into minutes. I shove off the floor and finish cleaning myself up. A temporary fix. With the way my stomach's churning, it won't last long.

A soft breeze ruffles my hair. Sigurd appears next to me, and I jump. In my haste, I nearly knock over half the stuff on the vanity.

"I'll never get used to that," I say.

Something passes across his face before he shakes it away. He holds up a vial of blue liquid. "Here. Drink this."

My nose wrinkles as I stare at the dubious substance.

He pops the stopper. I reach for it, but he shakes his head.

"I won't drop it," I mumble.

"Even so." He raises the vial to my lips.

It's cold, tingly, and tastes of mint and something I can't quite place. All my muscles relax as the liquid chills its way down into me.

"What was that?" Totally should have asked before I drank it but oh well.

"A healing tonic." The empty vial clinks when he sets it on the counter. "You'll be sleepy today but should be back to normal before tomorrow."

"Thank goodness." I sigh, my shoulders going loose. "Thank you."

"Of course." He brushes my cheek with the back of his hand, sending a shiver down to my toes.

I bite my lip, holding back a sheepish smile, and head for the bedroom. One step, and I stumble.

Sigurd catches me with reflexes faster than any human's, but instead of settling me on my feet, he lifts me into his arms, just like he did that first night he found me in the woods.

"Sigurd."

He stiffens. A brief glow emanates from his eyes. I swallow, still tasting mint. Should I have addressed him as king?

"Thank you," I add.

But it's gone as soon as it came. He settles me in the sheets, and I don't protest as he sits on the covers next to me. Already, darkness pulls at the corners of my vision. This stuff works fast, not like human medicine which can take ages to have any effect.

Silence settles between us, so heavy and thick I almost can't breathe. I have to break it. Say something. Anything. "Humans help your magic?"

"Yes, it's..." He glances down at my blinking eyes and stops whatever he was going to say. "It's a tale for another time but yes."

An embarrassingly large yawn erupts before I can stop it. He's right. I won't make it through a long tale, but I have to ask. "Then why don't you spend time with many?"

Sigurd huffs. " I should have known you'd ask about that." His fingers trail through my hair as if it's the most natural thing in the world. "Many reasons, but my father... spent a lot of time with humans. I refuse to be like him."

His father? I shift under the sheets, pulling them tighter. "Why?"

But I'm so tired. So pleasantly exhausted all of a sudden.

"Sleep, Wren." He strokes my head. "There'll be time another day."

Chapter 13

Sigurd's medicine worked wonders. I feel like I could run a marathon. Well, maybe a 5K. I've never been the best of runners. Sigurd is nowhere to be found when morning light crests over the mountains to spill into the room. Part of me frowns at the loss, but a bigger part is thankful. No awkward morning after—not that we did anything.

He was just being nice. That's all. If I tell myself that enough times, maybe I'll believe it.

My eagle friend swoops through the curtains and comes to rest on the bed. His talons pick at the cloth as he shifts on his feet. He gives a little squawk, and his head tilts this way and that as if he's asking a question.

"I'm much better today, thank you."

Tentatively, I reach out my hand and run my fingers along his feathered head. Like a happy golden retriever, he leans into my touch. I shake my head and smile. Ridiculous bird.

Satisfied, he ruffles his feathers and hops over to the table next to the bed. A large arrangement of white flowers spills out of a crystal vase. I blink a few times, and it's still there. Peonies? But the violet stems spearing into the water are unlike anything I've seen at home.

"Who..."

The eagle plucks a card in its beak and hops over to me.

I laugh and take the card.

Thick, white paper is folded in half. I open it to reveal words so looped and fanciful that, at first, I think it's some foreign fae language.

Wren,

I hope you enjoy these cadmum flowers. They only bloom in places that receive morning light and have plenty of water. They should be perfect by your bedside.

Warmth spreads through my chest, tingling all the way down to my toes. The note isn't signed, but it doesn't take a genius to know who sent me flowers. It's not Uncle Mark's style, certainly not his handwriting. Neither Moria nor Hawke seem the type.

"They are beautiful, aren't they?"

The eagle squawks in agreement.

An odd feeling clings to the tattoo around my wrist, almost like there's literally string there and someone is tugging it, but I convince myself it's just a trick of the mind.

No sooner have I washed, dressed, and scarfed down some food in the main sitting area than Hawke and Mark join me.

My stomach drops. I promised Uncle Mark a chat. Somehow being sick in bed would be preferable. I said I'd hear him out, and he'd kept his end of our deal. But still, one good act can't wipe away years of hurt.

"Good morning." I force a smile to accompany my words.

Uncle Mark laughs. "I'm glad today is. I came by yesterday, but you were unwell."

"Yeah..." I rub the pendant on my necklace. Good gracious, does he know Sigurd was with me? It's high school all over again, with Gran scolding me for making out with boys in the driveway. "I didn't know how strong the liquor is here."

"My niece, a drinker. Who'd have guessed?" The question is light and playful, but all it does is remind me how little he knows.

I shrug. "I'm a bartender. Usually, I can handle a drink or two."

Hawke raises his brows but says nothing.

The humor vanishes from Mark's face. "Really? I'da thought you'd go to college for sure. You had the grades for it. At least you used to." He rubs the back of his neck. "Maybe get a fancy job in the city or something."

Me too. I barely hold in the words. *I might have if you'd stayed.*

One minute together, and all the joy of the morning had trickled away. I bite my bottom lip and squeeze the pendant tighter. How on earth am I going to get through this conversation?

"Well," Hawke says, finally breaking up the tension in the room. "I'm sure you have much to catch up on, but for now, we need to take you to the competition. If you still wish to participate, that is." He inclines his head to me.

"Of course." I leap to my feet.

He nods. "It begins soon."

"Are you ready?" Mark asks. Genuine concern laces his voice, but that's not what settles heavily on my chest.

I assumed it'd be Sigurd taking me there. After yesterday—well, the day before—and the flowers. I'd been looking forward to seeing him way more than I should, especially since it's his fault I'm stuck here.

"Our king cannot show preference," Hawke says as if he can pick the words right out of my head. My skin turns clammy. Maybe he can. "He is concerned that your competition may already think the games biased in your favor, and such thoughts would not benefit any of us."

"Right." I swallow the tightness in my throat. "And they won't think that if I arrive with you both?"

"Mark is your family, and therefore, so am I. It's customary for family members to support their contestants."

Family. I hold back a snort. The old men at Jolene's are closer to me than these two, but I suppose someone has to take me there. Finding my way there on my own might be a struggle. That's assuming the guards at the main doors would let me out—they haven't yet—or my eagle friend has a larger buddy I could ride. A sigh slips out. A few of the birds lounging on the roof might just be big enough, but they haven't come down here.

"I don't suppose you can tell me what today's competition is?" I ask as I take their hands and brace for their horrible method of travel.

Uncle Mark opens his mouth, but Hawke speaks first. "No, but you'll find out with the other contestants soon enough."

"All right, well, beam me up, Scotty."

Hawke's lips twist as if I've splattered him with mud, but at least Uncle Mark laughs. I hold my breath and squeeze their hands in a death grip as the room bends and warps. No matter how long I'm here, I'll never get used to this. I pinch my eyes shut, begging the spinning to stop.

When I open them, I'm not prepared for the sight that greets me. Instead of the colosseum of two days before, we're standing in an open field. If I had to guess, I'd say we're likely somewhere in the valley below the castle. Wooden stands are erected around us in a half-moon. Fae cram them full, but there's a tenth of what there was last time. Today's attire seems more casual too, with more muted grays and blues rather than the riot of color from before. I guess it's like the Olympics, where the opening ceremony gets all the attention and the individual games draw a smaller crowd.

Hawke drops my hand almost immediately, but Mark clings to it. "Good luck today, Wren." He draws me in closer. "You'll need more than luck, but you can do it." His other hand clasps over mine. "I believe in you."

"Thank you." It's all I can squeak out as a sinking feeling takes hold. More than luck, huh? Unless we're making cocktails—un-likely—I'm probably the least skilled person here.

I join the other competitors where they cluster around a raised stage. The announcer from before—at least I think it's the same one, hard to tell with his outlandish outfits—speaks in low tones with a few other well-clad fae, likely preparing to present the day's contest.

Galen stands alone, and I weave my way toward him, dodging hard stares and words spoken in a language I can't understand.

"Good morning." I give him a little wave.

He nods his tanned head. "To you as well."

Unsure what else to say, I scan the crowd. I have to lean around Galen to see the royal box. Whatever strange tug I felt—or thought I felt—from the bond on my wrist before is gone, but it's still easy to find Sigurd. The royal box is uncovered today, and the light reflecting off the silver buttons and trim on Sigurd's attire gives him a regal look—no crown required.

I bob on my feet, hopeful to catch his attention, but his gaze slides right over me. A flicker of pain runs through my chest. Did I do something wrong?

"So, what could a human favored by the king wish for?" Galen asks, following my gaze.

"Favored?" The back of my neck heats as I recall Hawke's words from earlier. "I'm not favored."

"You're..." His brows wrinkle as he shifts on his feet. "Ah, I forgot you humans can lie."

I purse my lips. "I'm not lying." Okay, maybe a little. "Look, I just want to go home, but I can't, not without the cauldron's help."

He flinches and leans in closer. "You're here against your will?"

"Sort of." Without thinking, I grab at the fabric wrapped around my wrist. It's meant to look like an armband. My gaze drifts to Moria. She brought one to match each outfit. They came with stern instructions not to be removed outside Sigurd's quarters.

The look Galen gives me might as well burn straight through the fabric.

He knows. Oh shoot, he knows.

His jaw stiffens before he practically sneers in Sigurd's direction. "Just like his father."

"What?"

Galen shakes his head. It speaks volumes. Not here. Not now. Which probably means never, since I'm basically locked in a gilded tower when I'm not competing.

I refuse to be like my father. Sigurd's words echo through my mind.

"I could feel his presence on you," Galen says, "but I thought he'd marked you, that maybe you wanted to be fae."

"Marked? That's not—" I pick at the thick fabric bracelet, but he closes his hand over mine.

"No. A mark is a mating bond."

I wrench my arm back and screech far too loudly, "A what?"

Others turn our way, and it's all I can do to plaster a fake smile on my face and laugh like he'd just said a joke, not dropped a bomb on me. A mating bond? Seriously? My chest burns at the implication. That's what he thought hung between Sigurd and me?

"It feels similar." Galen shrugs.

"You can feel this?" I look at my arm then back to him.

"All magic can be felt."

"So everyone here thinks we..." My throat goes dry at the thought. Oh great. Just peachy.

"Most likely."

The laugh that bubbles from my lips isn't faked. At least Uncle Mark knows the truth, but all these fae... I stare at the other competitors. No wonder they dislike me. It wasn't just that I'd left Sigurd's box to join them. They assume we're lovers.

Just great. Maybe it'd be better if they knew the truth instead.

"So." I cough, trying to rid myself of his revelation. "What do you want if you win?"

All his features melt into a shroud of sorrow. After a lengthy pause, he says, "I want to go home too."

"You're stuck here?"

His gaze is somewhere far away when he answers. "There's a woman back home who I love. We left things...poorly." He shakes his head. "I at least owe her a proper farewell."

My chest tightens. Separated from someone he loves. It's a pain I'm all too familiar with. I reach for his hand to comfort him when a sharp whistle from the announcer commands attention. I knit my hands behind my back instead.

The announcer drones on long enough that I almost miss it when he switches to the important details.

"Today, our contestants shall search these woods to find this." He holds up a white flower with a purple stem, and a gasp catches in my throat. It takes everything I have not to look at Sigurd. It can't be a coincidence. It's not possible.

"The cadmum is a rare and beautiful flower," the announcer begins as his assistants carry flowers around for us to view up close. But all the announcer's remaining words are unhelpful. "All methods of hunting are permitted. The last ten competitors to return with a fully intact flower, or any who do not return by sundown, will be eliminated."

Find a flower in the woods? I groan and stare at my boots. They're comfortable enough but still. Freaking weird fae games.

"Begin!"

Fae race for the woods faster than champion sprinters. Some disappear completely. Another sniffs the air and then puts their nose to the ground, tracking scent like a bloodhound.

"Might want to hurry," Galen says before he takes off after the others.

CHAPTER 14

I JOG THROUGH THE woods until my lungs burn and I have to slow down. I repeat Sigurd's illicit clues over and over as I search for flowers or any sign of water.

Water. Morning light.

Water. Morning light.

I glance up at the blue sky above. The morning light is basically gone, faded into midday. A roar of distant cheers tickles my ears, and it's not the first. Others have already found a flower and returned, and yet, the only white things I've found are a few oddly shaped mushrooms.

"I'm going to need a miracle," I mumble into the surrounding forest.

It doesn't help that the trees here are weird. Spindly ones defy gravity as they spiral up toward the sky. Bulbous ones with violet trunks and golden leaves squat low to the ground. There are some pretty standard-looking oaks too, and I could see pines and firs from the castle. But the odd ones are so distracting that I might have jogged right past a flower without noticing.

"Human," someone whispers.

The fine hairs on the back of my neck rise. I turn this way and that, searching for its source. A gasp leaps from my throat when I find it.

A woman with pale pink hair peeks around a thick tree. Ears twitch on top of her head, ones like a cat's. A fae—there's no doubt of it—but one so unlike the others I've seen.

"Who are you?" I step back, heart thundering. "What do you want?"

She steps fully from behind the tree. Her clothing is tight like Moria's typical outfits but colored in greens and tans, as if to blend into the forest. Hard to do with that hair though. A tail flicks out behind her, like a cat at play. Maybe she has the reflexes of one too. I didn't hear a peep until she spoke. Not that I was looking for others.

"To help you." She blinks. "You are the human who was with the air king, are you not? At the ceremony?"

"Yes." Some of the tension holding my body straight and stiff slips away. "You were there?"

She nods, her whole body participating in the motion like a snake bobbing its head.

"Why help me?" Why would a fae want a human to win?

Her tail flicks again. "Because you can help me."

I rear back. "How?" How on earth could I help a fae? But memories come on me in an instant, settling hard in my chest. I know how. Sigurd told me. "I can't stay with you. There's the competition and..."

I fumble for words as I rub at the hidden mark on my wrist. *I don't want to?*

She appears next to me, and I gasp, stepping back. Her feline gaze—good Lord, she even has golden catlike pupils—lands on my wrist.

"I feel..." Clawed fingers hover over my wrist, but she doesn't touch me. Instead, she pulls them back as quickly as she reached for me. "He bound you? The air king?"

My throat goes dry. How could she know that? But she does. I can see it in the glimmer in her eyes.

"What do you play for, human?" she asks.

"My freedom."

"You do not love the king who bound you?"

"Love?" I jump back as if the word punched me. My chest aches in response. "No, certainly not. We haven't even kissed. He trapped me here. How could I—"

I catch myself. Here I've gone and spilled all my secrets to this strange woman just because she sets me on edge. And she eats them up, devouring every word in a slowly growing grin.

"You think to remove his bond," she says. "You believe he won't rebind you the moment it's gone?"

In a sentence, she murders my dreams.

The day is suddenly cold. Breath is hard to come by. I never considered, never thought... A whisper of his touch sends a shiver through my body. I remember the warmth of his body next to mine, the way he cared for me in my hangover, and the tingle of his fingers through my hair.

"That's why you may need my help," she says, circling around me. "Win this contest. Remove the binding, and I'll take you away before he can bind you again."

"He wouldn't," I stammer, and she stops.

"Are you sure?" The words are almost a purr.

I want to be. I yearn for it. But I'm not. So stupid, I've only known him a few days, but already, I trust him. I want to trust him. But...

My gaze falls to my wrist.

He did bind me here, accident or not, and I can't risk being away from Gran that long. I have to get home, have to check on her.

"What do you want from me?" I ask.

She hops back, her hands behind her back. "You'll see."

I swallow the lump in my throat. "And if I don't win?"

She grins. "That's why I'll help you." She holds up one clawed finger. "But you must tell no one about me. If you do, I will not help you."

My brows scrunch. How would she know?

"Oh, I'll know," she says as if reading my thoughts.

My skin turns clammy.

"You need a flower. Quickly, follow me." She doesn't wait for me to agree, just takes off into the woods.

It takes all my stamina to keep up with her. Limbs catch at my face and clothes. My chest burns. It's all too much, like my flight from Jolene's that brought me here, and I have to swallow down the hysteria threatening to choke me.

The fae woman picks her way through the forest with speedy, practiced ease, barely ruffling a leaf and leaving nothing to show her tracks. On the other hand, I might as well be a bull charging through, for all the noise and mess I make. When she finally stops, I double over with my hands on my knees, trying to suck air into my lungs. Sweat drips down my back and between my breasts. I have got to get in better shape. I wipe my brow and stare her down in envy. Her breathing is even, her countenance bright. Not a hair is out of place in her pink ponytail.

Ridiculous.

She points to the left with a grin.

Cadmums, a whole cluster of them, spring from the ground in a particularly shady spot near a bubbling creek. I let out a cry of relief and force myself toward them.

I glance over one shoulder. "How did you find—"

But she's gone. As if she never existed.

"Hello?" I call for good measure.

I didn't even get her name.

I examine the spot where I'd swear she was standing, but not a twig is disturbed or out of place. I shiver. Too eerie. Only time will tell if she keeps her word or not. I rub at my chest, trying to ease the ache that's settled there. She certainly gave me a lot to think about.

But there's no time to think about that now. I rush back to the cadmums and wrench a stem from the ground.

Distant cheers, barely audible, tease me.

My shoulders droop. Another jog is in my future, and it's going to suck.

Two minutes into the run, I know I'm not alone.

It's like spiders skittering down my spine. The odd rustle—too loud for a small forest animal—catches my attention.

Did she come back?

"Hello?" I stop, listening for any signs over my quick breaths.

Louder rustling sounds head my way.

I take off at a run. Whatever it is, I don't want to find out. Sigurd said the games could be dangerous. Wild animals? Enemies?

Shi-oot. I'm in a forest. War might be brewing with the Court of the Forest. Is this place theirs? Are they so close? Surely, they wouldn't hold their competition in enemy territory, but—

"Wren?" someone says.

I skid to a stop and nearly fall.

"Galen?" I twist around.

He stands a few feet away and has the decency to at least look winded.

"Have you—" But the words die as he notices what I hold. His eyes widen before narrowing. His jaw stiffens.

My feet flex in my boots, ready to run.

He shakes his head, and the look vanishes. "Anyone else, and I'd try to steal that from you."

"That's not against the rules?"

Galen shakes his head.

No, the announcer didn't say anything about that, did he?

I glance this way and that on high alert. I'm a sitting duck. If anyone finds me before I get back, I'm done for. My odds are terrible. It's amazing no one else has come across me, especially with all the noise I make.

Unless they're all back already and I've lost. It's not even close to dark, but that doesn't mean a darn thing with as fast as some of these fae can move.

An idea strikes me like lightning. "Can you carry me back?"

"What?" he scoffs.

"You're fast. You look strong. Could you run while carrying me?"

"Of course." He crosses his arms. "But why would I?"

Stubborn. I cross mine in return. "Promise to carry me back, and I'll get you a flower."

His lips thin, but he doesn't say no.

There were plenty of others where I got this one. He can be my transportation and protection. Other fae wouldn't come after us together, right?

"Fine, I promise." He spits out the word as if he tasted something foul. "Flower first."

I nod and jog toward him. "This way."

Thank goodness for my sense of direction. It only takes a few minutes to follow the stream back and find the cluster of flowers.

Galen snaps off a stem and sticks the stalky thing through his belt. He holds his hands wide. "Well?"

I stare at him. Right. He agreed to carry me back. Though until now, I didn't think about how he'd do that. Heat builds over my breastbone as I approach him. "How do you—"

"I'll just—" He breaks off and rubs the back of his neck. A hint of color touches his cheeks.

At least I'm not the only one suddenly feeling weird about this. I stare at the ground, unable to look at him. "However is fine."

He steps closer until we're almost touching. My boots shift on the dirt, and I don't miss the way he can't stand still either.

"Ready?" he bites out.

I nod. Whatever was I thinking?

Before I have the chance to second guess it, he bends down, scoops an arm under my knees, and lifts me up with his other cradling my back. With one arm around his neck and the other clutching my flower, he takes off.

It's a darn good thing I hold on tight. He flies through the woods, even with me in his arms. He's so much faster than I would have been and somehow manages to dodge limbs and shrubs with grace almost as fine as the pink-haired fae woman's.

Still, he's breathing heavier by the time the wooden stands slip into sight between the trees, and sweat dots his brow. With me in tow, he rushes toward the podium.

Wall-less tents dot the field on their side of the podium now. Fae lounge in their shade. Other competitors?

A wave of murmurs rushes through the crowd as Galen comes to a stop and plants me on my feet. With so many fae watching and talking about me, I'm frozen like a deer in headlights.

I guess it's only fair that Galen runs ahead and leaps up the stairs to the stage. Well, sort of.

A roar of cheers and applause rise as he hands over his flower.

I'm searching for Sigurd before I realize what I'm doing. And it's not hard to find him. A knot forms in my throat as I catch sight of him leaning on the edge of his royal box, palms splayed on top of the railing. His expression is hard to make out, but the lack of movement says enough.

He's pissed.

Because I got a flower or because Galen carried me?

Both?

"Wren," Galen calls to me as he hops down the stairs. He jerks his head toward the stage.

Right. I haven't won this game yet.

Chapter 15

With no time to lose, I race up the steps to the podium to claim my victory.

The announcer sweeps his arm in a large flourish, fanning out the faux—at least I think they're fake—feathered wings hangings from his arms as part of his attire. Today, they're a greenish color and match shimmering eyeshadow that creates a dramatic smoky eye any makeup artist would be proud of.

I hold out the flower, and he grabs my hand, raising it in the air.

The crowd roars. It might be my imagination, but their cheers are louder than ever before. Are they truly excited to see me move on?

I find Sigurd again, and the hope fluttering in my chest dies. The people are happy, even if their king is not.

Just peachy.

It takes everything I have to keep the smile plastered on my face until the announcer lowers my hand.

"Quite a show," he says with a wink before plucking the flower from me. "Rest, relax"—he gestures to the tents—"until this game is complete."

I dust the glitter from his hand off my arm as I make my way down the short flight of stairs. The other winning competitors cluster in the shade of the tents, reclining in plush chairs and enjoying the displays of food and drinks arranged in each. I count my blessings and search the tents. I find Galen nearly chugging a glass of water. He occupies a nearly empty tent. One more reason for its appeal. I've had enough odd conversations with fae today.

"Thank you," I say.

He wipes the back of his hand across his mouth and gives me a nod.

"I'm not sure I'd have made it back in time without your help."

A huff of laughter slips out as he grabs a plate stacked with fruit. "I should be thanking you. Who thought finding a flower would be so hard? You must be lucky."

"Yeah." Lucky. Right. I worry my lip with my teeth. Or getting myself in loads of trouble trusting some woman I don't know. Unsure what to say, I grab a glass of water and chug it back.

It's heaven.

Cool. Refreshing. The best water I've ever tasted.

The hint of relief calms the last of my adrenaline and makes all my aches known. My throat begs for more water. The muscles in my legs jump. Sweat sticks my clothes to my skin.

I grab a second glass and practically collapse in the chair near the one Galen claimed.

He pops something that looks like a blue strawberry into his mouth. Drool nearly drips down my chin. I probably should have gotten something to eat too, but now that I'm sitting, there's no way I'm getting back up. At least, not yet.

In an effort not to think about the weird fae woman or the king probably still scowling my way, I examine the man near me. He's handsome enough. Strong. A warrior, maybe? But there's a heaviness to the set of his shoulders, as if he carries the world on his back. Whatever did he do to anger the woman he loves? Does he seek her forgiveness? Is that why he can't go home?

I shouldn't ask. It's never proper to pry in other people's business. But curiosity eats at me worse than my hunger, and I need the distraction—anything not to think about my own problems.

"So." I lean in. "Is your home nearby? Why can't you go back?"

He coughs, almost choking on the berry. His fist slams against his chest as he clears his throat.

Oops. The toes of my boots press together. "Sorry."

"It's..." He shakes his head. "Complicated."

I roll my eyes and sigh. Is every fae going to tell me that? "And I thought we were friends."

Galen only blinks at me.

Okay, maybe friends is a stretch. "Allies?"

"Why do you want to know?" He cocks a brow at me.

To ignore my problems. But instead, I say, "I dunno. You left things poorly with the woman you loved, right? Well, I'm a woman. Maybe I can help you find a way to apologize?"

He throws his head back and laughs.

My stomach drops. I didn't think my offer was that ridiculous.

"I don't think an apology will be enough. But it doesn't matter. I can't get to her to apologize anyway."

My brows pinch together. "Why not? You don't live around here?"

"I was born here. But no." He looks past me, somewhere far away. "The Court of the Forest is where I belong. It's where she is."

A little golden leaf dangles from his ear, and he takes it between his fingers, rubbing it like I sometimes do my necklace. It must remind him of her. Or maybe she gave it to him?

"Why not just...go?" I ask.

Galen looks at me closely. "I see you know something about the courts?"

"Not much." I rub the back of my neck and look away.

"Tell me."

"This is the Court of Air."

He nods.

"There's a Court of the Forest," I hedge. He waits, and I swallow my nerves before continuing. "The two courts may not be on great terms."

Galen snorts and crosses an ankle over one knee. "No, not anymore."

"So that's why you can't go back?" I press.

He slides a sideways look my way. "You're not going to let this go, are you?"

No, not a bit. All I can do is smile.

"I'm oath sworn to Sigurd. He ordered me to stay here." His eyes pinch closed. "Unless he changes his mind, I don't have a chance of explaining things to Sylvie unless I can win this competition and force him to free me of my oath."

Poor guy. And stuck here because of Sigurd. I lean back in my chair, attempting to see the man in question. From this angle, I can only see the front edge of the box, and he no longer clutches the railing. Is he still there? Other than accidentally sticking me here, he's been mostly kind. Albeit a little flirty but maybe—

A thought strikes me.

"He can remove your oath if he chooses to?" I ask. "It's that easy?"

Galen shakes himself from the trance he'd fallen into. "Yes." His lips thin. "But don't expect any favors from *him*," he nearly spits the word.

I stiffen. Something hard settles in my chest. "Why not?"

He stares me down as if he could peel back my layers and see within. I squirm in my chair, everything in me yelling at me to flee, until finally he blinks and looks away.

His next words are so quiet I barely hear them. "You don't know what he's done."

A shadow creeps across my heart. I glance this way and that, but no one is close. Even so, I scoot my chair near him before I whisper. "He almost accidentally got the King of the Forest killed."

Galen stares at me. "Accidentally?"

Chills skitter down my spine. "He said... He told me he can't lie, but..."

"Maybe that was an accident, but everything leading up until that was no accident, Wren. He plotted for years. Watching. Waiting for the right moment to strike." His fist slams into his open palm, causing me to jump.

My heart races. Years. He plotted for years. "How do you know that?"

A pained grimace crosses his face.

Cheers erupt as competitors race into view, aiming for the stage. The two literally claw at each other, trying to be the first to the stage. Blood and shredded clothes leave a trail in their wake.

Color dots the edge of my vision, and I grip the chair for support.

That could have been me. If I'd run into someone else in the woods, it could be my blood painting the grass. One swipe would have done it. I don't have claws, fangs, or magic. My nails dig into the wood of the chair below me.

Despite their struggle, both make it to the stage, and each advance to the next round. A scream builds in the back of my throat.

This is ridiculous. What am I even doing here?

I glance at Galen, and he still looks ill himself, though his faraway gaze tells me it's not because of the violent show.

"A spirited struggle," a new voice says at my side.

I jump at the new voice and nearly tilt the chair over. My pulse beats against my ribs as I take stock of the competitor who joined us. Dark red hair trails down over his shoulders. His features are smooth and even, almost angelic. If I had to guess, I'd mark him about my age, younger than most of the competitors. Unlike most of us, he doesn't favor the blues and grays of the Court of Air in his attire, and suddenly, I remember who he is. My throat goes dry. The reds and yellows of his attire, the rubies dotting his earrings as bold as his hair—I've only had glimpses of him, but there's no mistaking the prince from the Court of Fire.

"Indeed," Galen replies, saving my tongue-tied self.

"You two made quite the entrance as well." He tilts his head in a way that's decidedly not human.

"Do you have a problem with that?" I bite out.

"Quite the contrary. It's most intriguing. A human woman with the King of Air's magic about her," he says, and my cheeks burn long after he slides his prying gaze to Galen. "And a fae of two courts."

Galen goes ramrod straight, and his gaze darkens.

"If you choose to ally again," the prince says, "perhaps you would include me?"

"You?" Galen scoffs. "That'd pit everyone else again us."

"Maybe." The prince shrugs. "But you may need my help in whatever is to come." His eyes cloud over, and his body stiffens.

I search Galen's face for answers, but his wide-eyed glance at me says he has none. This, whatever it is, is not normal, not even for a fae.

The milkiness departs as quickly as it came. With a shake of his head, the prince is back. "You'll need me. Think on it."

He smiles but doesn't wait on a reply before he walks away.

"That was..." I let out a sigh. "Why would he want to work with us?" I ask once the prince is a safe distance away.

"Don't know." Galen crosses his arms and stares at the retreating prince. "But I don't like it."

A roar of gasps and cheers rises from the crowd. People jump to their feet.

"Ah, our last winner arrives!" the announcer yells.

The last. I rise on my toes to see who it is.

A large bird, twice the size of my eagle friend, lands on the stage. It's feet away, but the wind from its wings stirs up my hair and flutters the heavy tablecloths. It looks to the announcer and caws.

The announcer nods and flings an arm in the air for dramatic effect. "And we have a race to the finish!"

I edge out from under the tent and spot a few more massive birds circling high above. Spiders race down my spine. They're watching, and somehow the announcer understands them? Magic of some sort, it must be, but then, did they see the cat fae too? I bite my lip. Her offer was strange, but having it voided already would suck.

The last competitor leaps onto the stage in a roaring bound.

Cheers and applause engulf us. This game is done. The remaining fae are disqualified.

I look over at Galen. So few came after us. I may not have made it in time on my own. I owe this man, this fae, and maybe I can help him.

Chapter 16

Hawke's healing magic soothes my aching muscles better than a hot bath ever could. Not that it stops me from taking one. The shiver of magic under my skin couldn't clean the sweat from my skin and hair, not to mention that the steaming water was a welcome respite from the revelations of the day.

Of course, tomorrow doesn't bode any better. The next competition is still two days away, but I promised Uncle Mark we could have our chat tomorrow.

It's going to suck.

But at least it'll be done with.

I'm finishing a painfully lonely dinner in the common room when a thunderous boom follows a rush of wind. The last bite nearly lodges in my throat as I jump to my feet, whirling toward the balcony.

Great, dark wings shield the last of sunset and cast fluttering shadows across the room. Warmth coils low in my gut even as my knees shake. Sigurd stands on the balcony, an imposing figure if ever there were one. His expression is dark and grand as his wings and cooler than ice. A king of the air in furious glory.

A deep, hidden part of me trembles, aching to fall to my knees to worship this being who certainly is not human—no one could mistake him like this. But another part, one that scares me even more, wants to caress and admire his wings, to feel their silken touch on my bare skin and let him cocoon me away from the world in his dark embrace.

You don't know what he's done. The echo of Galen's words buries itself in my chest, and I shiver.

"Wren," Sigurd draws out the last note, letting it coil in the air between us.

"Sigurd." My body goes into autopilot, and like an idiot, I curtsy.

His wings fold in and then vanish completely. One might think them an impressive illusion, had it not clearly been his landing that caused the castle to tremble and me right along with it.

No sooner do I step toward him than he appears in front of me. I screech.

He smirks.

"You have to stop doing that."

With casual arrogance, he plucks a piece of fruit from my plate and holds it between his fingers before shoving the juicy berry into his mouth. A hint of red smears across his lips in the process, which he wipes away with a slow slide of his tongue.

Before I know what I'm doing, I mirror the motion, an echo of the berry's taste teasing my memories.

His throat bobs.

The air between us is thick with unspoken words, and I have no desire to break it. For one terrible moment, I shove all the warnings in my head to a deep dark place where I can't hear them. He may be a dark angel, but I'm no saint.

Sigurd leans back on the edge of the table, away from me, and the yearning to rush to him and press my lips against his slips away. His features sharpen back to the steely blades from when he entered as he crosses his arms. "It looked like you made a friend today."

Galen.

So, I wasn't mistaken about his fury. Because he doesn't like him or because I was with him?

I drop into my chair. "We helped each other." I shrug. "There's no rule against it."

"He *carried* you."

"Well, yeah, he's faster than me. I might not have made it back in time without his help, so you should be thankful."

"Thankful to see you leave?" he scoffs.

"You did give me the flowers, didn't you?"

I'd swear his cheeks color before he looks away. He stares across the room, a slight pout on his features. "Don't human women like flowers?"

"Do you have much experience with human women?" I lean forward in my chair.

His shoulders droop. "Not for a long time."

The way he says it makes it sound like it's been an age, but he can't be more than mid-thirties at the very most, probably younger if I had to guess. Strange for a man of his age and position not to have a string of women to impress.

"I do like them," I say, tossing him a bone. He takes it, finally staring back at me and emerging from the raincloud he slipped under. "Cadmums. Such a rare and beautiful flower," I mimic the announcer's voice. "I thought you couldn't interfere in the games?"

That devilishly smug smile returns. "I didn't interfere. I simply gave flowers to the lovely woman in my keeping."

Lovely. I'm used to compliments. The men at the bar give them with ease, but from him, it stirs something warm and wild in my chest, yearning to break free.

"Yes, well, thank you for them. I thought you didn't want me to win?"

He snares the seat nearby, tugging it close until his legs almost brush mine when he sits. "I don't want you hurt, and the games will get more dangerous."

My stomach tightens. The Prince of Fire hinted at that too. "Well then, it's a good thing I have an ally."

His countenance darkens. "You talked to him afterwards. What about?"

I cross my arms and stare him down. "I'm not allowed to talk to others now?"

"Of course you can. I just..." His hand tightens in a fist.

"If you're so jealous, why not release him from his oath to you? Let him go home."

"Told you that, did he?" His laughter is dark, and gooseflesh rises on my skin. "They may not want him in the forest after what he's done."

"What—"

Sigurd scoots forward in his chair, leaning entirely too close to me. "He didn't tell you?"

I swallow, unable to speak.

"He's a traitor. Betrayed the King of the Forest and stole his human consort."

"What?" I gape. There's no way.

But fae can't lie.

"Didn't tell you that, did he?" His finger trails along my jaw, and I shiver.

He pulls away, and suddenly, I'm cold. Something is missing. It has to be. Galen isn't the type. Determined. Strong. But not cruel.

"He said he loved a woman," I say. "That they parted poorly. The king's consort?"

Sigurd gives nothing away.

"Then why order him to stay here? To keep him safe?"

"Not exactly. He knows too much." He gestures as he speaks. "About me, my court. If he told the King of the Forest all he knows, it could cause more trouble for me, and I can't have that. Not now."

"So, it's not for him. It's for you." I can't hide the bitterness on my tongue. "You trap him here against his will, just like me, and then are angry when he's kind to me."

"Wren."

"Am I wrong?"

His jaw stiffens. "No." I open my mouth to speak, but he continues. "A king has a duty to his court."

"Then why harbor the man who stole the Forest king's consort? If you have a duty to your court, surely that includes peace?" I stand, unable to hold still. My feet yearn to pace across the floor.

There's a piece missing, just out of reach. "You almost killed the king, right? Protecting Galen after he stole the king's consort?"

But even as I say it, I know it's wrong. I pace in front of my chair. There's too much anger between them, deep-seated distrust and hate. Had Sigurd protected him, Galen would be in his debt. He wouldn't loathe him so much.

"Wren." Sigurd draws me to a halt with his hand on my waist. His thumb rubs along my skin until all my thoughts vanish into the feel of that touch. So warm. Inviting.

He plotted for years.

I thought to pay him back.

Pieces click into place. Without Sigurd's hand holding me steady, I might fall. But that touch, the one I craved, is suddenly horrid. I jerk away, stumbling back.

"You ordered him to steal the king's consort," I say. "You made him a traitor."

Sigurd is still as a statue, all but his eyes, which glow an eerie blue.

Deny it. Tell me that's not true.

This man who flirts with me, who held my hair, who gave me flowers...

Who bound me here.

My heart cracks. I can't look at him anymore. I flee from the table, racing through the sitting room with no destination in mind. It's dark. The lights are dim. The sun has gone, and with it, all the warmth I savored in this horrible place.

The door to my room is near. Only a few steps and—

Sigurd appears in front of me.

I skid on the stones, slip, fall. A scream more fury than fear cracks through the silence.

Sigurd grabs my hand. And then I'm back on my feet, leaning against his chest, his arm around my back.

I shove against him. "Get off. Let me go!"

"Wren, please—"

My fist slams against his chest. Pain radiates up my arm. "Let." I hit him again. "Me—"

He frees me, and I stumble away, nearly falling again.

My nails dig into my palms as I stare him down, all simmering fury barely contained in my gritted teeth.

"Yes." His form is stiff, but his face is cold, emotionless. "I ordered him to steal the king's consort."

The confession knocks the wind from me.

"Why?" The word cracks, and only then do I notice the tears blurring the corners of my eyes. I blink them away, refusing to let them fall.

His expression breaks like cracking ice. His shoulders droop. The eerie glow fades from his eyes. All the hardness of his features softens out into deep sorrow.

Not that it dims my anger. Not one bit.

"There was a woman. I..." He glances at me under lowered lashes. "I loved her."

My traitorous heart clenches. "Evelyn."

The nod he gives is almost imperceptible, but it's enough. The woman he loved looked just like me. No wonder he flirts like he does.

"The King of the Forest kept her from me. I thought to return the favor and take someone he loved from him."

"Did the king hurt this Evelyn? Mistreat her?"

"No." His gaze narrows.

"Was she unhappy with him?"

"No." A gust of wind whistles through the room.

"Then why? Why be so, so selfish?"

He flinches, turning his head as if he's been slapped. His jaw stiffens. "You'd dare speak to a king this way?"

My boot taps a rhythm on the ground as I cross my arms "When you act like a petulant child. Yes, I will. I've sworn no oath to you."

His head snaps in my direction, the heat of his look scalding me. Fury and something much more dangerous threaten to consume me.

My back straightens as he stalks the space between us. I step back, retreating from his advance until I bump into the wall. My palms flatten on the cool stone, and oh, what I wouldn't give to climb up it or fly away as Sigurd slams a palm on the wall on either side of my head. His presence is dizzying—the glow of his eyes grows as he leans in, his hot breath warming my cheek.

"A selfish king would take what he wants," he croons.

Dear God. I suck in a breath. "And what is that?"

But I know. Oh, holy sweet baby Jesus, I know, and I might as well melt into a puddle for the effect it has on me.

His chest rises and falls. Our breaths mingle, the only sound in the room.

Sigurd angles his head. His lips part.

I stop his kiss with a finger across his soft lips.

His glow vanishes completely.

"I won't be some replacement for your lost love," I say.

I might want to—okay, I totally do—but it's the kind of wanting that leads to regret, to heartache. Being a replacement would never be enough for me, not even with someone I plan to leave as soon as I can. Anything we shared would stick with me like Super Glue, clinging to my heart and chaffing long, long after he's nothing but a memory.

One moment of pleasure isn't worth that pain.

He takes my hand, dragging it down his chest until it rests over his heart. It races as fast as mine. Maybe faster.

"You were willing to risk your whole kingdom for this woman, and yet you stand here and flirt with me?" My nails dig into his shirt, but he doesn't even flinch.

"Wren—"

"Tell me I'm wrong."

With a near growl, he shoves off the wall and turns his back on me. "She's dead."

"What?" I nearly slide down to the floor.

"She died years ago," he whispers.

Years ago. Again, he says it as if so much time has passed. The lingering sting of my parent's death creeps into the back of my mind, settling down in the wake of my anger. Even though it's been years, some days, the loss still cuts as sharply as the day my world shattered.

"Si—"

But he vanishes, taking all my anger with him.

I pull my arms around myself, suddenly cold and lonely as ever. As I walk the few steps to my room, thoughts chase me, but one calls louder than the others.

If Evelyn died years ago, then who exactly did Galen steal away for Sigurd?

CHAPTER 17

M Y EAGLE FRIEND KEEPS me company until I fall asleep. I don't have any words for him—thank goodness he doesn't need them—but his presence makes me feel better all the same. He's still there, snoozing near the cadmum flowers in their vase, when I wake up. I'd swear the darn bird nearly purrs when I stroke his head.

I wash and change but don't have the courage to venture into the sitting room. Running into Sigurd again after last night is just...

"Nope, not happening," I tell the eagle. "What would I even say to him?"

It cocks his head at me where I sit at the end of the bed, waiting for Uncle Mark to show up and retrieve me. Something else fun to look forward to.

"I'm sorry the woman you love died. That's no excuse for being an idiot and starting a war." I flop back onto the sheets. "What kind of king risks his people for petty revenge?"

The eagle squawks and hops near.

"Yes, petty," I say when he blinks at me. "What else would you call it? The other king didn't hurt her. She wasn't unhappy. Seems like she mighta preferred it there. Maybe? Anyhow, if it was years ago, he should have just let bygones be bygones instead of stirring up trouble."

He squawks, and I decide he must agree.

I roll over and prop my head on my hands, staring down the eagle. It might be dumb being this close to a bird who could pluck my eyes out, but if he really wanted to do that, surely he would have already. "What do you think? Is he horrible or just stupid?"

He snaps his beak, and I rear back.

"Hey, what the—"

A hard rap on the door startles the eagle as much as me, and he flies off through the balcony curtains. "Weird bird," I mutter, then louder, "Who is it?"

Don't be Sigurd. Don't be Sigurd. Don't be—

"Uncle Mark."

Thank goodness. I leap from the bed and throw open the door.

Hawke is with him. My smile falters. So we're to have a third wheel. This is awkward.

Mark must get my look because he quickly says, "Hawke offered to take us into town. I thought you might like to see it while we talk?" He looks between us, no more comfortable than I am. "There's a farm I visit sometimes. I remember when you were a girl, and we used to visit the animals, so I thought—"

"That sounds great." I beam. He doesn't need to convince me. All he had to say was outside, and I'd have been sold. Cute animals? Always a bonus.

"Well then." Hawke holds out his hand, and for once, I'm eager to take it.

The farm is a wonder. So much like the ones back home but more refined, like everything in Faery. The barns and buildings are pristine, not a fleck of paint missing or a board askew. The animals are well cared for, grazing in the green fields I could see from the balcony. Fresh air fills my lungs, and while the scent of animal droppings is still present, it's not as pungent as back home. In fact, it's oddly comforting.

It also distracts from the floating bits of land that hang in the sky near the mountains. As cool as they are, they somehow make me uneasy too. Like they might suddenly drop from the sky and squish someone.

Uncle Mark fits here. The fae know him, like him, and respect him. It's easy to see in their genuine greetings and friendly banter.

And though he's aged since he left us, I'd swear he looks younger. Maybe the effect of being here. Or maybe love? He walks with confidence, not dancing over eggshells all the time like he did with Aunt Virginia. He's loose, free. And though we've spent the past hour or so talking about the farm and the differences between animals here and at home, dodging all the important things we promised to discuss, this time has told me more than words.

He's happy in a way he never was at home.

I break the ice while brushing a sheep with lavender fur. "Marigold would love these," I say. "She's obsessed with everything purple right now. And unicorns. Don't happen to have any of those around, do you?"

His soft smile at the mention of the granddaughter he's never met eases the lingering tension. "No," he says after a moment. "Afraid not."

It's easy to talk about Tabitha and her kids. I've got plenty of stories, and while I brush the sheep, I can imagine I'm talking to them, not the man who left us all. Mark just listens and nods, for the most part, content with whatever tidbits I'll give him. I throw in some stories about Matt, Gran, and myself too. I leave out Aunt Virginia. She pops up in a few stories anyway, but no one needs to hear about their ex-wife running around with just about every man—single, taken, and everywhere in between—in town.

When the sun peaks in the sky and the day grows warm, we take a picnic break on a bench under some leafy trees. Honestly, I couldn't pick better scenery. The farm, with its joyful animals and forest stretching out beyond the fields, is a dream, away from all the hustle and bustle, away from most of the fae and the castle that's become a gilded cage. With the castle and sprawling town at our back, I can almost forget about them. There are many farms in the valley, some even grander, or so Mark says, but I understand why he likes this one.

It's quiet and simple, almost like home.

"Hawke and I met years ago, before you were born actually," he begins, rousing me from my daydreams.

"What?" I sit a little straighter. It's weird. As much as I dreaded this, I actually want to hear his story now.

"Virginia was pregnant with Tabitha. I'd always thought if she had the kids she wanted, she'd be more content with me, but it only made her see me as more of a failure. I never did enough in her eyes. Wasn't man enough. She only saw my flaws. And I tried to be a good husband to her, really I did. I gave everything I had until I was a shell of myself. It was never enough. One day after a fight, I needed space. Was in no frame of mind to get behind the wheel, so I just walked into the woods and kept going. I wanted to be somewhere else, anywhere else, and suddenly, I was."

He'd stumbled into Faery by accident, like I did.

"I ran into Hawke, and that was certainly a surprise. Didn't know a thing about fae. Thought I must have hit my head or something. I called him all sorts of things. Pretty sure he hated me at first, and that's why he helped me find my way back home. I was gone a day and night by then, and it only made Virginia angrier. She accused me of taking up with some floozy. As if I would." He shakes his head. "Over the years, I found myself going back, never for long, but just enough for a break. I met Hawke again, and over time, we grew close."

So long, and yet I never knew. None of us knew. It must have been so difficult for him, living a life in one world while yearning for a completely different one somewhere else.

His shoulders hunch, and he sighs. "I know what people thought of me. Even Ma. They assumed I was having an affair with someone. There was nothing physical between us then, but I suppose it was an affair of the heart. I was happy. There was no Virginia to yell at me and bring out all my ugly. Even Matt and Tabitha. I loved them more than anything, still do, but they heard their mom's words, her anger. What were they supposed to believe? The leaving didn't help, but I needed something, anything to keep going."

"We always did guess that you ran away with a lover," I admit with a weak smile. "Though I think everyone thought it was a woman. And a human."

"Another reason I left. Can you imagine what any of them would have thought?"

I take his hand in mine. "They'd have been surprised, but Tabitha, Matt, Gran—they love you, and they would love anyone who you do. They'd want you to be happy, and it would mean so much to them to know that you are."

Mark huffs. "I wonder."

"I don't." It's one thing I'm absolutely certain of. "But why disappear on us? Why not just tell them?"

"About Faery?" He looks at me askance. "Give them another reason to mock me? Humans who can see fae are rare, and most families guard the secret rather closely. It's odd, Hawke says, that ours didn't pass down the knowledge, but then he told me that not all humans in a bloodline will show the trait. If our family didn't have the knowledge, it would be likely our gifted blood was so thin that I was an anomaly. An odd one out among our family tree, like Uncle Dan."

Uncle Dan. Now that's a name I haven't heard in an age. He was a family cautionary tale, what happened when you went a little too far off the grid. He lived alone in a cabin in the woods, rarely came into town, and had little to do with anyone in the family.

"Uncle Dan used to tell us these stories when I was young," he continued, "about people in the woods and other places. He said no one could ever see them but him, not even our kin. Ma thought he just drank too much moonshine, but I wonder..." He rubs his chin.

"Maybe he was talking about Faery."

"Might have been."

I slide my boot along the ground, warring over the question in my head. But questions are what we're here for, right? "So, why stay? Why become"—I gesture to him—"fae? Don't humans help fae magic?" That's what they said anyway. "Seems...counterintuitive?"

"Wouldn't you want to stay with someone you love?" The smile that stretches across his features stirs up envy within me that I couldn't have predicted.

Love, true love.

"I guess I'd been drifting away for a while. Virginia made a show of her affairs and made me miserable every chance she could. The kids were mostly grown and involved in their own lives."

He shrugs, but I can see the way it pains him. The temptation to wrap him in a tight hug is almost too much to hold back, but I don't want to interrupt him now, not when his story is finally coming to light.

"It was selfish, but I wanted some joy for myself." He shifts in the seat. "As for becoming fae—"

Horses let out startled whinnies, disrupting the peaceful day. A small herd of them race across the far end of the field, away from the forested edge.

Mark goes still.

Fae rush from the barn, headed in that direction.

"What is it?" I ask. "What's happened?"

"I don't know." He rises to his feet with fae grace. "Stay here. I'll be right back."

CHAPTER 18

I REACH FOR UNCLE Mark as he hurries to the barn and whatever disturbed the animals, but he's already jogging toward the other fae, much faster than he ever could when he was human. Being fae does have some advantages, I suppose. Still, Sigurd said fae fade in our world. It makes sense they can't live there since I've never seen any, and boy, would that be prime-time news if people saw fae walking around. But being separated from your kids? I hug my arms around myself. I don't even have any, and still the thought makes my chest ache.

"Human."

The whispered word sends chills racing down my spine. I twist this way and that on the bench, searching for the source but coming up empty.

Uncle Mark's form grows smaller and smaller. Everything in me yells to run after him. I set the last of lunch aside and jump to my feet.

"Shh," the whisper comes again, just to my right.

I snap toward the sound, and this time I see her. The catlike woman, so unlike the other fae I've seen, edges out from between two leafy bushes. The commotion across the field tugs at my attention as realization sinks in.

"You disturbed the horses," I say. And how on earth did she get here so quickly and silently? "Why?"

Her tail twitches, a match for the amusement in her feline eyes. "To assist you in the games. No one can know. They might call you a cheat." Her head tilts to the side. "Disqualify you?" She stumbles a bit over the word. "We cannot have that."

I swallow. No, we definitely can't have that. "There's no game today."

"No, there's not. But soon. More dangerous for a human."

A hard knot rolls around in my stomach. Just peachy. Everyone has been hinting at danger. I fight back a sigh. What could the game be, a magical duel? "You're here to give me a hint?"

"No." She reaches out with her clawed hand.

I back away.

Her nose twitches. "You want my help. A protection spell."

My knees dig into the ground. "I was told magic can be felt. Won't they know if I cheat?"

Fangs peak from between her lips. "It can, but not mine." Cat ears twitch on her head, and her eyes narrow. "Do you want it or not? Hurry, human."

In the distance, I see forms disbursing, moving back this way. If it can help win, get me home, then I need it, whatever the source.

"Yes," I say. "Please."

Before I can second guess my choice, she latches onto my upper arm. Cool tingles roll under my skin, radiating out from her touch.

"Remember," she says, letting go of my arm. "Speak of this, and I help you no more."

I've no sooner opened my mouth to respond than she vanishes.

The bushes receive my deep frown. "I really hate it when they do that."

"What happened?" I ask Uncle Mark, feigning innocence as he nears our bench.

"Not sure." He scratches his chin and reclaims his seat. "Nothing looked amiss. I couldn't smell anything out of sorts either. The horses might have spooked each other."

"Smell?" My nose wrinkles. What does he imagine he'd scent? A cow pie?

He nods as if it's the most normal thing ever. "Fae sense of smell is so much stronger. It's incredible how much humans miss, how much I missed. The depth, the nuance." He slaps his knee, just like he always did when I was little and something amused him. "Bet I can put a hound dog to shame now."

"Stronger, faster, better senses. I suppose that's why you wanted to become fae?"

The joy of moments ago dims into sadness. "Fae have their advantages, it's true, but that's not it, not really."

"Then why?"

"When Hawke and I met, we looked about the same. Age-wise, anyway."

I lean away, my brows drawing together. "But you..."

"Look a good bit older than him now? Yes. Thankfully, he doesn't much mind that."

"Then how did he—" Knowledge holds my words hostage. Hawke didn't become younger. He stayed the same, while Mark aged as any human would. Until...

"Fae don't age?"

"We do." His smile is tight. "But much, much slower."

I rub my palms up and down my arms, fighting away the sudden chill.

"You see, as a human, our time together would be more limited. I was already getting older, weaker. It was harder to travel into the forest and visit Faery. Even once I came here to live full time, the years we'd have together—good, healthy, happy years—were fewer than either of us wanted. But as a fae..."

"You'd have more time together," I finish for him. It makes sense. As much as I don't want to, I understand his choice. He was an outsider to his family already. He found love, and he wanted it for as long as he could have it. "But at the cost of never going home."

Mark looks out over the fields. "This is my home now, Wren."

"You don't regret leaving your kids?"

Shadows cover his eyes. "Yes. I do. Though Faery has a way of making that easier too."

"Because memories fade."

He nods. "Even more now that I'm fae, but you've refreshed their memory. It hurts, but I'm thankful too. I'd rather remember them, hear about them, even with the pain it brings, than let it fade altogether. I know that now."

"So, Hawke is, what? Fifty? Sixty?" Hard to picture even when he looks thirty-something. An odd match for my uncle, but it's nice to know Hawke doesn't love him for his looks.

Mark points up.

"Seventy?"

A shake of the head.

"Eighty? Just tell me already."

"Over one hundred. The more powerful the fae, the slower they age, and my Hawke is... well, quite blessed."

A hundred. One deep breath after another fills my lungs as I watch the horses trot across the field, trying to process my racing thoughts. He'd have been late double digits when they met then, and yet he still looked so young.

Magic linked to age, how—

My hands tighten on the edge of the bench. I snap my gaze to Uncle Mark. "Then Sigurd is..."

"Older than Hawke by a few years. They're close in age for fae."

I leap to my feet.

When he talked about things happening years ago, about Evelyn dying years ago, it could have been decades. Or a handful. Who even knows how beings who can live so long measure time?

"Wren?" Mark says.

"I had no idea. I thought he— I mean, he looks young. They all do. And—I..."

He gives me a knowing grin. "You like him?"

"Uncle Mark." I roll my eyes and give him a look that says he should know better. "He's a king. A fae. And I plan to get out of here as soon as I can."

Mark shrugs, but it's the worst show of apathy I've seen. Clearly a fae's inability to lie doesn't extend to body reactions. "He's quite interested in you. More than any human or fae I've seen."

The sun overhead has nothing on the fire burning in my chest and creeping up my neck. "Nonsense." But all I can think about is last night, the warmth of his breath, the way his closeness nearly turned me into a puddle of need and desire. Our almost kiss. I bury my face in my hands. "Argh."

Uncle Mark stands, flexing his shoulders. "He may be my king now, but if I need to tell him to keep his hands to himself..."

I shake my head. No sense getting him in trouble. "I've got it under control."

Maybe.

Sort of.

"Evelyn," I say. "Do you know her?"

"Ah, so he told you about her?" He sits and pats the bench next to him.

With heavy feet, I drag myself back. "Not really, other than to say he loves her? Loved her?" I wave my hand in the air. "And apparently, I look like her. Do I?"

"I wouldn't know. Hawke says your coloring is similar, he thinks, though he can barely remember her. Hasn't seen her in over sixty years."

"What!" I shriek.

The horses look my way. At least they don't go running off.

"Sorry," I say with a wince and drop my voice. "I was under the impression the war he almost started—because of her, I understand—was recent."

Mark nods. "Hawke was furious, to say the least. Sigurd didn't tell him his true intentions beforehand. Hawke would have cautioned against his actions, of course. He's often the voice of reason with his cousins." Pride rings in his voice. "Fae grudges run far deeper than human ones, and King Sigurd is a bit mercurial. He tries not to be, I think. I do enjoy his company most times, but he had a difficult upbringing."

"A king? With a difficult upbringing?" I nearly snort. Oh yes, I'm sure being a prince comes with so many difficulties. A castle, plenty of food, no worries about money, schooling, how to pay the rent...

My lips purse. What would he know of difficult?

Mark pats my leg. "It's not for me to tell. But Evelyn... Whether he still loves her or not, it doesn't matter. She's long dead. Though it does seem strange that, if he still loved her, he'd try to steal her son's mate."

CHAPTER 19

"HER SON. THE KING of the Forest is Evelyn's son." I tell my eagle companion for maybe the tenth time. I still can't comprehend it.

Of everything Uncle Mark told me, that fact shocked me more than all the rest. His choice, how long he'd known Hawke, fae ages...

"What could he have possibly done to deserve to be almost killed and have his mate endangered?"

The word mate still tastes odd on my tongue every time I say it. It's so... I dunno. But Uncle Mark insists it's more fitting than consort, since they're an item now that they both lived. Partner or mate—fae preferred terms instead of spouse.

I turn my head to stare at the eagle across the bed where his talons pick at the furs, almost like a cat making biscuits with its paws. "Fae make no sense."

It turns, blinking this way and that.

Neither do birds apparently.

I shove to my feet and scowl at the outfit Moria brought me to wear in tomorrow's competition. Skintight, midnight black, and showing off everything. Seriously, if I ate a cracker, it'd show in that outfit, and goodness knows it shows enough of me in an unflattering way as it is.

"Doesn't bode well for me, does it?" I ask over one shoulder. If Moria thinks I need something to move in, with a few small knives like hers stored away in strategic pockets and seams, then I'm in a heap of trouble.

Music winds its way through the gloaming. A violin maybe? Some kind of stringed instrument, I think. The sorrowful notes tug at my very soul, rending it with each rise and fall.

Gran, how are you? Are you doing okay without me?

Spending the day with Uncle Mark brought the sharp ache of home sickness and worry back to the surface. It's been days, and I have no idea if Gran is all right. I'm sure she's not. I mean, I disappeared after a robbery, she probably thinks I'm dead. But I hope she's been strong and weathered the storm. I pray that someone is looking after her for me.

It's one more reason that no matter what waits for me in the next game, I have to give it my all. I need to get back to her as soon as I can.

I dress for bed, and the music falters. My chest tightens ever so slightly at the loss.

"What a shame," I murmur.

The eagle waits for me, watchful as always, as I return to the bed in my nightgown. The fae do make excellent clothes. Comfortable. Functional. Cute.

Well... I glare at my outfit for tomorrow. Sometimes cute.

"I wonder why they stopped?" No sooner do I say it than the tune starts up again, just as mournful as before and the perfect echo of my mood.

It lures me out to the balcony, where a few more eagles occupy the railing. They're not as brave as my friend, not yet willing to come inside, but they've at least decided it's safe to come down from the roof and don't fly away as I draw near.

I lean into the fading light, searching for the source of the sound, but there are few balconies on this side of the castle, and none of the ones below are occupied. Unerringly, I find the bird around my neck and rub the little pendant between my fingers. In fact, the sound is much quieter. My brows pinch as I turn back to the room.

The eagle hops on the bed and turns his beak to the door.

"Inside?" I ask, returning to his side.

He seems to nod.

I ruffle the feathers on his head. "Silly bird."

Songs have their own form of magic, the ability to transport someone far away or let them relive a memory from long ago. One note can say more than an entire speech and leave the listener reeling in delicious agony. This is that kind of song. It's more than sound, more than words. It speaks straight to the soul of pain, sorrow, loss, yearning, and maybe hope.

Ignoring it would be impossible, and I don't want to. They may as well have written this song for me given how I feel in the moment.

The main room is dark. Even the fairy lights have been put out. Only the glow of the moon slanting through the glass ceiling and peeking in through the balcony curtains provides dappled, blue-tinged light.

Music gathers me in its embrace, bold as if I'm in the front row of a concert. It tugs me to its source—the balcony.

Beyond the sheer curtains, a form lingers under the night sky, sitting on a cushioned stool taken from within the sitting room. With barely a glance, I know who it is, who plays this song that might break me and put me back together at the same time.

I should leave him to it, let him play in peace. Why else would someone play alone at night? But the pull is too hard to resist. Him or the song, I can't say.

Cool marble tickles my bare feet as I cross to him as silently as I can. The stringed instrument—maybe a large violin of sorts, but I can't be sure—rests against his shoulder. The body of it stretches down across his chest to rest in his lap, leaving his hands free to slide the bow and press the strings.

Sigurd's eyes are closed, and the planes of his face relaxed, as if in sleep. But he's certainly awake. Between the moonlight painting him in grayish blue and shadow, the music, and the peaceful aura he exudes, it's a sight more stunning than a masterpiece.

I curl up on a pillow with my legs tucked under me on the balcony floor, content to linger despite the chill of the night.

After some minutes, he draws the last note of the song to its end. His eyes blink open, and I'm treated to a rare and genuine smile.

"I hoped you might come." The words pierce me as deeply as the song, sliding into the cracks it left in my defense.

"Why is that?" My voice sounds harsh, grating by comparison.

"You had a good conversation with your uncle?" He sets the instrument aside, propping it against his stool.

"Yes." I smooth the silky nightgown down over my legs. "It was much better than I expected." So much more than I can put into words. I thought I'd want to run after five minutes, but we spent most of the day together and planned more in the future. Even if it brings the sting of being away from Gran back, it's completely worth it. "It was nice to be out too. To see the valley, the farm."

I glance that way, but the remainder of the balcony blocks my view.

Silence lingers, filled with his steady, relentless gaze that has my insides twisting themselves into knots.

"Your song was lovely," I say. "Sad, but beautiful too."

His genuine smile nearly cracks my heart anew. "Thank you. Music has a way of calming me. It always has."

"What bothers you that you need calming?"

Sigurd hunches over his forearms on his knees. "The better question would be what doesn't."

"The Court of the Forest?" I guess.

His jaw stiffens, and I know I've hit the nail on the head. "Moria has her commanders keeping an eye on things," he says. "They haven't advanced beyond their territory, but they haven't retreated either. Then there's the Unseelie."

That word sends a shudder racing through me. Everything about it screams wrongness. "What about them?"

He stands, stretching his arms above his head and rolling his shoulders. "They seem to be gathering together." He wanders to the balcony and leans on the railing, surveying the land beyond. "Bands moving around and joining up with one another."

I join him, keeping a healthy amount of space between us. "That's odd?"

Sigurd nods. "Odd enough. They've always been rather disparate, living in small groups, each ruled by a warlord or elder. This coming together is strange." Lines form on his forehead as he squints into the distance. "It's almost like they've found a new king. But it's been an age since the last one fell, and the magic failed to choose a new one. Why would one arise now? And how? For what purpose?"

So many questions, but they're not directed at me. This is why he played, the burdens and worries that he hoped the music would drown out.

"Why tell me all this?" I ask.

His fingertips slide across the railing in a smooth, hypnotic rhythm before he turns to me. "It's...helpful to talk about it. Moria advises we strike first and take an active stance before they can become more of a threat. Hawke, ever the opposite of his sister, suggests caution. Send in more spies, find out what they want, and negotiate before we strike." He pauses, his head tilting to the side. "What do you think?"

I look out over the valley and rub my necklace between my fingers, letting the metal settle my thoughts. "I don't like war or violence. But I believe in being prepared and not letting others take advantage. I suppose it depends on what these Unseelie are like, their nature. Monstrous, I've heard. How so?"

"Their magic is more...base—blood, darkness, and brute strength rather than the elements of our world. The ages have wrought their change on their appearance as well, turned their form more animalistic."

My blood runs cold. "Animalistic," I echo. "You mean they don't look human?"

"A mix. Most walk on two legs and have a similar structure, but yes—fur, fangs, horns, wings, and all sorts of animal features."

The world tilts on its axis, and I grip the railing to keep my feet. Sigurd continues to speak, but it's all a humming buzz I can't make out. The fae I met in the forest and today, the one like a cat, has to be Unseelie. It fits. More animalistic in appearance and different than the other fae I've met. But why here? Why help me?

"Wren." Sigurd's hand on my shoulder jolts me back to the present. He's so close, his scent filling my nostrils, his form blocking the rising moon and casting a shadow across me. "What's wrong?"

I swallow, trying to measure my breathing and calm my panic. He'll see. He'll know. And then any help she offers will be gone.

"You have wings. Sometimes. But you're not Unseelie." *Tell me I'm wrong. Tell me anything to convince me she's not Unseelie.*

As if on cue, wings spring from his back to tower behind him. I gasp and take a step back, but he holds me firm.

"Yes. I suppose we were all one race once, so there are some similarities. But my wings, my claws"—they glimmer in a thread of moonlight—"are summoned by my magic. Some of us can even transform into an animal completely for a time. But it's not who we are, not our natural form. Unseelie bear their differences as part of their nature. Besides, many Unseelie these days have little magic to change themselves at all, even if they wanted to."

Little magic at all. Except the one I met. The way she moved with the blink of an eye like them, whatever spell she cast on me...

I hug my arms around myself.

Sigurd wraps a wing around me. "You're cold?"

"I—" The way he looks at me makes me want to spill all my truth. "How can we be safe here? What if one swooped out of the skies and took me away?"

His arm encircles me, pulling me close as his other hand rubs the mark around my wrist. "No one can take you from me. Any distance between us I will feel, and our tether only stretches so far."

A tether? I muse. Maybe that was the strange tug I felt the other day, a reminder of our bond, a stretching of it when he was not near my side.

Sigurd draws my wrist to his lips, kissing my pulse over his tattoo. The intimate touch shatters my thoughts.

"W-what about Uncle Mark?" I ask. "Or anyone else?"

"My wards protect my territory." Another kiss on my wrist.

"Wards?" My voice is thick and raspy.

"Mmhmm," he mumbles against my skin. "Magical barriers keep the weak ones out. If a stronger one manages to cross, I'll feel it."

My nipples stiffen against the fabric of the nightgown, its silk cold against my heated skin. I really should have worn something more. "A-and have you felt any?"

His arm flexes around me, drawing me closer. Another kiss tickles the sensitive skin of my palm. "No."

I pull my hand away, pretending to adjust my nightgown. My gaze dips to his chest, watching the rise and fall of his breaths. Anything to avoid those eyes that see too much and that touch that makes all thoughts flee.

He didn't feel anyone cross. He hasn't remarked on the spell she placed upon me.

Either the woman is some weird figment of my imagination, some strange woman of the Court of Air, or something's wrong.

Sigurd pushes a lock of hair behind my ear, letting his fingers trail down the curve and along my neck. My thighs press together, a vain attempt to deny the moisture building there. All I want to do is reach out and stroke his wing, feel those feathers against my skin, lean into him and let him carry me far away from everything.

But there'll be no going back. Once I'm trapped in his pull, I'll become like Mark. In that, we're alike, and I can't let my heart get trapped here.

Gran needs me. My life isn't mine, not yet.

It takes everything I have, but I pull away, and he lets me go, releasing me from the embrace of his arms and wings.

"Wren."

I need a barrier. Something. Anything. And I know what will work. I hate it, but I know.

"The fae king you almost killed is Evelyn's son."

My heart thumps into the silence. I stiffen, waiting for his wrath.

"I see your discussion with your uncle was insightful indeed." Sarcasm laces his words. A snap and flutter echo behind me before moonlight spills in around me.

I twist, expecting him to have vanished, but only the wings are gone. Sigurd has his arms propped on the railing again, frowning into the night as if the moments before never happened.

It's not you he's interested in, the voice in my head taunts me. *It's her. The woman you look like. You're a replacement.*

"Why do it?" I ask, if only to drown out the voice in my head. "Why hurt someone she loved if you loved her?" When he'd talked about the King of the Forest keeping her from him, I'd assumed she was his consort. How wrong I'd been.

"Why do you really think I'm playing music out here?" He asks over one shoulder. "Why I wanted to see you?"

"Because I look like her."

Sigurd turns, his head tilting as he assesses me in the moonlight.

"I think you do. I thought it the moment I saw you, but..." His shoulders droop. "I find it hard to remember exactly how she looked anymore. There's one thing I'll never forget though." He pushes off the railing and crosses to me.

My back stiffens but I refuse to back away, meeting his hard stare and tilting my head up to hold it. "What is that?"

"The look in her eyes the last time I saw her. It's the look in yours right now." He reaches for me but halts halfway. "Fear. Anger. Staring me down like I'm a villain."

I swallow the tightness in my throat.

He huffs and turns away. "Maybe I am."

"Then why be that way? Why create conflict with the Court of the Forest?"

He's silent for so long I don't think he'll answer. But finally, he says, "A young, human woman came to the Court of the Forest. It was the first time the king showed interest, the spark of love. Or so my spies said."

"Spies..." I hug my arms around myself.

"A king must—"

"Work for the good of his people." Yeah, yeah. "I'm sure you had their best interest in mind." My words drip with sarcasm.

Sigurd snarls in return. "Humans are rare in the forest, especially young, fair ones. Her presence gave him strength, the ability to revive his whole court to levels they haven't been in years. If that happened, I'd lose my chance at revenge, perhaps forever."

"And you couldn't handle that?" I throw my hands up in the air. "Just had to be petty and stir up trouble."

"Petty? Rivenean kept Evelyn away from me after his father died. It was he who refused to let me see her again. Wouldn't even let me in his territory. For years, I lived off the words of my spies. Little tidbits about her, here and there. I watched her age in my mind, watched her human spark fade and die, all without being able to see her, to hold her again." He slams his fist on the railing.

My hands ball into fists, and it's all I can do not to smash one into his face. "He kept her from you? That's all? Maybe she didn't want to see you."

It's the wrong thing to say.

Sigurd whirls on me, eyes wide. His jaw stiffens. But I can't help myself. This man, this king, is acting like a child. Maybe no one else will call him out on it, but I've had years of putting stupid, annoying men in their place.

"I could have saved her. I could have turned her fae!" Wings snap from his back once more, towering over him larger than before.

I stumble back, my hands in front of me.

He flinches. The wings flutter and dip.

"She didn't have to die. Not yet." His voice cracks, something within me right along with it. This is the heart of the matter, the source of his pain.

"The cauldron?"

He doesn't answer, just scowls into the night.

Hesitantly, I step near. "Uncle Mark told me about how his presence helped Hawke and the Court of Air. Humans heightening fae magic and all, especially m-mates." I stumble over the word again.

"But they both wanted him to become fae anyway, to have more time together."

"Yes." He lets out a sharp breath. "And Evelyn could have had so many more years."

"But maybe she wanted to stay human, for her son, for the forest?"

Sigurd goes impossibly still. Doesn't breathe. Doesn't blink. "But I—"

"See, that's the problem." I scowl at him. "Everything is all I, I, I. Not what she wanted, not what's best for your kingdom." I gesture to the valley below. "A good king wouldn't be such an idiot."

He flinches, turning his head as if he's been slapped. His jaw stiffens. "You're bold to speak to me this way."

I notch my chin higher. "Maybe I don't care what you think of me." It'd be so much easier if it were true. Even easier if he hated me. Then I could win this competition, leave, and never look back. "You did a horrible thing. Wrecked lives. And for what?"

"A king is not allowed mistakes?"

"Some mistake. I was told you plotted for years. You said it yourself with your spies."

"I did." He admits, voice hard as the marble we stand on. "But it didn't turn out as I planned. I realized my mistake the moment a poison arrow plunged through Rivenean's chest. I wanted him to feel my pain, not...die. But I can't undo it. No magic can change the past."

"Then do better. Apologize."

Sigurd crosses his arms and looks back at me, nonplussed.

My lips thin. "But you'd have to be sorry to apologize, wouldn't you? And you don't entirely regret it, mistake or not."

A hot ache burns in my chest, and I fight the urge to rub at it. Why does he have to be so lovely and awful all at once?

"Maybe that's why she didn't want to be with you," I mumble. My hands clamp over my mouth, but it's too late.

Sigurd slams his fist on the railing, and it cracks. Little bits of stone clatter to the floor.

A sharp gust of wind tugs at my hair and plasters the nightgown to my legs. My skin goes clammy. He could toss me off this balcony without a thought, just like he threw Moria across the room. Just like that tornado tore apart my home years ago and stole away my parents. I back away, edging toward the room.

All at once, the wind dies. His expression shatters, and he flinches.

My heart clenches, but the damage is done.

"Sleep, little Wren." He looks away. "Tomorrow's game will need all your wits."

I turn to flee.

"Unless..."

My feet pause on the stonework.

"Unless you'll quit the game. Let me keep you safe, here with me until the binding fades."

Like I wanted to keep her.

He doesn't say the last part. He doesn't need to.

"I'm not her, Sigurd," I whisper without looking back.

He's quiet so long I assume he didn't hear me, and I retreat inside.

But before I can seal myself in my borrowed room, his reply comes as a whisper on an icy breeze. "No. You really are nothing like her."

CHAPTER 20

THE SETUP FOR THE third game is even worse than I feared.

I bob on my toes, nearly vibrating with the force of the cheers raining down on us. Fae crowd into steep stands that look down over the stage for today's game. A maze, or so it seems, from the little I can see. A long one. The stands run in two parallel lines facing one another, with the course between. High walls block the contestants' view beyond the entrance.

But the roars and screeches coming from beyond the walls say much—we won't be alone in there. I scan the crowd as they point out various things to one another, viewing the bits of the course they can see.

The only thing I'm grateful for is that I can't spot Sigurd in the crowd, wherever he is.

He's here. He has to be, I think.

But worse, I can almost feel his presence in my bones, not to mention the lack of a pull on the tattoo around my wrist.

You really are nothing like her. His words cut at me over and over.

Nothing like the woman he loved. I rub at my chest.

Fine. Whatever. My heel grinds into the dirt. It makes things simpler. Win the competition. Leave this place and him behind.

My stomach turns over as I think about Uncle Mark and losing him again, but at least I know why he left us and that he's happy. Maybe, just maybe, I can see him again. Maybe even bring my cousins to visit...if they can see fae.

Another roar rises from the crowd as something hard crashes within the maze.

I swallow. Before I can even think about home and what I'll do once I leave here, I have to make it through this game.

The outfit Moria selected makes sense. Easy to move in, possibly offering some camouflage in shadow, and no loose bits to get stuck anywhere. The only piece of jewelry is my necklace, tucked down inside my shirt. I don't have to worry about Sigurd's bond showing either, with the long, tight sleeves. The hidden knives are a nice perk, but the gnawing pit within me knows they won't be enough, not on my own.

"Hey there." I saunter up to Galen, where we all wait in a holding area of sorts, giving him my best smile.

"Wren." His brows rise as he takes in my outfit, giving me an appreciative nod.

"Allies?" I hold my breath, waiting for an answer.

He shifts on his feet. "This game, this challenge..."

"Look, I know we're not finding flowers, but I'm more determined than a hound dog at a hunt. You can't doubt that."

Galen rubs the back of his neck. "I don't doubt it."

"But?" My fists tighten, and I hide them behind my back.

He glances at the maze with its towering stone walls and half-dozen entrances and then back to me. "You're human."

He might as well have said I'm weak. A liability. No help to anyone.

Fine. Time to play my hidden ace.

"Yes." I slide near him, so close we're nearly touching, and whisper, "A human who has the favor of the king. You said so yourself, right?" I may not have Sigurd's favor anymore, not after last night, but Galen doesn't need to know that. As he said, I'm a human, and I can lie. I'll use every tool in my box if I have to. "I believe I can get the king to release you from your oaths."

His eyes widen.

I seize the chance to drive my arrow home. "If you help me. Think of it as an insurance policy."

"Insur—"

I wave my hand. "Even if you lose, I can get you what you want." My grin seals the promise.

"How can you be sure?"

I stare up at him from lowered lashes. "I look like his long-lost love. She won't be coming back, but I can be a convenient replacement." My stomach leaps into my throat just saying it, but I force the horror from my eyes and keep the confidence in my smile. "He's quite interested. If you know his scent, surely you smell him on me."

Good golly, the words coming out of my mouth. But I need this. I need his help. I even skipped a bath to make sure some of Sigurd's scent clung to my skin. If fae sense of smell is as good as Uncle Mark says and Galen knows him as well as I think he might, it should help my words ring true.

I may not be fae, but I have the determination of ten of them. Always have. Something gets on my list to do, I get it done. No excuses. No failure. There's no room to fail when your family depends on you bringing home the bacon and helping them get out of bed each day.

Except now I'm not there to do that. My chest constricts painfully.

But I'm fixing that. I'll get back and never leave them alone again.

Galen's hard stare has me holding my breath. He rubs his hand down his face and sighs. "Fine."

My smile broadens, and it's not a bit fake.

"But follow my lead, do what I say."

"Aye, aye, captain." I salute.

He nearly rolls his eyes. "You're worse than Sylvie."

"But, hey"—I nudge him—"you love her, so I can't be that bad."

His sideways glare says otherwise.

"Have you considered my offer?" comes a voice from behind us.

I jump. The prince from the Court of Fire stands in all his glory, wearing an outfit not that unlike mine. And oh boy, it does him all the favors that mine doesn't. It'd be a lie to say my mouth doesn't water a bit at the sight of those sculpted abs in his lean form. Or the thighs that any runner would envy. His deep red hair is tied back behind his head, and despite his warrior-like appearance, he exudes the strange calm of a scholar.

"Yes, join us." I share my blinding smile with him.

"What?" Galen says. "Now wait, we agreed I'm—"

"In charge?" I turn to him. "Once the game starts, yes, you are." I glance back at the prince. "If you wish to join us, follow Galen's lead."

The prince smiles and nods.

Galen rubs his hand across his face as if having a foreign prince and a human for allies is just about the worst thing that could ever happen to him.

"So, do you know anything about this game, Prince…" I incline my head and raise my brows. I should at least know my ally's name.

A quirky smile pulls at his lips. "You really don't know?"

Galen groans.

A touch of heat rises to my cheeks. Right, guess most people would have known that. I shake my head. "I'm new here."

"Lysandir."

"Right, well, nice to meet you, Lysandir."

"As for the game…" He looks up and past me toward the crowds gathered to watch. He steps near us and whispers, "Watch the crowd. See where they look. It may give us some clues."

I blink. He's right. Already their attention has been glued to certain areas.

Our announcer—and golly, I don't know his name either—traipses out onto a raised stage that overlooks the various entrances into the maze. His outfit today is garish green with highlights of gold and red, like some kind of parrot. He'd fit right in at a Mardi Gras parade, though the fae seem to love it too, their voices rising in a strange chant before he calls them silent.

"Today's game is a perennial favorite," he says. "The labyrinth!"

Fae clap and stomp their feet, creating a rolling thunder that echoes into my bones.

This time, I pay attention as he describes the history of the game. However, just about every sentence sends my heart plummeting further and further.

Beasts. Obstacles. Traps. And the whole darn thing is a maze.

As a teen, I was a champion over old man Murdock's annual corn maze. I held the record two years in a row. But the scariest things in there were the men who stumbled in after too much cider, and they were easy enough to avoid. I rub at my necklace through my shirt. This promises to be much more dangerous.

"The first fifteen competitors to reach the end will move on," the announcer continues. "If a competitor is incapacitated or must be rescued from the labyrinth, they will be disqualified."

The fae boo at the notion of disqualification. Or maybe the thought of any of us being rescued. I swallow the knot in my throat. The way they jostle each other in the stands like drunken college boys cheering on their favorite team, they might like a little bloodshed.

"No rules against harming other competitors, huh?" I say.

I mean it as a joke, but the hard look from Galen says it's true. Again. We have to make it through the labyrinth by any means necessary.

Literally any.

A resounding gong vibrates through the ground.

Several fae sprint toward the entrances. Others go at a more measured pace. The prince and I look to Galen.

"Well?" I say.

Indecision flickers across Galen's face as he watches the others before he points. "Second from the left."

I take off with them, running fast as my pitiful human legs will allow. It takes everything I've got, but the men at my sides might as well be walking for all the exertion they show. No sooner do we make it to the entrance than another fae—one who'd sprinted off like a cheetah—races back out the entrance and scrambles around a corner like the devil himself is on his heels.

Whatever lies beyond the quick turn ahead, I'd rather not find out. Thankfully, neither would Galen.

"This one, then." He tips his head in the opposite direction the other fae went, and we follow. The ground in this path is rocky and uneven like the remnants of a landslide. Galen and Lysandir practically hop from one boulder to another, racing through with ease. Showoffs.

My heart pounds in my ears as I leap from one boulder to the next, slip, scrape my shin, and scramble up the rock. Rinse and repeat. It sucks. It hurts.

But this is only the beginning, and I surely can't give up now.

A tall section of rock juts from the ground. Galen scales it with the speed of a Navy Seal and turns back, extending his hand. "Wren."

I nearly laugh. As if I could reach his hand way up there.

"Need a lift?" Lysandir asks. He doesn't give me time to reply before grabbing my waist and lifting me above his head as if we're an ice-skating duo.

"Wait," I say, "Ah—"

"Gotcha." Galen grabs my failing arms. "That's it. Use your legs."

My boots barely find purchase on the rock wall before he has me hauled up its side onto a narrow spit of land. I rock back on my heels, nearly tumbling down the wall.

A large pit gapes before us. It's way too far to jump and—

I lean over, just enough to look down.

Only darkness stares back.

"We have to go back," I say, just as Lysandir scrambles up the wall to perch beside me.

"We jump," Lysandir says.

"Jump! Are you crazy?" I gesture to the pit of no return. "I could never make that." No way, not even with the best jump of my life.

"Can you make it with Wren?" Galen asks, talking over me.

Oh no, no way are they jumping with me in their arms. Nope. Nope. Nope.

Lysandir scowls at the pit. "Too risky."

"We go back," I say. "We're wasting time."

"The path ahead is smooth, and look." Galen points to the crowd, just visible above the high walls. Their attention is focused further ahead. Someone, maybe many someones, are beating us. "No time."

Galen drops to one knee, his face creased in concentration.

"But— Then—" Words die on my tongue.

Thick vines spring out from the side of the cliff, braiding together and reaching across the void. Without thinking, I step back. My foot slips on rubble.

Lysandir moves in a blink, grabbing my arm to steady me. "Careful."

A humorless laugh echoes from my chest. Right. Wouldn't want to die being clumsy.

"That'll do." The prince's words have barely left his lips before he scoops me off the ground.

I clamp down on a scream as he runs out onto the vines with me over his shoulders like a sack of potatoes. Galen follows.

My eyes clamp shut. Lysandir leaps.

A silent prayer still rings through my head as we thump onto solid ground. I'm back on my feet before I can fully process what just happened.

"Come on." Galen races ahead as I watch his magical vines crumble to leaves and drift down into the darkness.

No going back now.

I race after the men, skidding down the slope to where they wait. Both look around the bend, not paying any attention as I nearly stumble the last few feet to the landing.

"What is—" I start.

But Galen pulls me into his arms and clamps a hand over my mouth. What the heck? I squirm against him until his harsh whisper fills my ears. "Shh."

He points ahead. I go utterly still, breath catching in my throat as I take in what they've seen. A large feline—twice as big as a lion—lumbers just ahead, hissing and roaring up at the crowd.

It hasn't seen us.

Yet.

"Torch it?" Galen whispers as he lets me go.

The prince grimaces but nods.

"You can't," I hiss.

Both men stare at me like I've grown a second head.

I plant my palms on my hips, staring them down. "You can't kill it."

"I doubt it shares your sentiments," Lysandir says.

Nausea churns in my belly. Maybe not, but killing for sport, for no benefit but our victory, feels wrong. Hunting for food is one thing. I still didn't exactly like it when Dad would bring home deer or ducks when I was a kid, but at least it was done to put food on the table. But this...

"The crowd has it distracted. We sneak by." I point to the side nearest us, behind the creature's back.

The prince's scowl deepens. "Should it turn on us, I won't hesitate."

Fine. No point in arguing, especially when it's clear he won't budge on this.

The crowd increases their antics, jumping up and down and shouting at the beast. They're on our side, and I'll take any help I can get. We sneak as fast as we dare down the side of the wall, the prince in front and me squished in the middle. The courtesy isn't lost on me, nor is the fact that they're going at my pace.

If I wasn't here, no doubt they'd have used their magic and zipped on by.

The beast occupies a corner. Whatever lies beyond the bend is a mystery. My heart hammers, each beat pleading for the creature not to turn—and for another not to linger just out of sight.

We've just turned the bend when the feline sniffs the air, inhaling with the force of a vacuum. Its whiskers twitch. The great golden head turns in our direction, its gaping maw sporting teeth long and pointed as daggers.

"Shit," I say.

Lysandir grabs my wrist and jerks me into a run. I stumble after, fast as I can go with his vice-like grip tugging me along. The way ahead is a honeycomb of rocky divots and caves. A sound like nails on a chalkboard sets my teeth on edge and scrapes against my mind as I sprint with all I have.

Several openings loom ahead.

"Which—" I say.

"No time." Lysandir jerks me to him and dives for an opening on the ground.

The impact knocks the breath from my lungs. Something sharp scrapes against my leg.

Darkness swallows us.

Putrid air swarms my senses and has me coughing into the dusty space. Lysandir groans as he gets to his knees in the little cave. It's so tight we can barely kneel.

I clamp my hands over my ears as the monster roars into the opening and swipes its claws along the stone. It dominates the exit, blocking the way out. Behind us—

Only stone. Shoot, shoot!

My heart skips a beat. "Galen!"

CHAPTER 21

G ALEN ISN'T IN HERE with us. My skin goes clammy. Tears prick the corner of my eyes.

"Galen!" My shrill scream is met by another growl from the monster.

I grab Lysandir's shoulders, all but shaking him. "What happened to him?"

He takes my face in his hands, far more gently than me. "I don't know, but we have to get out of here."

I suck in one breath after another, but it does nothing to calm me.

If is Galen hurt because of me, or worse...

"Back up. It's going to get hot." Lysandir shuffles toward the entrance. His words have barely registered before a bright glow fills our little cavern. Flames leap from his hands. The monster bellows and bounds away from the entrance.

Lysandir reaches back for me. Tendrils of flame vanish from his upturned palm. I take it, bracing for heat, but his hand is only pleasantly warm.

We skirt out the entrance, sticking to the wall. Another blast of fire from Lysandir has the monster backing up. Its long, rat-like tail swishes rocks across the ground at its back. The roar of the crowd is deafening as they cheer overhead, but I can barely hear them over the thump of my pulse.

"Up," Lysandir says. "Quick."

He has me in the air before I can get my bearings. I scramble onto the ledge, pulling up with all my strength as he gives me a shove from below. No sooner do I have a solid grasp on a rock than he lets me go, and I nearly fall backward. I yelp, straining onto the ledge as heat rushes below me. Another bellow from the beast follows. I twist around on the ledge as the monster shifts onto his hind legs. It's backside wiggles.

"It's going to jump!" I call.

A solid gust of wind crashes into its side, sending it skittering across the rocky ground.

I gasp, catching sight of a figure on some rocks to the left. My heart leaps. "Galen!"

Blood trickles down his face, but he's alive and on his feet.

"Find a way through," he calls before sending another blast at the creature, drawing its attention.

A wall pocketed with holes towers above me. At the top, rock arcs like a roof over us. It'd be impossible to climb—for me anyway. I race down the ledge, glancing into each opening, as Lysandir hauls himself up to my level. Some holes are no bigger than a cabinet, and none appear to go more than a few feet.

"Up?" I ask.

But the prince is busy trying to pull the monster's attention from where it claws at a pile of rocks, swiping precariously close to Galen.

I'm sure as heck not going back down. With no time to waste, I find a promising section of the wall and begin the climb. My nails dig into the rock for dear life, but in moments my arms are on flat-ish ground and I'm hauling my body up the last few feet.

A cry from below strikes me like lightning. I twist around to see the prince gripping his arm and the monster entirely too close.

"Lysandir!" I scream, but over the roar of the crowd, he probably can't even hear me. The monster sure acts like he doesn't.

With a cry of frustration, Galen sends a tornado of leaves hurtling the monster's way. Its claws dig into the ground as it braces against the offense but doesn't budge.

Fire erupts from Lysandir in a burst. It blends with the tornado, sending the leaves aflame. The beast roars and springs from the onslaught. I scream as it hurtles through the air straight toward Galen. He barely jumps out of the way in time, rolling across the rocky ground.

The hole in the wall behind me shows a glimmer of light at the end. A way through. I could take it.

But I can't leave them behind, not when they put themselves at risk for me.

Lysandir leaps in front of Galen, who is slow to rise. Fire races from him, singeing the animal's fur as it darts back and forth, looking for an opening.

I edge around to the course wall, slinking along an outcropping of rock that curves around the side. My throat grows tight when stones tumble off as I scoot by, dropping three stories to the ground below. One wrong step, and I'm in a heap of horse dung. If the fall doesn't kill me, it'll certainly hurt enough to make me a sitting duck for the monster—whatever the abomination is.

Fire surrounds the beast, but it leaps toward the flames, testing them, despite the way it singes its fur and no doubt hurts like heck. Guilt roils in my stomach. Lysandir is holding back. Because I asked them not to kill it.

Galen tries to make his way up the wall, but one arm sits at an awkward angle and he doesn't use it at all. Broken? My head spins. He'll need the prince's help, but with the beast as riled up as he is...

A diversion. I have to get its attention.

"Up here, you big dumb beast!" I yell at the top of my lungs.

But with the noise of the crowd, I might as well be a fly buzzing far overhead. Galen and Lysandir glance my way, but whether it's because I yelled or my flailing arms, who knows.

Shoot, I need...

Of course! I pull out one of Moria's hidden knives. The thin blade is light in my hand and gleams in the sunlight from above.

"Careful with those," she'd said. "They're razor sharp."

Let's hope so.

I rear my arm back and hurl the dagger at the beast with all my might. It hits its side, sinking deep.

Hurray!

The bellow it lets out is deafening, shaking the rocks around me and sending several tumbling to the floor below.

It rears back on its hind legs, looking between me and my allies.

"Over here, beastie!" I pick up a handful of rocks and hurl them toward it. My boots slide precariously close to the edge from the force of my throw.

The beast leaps through the flames, bounding toward me.

"Get up here!" I yell.

The monster leaps. Its great clawed paws crash against the wall, causing the whole thing to shake and crack.

Shit!

I cling to my spit of land. It snarls and leaps again, falling just a precious few feet short of my perch.

Lysandir and Galen are up the first ledge but not high enough. The beast follows my gaze and drops back to the ground.

Oh, heck no. I slide another dagger from its hiding place.

"Fur ball!"

It twists back to me and growls at the insult.

I hurl the dagger. It twists through the air and glances off its leg to clatter on the ground.

The monster leaps at me with another roar, its steaming breath nearly choking me where it wafts up in a stinking cloud. I grab up stones and chuck them down at the beast, ignoring the bloody cuts and dirt marring my hands.

"Wren!" Galen shouts.

The tension in me uncoils when I spot them in front of the tunnel. Safe. Finally.

The ground below me rumbles and cracks. My heart leaps into my throat as I wobble, trying to regain my balance. Claws as long as my arm dig into the ground not a foot away.

"Shit!" I clamp my hand over my mouth on instinct. Oh, frickety frick frack.

I scramble along the narrow path as the ground spiderwebs with cracks and fissures. Hot breath shrouds me.

Don't look back. Can't look back.

The crowd is wild, their screams drowning out whatever Galen and Lysandir say as they reach for me from the edge of the main wall.

Just a few more steps. A few—

Another rumbling shake nearly brings me to my knees. A horrible, rending crack grates against my senses, overpowering the roar of the crowd.

My ledge is coming down.

With a final burst of strength, I leap into the air.

Not enough.

I'm going to fall and be shredded to ruins.

A gust of air wraps around me, fierce as a tornado. Breath is sucked from my lungs. Terror grips me tighter than the wind, urging me to run, to flee, but I'm as helpless as I was as a child. Tears stream down my face, sobs racking the last of the air from my lungs.

Suddenly it stops. Strong arms are around me, settling my feet on the ground.

"We've got you," Galen says.

I blink, but the tears don't stop. I'm still sobbing, shaking.

"You okay?" Lysandir asks.

Humorless laughter bursts from my chest. Okay? I'll never be okay. Not where tornadoes are involved, monsters either.

"Wren?" Galen's hands are on me, searching for injuries, something strange tingling under my skin. Maybe it's residual fear making me so unsteady.

Eventually, I croak out, "I'll live."

He gives me one sharp nod before turning toward the tunnel. "Let's move."

Right. I wipe my eyes with the heels of my palms. We have a game to complete. There are worst dangers here than my memories.

I look back over one shoulder at the monster. Much of its hair is singed. Blood trickles from where my knife is still embedded in its side. It stalks back and forth, growling and roaring with what can only be hate.

My chest goes tight. *I'm sorry.*

"Wren?" Galen's hand flexes on mine. I don't even know when he grabbed it.

With a nod, we're off and running after Lysandir.

The tunnel spits us out into a miniature jungle full of thick trees, looping vines, large pointed leaves, and who knows what else.

"May I?" Lysandir looks back at me, one brow raised. Sparks float above his open palm.

"Do it." I won't endanger us again, not when there's an easier way.

But please don't let there be any animals—or worse, any people—in there.

He grins and turns toward the foliage. In moments, it's engulfed in a wave of fire. Heat draws beads of sweat on my skin. I squint against the gleam as Galen's hand tightens on mine.

The crowd is full of oohs and ahs, mixed with gasps. Such power. Such raw elemental strength. It doesn't just burn; it incinerates with a heat I can hardly fathom.

Lysandir unleashes it as if it's as natural as breathing.

A shiver races down my spine.

The wall of flames recedes, but the jungle still burns. Smoke rises in great clouds above us. Charred remains drift through the air.

The men glance at one another then me, and we're off, racing across the ash and smoldering remains. Smoke burns my lungs, sending me into a coughing fit. My eyes water.

Then crisp, cool air surrounds me, tugging at my braid and piercing the smoke ahead of us. But it doesn't terrify. It's not the whirlwind of before, but something calm and nourishing. I glance at Galen to see sweat mingling with blood and dirt on his face. His brows crease in concentration.

He's doing this, all the while never letting me go.

I push harder, stretching my legs and lungs to their limits.

Moments later, we race onto flat stone ground. Other paths spill out around us, all headed for the same spot: the stage.

Only open pathway lies before us.

I pull my hand from Galen's. "Go!" I gesture to the stage. Lysandir looks over where he keeps pace at my other side. "You too. Go!"

I held them back before.

I won't now.

They can run faster than me, beat me there. They deserve to.

"Go!" I say again.

Finally, they do, sprinting ahead at a dizzying speed.

My legs ache. My lungs burn. Sweat trickles down my skin everywhere. All I want to do is lie down and never get up, but I can't.

Not yet, not when I'm so close.

Galen and Lysandir reach the platform at almost the same time. Cheers rise from the massive crowd gathered in the stands just beyond and above the stage. So many fae. Multiples more than any of the other games. Maybe even more than the opening ceremony.

Some sections are framed off and covered. I have no doubt who lingers in one of them. Watching, probably grimacing in fury that I've made it so far. Or anger at who I emerged with.

Probably both.

"You!" A piercing shriek raises goosebumps across my skin.

I glance over one shoulder to see a fae—the woman who's tossed more scowls and nasty words my way than most of the others combined—race from one of the other pathways.

I push on. I can beat her. I've got a massive head start. I can—

She yells, and I look again. The fae presses her hands together and flings them toward me. Something rockets my way faster than I can make out.

My legs cramp up.

A bolt of pure, hard air barrels toward my chest. I can't stop it. Can't move.

It glances off, slicing a gash in my shirt and hurtling past me to crash into the stage. Wood explodes into a shower of splinters. Fae scream.

A hole three feet wide looms in the center of the stage. Fae—competitor and non—brush off splintered wood, a few bearing new cuts that gleam with bright red blood.

That was meant for me, to destroy me.

But... I touch the exposed skin on my side. Unharmed. A warmth pulses in my arm, then fades away.

The Unseelie woman's spell. It protected me.

And now it's gone.

The fae woman lets out another guttural cry and breaks into movement.

I can't let her beat me. I won't.

I bolt across the last few feet to the stage.

The announcer is still wide eyed, inspecting his mussed attire. He blinks at me as I leap up the few stairs and dodge the new hole. With a little shake, he comes back to himself and raises my hand in the air.

Cheers erupt. My heads spins. Colors dot my vision. Breaths come hard and fast.

But I made it. *I* made it.

"Our last semi-finalist, Wren!"

Chapter 22

I COLLAPSE AS THE announcer lets me go, landing hard on my backside on the stage.

The fae woman has reached the stage and spouts unintelligible curses my way, but I can't muster up the ability to care. Galen and Lysandir fill my vision, blocking out the angry fae beyond. Their questions are a buzz in my ears. All I can focus on is sucking in one breath after another.

Someone touches my exposed side, and I shiver.

I should be dead. I could be.

Did the Unseelie woman know this would happen? Why save me?

A shadow blocks the sun overhead. Suddenly, my friends are being pulled off me. Strong arms scoop me up, and I'm embraced by the scent of citrus and pine.

Sigurd.

I lean against his chest.

Safe.

The world twists around us, but I barely notice. A second later, we're somewhere else.

"Wren!" Uncle Mark's voice pierces the haze of my mind.

"Heal her!" Sigurd implores. His voice is panicked, brittle.

Am I that injured?

He lays me on something soft. Then Hawke is there, pressed in next to Sigurd, who still looms above me. Hawke trails his hands down my arms, my side. A cool tingling rushes under my skin, and I can't help but sigh.

The jumping, cramping muscles in my calves relax. My lungs no longer burn. My vision clears, and I can make out Uncle Mark and Moria near the end of the couch, leaning this way and that to get a good look at me.

"She's fine," Hawke says. "Some scrapes and sore muscles. Nothing serious."

Sigurd all but shoves him out of the way. His warm palm rubs over my exposed side where the shirt was torn away by the blast. "How..." He gapes, eyes wild. "I saw that blast come for you. It hit you. I thought, I—"

"It didn't hit me," I say. Although, I'm almost certain it did. "Grazed me. Tore my shirt, but I'm fine."

"Fine?" He steps away, pacing across the shaded space—one of the boxes in the stands? "I thought she'd hit you. If she had—"

Wind stirs up, racing through the box and whipping my hair.

"Whoa." Moria jumps in front of me, taking the brunt of his fury.

The wind dies in an instant.

He growls. "If she'd truly hurt you, I'd rip her apart."

I flinch back into the cushions.

"There's no rule against attacking other competitors," Hawke says.

"There is against killing them."

"She's not—" Moria starts.

Sigurd shoves her to the side and drops to his knees next to me. "Drop out. Right now."

"What?" I blink at him.

"You could have been killed. If something happens... The cauldron isn't worth your life."

My lips press thin. "But it's worth my grandmother's. What if something happens to her while I'm gone? Tabitha already has her hands full. She can't watch after Gran all the time. Aunt Virginia won't. Gran needs me. I have to be there for her. What if she falls? Forgets her meds?"

I shudder and shake my head, refusing to consider the worst.

"You can't help her if you're dead. Stop this, Wren. Stay with me." He reaches for me.

I scoot away, all the warmth and safety of moments ago vanishing in his words. "You. This is your fault, you know. You stuck me here with this stupid bond." I hold up my wrist. "You don't care about me. You said yourself I'm nothing like your lost love. You're selfish. Starting wars. Pursuing petty revenge. You want me to stay, to protect me, because you couldn't protect her. It has nothing to do with me!"

Deathly silence hangs around us with the buzz of the crowd in the distance.

Sigurd is completely still, his gaze dark. My chest rises and falls with all my emotions poured out and laid bare. It's too much. How dare he pretend to care after what he said the other night? How dare he order me to quit now after what I've been through?

Moria's mouth is parted, and she blinks as if she's just witnessed a brutal battle. Maybe she did, though not the kind I'd wager she's used to.

I can barely make out Hawke and Mark in the corners of my vision, but neither moves.

Sigurd's expression breaks. His shoulders droop, and he hangs his head.

The action cracks my heart. It is his fault, but this fury, this hate... He doesn't deserve it. Not from me.

"I—" I start.

But he's gone. Vanished into thin air.

"Sigurd." My voice cracks over his name.

"Where?" I look to Moria and Hawke, but neither speaks. Hawke just shakes his head. The bond on my wrist tugs, and I know he's nowhere close.

"He probably needs to calm down," Moria says at last. "That was..."

I drop my gaze to the floor. "I shouldn't have said all of that to him."

"No, you were mostly right in your words. He's heard them from others, but from you... They seem to have more effect. He takes them to heart, where most of us have little affect." Hawke sits in the chair next to me. "There's one point where you were wrong though." His hand closes over mine, giving it a little squeeze. It's the friendliest action he's ever had toward me. "He does care about you. More than I think any of us realized."

Then why tell me I'm nothing like Evelyn? I hug my arms around myself.

A tingle of magic ripples through the air, and a moment later, the announcer stands in the center of the room.

"What do you want?" Moria shoots him a glare so fierce that even the stalwart man, who held his place during the explosion meant to kill me, flinches.

He holds out the scroll in his hand, and his gaze drops to me where I lay huddled on a chaise longue. "Something for our brave competitor."

Moria's jaw stiffens, but she nods to him.

Slowly, he crosses the space between us. "You left before you could receive this. Something for our competitors to study before the next game." He passes me a scroll. "Well then." He looks to my companions before vanishing from sight.

Hesitantly, I unroll the scroll.

"What does it say?" Mark asks.

It's not just one page but many. Pictures of various plants dot the pages, surrounded by lines of text in a language I've never seen. "Another plant hunt?"

Geeze, you'd think they could be more creative.

Hawke leans over my shoulder, studying the top page. "No, these are poisons."

Moria curses and turns away.

The pit in my stomach opens up as I roll up the pages.

Maybe I should quit after all.

CHAPTER 23

I ASK TO STAY with Mark and Hawke. After my blow-up with Sigurd, I can't bear the thought of bumping into him again and having yet another conversation go awry. There's still tension in our bond, but when someone can travel in an instant, distance means little.

"Why does he push my buttons so much?" I ask my eagle friend the next evening.

My borrowed room is smaller here but still bigger than my one at home. The stone walls are draped in fine tapestries. Ornate furniture dots the room but refuses to crowd it. Honestly, the place could have been crafted by a zen fashion designer, and I'd have believed it. Though, its actual designer, Hawke, or so Mark said, is easy enough to believe.

There's no balcony on this room, just one off the main room of their sprawling apartment within the castle that apparently Moria shares with them. They've lived here since they were young, and why should she have to move all her stuff out just because Hawke has a mate? That's what she told me when I asked about it, anyway. Hawke didn't want to move either, and so they all live together, splitting the place down the middle.

Even so, my eagle managed to find his way here. A blessing because I need someone to talk to. Talking to Uncle Mark about Sigurd? Nope, no way. I tried, but the words caught on my tongue and felt all kinds of wrong.

He's their king, his mate's cousin. With how long we've been apart, Mark likely knows Sigurd way better than me, so venting about the insufferable man to him just didn't sit right.

"I know. I let him get under my skin." I give the eagle a scratch on his head. "I shouldn't. I shouldn't say things like I did either. He's not some drunk at the bar that needs a good chewing up and spitting out before being told to sober up. Really, other than trapping me here." Ugh. "He's been...nice."

Sexy. Ridiculous. Tempting.

I groan. "And such an idiot."

He has reasons for what he's done, but still, going to such lengths for revenge, possibly starting a war, almost getting someone killed? Not cool. We all make mistakes, but dang, that's...

I shake my head. "Do you think he's sorry? Do you think he can change?"

The eagle blinks at me. Its head nods, almost infinitesimally.

My chest clenches, and I force out a smile. "Guess it doesn't matter now, huh? I've blown it." I shake my head. "And I'm leaving soon anyway. Hopefully."

It shouldn't matter what Sigurd thinks of me, but somehow it does. He's not a man Gran would approve of. I'm not sure I can say I approve of him, given all I know, but he haunts my waking thoughts more than any man ever has. The only benefit of nearly getting myself killed in the competition was not thinking about him all the time.

A squawk pulls me back to the moment. Feathers brush against my cheek where I lay on top of the borrowed bed. A breath catches in my throat as the eagle nuzzles against my shoulder.

"Yes, I'll miss you too." I really will. More than I dare admit. It's probably why I haven't given him a name. It's too permanent, and I can't afford any more entanglements. Enough fae have imprinted themselves on my heart. Carving myself open more by naming my eagle like he's some kind of pet I can keep is a terrible idea.

A hard knock comes at the door. The eagle takes flight, soaring out my open window as I say, "Come in."

I expect Mark, but Hawke fills the open doorframe.

"Talking to someone?" He lifts one dark brow.

"Just myself." I sit up, ruffling the pages spread across the bed. I was supposed to be studying. To say I haven't been able to focus on it would be an understatement.

Hawke scans the room, doubt written all over the sharp angles of his face. His lips thin as he finishes his search.

I just blink in return. No point in dropping Hawke's opinion of me even further by confessing that I talk to animals.

"Anyhow," he says, "I finished translating the rest of these pages for you."

"Thank you so much." I lay on all the sweet, southern appreciation I can. I'd have been screwed if he or someone else hadn't offered to help. The pages they'd given out were all written in Faery Common, or so he said. It just looked like grand, looping swirls and squiggles to me.

He brings the pages over, and I expect him to drop them and leave, just like he did the last batch. Instead, he sits on the edge of the bed. The very edge. A centimeter more, and he'd probably slip straight off onto the floor.

I sit a little straighter.

"I wanted to ask about your grandmother," he begins without preamble. "Mark has told me some. You care for her?"

"Yes. I have for years." Worries creep into the edges of my mind, reaching out like grasping, spindly hands to strangle me. "Without me there... I'm sure Mark's daughter Tabitha helps but—"

He gives my knee a squeeze. "If your grandmother is anything like you and Mark, she will be okay. She'll be strong. Brave. Just as you are."

The compliment catches me more off guard than if he'd claimed the sky were red.

Fae can't lie.

"It's an honorable thing, caring for your elders," he continues. "We revere it quite highly here as well. However, you could get help if you wanted it."

I huff. "Who is supposed to help me?"

I'd told Uncle Mark all about his kids and how they help when they can, but they have their own lives, other obligations. Matt is not even in the country most of the time, for goodness sake. And Aunt Virginia? She's never helped anyone but herself.

"You could *pay* someone," he says. "Mark said there are places where the elderly can live where they are cared for."

I cross my arms. "That requires money, which we don't have."

Between Gran's savings and what I make at the bar, we get by, but affording a fancy senior living center? We wouldn't be able to do that for long.

"That's why I wanted to talk to you. We don't have your human money, but we have jewelry, gems, metals, things that may be of value. Mark hoped the gifts he'd left for you all over the years would help. They should have—"

I hold up my hand, cutting him off. "What do you mean, gifts?"

I hadn't gotten a darn thing, and if Tabitha had gotten anything from her vanished father, or anyone actually, I'd have definitely heard about it.

Hawke blinks at me. "The jewelry." His forehead furrows. "We thought it'd be the easiest for you to sell. Every so often, he'd take the risk to slip back into your human world and leave gifts at his old home."

"When?" I shake my head. A mistake. A miscommunication. It has to be.

"Since he left. The most recent was a few months ago now, but the piece was quite stately."

Simple words, but they hold so much.

"Whoa, whoa." I raise my hands in the air. "Uncle Mark told me Gran couldn't see him. He never mentioned presents. And he said fae fade in our world, so he couldn't stay? Just y'all, not your stuff?"

"He can't stay long. That's true. And it's dangerous." His gaze darkens. "If he were to get stuck or stay too long, he—" His hand balls into a fist. He nearly shakes. I've never seen such emotion, and all of it for Mark.

"Okay." I'll get to the bottom of that later. So help me if I'm not dragging his ass—butt—back with me to see his kids, at least for a few minutes. "This jewelry or whatever, we didn't get it. There have been no gifts."

Hawke practically leaps from the bed. "We need Mark."

No kidding. He holds out his hand to me, and I scowl. "We are not teleporting."

"Teleporting?" His head tilts to the side.

I roll my eyes and stalk past him into the hall. "Where is he?"

We find Mark in a library so cute and perfect with its floor-to-ceiling shelves and old book smell that I'd sigh and vow to stay forever if I wasn't so perplexed.

"You brought us gifts?" I ask the moment we step into the room.

Mark jolts in his chair and nearly drops his book before he looks between Hawke and me.

"I mentioned you brought you family things to help them after you left," Hawke says.

"Of course," he says, as if it's the most obvious thing in the world.

I stare him down, my hands on my hips. Then, a thought strikes me so hard I nearly double over.

Virginia... She loved to deck herself out in gaudy jewelry, anything to attract her next man of the month. I always assumed it was fake. How else could she afford it?

My head spins, and I have to sit down.

Bad enough that she rarely spends any time with her kids or grandkids, pretty much none with her mother-in-law and me, but to keep valuables from them? Things meant to provide them a better life?

"Wren?" Mark leaves his book behind and crouches by my chair. "What is it?"

Hawke curses.

"Would those gifts have included a long strand of pink pearls? A silver chain with a blue stone like this big?" I estimate the size with my fingers.

"A sapphire, yes."

Sapphire. I gasp. A stone that size would fetch a fortune. An-other reason I'd never thought it real. How could it be? But all this time, all these years, she'd kept it to herself, a tool to win new lovers.

"Virginia." Mark fills her name with all the bitterness churning within me.

All I can do is nod.

"She never told us. Kept them for herself. Never sold them that I know of, surely not for what they'd be worth." Though, as I say it, I can't help but wonder about that too. She loved to gush about the trips her lover of the moment took her on from time to time. Hawaii. The Bahamas. It seemed a lot for someone from our little town, but maybe her man of the moment hadn't been the one paying after all.

I hang my head in my hands. It wasn't just us she'd left to eke out a living but her own kids, her grandkids. With extra money in the bank, Tabitha's husband might have been able to take a different job, something closer to home, to let him spend time with the kids. Tabitha could get some help herself, maybe enroll the little ones in that new preschool they opened off Main Street.

Mark takes my hands in his. "We'll fix this. Everything will go to you from now on. You can make sure it gets to Tabitha and Matt?"

"Of course."

"Just do me one favor." His hands tighten on mine. "It wouldn't make Ma happy to know you put your life off for her."

"I—"

He levels me with a hard stare. "You have. And you wouldn't have if I'd been there or if things had worked out how I'd planned. We'll make it right."

Mark releases me, and I rub at the odd, burning ache in my chest.

"You could stay here if you wanted." Once again, Hawke sur-prises me. "Once you win, once you go home and see to the care of your grandmother, you are welcome anytime."

Turning my back on my family feels impossible, but the offer touches my heart all the same. I force a smile.

"I'll think on it." That's the best I can promise. For now, anyway.

CHAPTER 24

ORIA GUIDES ME TO the table she's set up in their massive sitting room. Sigurd's rooms are sparse—cold and formal compared to theirs. Here, life and history seep out from each gilded work of art, worn leather sofa, and rug showing years of wear and tread. Their pockets run deep, or so Hawke let on the night before last when I worried about Aunt Virginia's waste of their gifts. They could afford to redecorate, but Moria insisted their home was perfect as is. Why replace comfortable things they like?

"What is all this?" I gesture to the assortment of plants, vials, bowls, and other stuff strewn across the long coffee table.

"You don't know?" Moria says.

Some of the plants nag at me, pulling at threads, but they're certainly not ones we grew in our yard back home. I pick up a branch with purple leaves and small, white flowers.

"Careful with that one." She winks.

And then I know. I drop the branch as if it burns. It certainly can if the flowers are smashed. "Poisons."

Moria pulls out some folded papers, the original set of information I was given to study and which Hawke took to make a copy for me in English. "I thought it might help to see some of them in person. Though some of these"—she scowls at the page—"are quite hard to come by."

"This is okay? It's not against the rules?"

She snorts and tosses her ruby-dipped hair behind her. "Of course not. They gave you the information to study. It's only smart to get as familiar with it as possible if you want to win."

I reach for a crystal vial but think better of it and pull my hand back. "You don't think I need to drop out?"

"No. It's not that I don't want you to stay, but you should have a choice. Keeping humans in Faery against their will is something only the Unseelie do." She stares daggers at nothing across the room.

"Unseelie and certain kings..." I grumble.

Moria levels me with a flat stare, and I wince.

I'd promised myself no more jabs against Sigurd, particularly when he's not here to defend himself, but they keep slipping out on their own. The tug at my wrist has only gotten stronger, sometimes so forceful that it's almost painful and hard to focus on much else and then easing just as quickly. He must be moving, keeping busy, but he hasn't shown himself in front of me.

"Anyhow, I thought I'd help you study these for a bit. We don't know exactly what the game is, but the more you know..." She shrugs then grins. "Then perhaps you'll let me help you pick out a dress for the champion's ball?"

It's so hard not to groan. The ball was announced after the last game, though we'd missed the announcement with Sigurd's *rescue* of me from the stage. Another tradition of the games. All the remaining contestants are to attend, plus their families and previous champions, along with some of the royalty and nobility of the court.

Basically, it's one more opportunity for me to feel like a fish out of water and have fae shoot me dirty looks. Just peachy.

"You sure I can't skip it?" I ask.

"Nope. Though you don't have to stay long. Make an appearance, be introduced. It's usually a good time though. A lot smaller and more civilized than the finale celebration."

I sigh. Right, because fae love a good party. A ball for the contestants and a small selection of the elite now, and a rancorous festival for the rest of the people in the capital at the end. According to Moria, everyone looks forward to celebrating the winner of the games with food, drink, dancing, and all sorts of festivities. They hold it out in the valley. Mark had pointed out the preparations already in progress when we visited the farm again yesterday.

Secretly, I'd hoped to run into the Unseelie woman again to ask her what she wants of me, and selfishly, if she had anything to protect me against poisons. But though I'd found a few moments to slip away and linger in shadowy places, she'd never appeared.

"Hello? Wren?" Moria waves a hand in front of my face.

"Sorry, just trying to think how I'm going to keep all this straight." I gesture to the table.

"Uh huh. Well, I think he tries not to think about you just as much as you try to pretend you're not thinking about him."

Warmth rises to my cheeks. "I wasn't—"

She smirks. "You humans and your lies."

"Really, I wasn't." This time. Though admitting who I had been thinking about would open up a whole can of worms I can't begin to fathom.

"I know he can be impulsive. Foolish at times. But you've worked more change on him in a few days than I've accomplished in decades."

"W-what do you mean?"

"Sending an offering of goodwill to the Court of the Forest." She picks up a cluster of leaves, twirling them between her fingers.

"He did?" An apology, if not the words.

"Mmhmm. And he's paying more attention to the Unseelie threat, posting more sentries so that the rest of us aren't stretched so thin. Even taking more command. Why do you think I can afford to be here?"

I swallow and shake my head in wonder.

"Perhaps you'll give him another chance? Even if you do leave us soon, do it on good terms."

"Yes." Of course. How could I not? "I'll try."

"Good." She beams as if everything is settled and rosy in the world. "Now, let's talk about these poisons." Shining teeth glimmer in her vicious smile, though not quite as much as the ferocious twinkle in her eyes. "There are a few I'm *quite* familiar with."

Moria teaches me about poisons until my head throbs and the pages blur before my eyes. Several of the things she took her time detailing—the right dosages to kill a fae versus incapacitate them, how to apply it to a blade for best effect, how long the poison can linger on the tip of an arrow—probably aren't what the competition organizers have in mind, but after the last terror of a game, who knows. There's no dissuading her either. Once Moria starts talking about weapons and warfare, her whole demeanor changes. Focused, lethal, and unabashedly giddy.

She does love to talk about her knives. In fact, I'd say its second only to using them to carve out the beating heart of her enemies.

"You haven't heard a word I've been saying." Moria lays on the sofa across from me, her legs over the arm rest while she tosses one of her little knives into the air then catches it again. It set my teeth on edge until I focused on the table again while she talked, ignoring the casual danger she seems to enjoy playing with.

"I'm trying." I rub at my temples. "It's just...a lot."

We'd briefly stopped for lunch, but I'd long since hit a wall. I never was the type that could stay up all night cramming for an exam. After a few hours, my brain would just lie down and quit. Stubborn mule of a thing. It needs a decent break before it gets back up, and all my prodding at it hasn't helped it rest. Not to mention that her stories about the effects of one poison were so graphic I nearly lost my lunch.

"Fine, a break then." She flicks the knife across the room where it lodges in the wooden frame of a portrait. A number of other notches mar the wood. Moria jumps to her feet in one graceful motion that speaks of strength and agility. If I tried it, I'd likely face plant onto the coffee table and probably poison myself in the process too. "I want to show you this dress. It might be perfect for you."

I push to my feet with a sigh. Like I could ever pull off an outfit as well as Moria.

"What do you think?"

The dress she holds up is stunning—if one has the body of a runway model. Navy blue and sparkly, it shows off more than it covers, despite trailing down to her ankles. The deep V would need a whole roll of tape to stay in place, and the slits up the side would make most underwear impossible.

"It's..." My brows pinch as I search for the right word.

"For me, not you." She winks.

"Oh." Thank the Lord. "Well, in that case, it's perfect."

She trails her hand down the shimmering fabric. "I think so too. It's so nice to have another woman's opinion though. Hawke and Mark aren't the best judges of women's fashion."

"You'll certainly get a lot of attention."

Moria grins. "That's the idea."

Better her than me.

"I have another one in mind for you."

I nearly groan as she returns to her dressing room—it's way too large to call it a closet—to replace the dress.

"Is it similar to yours?" *Please say no, please say no, please say—*

She pops her head back out. "It's a surprise."

Great. I force a smile anyway.

Moria scowls toward the circular balcony that dominates a corner of the room. "For you and my cousin."

"Sigurd?" She hasn't mentioned another one.

I follow her narrow gaze. My eagle friend perches on the edge of her balcony railing, its head poked into the room.

"Annoying bird," she taunts.

It squawks at the offense. Poor thing.

"It's probably because I'm here," I say. "He likes to keep me company."

"Oh, it's definitely because of you." She crosses her arms. "He wouldn't dare perch there otherwise."

"You don't like birds?" How odd, given it's their family symbol and that of their entire court.

Moria blinks. Once. Twice. Laughter erupts as she throws her head back, chest shaking.

My chest burns like I've completely missed some obvious joke. "What's so funny?"

"You." She cackles like a Halloween witch. "You have no idea, do you?"

Unease prickles my skin, raising the fine hairs on my arms. "No idea about what?"

She grabs my arm and pulls me onto her bed, still trying to rein in her laughter. "That eagle"—she points to my friend across the room—"is Sigurd's."

Moria stares at me expectantly, her head cocked to the side.

"Yes. And?" Who cares if it's his pet?

She leans in, like a friend conspiring about a secret, and whispers, "He can see through the eyes of his eagles. When he chooses to anyway."

"He can..." My eyes go wide.

Moria pulls me closer, her arm around my shoulder. "Oh yes, and not just see. Listen. Feel. He can slip inside their skin for a time, should he choose. Based on the magic I feel in the air, I'd bet just about anything he's listening right now."

I go utterly still. All the things I've said to that bird... I've changed in front of it. Scratched his head. Petted it like a cat.

Oh. My. God.

"Hey, cousin." Moria waves at the bird. "Looks like I've spoiled your fun," she says, but she doesn't sound the least bit sorry. If anything, I'd say she's rather pleased with herself. "Why not quit lurking like a scorned child and show yourself?"

CHAPTER 25

I JUMP TO MY feet, and every inch of me stiffens. I'm not ready. I'm not—

Sigurd appears not two feet from us. He's dressed like a warrior in black armor with hints of silver and blue, an eagle emblazoned upon its front. His long hair is mussed and damp, possibly from sweat, but all I can smell is a whiff of pine and citrus that makes the fire within me burn in an entirely different way.

My eagle—*his* eagle—flies across the room to perch on his arm.

The movement snaps me out of the trance I fell into at his sudden appearance. "You're the fucking eagle!"

Moria collapses on her bed in a fit of laughter.

Thanks a lot.

Sigurd's lips twitch. "I thought you said pretty girls didn't have filthy mouths?"

"You-you." My nails dig into my palms. "You deserve every filthy, disgusting thing my lips can conjure."

"Yes, I think I might. Good thing I quite like your filthy mouth." A feral grin breaks free. He lifts his arm, and the eagle flies away, swooping out the window.

"How dare you? All those times I talked to you, confided in you!" My chest shakes, and I can't look at him. I'd rather be anywhere else.

His dark form nears, and I back away, but an arm around my waist stops me. "You were lonely. Hurting. I wanted to be there for you."

"But the things I said." Half of them or more were complaints about him. The mistakes he'd made, the horrible things he'd done, how much of an idiot he was.

One finger grazes the side of my jaw until it settles under my chin. Slowly, he forces my gaze up, taking his time, letting me take in every inch of the powerful warrior before me. His chest rises and falls, and when at last I reach his face, it bleeds with emotion.

"You told me what I needed to hear," he says, "even when I didn't want to hear it."

I could drown in his blue eyes. Dive in and die a happy death below their surface. It'd be so easy. I don't push him away as he tugs me close or as his fingers slide along my cheek, stirring up goosebumps across my skin and a warm, melty feeling low in my core.

A sudden cough cracks the tension between us.

Moria leans back on her arms atop her bed, a secretive grin spread across her face. "Perhaps you two would like to continue this discussion somewhere else? Like, not in my bedroom?"

Sigurd scowls. "I'll talk to you about this—"

"Later"—she waves one slender hand—"yeah, yeah. You can thank me then too."

"Wren?" His hand flexes on my back, asking a question so much bigger than my name.

If I don't want to go, he'll leave me here. He'll leave me alone for the rest of my stay if I want it. It's clear enough in the solemn lines creasing his pristine face. But I've learned about more than poisons in the short time since he left.

"Yes," I say.

My response still hangs in the air when the world around us bends and warps. I cling to him, to the metal armor formed around his chest and arms. My focus narrows to its design—etched to look like wings. It centers me, stops the world trying to twist me inside out as we shift to whatever place he has in mind.

I begin to worry we're trapped in some fae in-between when finally, a new scene shimmers into view. It takes my breath away.

Crystalline waters stretch out around us, catching the afternoon sun and reflecting it up—

I scramble back until I bump against Sigurd, who pulls me tight.

We're feet above the lake, the drop-off not far away.

"My lake home." Sigurd's voice slides down my cheek like a caress. So close. So...everything.

"It's stunning." Truly, there aren't words. Fresh air. Green trees. The lake itself. I haven't even seen the house, but the view alone is the thing of dreams.

"And safe. This little isle floats above the lake."

Floats? A gasp lodges in my throat.

"One would have to fly here or shift, but I warded the place to keep others out long ago. Only those I trust extensively can enter."

"Why bring me here?" I twist just enough to see the serenity smoothing out all the planes of his face. So calm and peaceful. Just like our surroundings.

Sigurd slides his arm around me until his palm is splayed across my waist. "I think you know. And I do believe you promised me more filthy words."

He may as well have lit me on fire. I pull away. Or maybe he's the flame because if I'd lingered in his embrace a second longer, I'd have certainly turned into a puddle on the mossy ground. A rather human-looking house, like an old, haunted Victorian manor, rises up behind him. Sigurd's lips quirk into a grin, and all those filthy words that I *never* utter rise to the tip of my tongue.

Instead, I cross my arms and scowl at him down the length of my nose. "I think you've gotten many more words than you ought to have."

"Not the dirty ones," he pouts.

I roll my eyes.

"I still can't believe that you... You..." I huff and turn away, but there's nowhere to run. Not unless I want to fling myself off the edge of this island. Clever man.

"Would you rather have been alone?"

I sigh and drop my arms. No, I wouldn't have. So many times, that eagle was what got me through. An outlet for my thoughts, a comfort in the loneliness.

"The things I said though." Gosh, I was cruel enough to him in person, and I never would have said a fourth of that if I'd known someone listened. And, oh— The fire is back, raging hotter than ever. "I changed in front of that eagle."

"Yes." His lips curl in a slow grin. "You did."

"You awful, perverted, peeping tom!"

He grins. "There's that mouth."

"Ridiculous." I stomp my foot. "Do you have no decency?"

"Of course I do. I looked away...most of the time."

"Sigurd."

"Say it again." He closes the distance between us.

My pulse hammers in my ears. My breath comes short and quick. "Say what?"

"My name on those delightful lips."

My mouth goes dry. "You don't think they're filthy?"

The back of his gloved hand trails down my cheek, and I shiver as he says, "I could never think you filthy, not even covered in mud."

"Si—"

His lips crash against mine, eager and demanding then soft and tentative, as if someone tugged on the leash of his restraint.

But the act shatters mine.

I lean into his kiss, stretching on my toes and wrapping my arms around his neck to tug him closer. He groans against me as my fingers slide through his hair, just as soft and delightful as I imagined.

Sigurd's arms are around me, holding me close as if he could make us one instead of two.

In that moment, we are. It's everything I dreamed of and feared. He's the smoothest whiskey, the highest high, and I run headlong into my desire for him, heedless of any risk of a future crash.

His tongue darts out, begging me to part for him. I do. Each flick of his tongue against mine sends my head spinning faster and faster. Nothing is left of the world but us. We could be flying high above it. I wouldn't know, and I wouldn't be afraid, not with his arms around me and him kissing me back like his life depends on it.

He's hard everywhere, all armor and muscle, but I don't miss the deep groan in his chest as I rub against him, eager to get as close as possible, or the way his stance shifts as he tugs me tighter. Everything in me is melty and warm—perfect.

Strong hands slide down my back, cupping over my backside. Then he lifts me. My legs twine around his waist, scrambling for purchase, but he never breaks our kiss.

"Wren," he groans against my lips.

I whimper as he pulls away, but he doesn't go far. Our foreheads press together, breath mingling in the ghost of a space between us.

A blue glow greets me as I open my eyes. His glow.

One second apart is too many. I lean in, eager to resume our kiss, but he lifts his head. My heart sinks as I slide down his solid form and back onto my feet. My legs wobble under me, and I cling to him, unwilling to let go.

"I thought I could show you the house." A deep flush colors his cheeks, and he won't quite look at me.

A hard, sinking feeling settles in my gut, and I turn away.

He kissed me first, yes, but then he pulled back.

Stupid. I kick a stone across the ground and scowl when it doesn't roll off the cliff. Should have known I could never be a good enough replacement. I don't want to be. Of course not. But for a moment there...

"Wren?"

A shadow cloaks my form. Tingles race across my skin as he slides stray hairs behind one ear.

"Why? I'm not the one you want here."

His fingers go still. Breath catches in my throat.

Each second is an eternity until he tugs my back against his chest. His breath is warm against my cheek, my neck, as he whispers, "You mistake me, Wren. I want you a great deal."

He can't lie. He can't lie. He can't lie.

"Then why?" I can barely form the words. With his hands on me, the warmth of his breath raising goosebumps across my skin. "What you said the other night on the balcony..."

"Ah." He exhales a long breath.

Yes, that.

"You are nothing like her," he says. I try to pull away, but he holds me tight. "But that's not a bad thing, Wren."

Sigurd turns me in his arms, forcing me to face him and all the sincerity in his eyes. "Evelyn accepted me for how I was. She didn't see me as a prince of the fae, as I was at the time, nor a commander of troops, my father's son, a disappointing heir, or any of the other ways people regarded me. You don't accept me for who I am."

I open my mouth to refuse him, but he shakes his head.

"No, you don't, not fully. But, Wren, I was content with who I was with her. But you—you make me want to be a better man. A better king."

"I-I do that?"

"Yes." His hands flex on my sides, stirring up all kinds of thoughts that mirror the desire in his slightly hooded eyes as he stares me down. "It's another reason I can't regret spending time with you as Zale."

My head tilts to the side. "Zale?"

He grins. "Your eagle friend. And mine."

A huff of laughter catches in my throat. I should have known he already had a name. Zale. It fits. And terribly, it may already be etched on my heart, even when I tried to avoid it.

"You said much to my face, but the honesty, your openness with him moved me even more. No one, not even Moria and Hawke, dared so much, and I needed it. More than I knew."

"Be careful. I might just give you all my thoughts to your face in the future. I'm known to do that sometimes."

"I hope you do." His voice is light and teasing, but the words are absolutely sincere.

They tug at me, begging me to wrap my arms around his neck and press my lips to his once more. His cheeks flush again, painting him much younger than his many fae years. Many more than I can comfortably think about.

"Well, shall we?" He partially releases me to gesture to the house. Such a fascinating building would have sucked me in with oohs and ahhs in a heartbeat back home. But here, it can't hold a candle in mystery or majesty to the man whose palm still lingers at my back.

"Just tell me one thing," I say. "Is this some grand plan to distract me from the competition and ensure I fail or drop out?" Honestly, he's doing a fabulous job of it at the moment.

"No. I won't ask you to quit again. It's your life, your choice. I hate to see you in danger. It eats at me in a way you cannot know." His voice rises, his hand tightens on my back. "But I won't cage you. Not like my—" He bites off his words, looking away.

"Like your father?"

His eyes fly wide. "How do you—"

"You mentioned him, and I've heard that he was not...well, maybe not the best of men."

"To some people. It's ironic, really. Some people despise me for being too much like him and others for being too different. He lusted for power. Ruled by fear. But enough of that." His fingers twine through mine in a way that sets every nerve ending alight.

The house is the opposite of his quarters in the castle.

The rooms are smaller—still large by my standards—with normal wooden roofs, but it's the furnishings that mark the main difference. Instead of being sparse and formal, these ooze life and memories from every crack in the leather and scrape on wood. This place is lived in, loved, comfortable. Him.

The dark wood, the masculine furnishings, and even the paintings of great battles and winged birds speak of the man who has barely said a word since we entered, just let me look in wonder.

"I grew up here," he says at last.

"Not in the castle?"

"No. After I was born, my father sent me away. He had the heir he needed to secure his legacy, but that's all I was to him. He had no interest in raising or training me. That, he left to my tutors."

"And your mother?"

His hand tightens on mine ever so slightly. "I never really knew her. My father took human women to his bed for the power they offered, as many as he could get his hands on. Some, he—" His voice catches. "Some even bound to him so they couldn't leave."

A hard knot lodges itself in my throat. A horrible man indeed. No wonder he hates the bond he forced on me, not that it stopped him. His father wanted power. Sigurd wanted...a ghost. But was that truly all? He'd mentioned the power humans give the fae before, and Uncle Mark told me even more.

Many ages ago, our worlds entwined with one another, and the fae became dependent on our human spirits. Without human presence, fae magic fades, and their land dies. A king, as the beating heart of his court's power, affects them all. If he takes a human mate, his power—all their power—grows. Yet, Sigurd hasn't done so, despite the power it would offer. Having other humans in their territory kept it vibrant. Even Uncle Mark's presence had been instrumental in strengthening the court—one reason many objected to his wish to become fae. It caused some dissention in the nobility trying to climb the ladder of power. But Hawke, and thus Sigurd as his king, was willing to relinquish that power for love.

"It's one reason I lost Evelyn," he says, a sad twist to his lips. "I—" He glances at me. "You probably don't want to hear this."

"I want to know." Some part of me needs to. I lay my hand on his arm. "Please."

Sigurd nods before swallowing thickly. "I met her when she was escaping the Unseelie."

My eyes grow wide. Of all the things I expected, that wasn't it.

"It was years ago. They tried capturing humans to revive their magic, but the effects were minimal without a monarch to sustain their land. She was one of the last ones they took before the last of their doors to your world closed as a result of their fading magic—or so we believe. Anyhow, they...did not treat her well."

The look in his eyes speaks to so many horrors he won't put words to, and for once, I'm glad. My chest grows tight at the possibilities, but something tells me the truth could be even worse.

"She managed to flee, and I found her while on patrol. She was scared and hurt, running for her life."

Just like I was the night he found me in the woods. No wonder he reacted as he did. Something in me softens at the comment. Perhaps, even then, he truly was just trying to help me.

"I protected her and helped her to come back to herself, and though I tried to keep her presence a secret from my father, eventually he noticed."

"He didn't," I say, suddenly terrified of where the tale may lead.

"No. I was close friends with Lutheon, the king of the Court of the Forest at the time. He was new to his reign, and humans were few in the forest. I asked him to take her in and keep her safe. I just never expected..."

He looks away. But I know where this part goes. She fell in love with Lutheon and gave him a son.

"You blame your father for that," I say.

Finally, he looks back at me. "Yes. But he's long dead. Any vengeance there is out of reach. It wasn't long after that when he passed, but by the time I returned to the Court of the Forest, well..."

I touch his face, savoring the way he ever so slightly leans against my palm. "Thank you for telling me."

Sigurd gives the briefest nod in return. "Anyhow, about my father, despite his lust for human women, he avoided an heir for many years, which is why I have no siblings. He didn't want the threat to his reign, I believe. But as he grew older and his power waned, he wasn't about to let the magic settle outside his bloodline or, worse, have it not settle at all, as happened to the Unseelie many years ago."

"Not settle?"

He glances down at me and forces a smile. "It's the transition of magic, when a monarch's power transfers to their heir. Long ago, the last Unseelie king died without an heir, and the power never settled on a new one. It simply left them and their land to fade."

The Unseelie woman's face flashes through my memories. I should tell him, warn him that an Unseelie fae ventures his territory. My gaze slides to the tattoo around my wrist. But maybe her offer is honest. Maybe she just needs to be near me a bit to keep from fading, and that's what she wants? Though sending me home is a bit counterintuitive to that.

"Wren?" Sigurd says. "You've gone quiet on me."

I swallow my thoughts and force a smile for his benefit. I *should* tell him. But there's a little voice screaming in the back of my head not to. He could bind me here longer, even if the cauldron releases me. Why wouldn't he—or anyone else—if I grant them power? I'd like to think he wouldn't do such a thing, that *I* wouldn't, but if I were desperate, if my family needed it, I just might, horrible as it is.

"It's just a lot," I say. "But your home is quite lovely, at least what I've seen." Yes, that's a better, safer topic.

"It was meant to be my prison. It was at first. The only way off the floating isle is plummeting to the water below or shifting out—which I couldn't do until my power matured."

"Didn't consider using your wings to fly away?"

"I didn't have my wings, either, until my power matured. But yes, I flew the moment I could."

"Where did you go?" A runaway prince escaping his tutors. Now that's a sight I can easily picture.

He draws me to a large picture window looking out over the lake and the forest beyond. "Where didn't I go is the better question." His grin steals my soul until it dims. "But I always came back. Father would have taken it out on my tutors if I didn't, and they didn't deserve that." He runs his hand through his hair. "The antics they had to put up with from me." He shakes his head before sliding a conspiratorial glance my way. "I paid them all well after I became king to compensate for the years of trouble."

"See." I bump my hip against him. "You can be nice when you want to."

"Oh, I can be *very* nice when I choose to."

My teeth sink into my bottom lip, hard.

"You always wanted to travel?"

No sooner has he asked the question than a gust of wind rushes against the windowpanes, throwing them open. It swirls around me, tossing my hair and urging me further into the crook of Sigurd's arm.

It settles as quickly as it came.

"Yes," I say, recovering my wits.

"Then fly with me, Wren. Let me show you some of the wonders of the Court of Air."

I gasp as his wings erupt from nowhere, filling the space behind him as they flex and stretch.

Oh, sweet baby Jesus.

Sigurd scoops me into his arms before I have time to protest. I cling to him, throw my arms around his neck, and clutch at his shirt for dear life, even though we're still on the ground.

He leaps onto the windowsill, filling its massive frame.

"I swear, if you drop me..."

A laugh rumbles from his chest. "I promise I won't let you fall."

CHAPTER 26

IT'S THE BEST FEW hours of my life and the most terrifying—at first, anyway.

Soaring through the skies with him, the wind in my face, pulse pounding in my throat, breaks the bonds of fear and worry binding me up so tightly. High above the land, there's no room for racing thoughts. Every single bit of my focus is glued to the moment, to wonders unfolding around me and the man carrying me through the clouds like a superhero.

I see more in the fading light of afternoon than during years back home. Waterfalls sparkling in a rainbow of colors from the setting sun. Mountains wreathed in puffy clouds. A herd of wild horses racing below us over the plains. Fae towns twinkle in the distance.

But the most wonderous sight of all might be Sigurd's face as he points out each one to me. His carefree smile, the twinkle in his eyes, and the laughter that rumbles in his chest and stirs up that warm feeling deep in my core. Gliding through the air with him, I can forget everything. All the tension in my body flees. My smiles aren't forced, nor are my laughs, and the competition is a world away.

Sigurd never lets me fall, and even if I did, I know with a certainty he would catch me.

Sweat slides down his skin and dampens my arms where they wind around his neck, though the fallen night hides it from view. I yearn to beg for more, but his chest already rises and falls with heavy breaths. Even a fae king of the air can only fly for so long.

Adrenaline still zips through my veins as we land back at his home. I bounce on my toes and roll my shoulders as if I have my own wings that I can use to soar back into the sky. It doesn't matter that it's night and a smattering of clouds obscures much of the weird bluish moonlight cloaking the world in shadows.

"That was so...so beautiful," I say.

"I agree." Sigurd leans against the railing of the porch where he landed, but his back is toward the world, his intense gaze glued to me. "The view is quite lovely."

Tingly warmth spreads through my chest and lower. I bite my bottom lip, trying to hide the sheepish smile working its way free. One comment shouldn't affect me so, not after our bodies were pressed together for the entire flight, but that look alone stirs up all the feelings that the excitement of the flight drowned out.

I cross the short space to him. "Are we staying here tonight?" *Just the two of us?*

"Would you like to?"

"I should probably study." I rub the back of my neck. Knowing these fae games, I'll need every single fact I can manage to memorize. But more than that, if I stay, I don't think I'll have the resolve to hold back from him. If we take things further, how will I focus on the games, on leaving him?

He captures my hand in his, drawing me into the shelter of his wings as they wrap around me. "Save it for tomorrow."

A cough somewhere behind me pops the bubble of tension between us.

Sigurd pulls me tight. His wings lock around me like a shield.

"Moria." He lets out a sigh, and his wings vanish.

I twist around as she stalks from the shadows of the open door leading into the house.

"I do hate to invade the love nest so soon," she says, "but urgent matters and all."

I didn't think I could blush any hotter, but the implications of her words set my skin alight.

"What's happened?" Sigurd's sharp tone cools my fire in an instant. A few splatters of mud mar Moria's boots, but otherwise, she appears unharmed.

"The Court of the Forest has rejected your gifts."

Oh no. My heart sinks.

"And they sent this as well." She holds up a small silver object.

"A ring?"

Sigurd winces.

A tangle of doubt coils its way around my neck as Moria advances. The ring she holds would look just like an engagement ring if its solitary stone were a clear diamond instead of blue.

"It was a gift to the forest king's consort," Sigurd says, though for whose benefit I can't say.

His words hit me like a blow to the chest. He doesn't need to tell me he gave it to her. His unwillingness to quite look at me says that clear enough. Funny how he left out that little detail when he told me about what happened with the Court of the Forest before.

Sigurd gave her a ring. He's given me…what? An unwanted bond that sticks me here far from home.

"The same consort you had Galen steal?" I have to know, have to be sure.

Moria whistles. "What else do you know?"

Enough. Too much. I hug my arms around myself.

"It's not like that." Sigurd runs his hand through his hair. Some of it stands on end.

"Not like what? You giving another woman jewelry?"

"Yes, I gave it to her."

"You wanted her away from the forest king, so you thought to… What? Seduce her away from him?" *Tell me it's not true. Tell me. Tell me!*

But he doesn't. Every second of silence that ticks by squeezes my chest tighter. Somehow, no matter how much of the story I get, there are still enough tricky details left to cut me up anew.

"We need to go." Moria's words are a death knell for my heart. The ring has vanished—slipped into one of her pockets or tossed off the balcony, who knows.

I look to her, only her. "Don't leave me here."

"I'll take you to your uncle," she says, but her eyes say much more important things. *I'm sorry. I shouldn't have mentioned it.*

I'm glad she did. Even though it hurts so much more than it should. Maybe she doesn't understand the words buried in my look, but that's fine.

Moria takes my hand. Over my shoulder, she says to Sigurd, "I'll meet you at the front."

"Wait," he says.

The word tugs at me, begging me to look back over my shoulder. Eventually, I do.

Sigurd's shoulders are hunched, his expression troubled. "I didn't care for her." Then he amends, "I don't care for her."

It doesn't ease the heaviness within me. It should. I want it to, but it doesn't.

"You're important to me, Wren. I can't change my past, but I can do better in the future. I've been a villain in so many stories, even my own." He swallows, his gaze never leaving mine. "And yours. But I don't want to be. I want a new story, Wren. Don't forget that."

CHAPTER 27

THE FOURTH EVENT OF the competition arrives before Sigurd and Moria return. It's not just the Court of the Forest keeping them away. The tug on our bond has been a tangible force the whole time they've been gone, like a string around my wrist that someone keeps a tight leash on. Sometimes, the tug is strong enough to nearly pull me down, bordering on painful.

Trouble with the Unseelie, Hawke said. Apparently, the enemy has been testing the wards at the borders in random places—no pattern to it. A distraction, he's sure, but for what, no one knows. I'd hoped to ask the Unseelie woman if I saw her again, but she's also been curiously absent. Probably for the best.

If the rest of the Court of Air knows of these troubles, you can't tell from how they cram into the stands, wave colorful pennants, and cheer loud enough that I wouldn't be surprised if half of them are hoarse tomorrow.

My heart races. A trickle of sweat runs down my neck. But it's not hot, and the game hasn't even begun.

The arena where we were first introduced is packed to the gills. How Galen and Lysandir manage to appear so calm and at ease is beyond me. It's a comfort having them at my sides, but it's not enough to keep me from bouncing on my toes and shifting from foot to foot as the finishing touches of the contest are set up in the large, grassy field before us.

We won't be able to help each other today if the setup is any indication. Tables are arranged in a broad circle. Cloths of varied, shimmering colors are tented above each, hiding whatever contents lie below.

Poisons, if I had to guess, or something related to them. *Please don't be weapons.*

A fae stands behind each table on the inside of the ring. Simple, flowing robes of gray and blue adorn their bodies.

I can't quite see into the royal box on the far side of the arena, but the little bits I can make out are empty. No Sigurd. No Moria. However, Uncle Mark and Hawke should be taking their places there soon, now that their obligation to deliver me safely to the game has been fulfilled.

I reach into my pocket and rub the little slip of paper I stuffed there this morning. A note from Sigurd, one of several his eagle, Zale, delivered on his behalf over the last two days. Apologies, mostly. Appreciated but unnecessary. I was jealous at first and caught off guard, but whatever he did with whoever before he met me is none of my concern. Even though that revelation may have taken a whole day to really sink in. The forest king's consort doesn't hold a special place in his heart? Cool, one less rival.

Not that we're anything.

We can't be with me leaving soon. Most of the notes left all my emotions tangled in knots and my words with them. I'd smile at my feathered friend and rub his head like I used to—or Sigurd's, I guess, if he looked through his eyes at that moment.

The last note though, the one delivered late last night, struck my heart and lingered. Even now as I rub the paper like a talisman, the words echo in my mind.

I believe in you.

Whatever awaits on those tables, I can handle it, even if they make me wield a poisoned sword or some nonsense.

I'll find a way. I have to.

The announcer's assistant blows on a massive horn. The deep sound rumbles through the air, and I fight the urge to cover my ears.

The crowd goes eerily quiet, taking their seats. The announcer's grin grows as he stretches his arms wide, displaying the silky black feathers stretching out like great wings on either side of him. He's the picture of somber elegance.

"Today," he says, "our remaining competitors take their very lives in their hands."

Peachy.

"Behind me stand tables bearing seven goblets each. Fine vintages fill each one." He moves his hands as he speaks, grand movements that have his feathered sleeves catching the light.

"Trying to get us drunk?" one competitor laughs.

My fist tightens around Sigurd's note. Oh yes, drinking fae booze went so well for me last time.

The announcer laughs and wags his finger at us. "Each goblet, however, is laced with a little something extra."

Poison. My mouth goes dry. Of course.

"Our competitors must match each goblet with an antidote for the poison lingering within. Will they rely on luck and instinct? Will they risk their lives and rely on taste? A little of both?"

The crowd rumbles with answering shouts and murmured conversations. They're quite pro tasting.

"The first five to correctly match the poisons and their antidotes advance. If our healers"—he gestures to the robed fae behind the tables—"must intervene, a competitor will be eliminated." The announcer looks back to us. "Competitors, pick a table."

I glance between Galen and Lysandir. No, they can't help me, but their smiles and nods give me strength. The prince takes my hand and grips it tight.

"Good luck," I whisper.

"And to you," Lysandir says.

Galen sucks in a deep breath. "To the finals."

I pick a table covered by a shimmering blue cloth. Sigurd's colors. May it grant me luck.

"No peeking at each other's tables." The announcer's voice is far too upbeat for what awaits us. "It won't help you. Each table is unique."

No wonder they all have their own uniquely colored cloths. It's probably some signal for the healers stationed behind them, so they know what antidotes to give. The one stationed on the other side of my table is a middle-aged fae woman. Her carefully blank face gives nothing away. However, she gives me the slightest nod. Encouragement, I hope.

Other fae step to the corners of the tables, lifting the edges of the cloths.

"Begin!" the announcer calls.

The cloths are ripped away.

Seven goblets sit closest to me. Various colored liquids fill each halfway. Beyond...

Sweet baby Jesus. There must be at least two dozen possible antidotes—liquids, powders, berries, leaves.

Breathe. Be calm.

I pull my necklace out from its place against my chest and rub the bird between my fingers. In a strange twist of fate, being a bartender might give me an advantage here. A humorless laugh catches in my throat. Gran always worried I wasn't making much of myself with my career. How ironic.

Even so, tasting them all straight away is risky, and guessing at random will take too long. Besides, I studied far too darn hard to rely on luck alone. The color of the liquid may be a clue. I lift the first glass and take a sniff.

Wine. It was probably a deep maroon to begin with. There's no telling how much poison is in there either. Enough to discolor it? Though some poisons have no color at all.

I swirl it around in the glass and lean in close. Beyond the fruity notes of the wine, another scent tickles my senses. Cinnamon? It could be Elscarion, if it tastes of citrus. I shake my head and expel a deep breath. One way to find out.

A sip of rich beverage washes over my tongue. Bitter notes speak out immediately, but there beyond them is something else. As I roll the liquid around in my mouth, I can just make out a hint of something like grapefruit, which certainly doesn't belong in a red wine. A white, maybe, but not a red.

I pull at my memories of the pages I studied. Elscarion induces severe itching that can last days.

I spit the wine onto the ground.

It's cured by... I worry my lip as I scan the possible antidotes. The cure snags my attention almost immediately. The little purple leaves present on the table are almost identical to the bunch on the scrolls. I grab said leaf and chew, despite its rough surface. I take another, place it behind the cup with a silent prayer, and move on.

Two more cups are easily discernable.

I'm almost halfway. I give myself a little shake and bounce on my toes.

The liquid in the fourth glass is clear with little smell. I dip a finger into the substance and swish it around. Water? But what could water disguise?

A memory floats to the surface of my mind.

"Silent maiden," Moria had said where she lay upon the sofa, tossing her knife up in the air. "It's one of my personal favorites. Colorless, odorless, but most importantly, lethal." She caught the knife and examined the tip. "It causes the blood to seize and thicken quickly. I usually keep the antidote on me at all times, just in case."

The best way to test it is with my blood. What a day to not have a knife on me. Moria would be disappointed.

I scan the table, looking for anything I can use. One branch of berries still has its thorns. It'll have to do.

"Let's hope they're sharp." Before I can second guess it, I rake my thumb across a thorn. Pain blooms. "Son of a—"

I bite off my words with gritted teeth. Blood trickles down my hand, dripping on the table as I draw it over the cup. The drops of blood find one another, cling together, and sink down into the cup without disbursing. A cold sweat breaks out across my skin. If I'd tasted that one, I might be done for, healer present or not.

I grab the silvery powder—one of the first antidotes I memorized—and place it beside the cup.

I'm on the sixth when the blast of the horn rattles my senses and nearly has me spilling the chalice in my hand.

The cheers are deafening. Someone has advanced.

I rub at my chest. There's no time to check the identity of the victor. It doesn't matter anyway. I've gotta move.

This glass contains whiskey, or the fae equivalent. Something I know well. But though I've sniffed, sipped, and glared at the way the light hits the liquid, I'm not sure exactly what it contains.

With no time to lose, I bring the cup to my lips. I barely let the liquid linger on my tongue before I spit it into the grass. Unfortunately, the small taste told me nothing. It might be something that needs to develop and bloom like the whiskey itself.

I block out my fear, worry, and the nearby noises trying to distract me. Instead, I pretend I'm back at Jolene's testing out a new vintage to see if we'll add it to the shelf. I take another dainty sip. The liquid rolls around my tongue and coats my mouth. How would I describe it to a customer?

Leather and cedar. I dare another slight swallow. *A hint of nuttiness, with a finish of...* My tongue tingles. *Mint?*

One of these things is not like the other, and I know what poison this is. I grab the bulbous roots from the table—ones of the same plant whose leaves are used to make the poison—and slam them next to the cup, ignoring the smear of blood from my hand.

Adrenaline tingles through my veins. Last one.

The horn blares once more.

The cheers rise in a swelling wave, not letting up long after the blast of the horn has faded. Others must be close.

The last vintage looks like a white wine. I give the cup a little swirl, watching bubbles form and rise. A sparkling wine. I tilt it this way and that, watching the light, the bubbles.

Then I see it, a faint sheen of pink when the sunlight streams in overhead and hits it just so. There's no need to taste this one. I know what it is. But the antidote... Now that's another matter. A liquid, I think. Syrupy to the point of almost being a paste but bitter rather than sweet.

I race around to the antidotes, lifting the various vials and bowls. Sniffing, tasting.

Finally, I find it.

I scoop up the little dish, careful not to spill it in my haste, and set it next to the final glass.

And then I wait, back rigid, eyes wide, and pulse fluttering wildly in my chest.

A soft buzzing fills my ears. The healer raises one hand.

Shit.

I have something wrong. But which one?

I reach for the table as the horn blares. The woman opposite me steps forward and waves me away.

"You're done."

No. I clench my hand into a fist. "But I—"

She smiles. "The horn was for you."

For me?

I blink once. Twice.

"They're all correct," I say, my voice almost a whisper.

She nods.

My breaths come short and fast. Tears prick at the corners of my eyes. I did it. I actually did it, and all on my own this time.

"To the stage with you." She ushers me away.

The crowd is still roaring as I hop up the last few steps to the blare of a fourth horn. There's only one finalist left.

I survey the competitors, and a heavy weight settles in my gut. Both Galen and Lysandir are still working on their cups. The prince has antidotes next to each cup, but something must be wrong. He lifts one, swirling it and sniffing at it. Galen has items by six and lifts the seventh cup to his nose.

Both are so close.

Only one can advance, if either.

So are many others. One man appears to be trying antidotes at random, picking one, setting it down by a cup, looking to the assigned healer, and then racing to swap it out again. He's hoping he's lucky. I'm hoping he's not.

The blast of the horn has me covering my ears on instinct.

I gasp, searching my friends.

Galen's healer has their hand raised. He smiles.

"Yes!" I bounced off my toes, my squeal caught up and carried away in the noise from the crowd.

He made it! We both actually made it to the finals.

But that spark of joy dims to almost nothing as I glance at Lysandir. He's still staring at the cups, trying to work it out, but the set of his shoulders and his downcast look say enough. He knows he's lost.

His chance for a wish, whatever it is, is gone.

Galen climbs the steps, and I force a smile back to my face. He deserves it, and I'm happy for him. I wanted him to advance. It was too much to hope we'd all make it, not that it kept me from praying for it anyway.

At least it'll make the final easier, whatever it is. Only one of my friends to defeat. Just the thought has my throat tightening.

To get my wish, Galen can't have his. Neither can the other finalists. Unless I can convince Sigurd to grant them somehow. If he's able. Though it might not be possible for all of them.

It's almost enough to make me want to quit. Almost.

But then I think of Gran, and I simply can't. Not when I've come so far. I'm in this. I've committed and come so far. I have to see it through no matter what.

CHAPTER 28

T HE DRESS MORIA SELECTED on my behalf for the ball is a work
of art. Shimmering fabric rolls down my body in waves of
blue, fading from bright sapphire to darkest night. Lacy, sheer
sleeves bare most of my arms, save the ribbons tied around my
wrists to act as decorative cover-ups for the bond Sigurd and the
others have tried hard to hide. Though, with all he's done, I can't
see how that would harm his reputation any further.

For days, I've worried about what monstrosity she decided on
for me, but I couldn't have chosen better myself. There's a deep
V down the front—figures—but little strands of beads in silver,
black, and various blues hold the sides together. More strands of
beadwork drape down my back, holding the dress together. My
boobs won't be escaping tonight. Good thing, since the cut leaves
no room for a bra and the fae don't seem to believe in pasties.
Or maybe they do, but Uncle Mark's face flushed beet red when I
tried to ask about them, so I gave up. Too bad Moria still isn't here
for me to ask her.

Or Sigurd.

I sigh and smooth my hand along the shimmering skirt of the
gown. I've never looked so grand, and of everyone, he's the only
one here I care to impress.

It's been over a day since the last competition, but they're
still preoccupied with whatever is going on at the borders. The
tug on our bond has been relentless, sometimes almost painful,
even waking me up once in the night. Whatever is happening, it's
nothing good based on the dark circles under Hawke's eyes and

how little I've seen of him the last few days too. He's been locked in meetings, or so Uncle Mark said.

Hawke would prefer to skip the ball, and the rest of the competition for that matter. But keeping up appearances is part of his role in the royal family, particularly with Sigurd and Moria absent. He suggested moving up the ball, and the finale of the games, but was told in no uncertain terms that such grand events could not be rushed. The message that would send could be more damning than the alternative.

In a way, it's a good thing. No sooner had Uncle Mark and Hawke retrieved me from the arena after the last event than a bout of nausea brought me to my knees.

Oh, the antidotes worked, or so they said. But those aren't always enough to prevent some ill side effects. Freaking figures. Thankfully, a little fae medicine, a touch of healing magic, and a day in bed have me back to normal. Mostly. All the semi-finalists are expected to attend, and my absence could be considered grounds for disqualification.

There's no way I'm letting that happen. I'd have gone even if it meant spending the whole time vomiting into a flowerpot.

"Almost ready?" I ask as Hawke fiddles with something on Uncle Mark's jacket. Leave it to me to be the first one ready. Though I had some help. Uncle Mark had some women work wonders on my hair and apply makeup with such perfection that any model would envy.

Another reason I wish—

Zale flies into the sitting room to perch on the back of a sofa.

My heart leaps.

"Sigurd." His name is a whisper across my lips. I race to the eagle and turn to the side just enough for him to see the front and back of the dress. "What do you think?"

He squawks. Warmth blooms in my chest, and I scratch at his feathered head. No messages are clutched in his talons today, but at least he's seen me and the wonder they've made me into.

"Are you going to be there tonight?" I ask him, with a stroke down his back.

I want him there. I want to tell him that I understand, to explain what his messages meant to me, what he means to—

"I don't think an eagle will be a welcome guest." Hawke's nose wrinkles as he takes in my companion.

"Well, no, not him exactly, but I assumed Sigurd might—"

Hawke's brows rise, cutting off my words.

Uncle Mark nods, a smile creeping to his lips. "I see."

See what? I surely don't.

"It's true. Sigurd sometimes looks through his eagle, but he isn't now."

Warmth crawls up my neck. "How do you know?"

"You can't feel it? Or the lack of it?"

"It?" I stare at them both.

"Magic," Uncle Mark says. "When he sees through his birds, it gives off a magical signature that we can feel."

Zale squawks. Even the bird agrees.

"Well, I can't feel it." I stroke the bird's head again. "At least you like my dress." And don't make me feel like an idiot.

The letdown at their revelation is a palpable feeling within me, like someone just took a little shine out of my outfit or squished me down too far in heels. No wonder the bond still remained tight and uncomfortable. I should have known he wasn't here.

The eagle squawks again and flies to the window.

I wave at him and turn to my companions with a deep sigh. "Let's get this over with, shall we?"

Getting caught talking to a bird was a little awkward. Being the only human entering a room of fae nobles, competitors, and other dignitaries, is somehow so much worse.

Everyone turns to look at us when we enter.

At first, I thought it might be because of Hawke—royalty and all—but oh no, they're definitely staring at me. Intrusive and prying, their piercing gazes inspect me head to toe, leaving nothing unscathed. My throat tightens, and it takes everything I have to put one foot in front of the other and enter the massive ballroom.

Or courtyard? Grand porch? Who knows. White marble pillars soar from the ground toward the sky, but there's no ceiling above, not even a glass one. Fae lights float above us like twinkling stars, with larger ones clinging to the pillars and other sconces dotted across the gleaming floor.

Fae pack the space wearing a riot of colors and designs. Everything from puffy ballgowns a meter wide to ones so infinitesimal they barely count as clothes. Attendants carry gilded trays with small bites of heavenly smelling food, which war with varying perfumes for dominance. Just about everyone has a drink in hand.

The announcer from the games weaves through the crowd to me without error. Shimmering white and silver drape from him in flowing waves. Sparkling pale eyeshadow sweeps out to his hairline to mingle with the white feathers woven there.

He takes my hand and gives it a little pat. "We'll be presenting the finalists in a little bit. Enjoy yourself until then."

Right, like that's so easy.

Maybe it is for everyone else, but not me. There's no presentation necessary for every single fae in this room to know exactly who I am. Several glance around each other, trying to catch my eye. A few head my way with unchecked determination.

My shoulders stiffen, and I look to Uncle Mark. But he and Hawke have already been drawn into conversation with another group.

A flash of red catches my attention, and my heart leaps at the familiar face. Even better, he's surrounded by a bubble of space as if no one dared get to close to a foreign prince. I weave my way to Lysandir, ignoring outstretched hands and calls of my name. How celebrities handle this nonsense, I'll never understand. A sigh escapes as I break out into the open space surrounding the prince and the pillar he leans against.

He nods to me before lifting the half-empty glass of sparkling liquid in his hand and taking a quick sip.

"How are you this evening?" he asks before ushering over an attendant to pass off his glass.

"Much better than yesterday. And better now that I'm here with you." I lean against the pillar, savoring the shock of the cool stone against my back. "I'm sorry about yesterday."

Lysandir forces a smile that fades as quickly as it came. "Me too. Though I'm not sure the cauldron could have granted my wish anyway."

"Why not? What do you wish for?" Instant regret follows my words. I probably shouldn't have asked, not with so many fae watching our every move like we're fish in a tank. In the moments since I've joined him, they've already managed to close the space around us, not much, but enough to know they likely listen to every word we say.

"Let us..." Lysandir glances around. "Get some air." He holds out his hand to me like the prince he is, and I take it.

He holds my hand in his and leads me to the edge of the throng. An intricate stone railing marks the boundary of the space and acts as a last defense to keep any wayward fae, or humans in my case, from plummeting off the cliffside to the valley below. Few linger here. These fae love to be noticed if their outfits are any indication, and so many stick close to the castle proper rather than lingering in the dim outskirts of the party.

I inhale the calm of night. "What a change. I feel like I can breathe again over here."

Lysandir chuckles. "I thought to skip this entirely, but I wanted to see you before I left."

My chest draws tight. "You're leaving?"

He nods. "In the morning. I've been away too long as it is. Besides..." He glances back at the party. "I think the Court of Air might be more at ease without me lingering in their midst."

"If they have an issue with you, that's their problem. Haters gonna hate. Just ignore them."

His shoulders shake, and I'd swear he's trying not to laugh. "It is refreshing to be around someone who treats me as...well, not a prince. Most come with expectations, demands, and favors waiting on the tip of their tongues."

A heaviness settles against my ribs. Sigurd said something similar. None of these fae royals seem to have an easy time of it, whatever their wealth and power.

"Well, I have no demands, only thanks for your help. Without you"—I shake my head—"I wouldn't have made it through that maze. There's no way."

"Oh, I don't know." A grin twitches at the corner of his lips. "Your other companion is quite capable."

Speaking of...

I scan the crowd, but there's no sign of Galen anywhere. He's probably lost somewhere in the mass of fae. As a finalist, he'll have to be here somewhere, unless he's running late.

"You asked what I would have wished for," Lysandir says.

My cheeks flush as I glance back at him. His former grin has turned sad and lingers on his downturned face.

"You don't have to tell me." I clasp my hands in front of me, twisting them together as they refuse to be still. "I shouldn't have asked."

"Strangely, I want to tell you." His brows wrinkle. "I'm not sure why. I suppose the future will tell us."

Such a strange thing to say. I lean on the railing as he continues.

"I see things sometimes," he says. "Not what everyone can see but likely futures."

"The future." I gasp and stand a little straighter, suddenly seeing him in an entirely new light. The first time we met properly, his eyes had gone strange, milky and distant.

"It's not a guarantee of what will happen, not always."

"That day after the cadmum game..." I start, but he doesn't hear me, or if he does, he ignores it.

"I came here because I saw something I wish to change. I'd—" His fist tightens until his knuckles go white, and a dim glow seeps from his eyes. "I'd do just about anything to change it."

A bad future. For him? Or someone he loves? I rub my wrist. My wish never seemed selfish. Gran needs me. So does Tabitha. But they've been without me for days already. Could they go longer?

"What if..." I say. "If I win—"

Lysandir lays a hand on my shoulder, the touch just light enough to turn me from my thoughts. "I won't take your wish, Wren. You're brave. Courageous. And you've risked much. Whatever you wish for, it must be dear to you."

"Still—"

He shakes his head. "I'm not even sure my wish could be granted, and I won't waste yours, should you win, on a maybe. Even the cauldron has its limits, but I had to try." His grip tightens before falling away. "And I hope you win. If it can't be me, I want it to be you."

Something cracks within me, and before I can stop myself, I wrap my arms around him and bury my head against his chest. His warmth envelopes me, comforting and safe, but so different than Sigurd. I could linger here all day, but the desire to brush my lips against his is curiously absent. It's not lust or desire I feel for him. Rather, the first bloom of a friendship that could be so much more if we had time. He grazes my shoulders, my back, in a tentative return of my affection. Formal. Respectful. The exact opposite of me practically leaping on him. I pull away, an apology on the tip of my tongue, but the sight of his smile silences it.

"You were right about that day after the second game." He takes my hand in his, his thumb rubbing across my knuckles. "I had a glimpse of the future. Your future."

I gasp and almost jerk away, but he holds me tight. My future. The beat of my pulse hammers against my ribs. "What did you see?"

"The future is mine to see, not to tell." He takes my hand and raises it to his lips. The chaste kiss is lost amid my racing thoughts. "I'll say only this—please remember that you have a friend in the Court of Fire, Queen of Air."

Lysandir drops my hand and bows his head, but I hardly register it over the echo of his words screaming through my mind.

Queen of Air.

CHAPTER 29

I GAPE AT LYSANDIR and his sudden revelation. "But I'm not—"

His shy, secretive smile nearly stops my heart.

A horn blares, demanding attention within the core of the celebration. Fae grow silent and still as the main doors open at the top of the stairs leading down into the party.

All the world narrows to that threshold as Sigurd fills its frame with Moria at his side.

He came. He's here.

My skin tingles. It's hard to breathe. With Lysandir at my side and his sudden revelation, I didn't even feel the tug on our bond vanish.

Queen of Air.

I turn to the prince, but the space next to me is empty. My shoulders droop. I don't have to search the party to know he's gone. I didn't even get to say goodbye.

Conversation resumes as Moria descends the stairs. She carries off her outfit with a confidence few could muster. How she keeps the sides of the dress in place is a mystery. I wager it's not tape, or no earthly variety anyway. Everyone dressed for the occasion tonight, even Sigurd. A silver crown twines through his dark hair. His outfit is the most elaborate I've seen, with a grand coat with silver stitching that shimmers and catches the light. A cape of some sort drapes down his back. I can't even see the rest, but the way he holds himself and scans the crowd with a mirthful gaze paints him king above all more than clothes ever could.

The crowd waits for him, glued to his form, but he's yet to move other than to turn his head.

He's looking for me. Breath catches in my throat. I move to the edge of one of the pools of light glimmering from the floating orbs.

I know the moment he finds me. Our gazes lock. He goes still.

And then he's in motion, gliding down the stairs and into the crowd that blocks him from view. I can't make myself move. In my mind, I see myself racing toward him, my heels tapping on the marble. I squeeze through the press of fae, craning my neck and bouncing on my toes to see above their shoulders. The crowd parts, and I leap into his arms.

It's a grand vision, something from a movie, but I can't make it happen.

Queen of Air.

I glance over my shoulder and confirm the worst. There's nowhere to run. As much as I yearn to see him, I dread it. It tears me in two, pulling, pushing, and leaving me frozen where I stand.

"Wren."

One word and suddenly my fears are gone. There's nowhere I would rather be.

Sigurd stands before me, only an arm's length away. Here, in the flesh, after days away. Other fae are a blur of intrusive color lingering just behind him.

Everything I'd planned and hoped to say flies out the window. Maybe it's for the best since we have an audience.

Instead, I dip a low curtsy, my ankles only wobbling a little bit. "King Sigurd."

"I believe they're looking for you to announce the finalists."

Oh. The word hangs on my parted lips. Of all the things I imagined he might say, that wasn't one of them. Nor was his vacant expression or the formality with which he holds out his elbow in an invitation to loop my arm through his.

It might be a show of indifference for the crowd. But that doesn't help my mind from thinking the worst and assuming something has changed between us without my knowing.

I loop my arm through his, savoring the little bit of closeness in my fragile heart. My shoulders are back, my head held high, but it's all an act. The too-pleasant smile on my face is as well. One jab could shatter me. I'd fall into a million pieces in front of these fae, and no amount of my stubborn will could piece me together.

"You look stunning tonight," he whispers as the crowd parts for us.

And just like that, he glues some of the fragile pieces together.

"Beyond compare."

My tongue flicks out across my lips. I reach for the bird around my neck, my anchor, the only thing keeping my mind from drifting away, caught up in his praise.

"I-I showed it off to Zale before the party," I whisper. My gaze lingers on the crowd ahead, where it should be, but it's so hard not to look at him, only at him. "I thought it was you. I hoped it was you. I wanted..."

He releases me as we step into a clearing where the other finalists already wait. Galen is there. He meets my gaze briefly, flashing me a tight smile.

"You wanted to talk to me? To see me?" Sigurd speaks out of the corner of his mouth. The words are barely audible, just loud enough to reach me.

"Yes."

He turns, his gaze meeting mine, and for the briefest flicker, I see beyond the shield of formality. It's a gale of desire, a lightning bolt of pleasure, and maybe a gust of hope.

And then it's gone, so fast I may have imagined it.

Sigurd gestures to the other finalists, who wait in a row on the sweeping stairs behind our eccentric announcer and host of the games.

Bolstered by that brief glimpse, I take my place at the end next to Galen.

The announcer projects his voice louder than should be possible and calls for silence. Fae cease their conversations and move in, eager to hear whatever he has to say. The brief respite I had from their examinations is over. They may pretend to pay attention as the announcer begins another, likely longwinded, speech about the games, but their focus slides straight past to me, skittering over my skin like spiders. Goosebumps race down my arms, and I fight the urge to turn away.

Uncle Mark, Hawke, and Moria stand far to the left, too far for me to watch without turning away, and that wouldn't go unnoticed. There's only one familiar gaze in the crowd I don't mind meeting, and he stands at the front, a witness to the games like any other of his court.

Sigurd's eyes lock on mine. The hint of a smile quirks at the corner of his lips.

I don't pay attention to the words being spoken. I don't care.

Galen leans in ever so slightly to whisper, "He's in love with you."

His gaze flicks from me to Sigurd, leaving no question who *he* refers to.

"Nonsense." I look away from Sigurd, staring at the announcer's back instead. So much safer. Why didn't I think of that before?

"You humans and your lies." Galen smirks.

"It's... It's not..."

But it is. That all-consuming look in Sigurd's eyes says more than words ever could. Maybe it's not love. How could it be, so soon? But it's certainly lust. My chest burns as I recall the feel of his lips on mine and his strong arms holding me tight. My legs wobble underneath me, and I nearly tip over in my heels. Without Galen's quick move to steady me, I certainly would.

"And you with him?" he says.

I have no answer for him. None that I'm willing to share anyway. Holy hell, when did this even happen? But then, Sigurd set my soul alight the moment we met. Even in that dark, rainy, terrible night, part of me clung to him with a need I tried to bury far down under all my fear and worry. No matter what I learned or how I tried to convince myself otherwise, the mere sight of him or whisper of his name would bring it crawling back to the surface.

Queen of Air.

But I can't be. I have family. Responsibility. And they're not here. Not all of them anyway. Maybe someday it could be possible, but that wouldn't be anytime soon.

Unless I fail. Unless Lysandir's portent means I won't win and I'll be stuck here for who knows how long until the magic runs its course and releases me from my bond. Would I be Sigurd's queen then? Could I, knowing he's the reason I would likely never see Gran again?

"Even with all that he's done?" Galen whispers.

The reminder is just enough to send my thoughts tumbling further into darkness. The chill in his words freezes me more than a dunk in ice water.

Oh, the things he's done...

Sigurd forced Galen to commit treason and then trapped him here. He tried to steal the forest king's consort. Nearly got the king himself killed. Almost started a war, one that might still happen. And those are just the things I know about, the recent events.

I close my eyes against the truths cutting my heart to ribbons. "I don't know."

My hands twist together behind my back, and I will time to pass, to fly, for this night to be done and gone. Already, it contains too many revelations I can't process. It has bred too many questions I don't have the right answers for or any answers at all.

The naming of the finalists begins, giving me the briefest distraction. We're introduced one by one. The competitors before me wave to the crowd, pump their fists in the air, and blow kisses. Well, Galen doesn't blow any kisses.

"Wren Dawson," the announcer calls.

Where the others are confident and bold, I curtsy, fanning out my dress and bowing my head in humility. Or I hope it seems that way. Truly, I don't want their praise and cheers. I want nothing but my freedom. With my eyes downcast, they can't see the horror churning there.

And then it's over. The formality is done. I sigh, ready to run to my uncle, to Sigurd, anyone to get me out of here.

But before I reach the bottom step, fae swarm me.

One touches my shoulder. Another asks a question I don't quite hear. A man with strong perfume looms inches from my face just before another dares to touch my waist.

I'm blocked every way I turn. Their tall forms loom above me. My dress is suddenly too tight, and I can't breathe. A scream fights against the knot in my throat, aching to break free.

And then the crowd parts.

A soft breeze wraps around me, clearing my lungs and teasing tendrils of my hair that have fallen free.

Sigurd holds out his hand to me. "As my cousin's mate's family, and thus my own, I request Wren's first dance."

Formal. Indifferent. As if he's fulfilling an obligation.

But I see it for the saving grace it is.

It doesn't matter that he barely looks at me as he leads me in a slow dance across the floor. With his arm around me and the hypnotic fae music that sinks into my very soul, I can almost forget where I am.

It's a pardon from the other fae demanding my attention.

It's sanctuary, if only for one song.

Uncle Mark claims the next dance. Then Hawke, who is a surprisingly good dancer. By the time Moria steps in to take his place, I've finally begun to calm down.

"I thought I'd get some lustful stares for my gown but not for dancing with you." She winks.

Dancing with a finalist is some kind of honor apparently. Galen and the other finalists have been passed from one partner to the next, though I'd wager most of theirs are not the familiar sort. Galen's posture is stiff, almost robotic, and the look on his face says he'd rather be anywhere else.

"How long do I have to keep this up?" I ask.

"Oh, not too much longer." She twirls me around, leading me expertly through the steps.

Good thing, since I have no idea what any of these fae dances are. Some of them seem a little close to dances on the ballroom dancing reality show Gran and I used to watch, but they're different too—more fluid and natural. Maybe it's the music's fault, but I have no trouble following along.

"So, who were you hoping would notice your dress?" I can't help but glance at the plunging V that—maybe magically—stays in place.

She shrugs mid-move.

"No potential mates?"

Moria snorts. "I do appreciate the male form." She glances meaningfully at a towering, well-built man at the edge of the dance floor. "But I prefer my conquests on the battlefield. There's nothing quite like a well-matched duel. Anticipating their moves. Meeting them blow for blow. Working up a sweat." She spins me again, and when I return, her gaze is far away. Still, she doesn't miss a step. "There's a feeling when you finally get an edge on your opponent, find their weak spot, and get them on their heels." The moan she elicits catches the attention of several onlookers and sets my cheeks aflame. "It is the sweetest ecstasy."

Right... I fumble a few steps before she guides me back into the rhythm. "Why the dress then?"

"I like the attention." Another half shrug. "Oh, look at how flush you are." She gives a dramatic pout. "We fae sometimes forget how much more delicate you humans can be. It would be a pity if you were to faint." Her pointed look speaks volumes.

Thank you, Moria.

I stumble during the dance, pulling her to a halt with me.

"I'm suddenly... I feel..." The back of my hand finds my forehead as I swoon in a display so dramatic Scarlett O'Hara would be proud.

I let my legs go limp as Moria swoops in with perfect timing to catch me.

Dancers halt mid-step. Fae gasp and clammer toward us.

"Wren?" The concern in her voice is impressive. "Back off, give her space."

I crack my eyes the smallest fraction. Bodies press in around us far closer than I expected. On instinct, I stiffen.

Moria immediately adjusts me in her arms, covering my error. "She might have had too much excitement. I'll take her to rest."

Tingles race across my skin. The air constricts. Everything goes weightless and spinney as voices, music, and light fade away. I could be fainting for real with the way the air presses in around me.

And then it stops. The pressure slides away.

A high chuckle fills the silence. "You can wake up now."

The party is long gone, as is the castle. A star-flecked night sky spreads above us. Bats or some other fae beasties flutter past as deeper shadows against the moonlit darkness.

As Moria settles me back on my feet, I finally catch a glimpse of the lake and realize where we are.

"The lake house?"

"You'd rather be back in the royal apartments at the castle?"

"No." I love this place. I've thought about it often since Sigurd brought me here. "But..."

Moria gives me a knowing smile. "Sigurd will be along in a little while. He can't leave the party too quickly after you, or the others will realize where he's gone. He doesn't want to give them a reason to doubt if you win or to think he interfered in the games."

No, we definitely don't want that. He's got enough trouble as it is. "How will he know I'm here?"

"It was his idea." She winks. "Have a good evening."

CHAPTER 30

MORIA DIDN'T JUST DEPOSIT me at Sigurd's favored home. She left me on the balcony outside his bedroom. There's no sign or anything, but it has to be his. It even smells like him.

My face flames so hot I have to fan myself. The navy sheets on the grand bed standing across the room are still rumpled and unmade. Somehow, it figures he wouldn't make his bed. A fae lantern emits dim light from the table separating me from that terrifyingly luxurious monstrosity. Simple foods are laid out with a decanter of wine.

I'm expected. Or someone was, and Sigurd doesn't seem the type to provide such a display purely for his own enjoyment.

I stir in delicious agony, waiting for him to arrive. Just thinking about the look in his eyes earlier tonight has moisture building between my legs. And that dang bed...

The implication isn't lost on me.

I'd have balked at it days ago. Smacked him on the shoulder and called him ridiculous, no matter that even then he made my mouth go dry and my heart race faster than any man had in ages.

Truth is, I may have wanted him from the very beginning. But with every step I took toward him, something pushed me back, some horrible revelation about his past.

We all have a past though, and not all of it good, no matter who we are.

Would it be so wrong to enjoy his company while I'm still here? My fingers wander to my lips. I close my eyes, remembering the heat of his kiss, the way the whole world faded away in his embrace, the flick of his tongue—

A stiff breeze comes from nowhere to race across my skin and tug at my hair.

And I know. My body, my soul, recognize his presence before I ever turn toward the balcony.

He's resplendent in the moonlight. It catches his hair, his crown, and the silver threads and buttons of his coat. Sapphires gleam in the rings on his hand and small earrings dangling from each ear.

Sigurd's chest rises and falls. His mouth opens and then closes.

But I don't give him the chance to speak, to find whatever words he searches for. I race across the balcony, just like I'd longed to at the ball, and don't stop till my arms wind around his neck and I'm standing on my toes with my body pressed against him. He sucks in a breath and his eyes go wide, but it doesn't stop me.

My lips crash against his, seeking that precious feeling from days ago.

He's stiff—still as a statue.

Suddenly, I'm sure I misjudged everything and made some terrible mistake. My belly twists itself in knots as I pull away.

And then his hands are on me, warm and coarse against the small of my back, pressing the beaded strands into my skin. His lips crash against mine in a kiss that steals my breath.

It's all consuming, like a dying man who finally found water.

Sigurd's tongue plays with mine, a game of conquest that neither of us wish to lose. His palm slides down to cup my backside and tug me closer. His other is in my hair, ruining the careful updo Uncle Mark commissioned, but I couldn't care less.

There are no words, but we don't need any. I want him, no matter what he's done.

And he wants me, not for the woman he once loved and whose face I may bear. Nor for my humanity and whatever power that gives him. The way he groans against me, the slide of his hands along my form, and the glow of his eyes that I can see beyond my shut ones tell me everything.

My core thrums with need. I'd take him right here and now on this balcony, bared for all the night to see without a second thought.

His fingers trail down my neck and over my collarbone, sending a shiver across my skin. They settle over my necklace, tracing the pendant.

I groan as he pulls back and lean in for more, but he denies me.

"A bird," he says. "As if you were fated for me."

A wren. Such a funny name for a girl. I'd never truly liked it until tonight. Maybe I was meant to meet him long before I ever knew his world existed.

His fingers continue down, sliding over each beaded strand holding my dress together and caressing the sensitive skin between my breasts. My nipples pebble against the fabric.

I pull at his coat, urging him to shed it, to shed everything.

Sigurd dips his head to my neck. His breath heats my skin as he whispers, "What do you want, Wren?"

A kiss follows his words.

"I want you."

"Mmm." He licks at the pulse fluttering in my neck. "In what way?"

Sigurd shrugs out of the coat with my help. It falls with a heavy thud to the floor. His shirt crumbles in my fist.

"You know," I say.

"Do I?" Slowly, carefully, he pulls a strap of the dress from my shoulder.

The buttons on his shirt stick. I can't get them. With a huff of frustration, I reach for his waistband instead.

He pulls me close, confining my movements and trapping my hands. His mouth leaves my neck as he stares me down with searing intensity. "Do you want me to fuck you, Wren?"

"Yes." Yes, that's exactly what I want.

Sigurd grins as he slides the other strap down my shoulder. The loose sleeves puddle around my lower arms before sliding off. The dress goes loose. Night air tickles my heated skin as the beads and fabric drop to pool at my feet, leaving me bare other than my silken underwear.

His gaze locks on my exposed breasts. I make no move to hide them, just bite my lip, to keep from squirming.

"Say it," his voice is hoarse. "Tell me exactly what you want."

"I..."

He takes my hand and raises it to his lips, pressing a decadent kiss to my palm.

Moisture grows between my legs, and for a moment, I forget what he's asked. "I want you."

He drops my hand and steps back, raking me with his gaze. "You want me to..."

"I want you to *fuck* me, Sigurd."

His eyes hood. "There's that filthy mouth."

I squeal as he takes me in his arms. His lips crash back against mine, hot and demanding, as he clutches my backside and lifts me to him. My legs wrap around him as best they can, and all that separates my needy core from him is the damp silk of my underwear.

I barely register anything other than him, his lips against mine, his breath in my lungs, and his caress that drives me wild. That is, until cool sheets press against my skin.

Sigurd lays me on the bed with care, staring down where I'm sprawled out before him.

He pulls his shirt over his head, ripping off a button or two in the process, and tosses it away. His boots follow. All the while, he never looks away from me. Finally, he grasps his silver crown and jerks it from his hair with a grimace. It's tossed on a chair as if it's worthless.

Clad in only his pants, he climbs onto the bed.

My pulse beats wildly in my throat. The last time I'd seen him shirtless was that horrible morning after our drinking game. I could barely see straight, much less appreciate the sight before me.

I do now.

All of him is a work of art—the hard, lean muscle, chiseled abs, and strong arms. A few thin scars add to his wild beauty. And that wicked one...

I trace a hand down the healed skin that dips into his waistband. Sigurd sucks in a breath, his stomach tensing under my touch.

"This wound must have been horrible," I say.

"It was. An attempt by an Unseelie to end my life long ago." His expression hardens. "He paid for it with his."

I swallow. Well, on a happier note...

I give his pants a tug.

"Mmm." He grabs my hand and twines it with his against my pillow. "Not yet."

"Si—"

He claims his name with his mouth. I cling to him as he lowers his weight onto me, the press of his cock hard and hot against my thigh.

Sigurd pulls back, a grimace on his face.

"What is it?" I graze his cheek.

"I can't fuck you."

"Why?" The fire within me dies. He may as well have slapped me or thrown me in the lake. I thought he wanted me. I *know* he does.

His forehead leans on my shoulder, pinning me to the bed. But after his previous words, I'd rather be anywhere else. He exhales a deep breath.

A thought strikes me so hard my throat burns. "This is because of Evelyn, isn't it? Because I'm not her."

"No!" He jerks upright. "No, Wren. This has nothing to do with her, with any of that." He cups my cheek. "The opposite."

"Then why?" I want to scream, to tug at my hair.

"Because I'd mark you, Wren. I'd mark you so hard no one in my court would doubt how much I want you."

Unwanted heat floods my face. "Mark me?"

"A fae mating bond. You want me, and I certainly want you. The magic of this world would bind us, mark us with a power that anyone, any fae, could feel."

Oh goodness. "But you don't want that."

"Oh, I do. I want it more than I've ever wanted with anyone. *Anyone*, Wren."

More than Evelyn. He can't lie. He really wants me.

"But I won't risk your chances in the competition. I won't throw doubt on you because you bear the mark of the King of Air. They'd assume I interfered somehow."

I melt into the sheets with a sigh. "Then after the last game, you'd— We'd..."

"It's your choice, Wren."

Because if I win, I could leave him. I could go back to my home, my world. My stomach clenches. Tears burn at the corner of my eyes.

How could I ever leave him? But how could I not?

I trail my fingertips across his cheeks, savoring the way his eyes close in contentment. My fingers glide through his hair and along the edge of one pointed ear.

Sigurd thrusts against me with a grunt, his hardness rubbing against my skin. A shiver rolls down his form as his eyes flash open. "You test my resolve."

"Do I?" I cock one brow and caress his ear again.

He growls deep in his chest and leans in, placing a little nip on my collarbone. "The ears are a fae male's second most sensitive spot."

"And the first?"

Pointed fangs peek out of a toothy grin.

I suck in a breath as his hand cups my breast. "Sigurd."

"When you do that, I—" His thumb rubs circles around my nipple. He pinches the sensitive tip, pulling a moan from my lips. "I won't fuck you, Wren, but there's plenty more I'd love to do with you." His hand slides down my stomach.

My muscles clench at his touch.

Sigurd holds my gaze as he ventures lower, dipping below my underwear. "If you'll have me?"

My core winds tight in anticipation, and all I can do is bite my lip and nod.

His fingers slide into the moisture between my legs. "So wet already, and I've barely touched you."

"Your fault." I spread my legs wider, giving him access. Every twitch of his fingers sends waves of pleasure coursing through my body.

"Greedy too." He's back at my neck, placing kisses in the tender spot near my collarbone.

"So greedy."

One finger delves inside me, and I nearly buck off the bed. Everything narrows down to the feel of him teasing me and searching for my most sensitive spot.

My hands fist in his hair as a second finger joins the first. Breaths come hot and short. I can't think, can't speak, can only feel as his thumb flicks across my clit, sending lightning searing under my skin.

"Wren," he groans against me. "So tight, so warm, so perfect."

His fingers slide free, and I cry out at their absence, the loss of him. "Sigurd. I need—"

"Patience." His warm breath caresses my skin as he trails kisses down my chest. That wicked tongue flicks out over my nipple, and I gasp. He kisses the pearled tip, taking it in his mouth and sucking until I writhe under him. "Delightful."

My release is so close, but I can't quite get enough. My fingers slide through his hair and rub against his pointed ear in a tease of my own, anything to get him to move on me, to finish the madness he started. Sharp teeth nip at my breast in return. The brief bit of pain blurs into pleasure.

I swat at him, but he slides lower, avoiding my reach.

His tongue flicks against my belly. Strong hands grasp my thighs, tugging them wider. Sigurd grabs the hem of my underwear, and I lift my hips, thinking he means to remove them, but in one quick move, he rips them off instead. I gasp, staring wide eyed as he tosses the ruined fabric away. Cool air tingles my skin, and before I can react or even form words, his mouth is on me.

"Sigurd!" I scream as his tongue laps against my folds.

He consumes me. All thought, all reason, narrow to the feel of him against me, twisting the knot in my core tighter with each flick of his tongue. His fingers return, meeting the aching need that has lingered since he retreated moments ago.

My vision blurs. My back arcs. I clutch the sheets to anchor myself to this world as he draws me to the precipice of release. I've never been this high, this wild.

Sigurd finds my spot with his fingers, and I buck against him, unable to be still against the surge of pleasure racing through me. He growls against me. The thrusts of his fingers quicken. Bolts of energy race out from my core.

Then he takes my clit between his lips and sucks.

I shatter.

Waves of ecstasy burst through me. My scream echoes in the room. All is white-hot light, joy, and a deep desire for the man wringing out my pleasure with the expert slide of his fingers.

"Wren. Beautiful Wren."

His thrusts slow, bringing me back to him. Sigurd's other hand caresses my hip, sliding along my stomach and down my upper thighs.

He kneels between my legs. His eyes glow a bright, ethereal blue. My dampness glistens on his fingers as he draws them to his mouth. His gaze locks on mine as he sucks them between his lips, tasting me.

Impossibly, more heat blooms in my chest, crawling up my neck. I pant on the bed, loose and liquid. Cool night air races over my heated skin and teases the moisture between my spread legs.

"More wondrous than I ever imagined." Sigurd crawls up the bed to lay beside me.

Waves of pleasure roll under my skin, and I can't will myself to move. Nor do I want to when he pulls me into his arms and hugs me against his chest. His pulse races, fluttering like the wild beast within me.

"You—" I search for words I cannot find. "That—"

Laughter rumbles in his chest. He claims my lips with his, sealing our passion and reviving my senses.

His manhood, still hidden within his pants, prods against my thigh, unmistakable in his proof of unfulfilled desire. I rub his length through the fabric, and oh sweet Jesus, what an impressive length it is. Enough to dry my throat and build the pleasure twisting within me again.

Sigurd groans in response and nuzzles my neck.

"May I?" I rasp.

He jerks back. "You would..."

The surprise on his features nearly guts me.

"Of course." I stroke him again. "I want you, Sigurd. More than..." My heart clenches. More than I should. More than I ever thought possible. I lick the sheen of perspiration on his chest. "Besides, what kind of person would I be if I didn't return the favor after such generosity?"

I yelp as he rolls, pulling me with him until I straddle his hips. His thumbs rub circles over my skin as he stares up at me, a satisfied smirk on his face.

"I'll take anything you'll give me, Wren." His smile fades. "For however long I can have you."

My throat tightens, but I swallow it down. The future won't ruin this night. The past won't either. This night is ours and ours alone.

"Good," I say ghosting my fingertips down his chest. "I have a number of things in mind for you too."

CHAPTER 31

T HE MORNING OF THE final game, we watch the sunrise from Sigurd's balcony at the lake house. I've always loved the pinkening of dawn just before the sun crests, morning dew clinging to the grass, and the happy chirp of birds just rising from their nests.

Not today though.

Leaning against Sigurd's chest, a blanket shielding us both from the cold, that light is a bringer of doom. The chill of my bare feet against the stone climbs up my body, causing me to shiver.

Sigurd snuggles me tighter and places a kiss on my hair.

But the cold, hard knot in my chest isn't one he can shield me from.

The last day was possibly the happiest of my life. From our night tangled together in the sheets to a day spent flying in his arms, splashing in the lake, and smiling until my cheeks hurt.

The rising dawn twists each happy memory into shards of glass that slice me up inside.

Either I'll win today and leave, or I'll be trapped here ages longer. Gran might be okay if I have to stay here. I hope so. But—I lean back against Sigurd's chest, listening to the steady beat of his pulse—how could I ever leave him then? Already the thought makes me ill. I tossed and turned so much in the bed that I couldn't sleep and eventually found my way out here. Sigurd was quick to follow and cloak me in his warmth. A blessing and a pity. Standing with his arms around me, knowing it can't last, is the sweetest misery.

A heavy sigh slips from me.

"You're still determined to leave if you win? To go home?" It's the first words he's spoken this morning, each as quiet as a distant whisper.

"Gran needs me." I say it as much for myself as for him.

"Your uncle can check on her. Even if she cannot see him, he can see her. I'll send others with him to speed his journey and see that he makes it back. We can send food, gold, jewelry, anything she needs."

Yes, it'd be good for Uncle Mark to see her again, even if the reverse isn't possible. Food, money, it would all help. But a key element is still missing.

"Those things alone can't see to her needs. Hopefully, my cousin has looked after her, but Tabitha has so many kids of her own to manage. Gran needs someone who can be there for the everyday things, getting up in the morning, taking her medicine, and helping around the house. She needs *me*."

"Wren." He turns me in his arms and forces me to look up into his still sleep-mussed face. "What do you think she would want?"

I rear back, but he holds me close in the warmth of the blanket.

"If she were here, if you could ask her, what would she want you to do?"

The lump that forms in my throat threatens to choke me. I know exactly what she'd say. Gran prodded me for years about going to college. For the education, yes, but more than that, I think she just wanted me to get out in the world, to experience life beyond our small town.

When I meet his steady gaze, I can tell he's read the answer in my silence.

Still, I say, "She spent so many years caring for me after my parents died. Years that should have been hers to enjoy. How can I leave her now when she needs me the most?"

A deep sigh slips from Sigurd's lips before he pulls me back against his chest. I cling to him, savoring his warmth, his scent, and his strength. I'd give anything to freeze this moment, if only just a few minutes longer.

"At least it will be safer for you in your world," he whispers.

Because war is on the horizon.

He hadn't wanted to tell me, didn't want to darken our day of joy, but I all but forced it out of him. The Unseelie *are* gathering together, amassing and joining forces for a purpose that cannot be good—at least not for the Court of Air or any Seelie court. Relations are no better with the Court of the Forest. Fae grudges run deep, and theirs is fresh, new and bloody. It could be war on two fronts at any moment. As a human valued by the king, I'd be a target here, maybe a significant one. There are more than enough people who dislike Sigurd and who would see him suffer. Harming me would be an effective method of that.

Even so, it doesn't dampen my resolve to stay at his side for however little time remains.

His arms loosen, and I almost cry out in protest. I know what comes next. I dread it.

"We should get you back," he says.

I nod, my cheek sliding against his chest before I reluctantly pull away.

One more challenge. One winner.

And it has to be me.

I'm numb walking into the roaring stadium. I'm as empty within as I was while Moria dressed me for the event. She said little, me even less. Moria blamed the looming war for her silence, her mind busy working through various strategies. At least she has a good excuse. My war is so much smaller, contained within me alone.

The winner will be announced after this last event. They will be presented before the king—before Sigurd—and drink from the cauldron to receive their reward.

Cauldron willing, anyway.

It should be able to remove our bond. Moria believes it. Uncle Mark and Hawke believe it. Their faith is enough to convince me it will work.

The winner receiving their blessing is the start of the celebration. I could see the preparations from high in the castle before Uncle Mark and Hawke brought me to the arena. Tents and makeshift structures were erected all around the great stadium set in an open field within the valley. Masses of fae have swarmed to the capital, to the arena, for the final of the games and the partying to follow. It's their Super Bowl, and these fae seem to love nothing more than a good celebration, looming war or not.

But then, the party is part of the act. Distract the people with enough fun, and hopefully they'll forget the shit they're in, if even for a day. Moria assured me there are plenty of guards stationed in the arena and the surrounding area. No enemies will attack the games. It would be suicide.

That's not quite what has me on edge though. This moment, this game, decides my fate. I could leave today or be stuck here, and the decider of my fate is a game I have no knowledge of.

Moria dressed me in a simple but elegant tunic and pants outfit of silver and blue, not even bothering with hidden weapons. Based on her outfit choices for me, it can't be a fight to the finish—thank God for that—but she's given nothing else away, if she even knows exactly what it is.

The remaining competitors, including me, each approach from a different entrance on the field. Our destination is obvious, despite no one telling me where to go. A large navy tent awaits in the center, cloth covering the roof and all sides. A raised area sits nearest us, the announcer of the games already standing on it, surrounded by other fae dignitaries. Beyond the massive tent, I can just make out the edge of what looks to be another raised area on the far side of the arena. This one is larger, more grandiose, and though we're not that far apart, I can almost feel a tug on our bond telling me that Sigurd is there. He waits for the winner to emerge, the cauldron likely close at hand.

I meet Galen just before the stage. He gives me a hard look from the corner of his eye, nose wrinkling with distaste.

"You stink," he whispers.

I bristle, standing a little straighter. I scrubbed in the bath for almost an hour this morning before being a little too liberal with the floral perfume Moria loaned me. Frankly, I haven't smelled so nice in ages. "I quite like flowers."

He snorts. "You smell of him."

An unbidden flush rises to my cheeks.

"Not surprising, given your disappearance from the ball...and who left not long after."

I swallow down the hard lump in my throat. I whisper back, "It was that obvious?"

"Only to those who bothered to look." He glances down the short row of remaining competitors where we've come to a stop in front of the stage and shrugs. "Most didn't."

But Galen did. He saw, he knew, and he didn't like it one bit. A deep hurt burns in my chest, and though I try to will it away, to push it down, it's persistent.

We were allies. Maybe friends? I kind of hoped we were. After today, though, we may not see one another again. If he wins, he'll ask for his freedom and leave here. Same if I do. The only way we could possibly remain together is if we both lose. But then I'd still choose to be with Sigurd, and it's clear that's a choice Galen cannot abide.

The announcer calls for quiet, somehow managing to bring the raucous crowd to silence. He begins another of his famous speeches about the history of the games, some kind of magic or fae ingenuity amplifying his voice for all to hear.

Galen shifts on his feet, inching closer to me so that he can lean my way and whisper. "Interesting he didn't forego the games and just let you have your wish of the cauldron."

"He wouldn't do such a—" I start, ready to defend Sigurd.

"But then that wouldn't work in his favor, would it? It benefits him to keep you here, just as you are."

Fury prickles under my skin, and I rub at my chest, trying to force it down. "He's not like that. He supports me in this." I gesture vaguely to the arena around us.

Galen raises one brow, his gaze straight ahead on the announcer. "Does he, or does he just want you to think that?"

Stop trying to get under my skin. My teeth dig into my bottom lip, barely holding the words in. If Galen's trying to mess with me, to unsettle me before this final game, it's working. "You hate him so much you refuse to think he could be honest in this or with me."

"Yes." He cuts his gaze to me. "I do."

My body nearly vibrates with rage. "Then I'll prove it. If the cauldron doesn't grant your wish, I'll ask him to remove your oaths. He can do that, right?" I don't know why I need to prove to Galen that Sigurd isn't as horrible as he thinks, that he *can* be a good person, a good king. Their history is their own. But Galen has pulled me into their messy web, and now I can't leave it alone.

Galen has gone utterly still. For a minute, I'm convinced he's not going to answer and I'm going to be left wondering, just listening to the announcer finish his speech, one he clearly has no intention of wrapping up quickly from the way he gestures to the crowd and has them laughing and cheering in response to his comments.

"You truly think he would do that because you ask him?" he asks, so quiet I almost miss it.

The comment emboldens me, and I turn my head to stare at him as I respond. "You said you still smell him on me. What do you think? He said he would remove my bond if he could, but he cannot. Do you truly think he would deny me a request?"

I teased Galen with this promise once before. Then it was really to gain his trust, and I wasn't sure Sigurd would bother with a request on my behalf.

Now, I believe differently, and I need Galen to believe it too.

Galen flinches. "He said that? He would free you if he could?"

"Of course." I fight the urge to cross my arms, a smug smile on my lips as I turn back to the announcer.

Queen of Air. Lysandir's words come back to tease me, and suddenly, I'm certain Sigurd would do this for me. In fact, I should have asked him before. Maybe I could have narrowed my competition before this final game ever started, maybe even gotten them all to resign if Sigurd could simply grant their wishes without the cauldron's power.

Regrets won't help me now. Could-haves and should-haves will only hold me back, chaining me to a past no force can change. But the future is still in play, and that I can make right.

"If I win, you'll have your wish," I promise Galen.

He shifts on his feet again. "We'll see."

It's not the warm and fuzzy reaction I hoped for, but it'll do. Maybe it will be enough to sway him in my favor if this last challenge demands we face one another head-on. I'll take every advantage I can get.

Eventually, the announcer settles his focus on us and the final game. "Our competitors will all enter the tent behind me, but only one shall emerge as our winner of the games. As for what awaits them inside... Ah, now that is a mystery."

I give a silent groan. He honestly couldn't make it more ominous if he tried.

"Keep alert," he continues. "Whoever emerges from the far end of the tent first will be our winner."

The announcer descends the stage and beckons us all to follow. One of the guards stationed outside the tent has raised a corner of fabric, revealing an opening, but only darkness looms beyond. Maybe these fae, with their sight so much better than mine, can see within, but it's a mystery to me, just as it has been this whole time.

"Good luck," I whisper to Galen. I mean it. I really do, even though I want to win.

He nods, silent. I suppose he can't say it back. It might be a lie on his tongue, if even a pleasant one, but I'll take what little support he offers.

Besides, only one of us can emerge as the victor.

CHAPTER 32

I T TAKES MY EYES a few moments to adjust once we enter the tent. Outside, the sun blazed overhead. Within, the fabric blocks its rays, creating a world of shadowy darkness, save a few balls of fae light that seem to float of their own accord near the ceiling, providing just enough illumination for us to see. Various fae guards stand around the inside of the tent at even intervals, and in its center, the only furniture of note are five podiums, evenly spaced and facing toward the center.

Not a duel. Nothing about this setup speaks to fighting. Some of the tightness between my shoulder blades eases. Besides, why would they deny the crowd that show? It almost looks like the setup for a political debate. If we have to argue our case for getting the wish, I'm not sure I'll win.

"Pick a spot, each of you. It doesn't matter which one. They're all the same," the announcer orders, shooing us like children toward the podiums.

The fae, two women and two men, including Galen, make a beeline for their chosen spots, making my decision easy. The announcer moves to the center of the ring, one hand clutching a large piece of rolled parchment that I'd swear hadn't been there a moment ago.

"Now, as you know, this is the final challenge." He takes his time, looking at each of us in turn. "One winner. Four losers. The winner, once determined, will exit through there." He points to a section of overlapping fabric panels flanked by two guards. I assume they'll pull the sections back to form a doorway for the winner to exit. As is it now, the fabric blocks out almost all sound from beyond, despite the thousands of fae cramming the stands. It must be magic at work. No fabric should be that soundproof, especially since the panels we passed through weren't particularly thick. "The losers will return the way you entered."

The entrance has been shut once more, the sections of fabric falling back in place and cloaking the processing from view.

"This final challenge is deceptively simple." He takes the parchment in hand, tapping it on his open palm. "A riddle. The first one to answer correctly wins."

I shift on my feet. Just peachy. I've never been very good at riddles, jokes either.

"You may give one response, but if your answer is incorrect, you will be disqualified and must leave the tent immediately."

My stomach sinks, and I already focus on keeping my lips pressed tight. As a human, I might not even know what the answer is to be able to give it.

"What if we all guess incorrectly?" one of the fae women asks.

The announcer turns slowly toward her. "Since a wrong answer disqualifies you, the last one standing after four have been disqualified will win."

So, I could just wait it out. Let them guess and hope they're wrong, and I win by default. But it seems like such a crappy way to win, not to mention that these fae already stand tall and alert, their minds honed to the challenge if the looks on their faces are any indication.

"There is no time limit. You may take the time you need to consider your answer, but the first one to speak the correct solution will be the winner. Are you ready to begin?" The announcer again takes his time looking at us each in turn, waiting for the bob of our head that indicates we're ready.

I flatten my clammy palms against the top of the wood podium, anything to center myself and still the panic stirring my thoughts into a mess.

Calm down. Pay attention.

Every word will be important, and I can't miss one stuck in my worries.

"Let us begin." The announcer snaps the seal on the scroll and unrolls it with care. He adjusts his form just so, probably so that no one can see the words before he reads them aloud. The fae might be able to, but my eyesight is way too poor to see anything more than scribbles at this distance, even though my vision has always been good by human standards. I bob on my toes, waiting impatiently, when he begins.

"It's one of the most valuable things in existence.

You can have it but cannot hold it.

It's a—"

"A heart!" one of the fae men yells.

The room goes eerily still, the thundering of my pulse the only sound in my ears. Could it possibly be so simple? The announcer never said we had to wait until he finished speaking to guess, but to lose now before I even had a chance—

"Incorrect."

A tangible sigh slips through the room, all except for the loser. He slams a fist on the podium, uttering some expletive not in English or anything I understand.

"Out with you," the announcer says, gesturing to the entrance. "I will continue once he has left," he says to the rest of us. "I advise you to listen to it all."

Murmured agreement drifts around our circle as the failed contender exits. The moment the tent flap is raised, cheers erupt, bursting into the quiet of our space. But they fade off even more quickly than they rose, the audience likely realizing this is not their awaited winner. The flaps fall back in place, and the room is silent once more.

The announcer clears his throat and begins again.

"It's one of the most valuable things in existence.

You can have it but cannot hold it.

It's a tremendous gift but can be hard to receive.

Giving it can make you stronger or weaker.

Once it's broken, it may be impossible to repair."

He pauses, and I think he may continue. But he doesn't. He simply looks at us each in turn, waiting.

Oh, sweet baby Jesus. That's it. That's all the clues.

No sooner have I started to repeat them to myself than a woman calls out, "Love!"

My heart sinks. To my left, Galen groans aloud. Blast it all. Of course it's love. Isn't it always in these kinds of riddles? I should have known, should have guessed, but I was too slow, too stuck trying to process the lines I'd just heard to even formulate the answer. I can't look at the woman, can't see the joy on her face. All I can focus on is the wood of the podium below my hands and the way my knees are suddenly weak.

"Incorrect."

I snap my gaze to the woman who spoke. She's no less shocked than me, her mouth agape and confusion written all over her pinched features. I'd have sworn she was right. Her answer made sense with the clues, especially as I think back through them.

"But I—" she sputters, blinking.

"To the exit," the announcer says, though there's something akin to pity in his voice, or at least a gentleness that wasn't there with the other contender.

She's still blinking, shaking her head slightly as she makes her way to the exit. The fabric parts, and an audible gasp and murmur rumbles through the crowd but fades quickly. The fabric doesn't quite close all the way when the guards release it, leaving a little gap, but you wouldn't know it for the lack of sound disturbing us, as if we're a world on our own.

The pause and silence outside is palpable, as if everyone is stretching on their toes and looking toward the other side of the tent, waiting for someone to emerge at any moment.

But none of us are moving. No one has spoken.

The wrong word, and we're out like the other two, making the long walk of shame across the arena for all to see.

"Shall I read it again?" The announcer unrolls the scroll and reads through the clues again, but all I can think about is the woman's answer and how love seems so perfect.

I glance around the tent. The woman on the far side has her brows knitted in concentration, staring at nothing. Galen, however, looks directly at me as the announcer reads, almost as if he wants my attention.

To distract me or something else?

Galen inclines his head ever so slightly in a brief nod. Then he reaches for the golden earring he always wears, one that must have been given to him by the woman he loves, for he touches it almost every time he speaks of her. When his fingertips graze it now, he's looking at me, something written in his gaze.

And then it hits me, sending a wave of tingles racing across my skin.

He knows the answer.

But he wants me to figure it out. He's...trusting me.

I slam my hand on the table in front of me as if it's some kind of buzzer. "Trust!"

Galen's eyes widen. Good or bad? A heady buzz of adrenaline surges through my veins, and I can hardly process that I've spoken, much less his reaction.

I twist toward the announcer, who has startled at my outburst, his hands fumbling as he rerolls the paper. But then he blinks, and the look is gone. His hands still in their motion, and a slight smile curves his lips.

"Correct."

I blink at him. A groan of despair from the other woman fills the air. It takes a minute for the word to soak in and realization of what it means to have me swaying on my feet.

I've won.

CHAPTER 33

I GO ALONE THROUGH the exit on the far side of the tent, the winner's exit. Apparently, the others will depart the way we all came in and meet me in front of the stage, where I'll claim my victory.

The light is blinding as I step out into the sun. I pinch my eyes closed then blink against the change. Roars erupt from the stands. It's so loud it shakes the ground under my feet. The air vibrates with the force of their excitement, a power so tangible it has me standing a little straighter and adrenaline zipping under my skin like an electrical current. If this is how pro athletes feel when they step onto the turf, I understand why they do it—why they stress and risk their bodies. Okay, the money doesn't hurt either, but the feeling is a high unlike anything I've felt.

Without thinking, I raise my hand to the crowd, still a blurred colorful mass to my adjusting eyesight. The simple action feeds the frenzy. I'm probably supposed to go somewhere, advance on the stage, but the force of this moment keeps my feet rooted to the ground.

Finally, my vision clears, and I get my first glimpse of said stage. What I spy there nearly brings me to tears. Sigurd stands at the very edge, a broad grin on his features as he beams with what can only be pride.

I knew you could, I see him mouth, the words lost in the chaos.

I swallow down the tightness in my throat and give an answering nod. He believed in me, a simple human that the odds were surely against.

I don't know how long I stand there taking it all in, lost in the wonder of the moment and unable to move, but suddenly the announcer is there at my side, escorting me to the stage. Sigurd waits for me there, hand outstretched, and the announcer passes me off to him like a father delivering the bride to the altar.

The roar of the crowd finally dims. All eyes are on me, and without their boisterous cheers, anxiety grips me in a death vice. Sigurd must sense it because his hand tightens on mine.

"You did it, Wren. You won," he says, only for me.

I stare up at him, and the moment becomes less intimidating. If I stare at him, only him, I can almost forget the massive crowd filling the stands and the other important fae sitting in rows of chairs at the back of the stage—Uncle Mark and Hawke included.

But there's something else on the stage I cannot ignore. Placed in its center and bound by heavy chains of gray metal stands what must be the cauldron. It's smaller than I expected, not too much larger than a gumbo pot, but this is no cooking tool.

Strangeness radiates from it, pulling my attention and beckoning me near. Beyond the noise of the crowd, I can almost hear a strange song, both harmonious and discordant all at once, and I know deep in my bones it's coming from that black metal cauldron. So deceptive in its appearance, but the sight is misleading. If even a human like myself can feel its power, it must be vast, a tool for granting wishes if ever there was one.

"The cauldron," Sigurd confirms, turning me toward it.

I nod. That much I've deduced, but one thing I have not. "Why the chains?"

He leans in, his body brushing mine. "It would be most unfortunate if a fae were to attempt to steal it by simply grabbing it and shifting away."

My brows rise. Unfortunate indeed. And if these fae are as similar in nature to humans as they seem to be, I'm sure it's been attempted.

"Are you ready?" he asks.

I'm still stuck staring at the darn thing when Sigurd turns us back toward the majority of the arena and raises our bound hands in the air.

"Your winner, Wren Dawson!" His voice is unnaturally loud, so much that I wince and wish I'd known to cover my ears. The crowd has barely quieted when he adds, "She will now drink from the cauldron to receive her wish."

It's then that I spot the row of other finalists standing in front of the stage, all lined up to witness me claim the prize that they so recently lost.

My gaze lands directly on Galen and holds.

I'm trusting you. At least, I think that's what he says, his words silent or lost to the noise.

A heaviness settles in my chest, and I know this is the moment I must make good on my promise. If I don't, he'll think I betrayed him, and I can't do that, not after he gave up the win for me. He gave me his trust, his most precious gift, and I will not break it.

Sigurd lowers our hands and leads me toward the cauldron. I give a firm tug, drawing him to a halt. "Wait."

"Wren?" His brows wrinkle as he looks at me.

"I have to ask a favor of you first, a few favors actually. I want you to grant the other finalists their wishes." The press of his lips only grows thinner. He opens his mouth to protest, so I hurry on. "If it's within your power, if it doesn't hurt the Court of Air or another fae or human, if it's a good and noble wish, please grant it to them. For me."

His throat bobs. Murmurs have risen around us from the stands, spectators likely trying to understand the delay. Even Hawke has risen to his feet, though he still stands at his chair.

I draw my wandering gaze away and stare Sigurd down.

"This is an odd request, Wren. The cauldron only has the power for one wish, and by tradition, that's all that's granted at the games."

Stubborn fae and their damn traditions. I notch my chin higher. "Then do this for me. Not for the games but simply because I asked, because I want this with my whole heart."

His head tilts to the side as he looks at me anew. "Do you even know their wishes?"

"No. Not all of them." They could be selfish, petty, or even vengeful things that shouldn't be granted. I have no idea of most of them, but if it means that even one wish, Galen's wish, is fulfilled, it's enough.

I sense the indecision as Sigurd looks between the finalists and me and then back toward the cauldron and the other fae, as if seeking counsel in the silence. But I have one last card to play, one thing that I feel certain will sway him in my favor, and if I'm honest, it's something I'd give without the promise of a favor in return.

I squeeze our joined hands, drawing his attention back to me. "Do this for me. Grant their wishes if you can, and I will be yours."

His eyes widen, a soft blue glow lighting them from within.

"I'll bear your mark gladly. And after I return and check on my family, once I've ensured they are well and cared for, I'll return to you."

"You'd come back?" His lips part in wonder. "You'd stay with me for this favor?"

"Yes."

Sigurd rubs the back of my hand with his thumb. "My Wren, I will grant you this. If their wish is honest and true and within my power to grant, I will see it done. I promise you this."

A pulse of some magic passes between us like a wave through the air. Fae gasp. One of the other finalists even takes a step back, disrupting their perfect row. This isn't a simple promise. It's bound in magic, a force so strong even I felt it.

My eyes well with tears as I take in what he's done.

A smile breaks across Sigurd's face, so honest and true that it nearly breaks me. It's still there, the glow in his eyes bright as ever, as he looks to the crowd and raises his voice to that unnaturally loud tone once more. "Wren, as the winner of the games, has asked a favor of me, and I have promised to fulfill it."

The crowd goes deathly silent, hanging on every word their king speaks.

"I shall hear the wishes of the other finalists," he says. "If they are well intentioned and within my power to grant, I shall see them done."

If I thought the crowd excited before, they're losing it now. The cheers are deafening. The stage vibrates. The female finalist who guessed incorrectly literally leaps on another in her joy, but it's to Galen that I look.

He hasn't moved, only blinks before shaking his head and finally, finally letting free a smile. His gaze meets mine, and I see the relief there. Whether he doubted me or Sigurd, or both of us, I can't say, but this is a surprise to him. A welcome one. I wish I could rush down the stairs and give him a hug and celebrate with him, but this isn't the time. Hopefully, maybe, I'll be able to see him later before he leaves.

"Claim your wish now, Wren," Sigurd says at my ear, his lips so close that warm breath ghosts across my skin, stirring up an entirely different kind of tingle.

I turn toward him, daring to cup his cheek in my palm for all the crowd to see. His leans into the touch, his eyes hooding, the mirth dancing there promising so many delights and sending a flush racing to my cheeks.

"Thank you," I tell him.

I promised to be his, to return to him, and I plan to. However long it takes, I will stand by his side.

Before I can doubt my resolve, I drop my hand and stride toward the cauldron. The thing rises almost to my waist, so I kneel beside it. However, no liquid fills the basin as I expect. Instead, a thick misty fog swirls within, obscuring much of the view. Its song is louder here, calling and beckoning me above the numerous voices that buzzed around me moments ago. The cauldron offers peace, a moment of respite amid the excitement of the moment.

No one has told me how exactly to drink from the cauldron, but I don't need to ask. The cauldron itself speaks to me without words, inviting me into its magic with temptations beyond all that I've considered. It could grant me much—it would—if only I were to ask.

But I entered this competition for one reason and one reason alone, and that's what I focus on as I cup my hands together and lower them into the fog.

Unnatural chill prickles across my skin. If someone could touch a ghost, it would probably feel a lot like this—cold and insubstantial but present all the same. Still, I don't pull away. In truth, I'm not sure the cauldron would let me, almost as if it controls my actions as much as I do. I watch, transfixed, as tendrils of the mist swirl within my cupped hands and seem to partially solidify. A golden glow threads its way through the fog as it someone sews the glimmer into the clouds.

Suddenly, my hands are rising toward my face, bringing that golden mist to my mouth. There's no fear, no panic, just utter calm and peace as the cauldron's song consumes me, blocking out the world.

That misty liquid touches my lips. The sweetest, warm honey floats across my tongue, coating my mouth and sliding down my throat. I might groan at the pleasure of it, the taste so extraordinary that I know no food will ever compare. A tingling warmth starts in my chest and spreads through my limbs until all is warm and satisfied. I feel a tangible change in my wrist, like a handcuff being undone, and watch in wonder as the ink of my bond with Sigurd lifts from my skin as smoke and then is gone.

It's worked. I have my wish.

Laughter shakes my shoulders as I gasp in relief. I can go home. I can see Gran and make sure she's safe. But even though I have the wish I wanted, something heavy still lingers in my chest.

As quickly as the tingling came, it seeps away. The cauldron's song fades into nothingness, and the world around me rushes back in full force. I look up to find Uncle Mark and Hawke not far away, looking on with pride and maybe a bit of wonder. Other fae smile as well, and the crowd is boisterous as ever.

Finally, I rise and turn to Sigurd. His look is unreadable, the silence between us punishing, so I speak, "It's done."

"It is," he says, his smile dropping for the briefest moment. "Come." He holds out a hand to me. "I have wishes to hear, and you should hear what your request has granted as well."

CHAPTER 34

I F I HAD ANY doubts about fae affection for a good party, this night would erase them. I suppose when lives are measured in decades, not years, you need something to look forward to, to mark the passage of time, and this event is certainly it.

The party spreads through the valley as far as I can see. Bonfires add their color to the fading rays of sunset, as do fae lights that float above the crowded spaces. Something I can't name perfumes the air, giving it sweet and smoky notes that aren't just from the copious amounts of food or the fires. The scent alone is almost intoxicating. Drinks flow liberally, and so far, I've done my best to avoid those, other than a few sips of a particularly delicious whiskey. It'd be impossible to forget what happened the last time I had too much to drink here, and I won't let that happen again, not tonight.

I haven't been this giddy since I was a teenager, waiting for my date to pick me up for my first school dance. But the king who lingers at my side this evening is so much more of a man than that boy will ever be, and the dizzying effect he has on me every time I glance at him is palpable. His hungry, hooded looks and the reminder of the promise I made to him only build my anticipation.

Sigurd kept his word. He heard the wishes of the finalists and granted those he was able, including freeing Galen of his bond. I'd hoped to see Galen tonight, to say one final farewell before he ventured off to return to the woman he loves and beg her forgiveness. It hurts a little that his face hasn't appeared in front of me along with the seemingly endless line of so many others coming to see the victor of the games and offer me congratulations. I swear, it's like a greeting line at a wedding, and Sigurd standing at my side doesn't lessen that feeling. But of all the many fae, and two rare humans, who have come before me before going off to join in the revelry, I haven't seen my friend.

Galen gave me this victory. He should be here celebrating with me and basking in it himself. Still, I guess I can't blame him for wanting to leave now that he's free of his oaths. He must love her very much.

I shift on my feet as I smile at another group of passing fae offering congratulations that flow in one ear and out the other. I'm grateful, really, but it's felt like hours of this now. My feet are sore, and my cheeks ache from keeping up the happy grin. It's not that I'm unhappy—honestly, I feel like I could float I'm so excited—but standing here isn't where I want to be.

Moria saunters over, drink in hand, and shoos away the approaching fae. "Give our victor some air." She winks at me before coming to stand before us, close enough that one might assume she converses with us, though she doesn't say a word before turning back to the line of fae. "It's time for Wren to celebrate her victory and enjoy this night."

The assembled fae let out a groan, and I do too, though for completely different reasons. This is the reprieve I've been waiting for. Appropriate that it comes from Moria so the king isn't the one turning his people away. In fact, that's probably why we've been standing here so long. The more he can project the appearance of a contented monarch who is not worried about impending war or anything other than celebrating the champion of the games, the more the fae might just believe it.

"Can I escort you somewhere more relaxing?" Sigurd offers me his arm, eyes dancing with mirth as they coast across my form.

The look alone makes it hard to breathe again. Suddenly, I'm grateful that much of his attention had been on conversing with the endless line of fae this evening. If I'd had to see this expression all night, I'd have faked a swoon again, if only so he could carry me off and make good on all the unspoken promises dancing in his blue eyes.

I slide my arm through his, savoring the warmth of his body and the way it sends a tingle under my skin. "Yes, please."

I look back once over my shoulder, just enough to catch Moria's eye.

Thank you, I mouth.

She winks again before going to rejoin Hawke and Mark where they converse with a few other fae in an open tent full of plush chairs, pillows, and the coziest looking blankets I've ever seen.

Maybe Sigurd has something similar in mind for us, but he leads us away from the area we've been occupying and along a wide pathway through the festivity. Some spaces are left open for dancing, gathering, and games. Others are spotted with tables and chairs or other more elaborate resting places like the one Hawke and Mark occupied. Still other sections are full of tents, these with walls, presumably for when the fae have had their fill of partying and need a place to rest for the evening.

"It's like a giant campsite," I remark as we pass one.

"It is," Sigurd agrees. "It's a tradition that goes back generations. On this night, everyone is invited to celebrate their fill. Some will barely be able to stand by the time the morning light crests the mountains, and many cannot simply shift themselves home. Rather, it's tradition to stay on the celebration grounds."

"Even for royals?" I arch a brow at him.

He grins down at me. "Yes. Thankfully we have a tent all to ourselves this night."

My cheeks heat. When I promised to stay with him tonight, to be his, I had no idea that meant in a tent, during a celebration no less.

"I hope it's private," I mutter.

Deep laughter rumbles in his chest. "I had the tent walls spelled."

Of course he did.

"So presumptuous of you," I say.

"Can I not be hopeful?" he teases, only adding to the moisture building between my legs.

We pass many other fae in our walk, but all of them give us respectful space. Many bow to their king. Many more whisper after we pass—at least, it's whispers to my ears, but the various amused expressions that cross Sigurd's face tell me he can hear much more.

"Do I want to know what they're saying about me?" I ask.

"Good things," he promises. "Most are more surprised at me."

"Oh? And what would you normally be doing on this night?"

"Drinking," he says plainly. "And retiring to my tent as soon as I reasonably can."

That, I did not expect. He hasn't touched a drop of anything tonight that I've seen. "You're not drinking tonight."

"No." Sigurd halts, turning to face me. He cups my cheek, his fingertips ghosting across my skin in a way that makes all thoughts vanish. "I don't want a drink to cloud even a moment of this night."

I blink at him, waiting for him to close the distance between us and kiss me. I lean in—

He drops his hand and resumes our stroll. "Just ahead. This one is ours."

I'm still regaining my senses as we approach what's arguably one of the biggest tents I've seen this evening. It stands a respectful distance from the others—thank goodness, spells or not—and is surrounded by several guards with the eagle crest emblazoned on their breast plate.

A king takes no chances, not even during a celebration. At least no drunk revelers will be stumbling into our tent.

Our tent.

The thought flows through me with a shiver as Sigurd acknowlededges his guards and leads me inside. This tent puts the others I've glimpsed to shame. Rich carpets line the expansive floors. Sitting areas are arranged with chairs, low tables, and heaps of pillows. One table is laid with a display of various food items, whose scents make my mouth water, even if I can't quite place what they are.

Sigurd mentioned the fae sleep here during the festival, yet the sight of the massive bed still steals the air from my lungs. The mattress is low to the ground and piled with lush coverings and still more pillows. The absurdity of them all sparks a fit of giggles I can't fully contain.

"Is it not to your liking?" Sigurd asks, drawing me closer.

"It's—" Ridiculous. "It's so much for just one night."

He shrugs as if it's nothing and releases me. But only a fool would call any of this modest.

Sigurd wanders toward the other object in the room that I couldn't fail to see—a large copper tub that might as well be a hot tub for its sheer size. "In case you wanted to bathe or relax."

A small tendril of steam floats up into the otherwise cool air. Maybe that's why we had to stay and greet the fae for so long, so they could prepare this room.

There are no curtains around the tub, nothing to shield the bather from the rest of the room. A sprig of modesty tries to prod me into embarrassment, but then I remember why we're here, what I promised, what I *want*. To say nothing of the way Sigurd made me feel when we stayed at his house above the lake.

I bathed before the final competition, one that didn't require any exertion. And though I'm eager to scrub away the touch of the various fae who took my hand in theirs as part of their odd fae handshake after my victory, it's not the reason I bite my bottom lip at the idea of sliding into that tub.

It's time to make good on my promise. Almost.

"You know," I say, giving Sigurd a meaningful look. "Maybe I could use a bath after all."

CHAPTER 35

S IGURD GOES STILL, EYES wide, as I pull my shirt over my head and toss it away. The instant effect I have on him draws a grin to my lips, particularly as I kick off my boots and shed my pants. Clad only in delightfully comfortable fae underthings that leaves little to the imagination, I stride across the room to join him.

He rakes a hand down his face. "So easily you undo me."

That's the idea. The cool air of the room tickles my flushed skin as I halt in front of him. The warmth from the tub at my side tempts me, urging me to sink into it, but it's less appealing than the man in front of me who looks like he might devour me at any moment.

But he hasn't touched me. A pity.

I trail my hand down his chest, savoring the way his muscles go rigid beneath his clothes. "I thought you liked me filthy?"

His chest rumbles under my touch, something akin to a groan slipping from his lips. "I like you however you are."

"Good. Wouldn't want to spoil things by taking advantage of the bath." I turn and give him my back. "A little help?"

I don't actually need his help undoing the barely-there clasp that holds this bra in place, but I want him to undress me. I want to feel his hands on my skin. I squirm in anticipation, holding my breath, before he finally rewards me with the touch I crave, sending a delicious sigh throughout my body.

Sigurd is absolutely silent as he works. I can't even hear him breathe. I don't dare look back at him for fear of disrupting the delicious tingling low in my core or, worse, igniting an inferno that makes things spiral out of control too fast.

I want him, but I want to linger in this moment, to enjoy this thing that's as much a victory as winning the competition.

My heart gives a little jolt as the clasp pops free, and then he's moving the straps down my arms, taking his time coasting his palms along my bare skin.

When the bra falls to the floor, I finally turn.

The bright glow of his eyes makes my knees go weak. They're a tell, stronger than anything else, how much he's affected by this simple touch.

"A little help with the rest?" I glance down then back up at him.

Sigurd rewards me with a devastating grin. "My champion is needy this evening."

At first, I think the comment a dismissal, until he drops to one knee. He glances up at me, and the sight of a king on his knees, staring at me like I'm his world, has me gripping the edge of the tub for support. I gasp as he leans in, placing a kiss on my stomach. His hair tickles my skin, the sensation so much more intense than it should be. Another kiss follows the first, this one right on the hem of my underthings.

"Sigurd." I gasp his name, my free hand slipping through his hair.

Just when I think he might rip them off with his teeth, he pulls back and stares up at me once more. His gaze never leaves mine as he grips my underwear and tugs it down. His hot breaths ghost across my skin, but he doesn't look at the sight he slowly reveals, just my face—just me.

I step out of my underwear on shaking legs, unsure of what comes next. I had planned to bathe, truly, or at least enjoy the warm water, but all I really want right now is to peel his clothes off and lead him to the bed.

Before I can give in to that temptation, I step into the tub, intentionally baring myself to him in the process.

Sigurd growls as he rises to loom above me where I sink into the almost too-hot water.

The water is clear. He can see everything. But I don't bother to shield myself from view or pull my hair around me. Instead, I blink innocently up at him.

"There's plenty of room for two." In fact, the tub feels oddly empty with just me.

"Now, who would turn down that invitation?" He sheds his clothing one piece at a time, giving me a show that I eagerly drink in. Every inch of skin he reveals increases my need. It's so tempting to ask him to hurry it up already, but I hold myself still, admiring the view. The scars on his body entice me, and I can't wait to trace them once he joins me.

I've seen him bared to me before, taken him in my mouth and savored each ridge and line of his body. Even so, my throat goes dry as he sheds the last of his clothes.

He's glorious, a work of art, and I will never tire of this sight.

Sigurd takes the other end of the tub. Despite its size, he manages to fill it up, one arm draped over either side as he stares at me across the water.

He crooks his fingers. "Come here, Wren."

As if I would say no. I go to my knees and make my way through the water as gracefully as I can muster. I'm barely halfway when he reaches out like a viper, grabs my waist, and hauls me into his lap. I gasp as we slide together, my knees on either side of him, his manhood prodding my lower stomach. His fingers trail down my side before cupping my backside in his palm and urging me closer. I grind against him in the process, the planes of his chest teasing my nipples at the water's edge.

"Not yet." He squeezes my ass, almost like a warning, and I still. "I do believe we were bathing first."

"You're that eager for me to wash you?" I flick water at him in return, earning a wicked grin.

"I've fantasied about it more than I'd like to admit." He reaches for the little table near the rim of the tub and grabs a vial of something blue. "Though as much as I'd enjoy that, I think I'd enjoy washing you even more."

He pops the stopper, and I'd swear the scent alone transports me to the beach, a place I haven't been in years, and never with company this sexy.

"Do all victors get pampered this way?" I ask.

Sigurd laughs, pouring some of the substance into his hand before rubbing his palms together to form a bubbling lather. "Not by me."

He starts tame, washing my arms, my sides, and seeming to carefully avoid the more sensitive regions of my body that his gaze tends to linger on. When he tells me to turn around, I can't help the little pout before I twist to give him my back.

Sigurd is methodical in his approach. He takes his time soaping my hair, using his fingers to massage my scalp and remove errant tangles. I don't protest when he tips me back to wash out the soap, even though I catch only the barest glimpse of his focused expression. The way he washes my back, using his thumbs to soothe the tense knots in my muscles, earns a groan of delight that's in no way sexual but just as satisfying. I can't help but relax into the warmth of the moment and the deft touch of his hands. If I didn't know better, I'd say he was trying to soothe me into a restful sleep.

I lean back against his chest as his arms come around to wash my front again. The slick heat of his skin against my own is a delight, one I'd happily rest against for hours if not for the clock ticking in the back of my mind, reminding me that this night can't last forever, no matter how I may want it to. I'm about to protest the lack of certain attentions when he cups both breasts in his rough palms, and I jolt against him. Whatever edge of sleepiness he coerced my body into vanishes instantly.

"Do you like that, Wren?" His thumbs make broad, soapy circles, coasting over my nipples with each swoop.

"Y-yes." My nerve endings come alive, urging me to lean into his touch. Slickness builds between my legs that has nothing to do with the bath water.

He continues the touch under the guise of cleaning, but it's so much more than that—so different from his almost clinical touch thus far. A sigh slips from me as his hands slide away to vanish under the water, but my disappointment doesn't last long. My body stiffens as he palms me between my legs.

"Sigurd." My voice is hoarse. My heart races.

"Do you not want me to touch you here?" He flexes his fingers for emphasis, the tip of one dipping into my opening as he places a kiss on my shoulder.

"Yes, please touch me. I want you to." Now that he's started, I *need* him to. Leaving this tent, his world, without having all of him and giving him all of me? Impossible. I meant what I told him with every ounce of me. I want to be his—in all ways.

He places another kiss at the base of my neck. "Good. Then relax. Enjoy. Let me take care of you."

"But you—" I protest.

"This"—he slides one finger deep into my heat—"is exactly what I want right now."

The firm and insistent stroke of his fingers silences all of my protests about him prioritizing my pleasure over *our* pleasure. All words vanish, as do my thoughts when he adds another digit, stretching me in the most delightful way. Finally, I let my body go loose, my head falling back to his shoulder, as I give myself over to his touch.

"That's it," he croons. His other arm is banded tight around my middle, sealing us together, and it's impossible to miss the hard prod of his erection against my back.

In moments, I'm squirming against him, water sloshing near the side of the tub. His fingers alone would be enough to bring me over the edge, but the slick slide of his palm over my clit is maddening, drawing me toward my orgasm far too soon.

Sigurd takes my earlobe in his sharp teeth, eliciting a little yelp. No sooner does he release it than his lips are there, whispering, "Do you know how I felt when you said you'd be mine?"

My teeth dig into my bottom lip as I shake my head side to side, unable to think of a response, much less form the words.

His deep chuckle echoes into my body, bringing me ever closer to the edge of release. Sigurd grinds his palm hard against me as he thrusts his fingers deep. "You will when you come."

Release barrels into me. I clamp around his fingers, bucking in Sigurd's lap as I moan his name. My fingers dig into his thigh for purchase, anything to steady me as he draws out the waves of my pleasure with his continued slow thrusts.

I'm still coming down from my release when he rises from the water with me in his arms.

"I didn't get to wash you," I say in breathless protest.

He steps from the tub with ease, dripping all over the carpets. "Do you mind if I'm filthy?"

"No." I circle my arms around his neck, though I've never felt so securely held, despite being soaking wet. "I think I like you filthy."

Sigurd lays me on top of the bed. His gaze rakes my naked, panting form as he says, "Good, so do I."

A needy whimper escapes from me as he crawls onto the bed. I let my tented legs fall open, giving him a view of where I need him. Yes, he just made me come all over his hand, but the release did nothing to dampen my need. If anything, he only made it worse.

"My beautiful Wren." He pushes my thighs even wider as he fits himself between. Sigurd leans over me, bracing himself on one hand to keep his weight off me. With the other, he runs his cock along my folds, making me squirm in anticipation. "I need you to tell me you want me, Wren. Tell me you'll accept my mark."

I'd almost forgotten that part, the reason he wouldn't give me what I wanted before. His mark would be a magical and physical signature on our bodies. Proof of our bond. Something no fae would fail to notice.

"Please," he says, "promise me you want this."

"Yes, Sigurd." I caress his cheek, savoring the way his eyes briefly flutter closed. "I want this. I want to be yours. I want your mark. I want all of you." Now. In the future. I don't know exactly what lies beyond this night, but I promised to come back to him. I *will* come back, no matter how long it takes, and I hope he'll be waiting for me. No matter what though, I know I want him right now. No doubts. No second guesses. "I want you so much I can't stand it. Mark me. Make me yours."

Sigurd notches himself at my entrance, sliding in the barest bit, before he takes my hand in his, lacing our fingers together on the sheets next to my head. His face hovers an inch from mine, heavy breaths mingling, and then he fills me in one sure stroke.

I cry out at the fullness of it, the rightness. At that instant, his eyes blaze as blue as I've ever seen, the bright light basking us in its glow. It fades a bit but doesn't recede as I grip his hand tighter, savoring every point of connection as he moves in a steady rhythm.

"Wren. My Wren," he murmurs, never breaking eye contact.

And then his face is buried in the crook of my neck, planting one kiss after another as some of his weight settles atop me. My free hand tangles in his hair. No matter how eager his movement, I want this to last. I want to hold on until I can't breathe and my mind is numb to everything except the touch of this man—this fae.

My release dances closer, and I move my hips to meet him. He's relentless, but somehow I want more. I *need* more. In my eagerness, my palm brushes over his pointed ear. He moans, thrusting deep and wrenching a shocked cry from my lips.

"Are you—" Sigurd jerks his head back, stilling within me. "Did I—"

His gaze rakes me, but there's nothing to find.

"Fine. I need—" I try to pull his face down to mine as I wiggle under him, but he holds firm.

"I think I know." And then he's flipping us, moving me so quickly I barely have time to register what happened. He slides free in the act, and I whimper at the loss, even as I straddle his abdomen, grinding myself against him.

Not enough. Not near enough.

Then his hands are on my hips, urging me up. "Ride me, Wren. Take what you need."

My lips part in a silent O. I follow his lead, giving him space to position his cock at my entrance once more. But he doesn't move. He holds absolutely still, waiting for me to take control. So I do. Without another thought, I take him in hand and begin to slide down his impressive length. In this position, he fills me so completely I can't help but gasp at the way we fit together, the way it brings every nerve ending in my body to life.

"Good girl." His hands slide up and down my hips and thighs, his thumbs working little circles across my skin as he urges me to move. "I want to watch you as you come all over my cock."

"Filthy fae," I tease as I move on him.

His gaze sweeps over my body, so intense I can almost feel it on my skin. The way he watches me, drinks his fill, is more intoxicating than any whiskey. Pleasure coils tight within me. My motions are no longer my own, given over to pure instinct. Sigurd's fingers find their way to the apex of my thighs to rub against me, and then I'm coming harder than I ever have before. Tears leak out the corner of my eyes. Words flow from my mouth, but I couldn't say what they are.

And then his arms are around me, cradling me on the sheets as he thrusts into my warmth, drawing out the last of my release and following me himself. My name is a hoarse cry on his lips, our bodies a tangle of damp limbs and wet hair.

Something cool tingles across the skin of my hip, so different from the inferno still raging through my core or the warmth of Sigurd's body against mine.

Smooth palms caress my face, pushing away tangled, wet hair. Sigurd stares at me in silent wonder, our heavy breaths mingling. His heart beats so hard I can feel his pulse against my skin as I come back to myself.

"Did you do it?" I ask, still breathless. "Did you mark me?"

Laughter rumbles in his chest as he places his forehead against mine. "You truly have doubt?"

I bite my lip and stare at him sheepishly. "It was my first time with a fae, after all."

His palm coasts down my side, stirring up goosebumps. "I hope I lived up to expectations because I have no intention of sharing."

"More than," I promise.

"Would you like to see it?" His brows lift.

At my nod, he gently disentangles us and sits on the bed, helping me to do the same.

I'm not even fully upright before the sight of it snares my full attention, but the mark I see is on him, not me. Hesitantly, I reach out tracing my fingers over the soaring eagle emblazoned on his hip. It's stunning—a work of art that even the most renowned tattoo artist would be proud of.

"You have one too," he says.

His touch on my hip draws my eye to the matching mark on my skin, just as beautiful and perfect as his. It's right where I felt the cool tingle moments ago. It must have been the magic of the thing settling into place upon my skin.

"What do you think?" His look is suddenly guarded, his body rigid, as if I might declare it a disaster. This matters to him, more than just sex and a night of pleasure. Something about this means the world.

I smile. "It's perfect."

"You don't regret this tie to me?"

I cross the space between us and place a gentle kiss on his lips. "Never."

"Good." He pulls me into his arms and back down onto the bed.

It'd be so easy to close my eyes and fall asleep in the safety of his arms but not yet.

"Maybe we should return to the bath?" I suggest, if only to clean up.

Sigurd cups my backside, pulling me tight against him so I feel his length start to harden once more. "Soon, but not yet."

I raise my brows and give him a meaningful look. "You really are quite powerful, aren't you?"

His chest rumbles with laughter. "And yours, Wren. All yours."

CHAPTER 36

I'VE STARTED TO DRIFT off a few times, but something always jolts me awake. My body is still filled with languid contentment from making love to Sigurd...more than once. His arm around me has me feeling as safe and cherished as I ever have. In fact, a large part of me never wants this moment to end.

But that's not the thought that keeps creeping in and waking me up.

I have to leave soon. Every moment I delay is another that Gran is without me, and a large part of me is terrified of what I'll find when I return. She probably thinks I'm dead or kidnapped or something—that's assuming this whole thing didn't give her a heart attack, leaving her in the hospital or worse. It's a possibility, and just the thought of it makes me ill enough not to be able to enjoy the afterglow of this night the way I should.

Carefully, as not to disturb the sleeping fae king, I slide out from under his arm and across the sheets. He's peaceful in sleep, chest rising and falling in an even rhythm. The hint of a smile lingers on his kiss-flushed lips, and his dark hair is tousled on the pillow. The sight stirs up desire deep within my core, and I nearly wake him up to resume our previous activities.

But even kings need to rest.

I'm tired too. I can feel it in my body urging me to slip back down into the sheets and curl up against Sigurd's chest, but my mind simply won't be quiet yet.

I don my clothes, pull back my still-damp hair, and slip out of the tent into the night. Immediately, sound hits me. It was quiet within, but outside, the party carries on late into the night with plenty of laughter, conversation, and music still filling the air. Sigurd wasn't kidding about the soundproofing magic. A darn good thing too after everything we did in there. My cheeks flush a little warmer against the cool night air.

Guards linger nearby, no doubt keeping a close watch on their king. They eye me with interest, their focus glued to every step I take.

"Lady Wren." One steps forward into my path and gives a slight bow. "How may we assist you?"

The formality of it all has me shifting in my boots and standing a little straighter. The guards haven't been so focused on me the whole time I've been here, but then, I was always in a game or with a member of royalty. Not to mention, that was before I won the games or bore their king's mark. My face heats as I remember the symbol now emblazoned on my hip, one he said fae would feel, even if they could not see it.

"I just wanted some air for a moment." *Alone.* If these guys insist on trailing beside me the whole time, there's no way I'm going to be able to sort myself out.

He nods, seeming to understand. "An audience was requested with you, but we said you were not to be disturbed. However, they chose to wait, if you'd see them?"

Who? My brows knit together. I half expect Uncle Mark or even Moria, but that's not who I spy sitting on a bench some yards away when the guard moves to the side and gestures in his direction.

"Galen," I whisper. He's too far away to hear me. He sits with his face in his hands, possibly half asleep. He ought to be, given how late it is. I turn to the guard. "I'll speak to him now, please."

The guard leads me over to where Galen sits. He spots me halfway here and rises to his feet. Not asleep after all, though the worn look on his face paints him as far from rested.

"Thank you," I say to the guard. "I'll be fine with my friend."

He nods and moves a distance away, though it's clear I'm still his focus—the focus of several of the guards stationed outside Sigurd's tent.

Once we have the smallest bit of privacy, I say, "I thought you'd have left by now."

Sigurd granted his wish. Galen is free of his oath. He could have left that very moment, off to the woman he was so desperate to get back to, but he hadn't. Selfishly, I'm glad.

"I wanted to see you again first," he says.

That brings a smile to my lips. I guess I'm not the only one who felt that way.

"Walk with me?" He offers his arm like some kind of historical gentleman, and I take it.

"Please," I say. Anything to be rid of the feeling of multiple people's attention glued to me, though even a walk may not help that. I wouldn't put it past them to follow along behind us like dutiful chaperones. Still, I do my best to block them out and focus on Galen. This may be our last time together—at least for a while—and I won't let others ruin it.

"He marked you," Galen grates out.

So much for not ruining the moment.

"It was mutual." Why deny it? Besides, if I understand this fae magic correctly, it had to be a mutual decision for the mark to form and appear.

"So you won't be leaving after all?" Galen says. "You win the tournament for your freedom and then decide to stay?"

The words cut deep. He got his wish and so did the others, yet his comment still holds an edge of betrayal, one that demands I defend myself. "No, I still plan to return home. In the morning, in fact."

This surprises him enough that he stumbles slightly as we walk.

I don't fight the satisfied smirk rising to my lips. "My family needs me. That hasn't changed. I plan to go home and care for them, see that they're well."

"And then?" he prompts, as if he knows there's more.

I swallow against the sudden insecurity holding my tongue. "I want to come back" I shrug, but indifference is the last thing I'm feeling. It's one of the reasons I couldn't sleep. "Maybe go back and forth for a while."

"I see."

Silence stretches for a minute before he finally speaks again.

"Thank you, Wren, for asking for our wishes." Galen rewards me with a smile, though it doesn't quite reach his eyes.

"It's nothing," I say. Truly, I'm ashamed I didn't ask it for him sooner.

"It's so much more than that," he says. "You had such confidence that the king would listen to your request, but I still doubted it. I thought, at best, it might be a deception, something to make it seem like my oath was revoked but holding me here just the same. But it's not. I'm truly free." The last part is so quiet it's almost swallowed up by the sounds of the night.

Not too far away, music blares into the darkness, accompanied by conversation and laughter. A large bonfire and fae balls of light illuminate a clearing where many fae still dance and drink. They weren't kidding about the party lasting until dawn. From the noise all around us, I'd wager more are still awake and celebrating than have returned home or retired to tents on the celebration grounds. At least the area where we are is devoid of partiers, likely some kind of deference to their king who slumbers nearby.

"I'm happy for you," I say. It's true, even though it stings that he doubted Sigurd so much. "You can return to Sylvie."

His whole countenance brightens at the mention of her name. He reaches up to rub the little golden leaf dangling from an ear. But the joy vanishes as quickly as it came, and he drops his hand.

"If she'll have me. If any of them will after what I've done." He releases me, putting space between us where we've stopped walking on a grassy pathway.

My gaze wanders, unable to stand amid his sorrow. The distance between us might as well be so much more. A quiet, dark tent blocks the view of the guards, but I'm sure they're nearby. With fae hearing, they're probably listening in, or trying to.

"Forgiveness can take time," I say, just above a whisper. "It may not be immediate, but once they hear your story, it may come sooner than you expect." He huffs air through his nose, and I press on, forcing myself to stare at him. "My Uncle Mark, Hawke's mate, left my family. Just up and disappeared one day. We didn't know why or where he'd gone or even if he was alive."

This revelation seems to catch Galen off guard. He shifts on his feet, various emotions flickering across his face that I can't quite make out in the dim light.

"It's true," I continue. "I was so angry with him for years for leaving like that. But I found him here. I heard his story. It doesn't make what he did right, but I understand his side of it, why he did what he did. If a few conversations can help overcome years of hurt and pain, then I'm sure they can do the same for you."

"Perhaps," he muses, staring off toward the nearest group of partiers. "But they'll have to listen to me first."

True. In other circumstances, I'm not sure I would have heard Uncle Mark out.

Something catches my attention from the corner of my eye. A flash of pink hair slipping between two tents not terribly far away. My skin goes clammy, and I suddenly wish I hadn't left the tent.

"Galen." I tug his sleeve. "Did you see that?" I gesture in the direction of the movement.

"See what?"

"I thought I saw someone." Though no matter how I stare, I don't see them again, nor anything else.

Maybe it was a trick of my mind, but I can't shake it. With all the excitement and revelations of the last few days, I'd forgotten about the Unseelie woman. I should have told Sigurd about her. I should have told him long ago. My heart picks up its pace, hammering against my ribs. I never learned exactly what she wanted, but it seemed to involve me winning the games. I have. If she has some kind of plan, I've played right into it without even considering the consequences.

"I should go back. It's late." I turn back toward Sigurd's tent.

But Galen stops me with a soft touch on my arm. "Wait."

I turn to him, waiting patiently as he asked, even though my breaths are coming short and quick.

"You truly think betrayal can be forgiven?" he asks.

His eyes are wide, filled with so much emotion that it's pouring out of him, visible even in the night. The corners of his eyes even seem to give off a soft, bluish-green glow.

"Yes, I truly do."

He nods, visibly swallowing. "Good." He takes my hand in his, squeezing almost painfully. "Because I am so sorry about this, Wren."

CHAPTER 37

I JERK BACK AND open my mouth to speak, but it's too late. His grip is like iron. The world around us already bends and warps, the air around me constricting and drawing me back to Galen. This shift takes a long time, enough for nausea to take hold and for me to scream at myself about being an idiot.

I thought I had to worry about the Unseelie, but instead, it was my friend who led me into the dark to betray me.

Will Sigurd even know what happened? Or will he think I chose to leave him? I planned to return home, but somehow, I know this is far from the destination I had in mind and not at all how I planned to leave things with the man I'm falling in love with.

I'm in love with him.

No sooner has that thought screamed through my brain than the spinning stops, and I nearly fall to the ground. But Galen has me, his grip as absolute as before.

"How dare—" I stumble, the rest of my angry outburst ending in a grimace.

"You'll be safe. The Court of the Forest will get you home."

"He'll come for me." It's a hope more than a certainty, but humans are not bound by fae laws of truth.

Galen grimaces. "I know."

At that, my heart gives a tiny leap. He's certain of it. "Then why?" Why risk angering the king who just freed him?

"Proof of my loyalty to the Forest," Galen says.

So I'm a pawn. A tool. So much for me thinking him my friend. Tears prickle the corner of my eyes anyway. At the moment, he's the last person I should be sad over, but it hurts all the same.

"If I give them you, the King of Air's marked mate, they'll have to listen to me."

I can't help but wonder if he planned this all along or if it was a spur-of-the-moment thing. Was it all a lie? Everything? I can't make the questions take shape on my tongue.

Galen grits his teeth as he steps forward, almost like he's pushing against some invisible barrier. It's a slow tread with me tugged behind him like a dead weight. A quick glance at the ground shows a literal line of sorts between the sparse, rocky ground we stand on and the verdant grasses beyond looming at the edge of a thick forest. He gives a groan, and whatever was holding him back releases. He stumbles forward. I'm pulled after him into the thick grass.

All at once, the air is different. What was almost devoid of scent now is full of life, of leaves and loam and floral notes. Without being told, I know we've passed into the Court of the Forest. It's the only thing that makes sense.

He's quiet for a minute, almost like he's waiting for something. In my anger, I have no words for him. All efforts to free myself from his grip are unsuccessful.

"Be still, Wren," Galen says. "I won't hurt you."

I snort and jerk against his hold even harder. As if he hasn't already caused me a different sort of pain.

"You," the female voice cuts through night.

"Sylvie." Galen turns us, finding her unerringly in the night, where she looms at the edge of the tree line.

I gasp, catching sight of the long sword held at the ready and the hard look on her face, barely visible in the moonlight. This woman, the woman he loves, is the spitting image of a fierce warrior. Though short by fae standards, she holds herself tall, her chin raised and proud, her blond hair pulled back behind her head, displaying her pointed ears as she stalks toward us.

Galen releases my hand and takes a half step in front of me as if to shield me from Sylvie. Suddenly, I'm far less certain about his promise of hospitality from this court.

"What are you doing here?" she demands.

"I'm free of my oaths to Air. I come to pledge myself to the Forest—to you."

That draws Sylvie to a sudden halt a dozen or so feet away from us. Meanwhile, I can't help but glance this way and that, trying to gain my bearings. We're at the edge of the Court of the Forest for sure, but the land we entered from is something else—not Air, I don't think. It looks sick, almost dead, with barren stretches of nothingness pocked with the twisted and gnarled remains of old trees. Everything in me says to run, but to where? To say nothing of the fact that they'd catch me in a heartbeat.

"Who is she?" Sylvie looks past Galen, straight at me, all but pinning me in place with her sharp gaze. "I feel..." Her gaze dips to my hip, to Sigurd's mark, though my clothing hides it.

"She bears Sigurd's mark," Galen replies.

I can't help but shift on my feet, my cheeks heating. *Thanks for talking about me like I'm not even here.*

Sylvie swears. "One consort to repent for the other?"

Galen merely nods. "She wishes to return to the human realm."

Her expression sours. "Provoking Sigurd will not help the Forest."

No kidding.

"You bring war to us. You—" Her mouth gapes open, whatever she planned to say lost in that void.

There's no time to wonder why before a hand clamps over my mouth, and I'm jerked back against a solid form. It's not Sigurd. I know that instantly. He'd never be so rough with me—not after what we've shared. The smell is wrong. The feel is wrong, as are the claws that prick against my skin.

"Fools."

The instant she speaks, I recognize the voice—the Unseelie woman.

Galen whirls, wide eyed. "Katiya."

"How?" Sylvie raises her sword like she may charge, but a cluck of the woman's tongue stills her movements.

Katiya's clawed fingers drum on my cheek in warning. "Thank you for the Air king's mate."

My stomach drops just before I register the warping of the air around us. Galen lunges forward, but it's too late. We're gone, traveling somewhere else. The shift is short. Suddenly, we're in what looks to be the same forest but a different spot—it's hard to tell, though, with the world spinning around me. Katiya releases me, and I stumble forward.

"Why?" I cry. It's all I can think to ask.

She shrugs one lithe shoulder, her pink hair swaying. "We need you."

"We?"

The question has barely left my lips before she lashes out, grabbing me once more and shifting us again. We land in a new spot, and once again, she lets me go, almost like a cat toying with a mouse. Fitting, given the cat ears atop her head and the strange vertical pupils of her eyes.

"The Unseelie," she says, picking up the conversation as if shifting were as easy as taking a step. For her, maybe it is.

She grabs me again, moving us a third time.

"You're taking me to them?" I confirm when I can speak again.

Katiya nods. "As soon as I finish leaving bait for your king to follow."

I swallow the hard lump in my throat. Bait has to be me. But so far, she hasn't left anything behind.

Her nose twitches as she takes me in. "You bear his mark." A fierce grin spreads across her face, pointed fangs peeking free. "He'll feel you here and come, but you'll be gone by then."

"You're trying to start a war between Forest and Air."

"Partially."

I'm too slow to move before she latches onto my arm and shifts us again.

When she releases me this time, I wobble from dizziness and fall to one knee. "He'll just follow me wherever you take me. Why this nonsense?"

"He can't follow me, little human." She circles around me, her tail flicking behind her. "I'm a null. A shield to my brother's sword. If I am touching you"—she takes my hand in hers, almost gently—"he won't feel you at all. Almost like you don't exist."

If I wasn't already kneeling, I'd have swayed on my feet. "That's why no one noticed you in the Court of Air, or the protection spell you placed on me that one time."

"Smart little thing," she says. "Enough. My brother waits."

This time, the shift is slower, more jerky and awkward, and I know wherever the magic brings us, I'm not going to like it.

CHAPTER 38

T HE WORLD FINALLY STOPS spinning around us. I'd have fallen again if not for Katiya's solid grip. She's not letting go, not this time. Shifting at all is a horrible feeling. Shifting so many times in a row is far worse, like being stuck on a rollercoaster that I can't get off of.

I squint against a spill of bright light flickering in front of me. My vision clears quickly, revealing rough-hewn rock walls on either side of the little pathway we stand on, almost like we landed in a narrow gorge. I glance up, expecting a roof, but beyond the narrowing of the walls high above us looms a starlit sky.

"Come along." Katiya gives my arm a gentle yet insistent tug.

My heart tries to climb into my throat as we traipse the narrow pathway. I have no idea what waits ahead, though the whisper of conversation growing louder with every step indicates we aren't alone. Somehow, I know we aren't in the forest anymore, nor anywhere near Sigurd. This is somewhere new—the Unseelie's home, if I had to guess. If Katiya is to be believed, Sigurd won't know where I am either.

The sides of the gorge open into a wide space. Everything in me screams to run, but Katiya's tight grip pulls me forward toward the cluster of Unseelie lingering near a large stone chair—a throne.

The man sitting atop it grabs my attention instantly, especially as he demands silence with nothing more than a raise of his hand. Authority clings to him like a second skin, radiating power that even I can sense. But the most peculiar thing is his look. His hair so pale it may be white and hangs loose past his shoulders, contrasting with the black of his clothes and the golden tan of his skin. This has to be Katiya's brother because they share the same set of cat ears atop their head. If he has a tail, I can't see it yet.

Other fae stand nearby, just as strong and sculpted as their leader, each bearing animalistic traits that boggle the mind. One, however, is more massive than the rest, with rams' horns curling back on his head, a snarl on his features, and a glint in his eye that says he'd love to eat me alive.

"You got her," the pale-haired man speaks from atop his throne. His voice isn't the sharp, hissing thing I imagined—nothing like his sister's. It's deep and rich, the kind that resonates through a person and slips into their memories, only to play itself over and over again. "Were you seen? Do they know it was you?"

Katiya shoves me forward, sending me stumbling to a stop before this intimidating group. Despite my best efforts, I can't quite hide the quiver in my limbs. But she let me go. Maybe it's an error, or maybe it's a trap, hoping Sigurd will shift right in here to try and save me. Despite my worry for him, I can't deny the bit of hope burning in my chest that he'll appear and take me away from here.

"There was a complication, but I believe I used it to our advantage," Katiya says, circling around me. The other fae move out of her way as she stalks toward the throne and leans on the armrest at her brother's side. "Another fae had already stolen her to deliver her to the Court of the Forest," she says smugly. Her brother merely raises his brows, waiting for her to continue. "I took her from him and left a trail of her presence through the Court of the Forest. With any luck, the Air king will take the bait and rush in to save her."

Poor Galen. My chest grows tight. I'm still pissed that he would dare to use me as a pawn for his advantage, but this is the very opposite of what he planned. At this rate, he truly will have started a war, angering both sides, instead of receiving the forgiveness he longed for.

"They are impulsive, these Seelie monarchs," her brother says, his gaze coasting across me.

Katiya smirks. "Don't look so hopeful," she says to me. "I've created wards around this place. He won't feel you here. He won't feel any of us. Most likely, your king is already invading the Forest searching for you."

The little spark of hope I cling to dies a stuttering death. The fae laughter that follows it chips away at the last of my resolve. It's almost like they want to see me suffer, though I haven't met a one of them before except Katiya.

"Excellent!" The biggest fae bellows in a grating voice like tumbling rocks. "Let them destroy one another, and we shall conquer the ashes."

I might be sick right on their floor. They're right. Sigurd already holds a grudge against the Court of the Forest. If he thinks they took me, he'll be his impulsive, reckless self and light the kindling that's been building between the courts. And the Court of the Forest needs little incentive to retaliate. From all I've heard, they're just waiting for the right moment, and this could well be it.

Despite the dark humor of these Unseelie, one person isn't laughing. Katiya's brother rises from his throne, and the laughter dwindles. He does have a tail, just as pale as his hair. It flicks to one side of his legs. A wicked-looking scabbard hangs from his other hip.

I force myself to hold still and face him down rather than run or cower like the voice in my head is screaming at me to do. Or break apart like my heart is right now.

Sigurd could die. Moria. Hawke. Galen. Any of them.

And I'm just stuck here, a pawn in this game of courts. Worse, what if Sigurd thinks I left on purpose? Just snuck out in the night after all that we shared? I twist my hands behind my back, if only to hide their shaking.

"You bear the King of Air's mark," the pale-haired Unseelie says.

It's not a question, but I give a short, jerking nod all the same.

"Yet my sister says you wished to be free of him?" His stare is so penetrating he may well be looking into my soul. "That he bound you against your will?"

When I don't respond, he lifts one pale brow.

I swallow the thickness in my throat and blink away the tears burning to be free at the corners of my eyes. "He did. I did. But things...changed." They changed more than I would have ever imagined. "I still want to go home," I add, filling my voice with a desperate plea to pull at any heart-strings this male may have. "I care for my grandmother. She's old and ill. She needs me. I cannot stay here."

But I want to come back. I planned to. I *promised* to. That won't help me here though.

His impassive features give away nothing, but his gaze dips for the briefest moment.

"Just spill her blood and be done with it," the bulky one grumbles.

"What!" I squeak. This time, I do step back, fear moving my body away from this monster before me.

The pale-haired man raises his hand toward me. A sign of peace? "You're too important to kill," he says quickly before turning to look back at the gathered fae. "And I don't abide mistreatment of humans."

Katiya hisses at the bulky fae, as if adding her own condemnation to her brother's words.

The other fae grumble and go silent. I scowl at these brutes who think kidnapping me and using me as bait wasn't mistreatment enough.

"You're here for two purposes. One, you know. The other..." He pulls the sword from its scabbard.

I take another step back on instinct. Fae supposedly can't lie, but maybe that doesn't extend to the Unseelie. His actions sure don't line up with his words.

"Do you know what this is?" he asks, holding the sword aloft so it catches the light.

"A sword," I answer. A beautiful one at that, polished to a shine, its blade decorated with some kind of intricate designs I'm not close enough to make out. A musical hum seems to emanate from it, so soft it might be some trick of my sleep-deprived mind.

The corner of his lips twist up on one side. "Indeed. It's quite ancient." He twists it this way and that, admiring the blade. "Crafted by Áine herself, or so the legends say."

The name pulls at my memories. An ancient fae queen?

"But it's lost its power." He lowers the blade.

"What does that have to do with me?" I ask.

"We found some ruins recently." He narrows the space between us. "In them were ancient carvings, one about the sword. It's believed the blood of a marked human can help revive it."

My blood.

"Give me your hand." He offers his.

I stare at it, warring with my decision. Really, there's no choice. I doubt I could escape if I tried.

"Just a cut. I'll make it quick."

Katiya appears at his side, a bundle of something in her hands. At my look, she says, "To heal the wound."

"I thought you didn't like mistreatment of humans," I say to her brother.

He frowns. "I don't."

Even so, he flexes his fingers, beckoning me.

Reluctantly, I stretch out my arm. He grabs it with his calloused hand and positions it just so, palm out toward him. I grit my teeth and pinch my eyes closed, prepared for the worse.

I cry out as the blade slides the sensitive skin of my palm. It's the worst fire, blinding and sharp. I try to jerk away, but he holds me firm, pressing my wounded hand against the flat of the cold blade. I snap my eyes open and stare in horror at the sight, my blood sliding down the metal and some dripping onto the dirt below us.

Just a cut, my butt. He didn't take the whole hand, but sweet baby Jesus, it hurts like heck.

Whenever he decides he has enough, he pulls my hand away and lets it go. Katiya is there, wrapping something around my hand that almost instantly cools the burning pain—thank goodness.

Her brother stares at the bloody blade as if waiting for something to happen. After a moment he orders, "Take her to the cell."

"A cell!" I snap. Not that anyone listens.

"See that she has food, water, blankets. Anything she needs." Then he turns his back and stalks away.

Katiya finishes wrapping a cloth around the wound, sealing in whatever tonic she's applied and stopping the drip of my blood everywhere.

"Come with me," she says, albeit somewhat gently.

"What happens to me now?" I can't help but ask as she leads me away toward another narrow pathway.

"Whatever my brother decides."

He's not even looking at me. I might as well not even exist anymore. If he leaves me to rot in this horrible place, I'll never forgive myself for leaving Sigurd's bed.

CHAPTER 39

T HIS IS A NIGHTMARE. A prison so much worse than the bond I
worked so hard to free myself of.

I'm not sure how much time has passed since Katiya led me into
this cell and locked the door. I fell asleep at some point in a heap of
blankets on the floor. Exhaustion—physical and emotional—had
finally won out.

Light doesn't reach me here, if it reaches the land of the Unseelie at all. At some point while I slept, a tray of food and water
were left in my cell, though I haven't been able to muster much
of an appetite for the strange-looking brown fare. The food is as
unappealing as the rest of this place.

I've always thought of cells as damp and musty places, but this
one is dry and hard, the walls made of solid stone other than the
rough metal bars running from floor to ceiling on one narrow side.
A few of them make up the door, but it's locked.

My thoughts are even more turbulent than the night before, and
being trapped alone with them might be the worst punishment of
all. Over and over again, I see Sigurd racing into battle, Moria at his
side, an army at their backs. But their foe is monstrous, the battle
ferocious, and the result...

I shudder, shutting down the dark vision.

I'm not sure which taunting outcome in my head is worse:
Sigurd thinking I left of my own accord and following the trail
Katiya left to the Court of the Forest, sparking war there. Or him
somehow figuring out what happened and attacking the Unseelie.

Though there's another part of me that wonders if neither thing happened. Maybe he thought I left as planned and has done nothing. Maybe he truly doesn't know I was taken. Or if he does, maybe it's not worth risking a war. Heck, he wouldn't consider canceling the games to let me drink and reverse our bond at the risk of making his people unhappy. So many times, I accused him of being petty, holding a grudge, and risking his court foolishly. Maybe he finally listened and has decided I'm not worth the trouble despite the night we shared.

He never claimed to love you, the rational part of my mind taunts me.

Nor did I share the true depth of my feelings for him.

I pull up the hem of my shirt to gaze at the edge of his mark—our mark—where it climbs up my skin above my pants. I trace my fingers along it for the hundredth time, confirming it's still there. Maybe it's proof that Sigurd lives. I hope it is.

"He'd be a fool to risk himself or his court for me," I whisper.

"Perhaps."

I scream and lurch backward as a shadowed figure detaches from the wall and stalks into the puddle of torchlight outside my cell. My racing heart doesn't slow as I recognize Katiya's brother, that nasty sword still strapped to his side, if anything, it intensifies. His clothing has changed. Dark armor hugs his form, accenting the power of his build. Give him a hood, and he could be my executioner come to finish what he started the day before.

"But I still expected him to," he says, completely nonplussed by my reaction.

I scoot back further, my back coming against the rough stone wall. Somehow, the prick of stone through my clothes centers me. His words spark a traitorous bit of hope.

"Then he's..." I dare not say it.

"Alive?" He kneels before the cell bars. "I suspect as much."

Alive, he's alive! Relief shivers under my skin, all hot and cold at once. The worst of my imaginings did not come to pass.

"Curious that he wouldn't come after his marked human." His gaze narrows. "Did you plot this?"

"What?" I squeak. "How could I possibly plot my own abduction?"

"Hmm." He continues to stare me down, arms braced on his thighs where he balances on the balls of his feet. "And yet my sister reports that you are the first human he's marked, that we are aware of."

Somehow, despite the situation, this comment still brings a blush to my cheeks. After all, it isn't every day that your enemy discusses your sex life like a host on a gossip show.

"I guess I'm not that important and you can just send me back."

"I think not."

"Back to my world?" It's a foolish hope, but I have to try. "You said you don't like humans getting hurt, right? And I'm no use to you here."

He tilts his head, brows scrunching. His eyes widen as if he's finally realized something. "Human lies," he grumbles. "You are quite useful yet."

Dang it.

I need a tactic change, especially before he decides to just walk away and toss out the key, leaving me in this blasted cell forever.

"What's your name?" I ask.

"My name?" He adjusts his stance and sits cross legged on the floor like he might stay a while.

Good thinking, Wren. Good progress.

"Yes. You're holding me captive, and you stole my blood. I think it's only fair you give me your name. I know your sister's, after all."

He lets out a soft grunt in response and glances away. A tingling fear that I've lost him courses through my chest before he glances back at me.

"Speaking of blood, perhaps you'll explain something to me." He grips the hilt of his sword and manages to pull it free, laying the now clean blade across his lap. There's enough space from the bars to my wall that he can't stab me without coming in here, I don't think, but the act makes me uneasy all the same. "Why didn't your blood work?"

"Excuse me?" I say before I can think better of it.

"The blood of a marked human should grant power back to the sword. Your blood did not work."

"That's not my fault." I cross my arms and stare him down. "Maybe you read your instructions wrong."

He raises one brow, a calculating glint in his eye, and for a horrible moment, I feel I've made a terrible mistake and encouraged him to shed more of my blood.

"What's so important about this sword anyway?" I blurt, if only to distract him. Ancient he said, sure, but there has to be more than that.

"You can't feel it? Hear its song?" he asks.

Now that he mentions it, there is a soft hum in the background that wasn't there before. Absently, I nod. It's the same sound I heard when I saw it before. The whispers of a song are much like the one the cauldron sang to me. But its song stopped after I drank from it, becoming little more than this. Maybe they are the same in a way, their power used up and dormant. But the cauldron was said to recharge over time, not through some sacrifice of blood.

"It's the sword of the Unseelie king," he says. "A symbol of our people and source of great power that could lead us on a path back to prosperity."

"Your people don't have a king. Maybe that's why it didn't work."

A sad smile touches his lips, painting him far less fierce than moments before. "They did not for a long time, and it has brought us to ruin. You know that much, but your king's spies have failed to discover much, other than the information we grant them."

"What?" I straighten. Sigurd mentioned spies, but this guy knew?

The look he gives is almost pitying. "Seelie are not good at hiding their tracks in our territory. Of course I know of them. You don't need to try your human lies and deceit on me. Mostly, they have only learned what we want them to, but it seems it's time they know more."

Gooseflesh tingles up my arms. "What do you mean?"

"You asked my name. I am Kallan, and the power of the ancient line has settled on me and become my burden to bear—mine and my sister's. I am the Unseelie king. I am the sword of my people, as my sister is our shield."

It was clear enough when I was brought before him that he was their leader, but king? Of all the things I expected, that was not it. Though it makes a certain sense now. The Unseelie king. My mouth hangs open, any words I could think to respond with lost.

He's Sigurd's enemy—a boogie monster of their stories come to life—and yet he sits across the cell bars from me on a cold stone floor, having a tame conversation with his captive.

"I see you truly did not know," he says.

Finally, I snap my mouth shut. "Why tell me this unless you plan to kill me?"

Kallan huffs air through his nose. "The Seelie need to know that the Unseelie have a king once more. We will no longer cower in a land dead and dying. I will see my people prosper once more, if it takes unto my last breath."

The Unseelie king rises to his feet before shoving the sword back in the scabbard at his side. He turns to leave, and the act urges me up as well. I'm rushing to the bar before he can leave me alone in this place again. The only thing worse than being stuck with the enemy is being trapped alone.

"What does that have to do with me?" I ask.

He glances back at me over one shoulder. The flickering firelight paints him as the king he claims to be—dancing in bright colors over his pale hair and accenting the hard angles of his face with shadows. The cat ears atop his head twitch as his lips twist up at one side. "If taking you will not spark the Seelie into a war with one another, perhaps I can weaken them in another way."

As if on cue, Katiya appears. She's also dressed for battle in armor of dark gray that hugs her more lithe form. Her amused look says she's been listening to much of our conversation.

"What do you plan to do to me?" I can't help but ask.

"To you? I hope little. But we shall see how much the King of Air desires his marked human returned to him."

I bounce on my toes, gripping the bars in my fists. "You're giving me back to him?"

"Giving? No. Bartering? Perhaps."

So I'm to be bait of another type. But it's the best hope I've had since Katiya stole me, and I let that little ember sustain me and sharpen my wit.

Katiya moves to the door, using some quick motion of her hands to disguise how she unlocks it.

Whatever comes next could have vast consequences—for me, for Sigurd, for multiple courts of fae. I have to be prepared. I will not be a liability. Of all the trials I've faced in Faery, this is the final test, the last challenge, and I will not fail.

CHAPTER 40

WE MEET UP WITH a small host of Unseelie warriors, a few of whom look familiar from the small gathering when I was first brought before their king. Everyone links hands—Katiya on my left, Kallan on my right—and then we all shift as one.

Normally, it's a disorienting process at best—for humans like me anyway. But this is much worse. It's not just the world around me spinning, I feel like I'm being twisted inside and out, reshaped in this journey that seems to stretch on forever. Colors blur and shift around us in a nauseating display, forcing me to squeeze my eyes closed against the onslaught.

When it finally stops, I feel like I've been shoved in a clothes dryer and left to spin around and around with the socks until someone finally remembered I was in there and chose to let me out. I would certainly fall if not for the two Unseelie holding my hands in a death grip. Even so, I can't help sinking to one knee and trying to keep my stomach from climbing up my throat.

"Wren!"

My heart lurches against my ribs at the familiar voice. I snap my head up, the world still spinning around me, but across a stretch of cracked, dead land of grays and muted browns, I spy Sigurd.

The sight of him takes my breath away. He's worn his armor today too, including a winged helm I've never seen before, but he's impossible to miss, as if my heart would know him, even if he wasn't standing tall at the front of a mass of fae warriors. Moria is at his side, holding him back by one shoulder like he might sprint across the wasteland to me.

It's daylight, but thick clouds hang overhead as though even the sun doesn't want to grant its light to this dark meeting.

"Sigurd!" I reach for him, but a firm tug on my arm draws me to my feet. Katiya's grip on my arm is solid as steel, even as her brother releases me and steps forward in front of our group.

"King of Air." Kallan's voice booms across the plane, both sides eerily silent behind their monarchs. "I believe I have someone you'll want returned. Let us discuss terms."

The Unseelie are vastly outnumbered, but that doesn't seem to bother them. Despite the armor they wear, they're not here to fight. At least, I don't think so. They want to barter, with me as the bargaining chip. If things go south, I have no doubt they'll shift away again, me in tow. With Katiya here, I doubt Sigurd or any of the others could track them, no matter how awkward and strained the shifting.

Sigurd and Moria detach from their group and advance. Kallan and Katiya do the same, with me in tow. It's almost like a stage play with how perfectly choreographed their actions are, but I doubt the show will be met with thunderous applause.

Sigurd's gaze never leaves me as he advances on the enemy. It warms me, heart and soul, but at the same time, I can't miss the chill sliding down my spine.

I'm a liability, the last thing I want to be.

"You're okay?" Sigurd asks. His wide-eyed gaze holds more questions that I can process, but one thing I know for sure—he's truly worried.

He cares. He...loves me?

"Yes," I say. *Focus on them, not on me. I'll be fine.* I will the message to him, hoping that somehow it can come across without words.

Kallan snarls. "I do not condone harming humans."

"Oh?" Sigurd says, a dangerous lilt in his voice. "That has not been my experience with Unseelie."

Because they hurt Evelyn long ago, possibly before this king came to power. She was harmed by them in ways even Sigurd refused to voice.

"It's been long since such atrocities occurred," Kallan says. "And you're one to speak, Air King. Did you not bind this human to you, as your father bound others before you?"

Sigurd roars, a sound both vicious and pained all at once. Great wings sprout from his back and linger high in the air, a few feathers drifting down to the stark ground. My chest grows tight at the sight, the uneasy tension hanging in the air. If Kallan hoped to unsettle Sigurd, he's done it.

"How can you—" Sigurd starts.

"Know?" Kallan speaks for him, completely unruffled.

This earns another snarl in return.

"We know much, King of Air. Much more than you."

Moria puts a hand on Sigurd's arm, a vain attempt to calm him. "Who are you to speak for the Unseelie?" she asks Kallan.

Katiya smirks at my side, a little huff of laughter slipping from her lips.

Kallan pulls his sword—an act that has Sigurd and Moria reaching for their blades—and plants the tip in the ground between his feet. "I'm Kallan, King of the Unseelie."

"How?" Moria asks, wide eyed.

Sigurd's wings twitch, collapsing down behind him before springing out again. His face gives little away, but his silence says much. When the quiet lingers uncomfortably long, he finally says, "The magic did not settle after the last Unseelie king died."

"It has now," Kallan replies.

"That sword," Moria says on an inhale. If Moria recognizes it, it must be the blade Kallan claimed. She knows her weapons and her lore, maybe as well as anyone.

I'd swear the air around us drops a few degrees as the revelations sink in, one after another.

"This changes nothing," Sigurd snaps. Whatever thrall the pronouncement held him in is gone, and the fierce warrior has returned. He steps forward, hand outstretched. "Give Wren back to me."

"Watch your tone, Air King," Katiya mocks. "One wrong move and I take her with me."

Moria shoots Sigurd a hard look. Katiya is right, and I hate it. If Sigurd pisses them off any more, they may just abort this whole venture and take me with them.

"I assume you've realized by now that my sister is a null," Kallan replies, calm as ever. He's pulled the tip of his blade from the soil, leaving it gripped loosely in one hand. "If we take Wren, you won't be able to follow, just as you weren't able to before."

It's the first time he's said my name, and something about it leaves me unsettled.

Sigurd locks eyes with me, and I can see that he knows they're right. He's stuck between a rock and a hard place unless I can get free from Katiya somehow. I know what I have to do, but without some kind of distraction, it'll be impossible. I try to relay as much without words, but I have no blasted idea if any of it is getting through.

"What do you want?" Sigurd turns his attention back to the Unseelie king.

A silent look passes between Katiya and Kallan before the king turns back to Sigurd. "You have the cauldron of Áine. We want it."

My heart sinks. Of all the things they could ask for, this one hurts, though I shouldn't be surprised. Of course they would want something powerful, and they already have Sigurd dancing to their tune.

"Don't do it," I say.

"Hush." Katiya's order is a hiss in my ears.

I shake my head from side to side in echo of my words. He can't give that up. It will weaken his reign, the entire court, and I... I manage to swallow down the tightness in my throat.

I'm not worth it. One human can't outweigh that kind of power. How could I forgive myself if he sacrificed that for me when I was the idiot who left his side and failed to mention Katiya's presence in the first place?

"Sigurd." Moria packs a lot in his name, her tone echoing my thoughts. They can't do it, no matter if he wants to.

I'm still staring at him, still shaking my head, but Sigurd gives away nothing. His entire form has gone rigid, harsh, and unblinking.

Unbidden tears prick at the corner of my eyes. He's considering it. Dang it, he really would sacrifice that for me. I can tell the moment he has his decision. Something softens in his face, and he focuses his attention back on me.

Adrenaline spikes through my veins. It can't happen. "Don't!"

Sigurd shifts his attention to the Unseelie king. "Duel me."

"What?" Moria and Katiya screech at the same time.

"That wasn't—" Kallan begins.

"Duel me," Sigurd commands again, letting his wings vanish into nothingness. "The winner gets their desired prize."

"And the loser?" The Unseelie king adjusts his grip on the blade, hoisting it in front of him.

Sigurd's slow, vicious smile sends gooseflesh rising on my skin.

"No. You can't!" I shake my head, but no one is looking at me anymore.

"One on one. No interference or it's null," Sigurd continues, pulling free his own blade.

Shit. No! This is happening, and it's wrong, so wrong.

"Fine," the Unseelie king replies, with a look at Katiya.

I feel the shiver of rage vibrate through her. Sharp nails dig into my arm, nearly drawing blood. She hates this as much as I do.

"You risk much, Air King," he taunts.

"A worthy risk for my court." He glances over one shoulder then back at me. "For the woman I love."

The confession breaks my heart, sending the tears I tried so hard to hold back sliding down my cheeks. Stupid, glorious fool.

Katiya pulls me back toward the Unseelie, and though I try to jerk away, her hold is far too firm to budge. Moria moves to join her warriors, and just like that, the two kings are left alone to fight for the fate of their courts.

CHAPTER 41

Watching the duel is the hardest thing I've ever done. Not watching would be impossible.

Sigurd fights for me. For his court too and the pride of his people, but I'm the reason this duel is happening. I'm the reason his court could lose their treasure.

I'm the reason he could die.

And I hate it. I hate myself for the position he's in. Worse, I hate that I feel helpless, like some damsel in distress that I vowed at a young age never to be. From the moment my parents died in that tornado, I've had to act above my age—to be strong, when I really just want to fall apart. Gran was hurting too. Me being miserable wouldn't help. And then she needed me, and Tabitha needed me, and I had to be strong—for them, if not for myself. Someone had to keep my family going, and it had to be me.

The fae aren't my family exactly—well, except Uncle Mark—but I love Sigurd. I've come to love and appreciate this world. I will not fall apart while everything hangs on the line.

I have to do...something.

Sigurd blocks another blow from Kallan and his wicked sword. Fully charged or not, it sings through the air and meets Sigurd's blade repeatedly in a crash of metal that rings down to my bones. Even from a distance away, I can see the focus both fighters possess. I'm glad of it, that Sigurd has his head in the game. He's fighting well, but Kallan seems just as strong and shows no sign of slowing down.

This duel has been clean so far, blades meeting in a lethal dance, but I'm under no illusion it will stay that way. Sigurd has an arsenal of magic at his disposal, and I have no doubt he'll use it if he has to.

If only I can get free, maybe I can invalidate their duel somehow—make them stop.

Both sides look on uneasily, the Court of Air in a tight formation behind Moria, who stands eerily still, and the Unseelie jostling behind Katiya and me, a few adding commentary when their king lands a blow.

With effort, I pull my attention from the duel to Katiya. "You don't have to hold me here. They're already fighting."

She tracks the duel with her eyes, both sets of ears twitching atop her head as if she hears things too quiet for my human senses. At first, I think she hasn't heard me, but then her grip tightens painfully. "You're my one task," she says without looking away. "This is all I can do to help him now."

Darn it if she isn't right. But maybe I can distract her from that task, if even briefly.

"What happens if your brother falls?" I ask.

She twitches, and I know I've struck a chord.

"Do you become king? Or rather queen?"

"Hush!" Her nails dig in so hard I bite my lip to hold back a whimper. Blood pools underneath one of her nails and runs down my arm. She's holding me so tight I've started to lose feeling other than the pain of her nails gouged into my skin.

Painful for me but working. I can handle a little pain.

The ground shudders, a stiff breeze whips at my hair, and I snap my attention back to the duel. Breath catches in my throat. Sigurd's wings are out again, and he's taken flight, sending volleys of air from above toward his opponent.

And I see why. The ground has split in two, leaving a deep chasm where they were standing.

The fight has escalated, and though it looks like Sigurd has the advantage from the air, I can't hope it will last, especially not with

Kallan literally cutting through Sigurd's magic with his sword. The gusts aren't landing, not on their target anyway.

"Would the Unseelie follow you?" I ask Katiya. One glance behind us shows they aren't paying us any attention. Every single one is focused on their king fighting for his life and their futures. "Do you think they'd stand with you the way they do Kallan?"

She wrenches my arm, and I cry out. Blood runs more freely across my skin to drip onto the ground, but I have her attention. I pointedly look to my bloody arm then meet her sharp, feline gaze. "Your brother doesn't like harm to humans."

With a hiss, she releases me. Feeling returns to my arm in a heady rush.

A loud gasp cuts across the field of battle. I shift my attention just in time to see a blast of wind barrel into Sigurd's wing, leaving it askew and him floundering to the ground.

"No!" I cry.

He hits with a hard thud, sending out another wave of air that visibly ripples across the ground. This time, I see what caused the gasp. Instead of cutting through the magic, Kallan uses that ancient sword to reflect it back at Sigurd. The blast sends my mate rolling across the ground, tumbling over his wings, which must be ruined.

"The sword reflected the blast!" one Unseelie roars.

"It can do more than that," Katiya says, her voice filled with awe. "It can open up the world to us."

I hold my breath, waiting, praying, hoping for Sigurd to rise. A deep sigh slips from my lips as he does. He's hurt but not out. Sigurd pulls his sword from its scabbard again, apparently ready to resume a more physical battle than one of magic. His wings vanish.

It takes everything I have not to run to him. I yearn to, but I'm no fool. Katiya would catch me before I could disrupt their duel. At best, I'd be a distraction. At worst, a fatal one.

I need—

A strong arm wraps around my middle. There's no time for fear before magic tingles across my skin. Katiya lets out an inhuman screech, lunging in my direction, but she's too late. Suddenly, we're yards away, staring at the group of Unseelie. Other fae surround them, dressed in greens and tans, trees emblazoned on their chests, and blades at the ready.

I push on the arm around me to no avail. "Get off—"

"Don't panic."

"Galen?" Instantly, I stop struggling. His hold on me lessens, allowing me to turn enough to confirm his identity.

He tries to force a smile, but it doesn't quite hold. "I couldn't leave you with them."

I should be furious since he's the one who got me into this mess, but all I feel is relief.

A screech cracks through my moment of peace. Katiya stands a few feet away, twin short swords drawn, her stance filled with simmering fury as she stares us down.

No sooner have I seen her than Galen is shoving me behind him and drawing his own sword.

"How dare you!" Katiya races toward him.

They meet in a clash of blades. I barely have time to jump out of the way to avoid becoming an obstacle as Galen retreats a step in the wake of Katiya's onslaught.

Adrenaline pumps through my veins as I scramble further away and scan the plane. Fae, who must be the Court of the Forest, surround the group of Unseelie. Moria and the Court of Air look uncertain, shifting from their tight formation into a jumble of hesitation.

Sigurd and Kallan still fight, and the sight makes my heart skip a beat. Blood coats Sigurd's arm. His stance is haphazard at best. My heart leaps into my throat, choking off the screech building in my lungs.

He's losing.

And for what? I'm not even in the possession of the Unseelie anymore.

Without thinking, I race for them across the field of cracked soil and yellowed grasses.

I have to stop them. I can't let him die.

Sigurd knocks Kallan back with a powerful blow, but it's a momentary victory. He catches sight of me, his whole form going still.

Shit. Don't look at me, you idiot!

Suddenly, he lets out a roar, air flying out from him in all directions.

I gasp, stumbling to a halt and nearly twisting my ankle on the rocky ground. Dust from the ground gives the magic tangible shape, showing the air twisting in a circle around their dueling ground. It rises high in the air, blocking my path—blocking everyone.

A terrible chill races over my skin as I realize what he's created. Not just a blast of air like before.

A damn tornado.

The worst memories of my childhood flash before my eyes, scenes from that awful night, which started so normally. I came home from school. We ate dinner—spaghetti, which is probably why I can't stomach it now. The tornado sirens went off, but we didn't think too much of it. They aren't exactly uncommon where we lived. Even so, we went into my room, the most central place in the house. The storm went quiet. We thought it was gone, but it was just the beginning. I'll never forget the roaring and whistling sound that filled the air just before the tornado struck or the way all the hair on my body stood on end.

It's the same sensation now, the rush of the wind that sounds like a racing train, the charge and pressure in the air that tells you something is wrong, even if you can't see it yet.

I'm frozen, trapped in that nightmare again, my legs shaking beneath me.

Sigurd knows my fear, what happened in my childhood, and the way it still scars me. I told him about it.

Despite that, he chose to waste his magic and construct this monstrosity.

Not despite. *Because* of me.

He created this to keep me away, the one thing he knew would make me halt in my tracks, just like I did. Part of me hates him for it. Part of me admires the reckless fool.

"Stop this," I yell into the twister, though it's a vain hope to believe my words can reach him through this gale. "I'm free!"

A deep groan reaches me over the gusting winds.

I turn toward the sound to find Galen down on one knee, blood soaking one pant leg. Katiya stands before him, bloody blades raised to strike. He has his sword up, but his arm is bloodied too and shaking so hard even I can see it.

"No!" I yell.

My stomach roils. It's difficult to breathe as I stare in horror at my friend.

Galen can't lose. It can't end this way, not after he risked himself to free me from his mistake.

Please!

I clutch my necklace, unable to look away as Katiya's blades begin their descent.

"No!" I cry again.

My screech is met with the ring of metal.

I blink once, twice, trying to comprehend the sight before me. A blond fae appeared next to Galen. The sword she holds, poised just above and in front of him, took Katiya's blow. Galen gapes, wide eyed, staring at the weapons that would have been his demise.

Sylvie. A shuddering sob racks my form. *It has to be Sylvie.*

Katiya leaps back with a roar of frustration, and I can breathe again.

Galen is alive. Even better, he has backup.

Sylvie takes a stance in front of Galen, facing down Katiya. It gives him the moment he needs to recover and, albeit wobbly, take his place at Sylvie's side.

Two on one.

They can do this. They must.

I whirl back toward the tornado and the barely visible battle raging within. The torrent of dust and debris caught in the wind's thrall swirl around them, obscuring some of the view, but what little I can see is grim. Sigurd is injured and flagging, his back nearing the gale.

My nails cut grooves in my palms as I stare them down.

I won't lose him. I refuse to lose any more people who matter to me.

Without another thought, I rush toward the twister. Each step is a fight to stay upright and move forward. My hair whips around my head, obscuring my vision. My clothes risk being ripped from my body. Little bits of grass and dirt find their way up my nose, causing me to cough and gag. I throw an arm in front of my face, trying to block the onslaught as best I can.

There are feet to go, but I can't stop now, not this close.

A sudden strong gust sends me to my knees. I dig my nails into the soil, trying desperately to find purchase and not be swept away. Dust stings my eyes, causing them to water. I manage to crawl forward, but the sight ahead roots me in place.

Sigurd kneels on one knee, blade raised, deflecting a blow from Kallan.

The Unseelie king is wounded too, blood dripping down one arm, but he shows no sign of backing down, even as he takes his time readying for the next blow.

"Stop this!" The tornado steals my words. Neither react.

I dig deeper into the dirt, feeling a sharp bite as my nail cracks. "Sto—"

The rest of what I planned to say ends in a scream as vines erupt from the ground under Sigurd and Kallan. They climb skyward, twisting and flailing like a giant squid emerging from the ocean to pull a ship into the depths. But their actions aren't random. In seconds, both Sigurd and Kallan are wrapped tightly in their embrace. Arms are wrenched until blades fall to the barren land. The tornado vanishes in an instant. The cloud of debris drifts to the earth, bits of grass landing on me where I still crouch upon the ground.

As the dust settles, something new looms between the two bound kings—a third.

CHAPTER 42

I RUB AT MY watering eyes, trying to blink away the dirt and dust causing them to sting and burn. I wasn't imagining things. The figure standing between the two kings is dressed like a druid knight in the video game Matt used to play when we were younger. The colors of the forest are painted across him, a giant golden tree on his breastplate. No crown adorns his long, golden-brown hair, but it doesn't take a genius to know who just stopped this duel. Who could but another fae king?

The vines twist tighter around their captives. A groan of pain from Sigurd has me shoving to my feet, my own cuts and bruises forgotten.

"Sigurd!" I call.

He stops squirming against the vines and snaps his head in my direction. "Wren." His eyes glow that eerie blue, which I know means strong emotion. "You're hurt."

"I'm fine." I probably look much worse than I am after braving the literal storm, but my injuries are nothing on his, which I know must be punishing.

The newcomer king doesn't stop me or bind me with vines as I approach Sigurd, but I can feel his steady gaze on me nonetheless.

"Brave, foolish woman," Sigurd says, but his eyes hold so much more, a deep longing that sends tingling warmth throughout my limbs, pushing away my aches and pains.

"I could say the same of you." Tentatively, I touch the vines that separate us. I can't quite reach Sigurd through their bulk, and the thorns protruding along their length dissuade me from climbing them or trying to push through. A new horror catches my attention within the twisting mass as I spy a thorn digging into Sigurd's side, blood running down its surface. My eyes go wide. My hand flies to cover my mouth.

Without thinking, I turn on the Forest king. "Free him! He's hurt, and your thorns are doing more harm."

"Wren." My name is full of pain when Sigurd speaks, and it nearly breaks my heart.

But I don't heed his warning, don't back down. Instead, I stare at the king, unflinching.

"You're the human they stole," he replies, as if this is some casual conversation and he's not bleeding out two other kings as we speak. Not to mention that his people hold not just the Unseelie but the Court of Air at bay. I didn't see weapons drawn on the Court of Air, but the threat is the same: Don't move. Don't interfere.

"Yes." My brows pinch as I stiffen my spine. "You interrupted the duel. It's invalid, and I'm free anyway. Now let Sigurd go. Let us leave this place."

"You fought for this human woman?" The Forest king looks past me to Sigurd.

"For Wren," Sigurd says. "Yes. I love her, Riven. I will always fight for her."

He loves me. I sway on my feet, bracing myself on a vine and nearly earning a nasty cut from a thorn.

As much as the comment caught me by surprise, it does just as much to the Forest king—to Riven. His eyes glow emerald green. His gaze goes far away, even as he blinks rapidly at the revelation.

"And you? What did you fight for?" Riven asks the Unseelie king.

"The cauldron." Kallan groans, still fighting the vines. "The cauldron for the girl."

The ground below us trembles, and I edge back farther against the vines. Only minutes ago, he opened up the earth. The chasm lingers not far away. Would he do the same again?

Riven raises his hand. The forest fae respond, as do the Unseelie who cry out in alarm. The ground stills immediately.

"None of that," Riven says. He narrows his piercing gaze at Kallan. "I don't like Unseelie who capture humans."

The half laugh that slips from the Unseelie king is a thing of nightmares, twisting and vicious all at once. "How ironic, given the shameful way you used my people for your twisted game."

"Your people?" Riven asks.

"He's the Unseelie king," Sigurd replies, voice laced with pain.

Riven goes utterly still, his eyes flaring with a bright green glow.

"The magic has settled, even after so long," Riven says, almost to himself. With a little shake, the look of shock is gone, and he spears the Unseelie king with his attention and snarls, "It was no game."

"Tell that to my dead brethren."

"It's your living ones you should worry about."

Kallan twists as much as he's able, trying to see behind him. He grunts and groans, pulling against the vines to little avail, but he's able to shift enough to see the group of Unseelie we'd parted from. Members of the Court of the Forest ring them in, holding them at sword point in a tight cluster. Katiya is nearby, physically held by Sylvie, probably to keep her from shifting away. Galen stands next to her, leaning heavily on the hilt of his sword for support, the tip wedged deep into the ground.

"This doesn't need to end in bloodshed," I say, garnering attention from the group.

"Doesn't it?" Riven asks, though I sense he's not looking for a direct answer.

I swallow, summoning my willpower. "The Unseelie didn't come here for a fight." I know that to be true, even if they refuse to say it. "The Court of Air didn't either. They didn't attack the Unseelie. Nor did they attack your court, despite Katiya stealing me from there and planting a trail for Sigurd to follow."

Somehow, I know that to be true—I'm betting on it. If Sigurd had stormed into the Court of the Forest, an army at his back, there'd be an entirely different battle underway.

"Two of my greatest enemies weakened and in my vines. You think this ends any way but in blood?" As if to emphasize Riven's position, the vines twist. All I can think about are the thorns digging deeper into Sigurd's body, bleeding him out.

"Stop!" I beg. "You already have your blood." Sigurd can't possibly lose much more. "They were both trying to save people they loved. How dare you barge in and take advantage of that?"

The vines stop abruptly.

"Wren." Sigurd groans. A warning. I don't listen.

"It seems you've fought dirty with the Unseelie already," I prod. "You love a human woman, don't you? What would she say about this?" *Please, dear God, don't let her be bloodthirsty.*

The jab hits home. Riven snarls, baring a hint of fanged teeth, but doesn't retaliate. His look softens, and he whispers something I can't make out. He glances at the Unseelie king. "If I free you, you will take your people and leave this place immediately. Vow it."

Kallan snarls, baring his own fangs. Wicked, black claws on one bound hand rake against the vines, digging grooves that appear to heal over the moment they're made. Blood runs down several of the vines, and for some reason, it strikes me as odd that it's red. Apparently, even dark fae bleed the same as humans and Seelie.

Seeming to realize his struggle is useless, Kallan stills. He gives one glance back to his people, his sister, before turning back to Riven. "I agree."

Some kind of magic tingles through the air, and then the vines around the Unseelie king vanish. He falls unceremoniously to the ground.

"My offense against your people is repaid. Do not let us meet again," Riven says. "If we do, there will be no mercy."

Blood mars Kallan's pale hair and streaks down his ruined armor. Without a word, he lifts his blade, sheaths it, looks between the other two kings, and vanishes.

A gasp at my back alerts me to his reappearance. I turn to see him in front of Katiya. Words pass between them, but I'm too far away to hear. A moment later and the Forest fae part to allow them to rejoin their comrades. The whisper of more conversation and hint of a barked command are all I make out before the Unseelie slowly fade as one. It's not the clean and instant shift I'm used to seeing. Maybe that's why it felt so nauseating on the way here.

When they're gone, I turn back to Riven. "Free him." I gesture to Sigurd. "Please."

I refuse to look too closely at the vines anymore. It was one thing to see Kallan bleed. If I have to see more of Sigurd's blood marring the greenery, I'll lose my resolve.

"You asked what my human woman would say about this," he says to me. "Let's find out."

CHAPTER 43

RIVEN, THE FOREST KING, makes some kind of hand gesture, and moments later, another fae appears at his side. A new face to me but one who carries authority in his stance and cuts an intimidating façade with the scar down one side of his face. He's dressed similarly to his king—a commander of some sort?

"Ambrose, bring Lia to me," Riven orders.

"Here?" His gaze pans across Sigurd and the members of his court looming in the distance. He must be of authority to question his king.

"Yes, here. As soon as possible."

Ambrose grumbles but vanishes a moment later.

Silence lingers uncomfortably in the wake of his absence, particularly when he does not quickly reappear.

I chance a look at Sigurd. His head lolls slightly to the side, but he's awake, a terrible grimace etched on his face though I sense he tries to hide it. I bite my lip, barely holding in the whimper aching to break free.

"Let him out of this mess," I say, turning to Riven. "He's badly injured."

"The things he's done…"

"I know exactly what he's done," I retort, failing to keep the bite out of my voice. Probably not all of it, but I know enough. I know why Riven hates him, but leaving him bound and bleeding is cruel. It might as well be slicing me up as much inside. "But if you don't let him down and get him help, he won't be conscious to hear whatever your human has to say."

Riven looks past me. "If you shift away before our discussion is complete, I will consider it an act of war."

"I agree," Sigurd says.

Riven projects his voice, sharing the same message with the fae from the Court of Air across the field. There will be no easy escape, even if Sigurd is unbound. But even small victories are just that. Satisfied, Riven releases his vines, thankfully, letting Sigurd down more gently than he did the Unseelie king.

I'm there before his feet ever touch the ground.

"Sigurd," I whisper, brushing matted hair back from his face. Some of his weight leans on me as the vines release, but he tries his best to stand. That only lasts a moment before he drops to one knee, me at his side, cradling him close.

"You're okay," he whispers to me. "You're here, and you're okay."

"I am. I have you now. You'll be fine." I wish, I pray. I may not be fae, but I hope my words hold no lies for him. "Can you heal?"

A sad smile touches his lips. His bloodied hand caresses my face. "I've never had that talent."

A soft tingling runs across my skin, and I know without turning that Ambrose has returned.

Sigurd swallows, turning to face the newcomers, and I do the same.

The human who stands at Riven's side, one hand still clasped with Ambrose, is nothing like what I pictured. Somehow, I thought she'd be almost fae-like—tall, ethereal, radiating power and beauty. After all, this is the consort that Sigurd ordered Galen to steal, one that nearly sparked a war. But she's no Helen of Troy.

Rather, she's a lot like me, really. Maybe slightly younger with brown hair instead of blond, but she could be anyone in our world. A girl I went to school with. Someone I met in town. She's not clothed like one, not in the flowing green dress whose light and airy construction speaks to fae clothing, but otherwise, she's...average.

Her gaze fixes on Sigurd, and she pales, almost swaying on her feet. A look of pity crosses her face as she covers her mouth with one hand.

A dark side of me is smug. Good. Let her see her king's nasty handiwork. At least she's affected by it, even if the fae seem nonplussed.

"Lia." Riven holds a hand out to her.

She releases Ambrose, shuddering slightly, her gaze still glued to Sigurd and me, before she recovers and moves to join her king.

"My consort and future queen," Riven finishes once she's at his side.

Sigurd stiffens a little. It's at that moment I notice the giant emerald set in the ring around her finger.

Riven cuts his gaze to the other woman who returned with Ambrose, a stunning dark-skinned fae who is every bit the elegant princess I expected Lia to be. "And Solona," he says, a hint of a question in his voice. "My advisor."

"I thought I might be of help," she replies.

Lia shrugs and looks at Riven. "We were already together."

Enough chat. Every moment we sit here, Sigurd gets worse, and I won't let him linger in pain, not now that he's free. "Past grievances are done," I say with all the strength I can muster. "Let them die. Let this be a new start, a fresh one. Let us leave so he can be healed."

"Are they?" Riven asks. One brow rises. "Despite my feelings, I took no direct action against him, but he—"

"Made mistakes." I interrupt. "Haven't you?"

He flinches, and I know it's no little thing he regrets, whatever it is. Lia looks up at him, and I can see it written in her features too.

Something recent then? Good. Even fae kings are fallible, mortal.

"Everyone, fae or human, makes mistakes," I say. "But it's how we move on from those that makes the difference. It's done. The past cannot be changed, but the future can. Let it be done." *Please.*

The four look between one another, some silent conversation occurring that I'm not privy to. I straighten my spine, meaning to speak again, but Sigurd beats me to it.

"I loved your mother." That gets their attention immediately. "You know that. But I respected her wishes until the end and stayed away after your father died, despite the pain that it caused me. I was angry at you because I believed you kept her from me and were an obstacle to the future I wanted—a future with her by my side. Human or fae."

It hurts to hear him talk of Evelyn. I can't deny that. No matter that she's dead and he professed to love me, the lingering scar she left on him pains me too. But it's in the past. I told them to let the past lie, so I have to do it as well. Move on. Look to the future, to the injured male pouring out the last of his heart in an effort to stop a war—to save us.

"But Wren," he says, his arm tightening around me ever so slightly, "helped me see the error in my ways, the selfishness of my desires. She—" He pauses, staring at me, the corner of his bloodied lip lifting ever so slightly. "She saves me from the worst of myself."

Sigurd... As if I didn't already love him, and he goes and says something like that, which only makes my heart beat for him even more.

"I know you blame me for your father," Sigurd continues, focusing back on Riven. "But his death is not my fault. I hesitated on the battlefield. For one brief and fleeting moment, I saw a future without him, where Evelyn was mine. But I chose to defend Lutheon. I could have been at his side sooner, but it would not have stopped the blade that ended him. He was my friend. A dear friend, and he died in my arms. Despite your mother's love of him and the way that wounded me, I did not wish him harm."

Tears sting at the corner of my eyes, and I'm not the only one affected. Riven seems to have shrunk in on himself, no longer able to look at Sigurd. Lia leans into him as if to offer support, all her focus on her king. Solona and Ambrose share a look full of grief.

"You didn't know that part, did you?" Sigurd says with a heavy sigh, letting a little more of his weight settle against my side, which I embrace. "I killed the Unseelie who slew him and then held Lutheon as he died. For all my skills, I could never heal. Not to save myself or those I cared for. I felt his power leave and pass to you."

It's hard to hear, and I wasn't even there. I didn't know Lutheon, but I know Sigurd. I know the grief in his voice is real, that this is true and cuts him deeply. Even if he could lie, no one could mistake this for anything other than painful reality—a scar that's lingered for far too many years.

"I ask for peace," Sigurd says. "This new Unseelie king is a threat to us both. Let us—" A deep coughing, choking sound cuts off his words.

"Sigurd!" I screech.

Blood dribbles down the side of his mouth. Sharp nails claw into the ground for purchase, but he somehow manages to keep his other hand, the one on me, normal, clinging to my shoulder so he doesn't collapse.

Dear God. Help him!

"Please!" I turn, looking for tangible help and finding only surprised and wary looks. There's no time left, and I know the card I have to play. Keeping a firm grip on Sigurd, I twist toward the King of the Forest and yell, "The Court of Air, Sigurd, will be a threat to you no more. As the future Queen of Air, I vow it!"

"Future queen?" someone asks.

Over my pulse pounding in my ears and the panic racing through my veins, I couldn't tell you who it was.

"It's been foreseen," I say. "Now heal him!"

I gasp as Solona appears next to us. I panic as she reaches for Sigurd's still struggling form and try to pull him away, but her hands are on him in an instant. His choking cough ceases. Blood stops flowing from his wound. Something tingles across my mark—Sigurd's mark—and all at once, I know what's happening.

"You're healing him," I say.

Her eyes flutter closed then open again, the mirror of Sigurd's. His body shudders, but he's twisting in my arms, half sitting up and rubbing at the blood trickling from his lips.

Solona pulls away. "He'll keep until more healing can be provided," she says to me. To Sigurd, she says, "Evelyn would not have wanted to see you hurt and suffering." She places her hand on mine, and I gasp at the warmth of it. "Take care of him."

"I intend to."

In a blink, she's standing back beside her king. Solona looks at Riven, but he only nods.

"Peace then," Riven says, though his lips twist as if he tastes something bitter.

"An alliance," Sigurd corrects. He pushes to his feet, bringing me with him. "Against the Unseelie."

Riven crosses the space to us, his look impassive. Sigurd steps forward without me to meet the other king. There's a moment of tense silence where the two stare at one another, neither moving nor speaking.

A tingle of dread slides down my spine as I wonder whether this meeting will turn to bloodshed once more. But finally, *finally*, the two clasp hands, their palms on each other's forearms.

"Agreed." They say at once.

Magic pulses out from them in a shimmering wave that even I can feel.

"A promise sealed in magic," Lia says with awe, answering my unspoken question.

A true alliance. A reluctant one, to be sure, but it's so much more than I could have hoped for. *Thank you, Lord.*

"Never thought I'd see the day," Ambrose mutters, but there's warmth in his tone, something like joyous awe. Maybe this can be a new start for both courts.

The other fae must feel it too because no sooner have the kings released one another than Moria appears at Sigurd's side. Fury rolls off her in waves, even as she gathers Sigurd in a tight hug, causing him to cry out in pain.

She releases him instantly, but the scowl on her face remains. "You could have died!" she snaps, berating him in front of everyone. "I'd have cursed you into the beyond if you lost your life so foolishly and left me behind."

The hint of a grin twitches at the corner of Sigurd's lip. "I think you've said that before."

"I mean it." She wags a finger at him. "And you—" She shifts her focus to me. In an instant, she's before me, pulling me into an equally tight hug that steals my breath. As she releases me, she says, "You humans cause my family such trouble."

"I worried about you too," I reply.

The smallest touch of color rises to her cheeks, and for Moria, that speaks volumes.

"I'll be taking them home now," she says to the assembled from the Court of the Forest.

"Thank you," Sigurd says, nodding to the king and then to Solona.

Riven nods in return but does not speak. Lia elbows him in the side, and he scowls down at her. All at once, the look softens, speaking volumes of whatever lies between the two.

"And you," Riven responds like a scolded child. "Thank you for peace."

"Good to see you, Moria," Ambrose says.

She snorts air through her nose by way of response, to which he laughs. Whatever history is there, I'm not sure I want to know.

Moria reaches for my hand, presumably to shift us away.

But I step back. "Wait."

"What—" she begins, but I've already turned back to the King of the Forest.

"Galen." I haven't seen him since he vanished with Sylvie earlier, but I have to believe he's okay. "Please, don't be too hard on him," I beg them one and all. "He didn't want to betray you." I leave out exactly why he did. There's no point bringing up sins of the past that may have them rethinking this deal. "He thinks of the Forest as his home. He wants to be with you all."

I turn to Sigurd, this part as much for him as the others. His scowl shows exactly how he feels about Galen, but I won't let that deter me.

"He tried to make things right in his way by bringing me to you all. That was his intent, but things went...not as anyone planned."

Except maybe Katiya, now that I think about it. We all played perfectly into her and Kallan's hands, though it seems like this outcome is different from what they hoped. Actually, I know it is.

"He was my friend while he was in the Court of Air," I continue. "He helped me. Please—"

"He's my friend too," Lia says, surprising me. "I don't think he wanted to hurt us. Or you."

I nod along, so grateful for someone who understands, even if the men don't.

"He didn't," I confirm. He may have abducted me, but if he didn't care, he wouldn't have saved me from Katiya. "Even today, he protected me. He's the reason I got away from the Unseelie."

At least that bit got Sigurd's attention and in a good way, if the loosening of his crossed arms is any indication.

"Galen was hurt in the battle," I say. "Please..."

Ambrose nods along, scratching at his beard. "I'll talk to him."

"As will I," Riven echoes.

I'll make sure he's okay, Lia mouths, or at least I think she does.

It's enough. He'll be okay. He has to be. And I sense I won't be getting anything more on this front, not immediately.

"Thank you," I tell them. *Please, let it be enough.*

Without another word, I take Moria's hand, and she shifts us from the battlefield.

CHAPTER 44

HE HEALERS SEE TO Sigurd the moment we return, tending his wounds and encouraging him to rest and recover from the fight. Of course, he insists on them attending to me first—ridiculous man. Not that there is much for them to do. Katiya's concoction of herbs, whatever it was, worked wonders on my hand already, and my other wounds are minor scrapes and bruises. The blood on me is the worst, but it mostly isn't mine, just another reminder of how close Sigurd came to losing today, first to the Unseelie, then to Riven.

Two kings against one truly wasn't fair, particularly not given his condition before the battle. Moria informed me that Sigurd hadn't slept since I was taken, and it basically took both her and Hawke staying on him constantly to make sure he didn't run off on his own to try to save me, not even knowing exactly where I was.

Now that would have been something to see.

After I bathe, Uncle Mark basically force feeds and coddles me like the child I no longer am. Once he asks for the millionth time if I am truly all right and I tell Hawke and Moria what little I saw and learned while with the Unseelie, I am finally allowed to see Sigurd.

They placed him in the private chambers of the King of Air, a place I know he hates, but I'm secretly excited to finally get to see them. I always wondered what lurked beyond the other locked door off the main sitting room.

Now, I finally get to know.

Stone stairs twist upward, lit by floating balls of light evenly spaced along the walk. Bright light floods in ahead, alerting me to the end of the staircase. It spills out into a massive open room. Pillars reach skyward, supporting a roof of glass that arches high above. Even more eagles roost on its surface than they did atop my former room, creating odd spots of shadow against an otherwise bright blue sky. There are no walls in this room—I guess magic must keep the rain and cold out, but light curtains flutter between the pillars, providing the illusion of privacy from the balcony running in a circle around the room and the open air beyond. Sparse but ornate furniture punctuates the space, and there, near one side and laid atop a massive circular bed, is Sigurd.

Pillows are propped behind him so that he's half sitting where he speaks with a pair of fae healers who crowd next to his bed.

"Finally, someone I want to see." The pleasure in Sigurd's tone adds lightness to my steps as I cross the room. Already, I can tell he's much better. He shoos the healers away, insisting he'll rest as they request. As they disappear down the stairs, he grumbles, "Fussing over me like I'm some foolish child."

I arch a brow at him. "You were quite badly injured."

"And you?" He reaches for me, nearly tumbling off the pillows, so I take a seat on the edge of the bed next to him. The skirts of my dress float out around my legs to drape down the sides of the comforter.

"I'm fine. Really," I promise. "You had the healers see to me yourself, right? I'm sure they reported my condition."

His hand tightens on mine. "In the past, they've..." He trails off with a shake of his head. "I have to know, Wren. If they did anything to you, if there's anything you didn't tell the healers."

The look in his eyes speaks volumes. He's worried that whatever happened to Evelyn all those years ago happened to me too. Thankfully though, these Unseelie didn't treat me so poorly.

"I promise. All they did was take some of my blood to apply to the king's sword. Just a scratch," I add quickly at his wide-eyed look. "He said something about how the blood of a marked human was supposed to help it regain its power, but I don't think mine worked."

"But you bear my mark." Sigurd drops my hand to run his fingertips over my hip, stirring up a flock of butterflies within me.

"I know. The sword felt different after. There was a slight humming sound like the cauldron but much quieter. Kallan said my blood wasn't enough. It didn't repower the sword as he'd hoped."

And thank goodness for that. The Unseelie king was powerful enough as it was, even without his magical sword. If he finds a way to repower it, I shudder to think what he'll be able to achieve. Katiya said something strange too. Something about opening the world to them, whatever that means. Nothing good, I'm sure. I wish I could have learned something more helpful, but at the same time, I'm so glad to be free.

"I guess it's a good thing they didn't decide to spill more of my blood, just to be sure." I shrug and try to make light of the situation.

But Sigurd takes the comment to heart. His eyes flare with a bright glow. His lips pull back in a snarl. "If they'd dared—"

"They didn't." I lay my hand on his, giving it a gentle squeeze. The glow from his eyes dims, and he seems to relax back into the cushions. "More importantly, how are you?"

He sighs and forces a weak smile. "Much better now," he promises, lifting my hand to his lips and placing a gentlemanly kiss upon its back. "Though they still insist I stay abed today."

I shrug. "You can't blame them for worrying. I—" Emotion chokes off my words, and I swallow it down. "When I saw you fighting..."

"You ran for me," Sigurd finishes for me. "That might have been a more terrifying sight than seeing you shift in with them. At least then I knew some of what to expect and could brace for it. But watching you rush into danger..." He shakes his head. "I never want to see that again."

"Then maybe don't duel the Unseelie king?" I give him a pointed look.

His thumb rubs little circles on my palm. "You think I wouldn't risk that or more to see you safe?"

The look he gives me has my stomach doing little somersaults. I pull my bottom lip between my teeth.

"Keeping me safe—is that what you call that tornado you conjured?" What a waste of magic.

He winces. "I'm sorry. I know what that means to you, but it's the first thing I thought of that might make you stop—keep you safe."

"You weren't wrong. It did make me hesitate." If not for all that we'd already shared, I might have stopped or turned and run.

"But I underestimated you." He kisses my hand once more. "I should have known you would find another way to surprise me."

I lace my fingers through his. "You thought I'd just let you fight, even though I was already free? I wanted to interrupt the duel—nullify it."

"I know," he says. "But I intended to win that battle and take out two birds with one stone, as it were." He adjusts his grip, tightening his hold on me. "It seems things often don't go as I plan. It's a good thing I have a delightful mate to balance out my impulses. Or should I say, future Queen of Air?"

A fierce blush rushes to my face, and I jerk my hand away. "I'm sorry I said that. I couldn't let you be in pain anymore. I had to make them agree, and that was the first thing that came to mind."

"And so you did. You stopped a war, Wren."

I shake my head. "That was you. You fought. You told them about what really happened in the past."

"No." He takes my hand in his again. "I merely said the things I should have spoken long ago. Without you there, they never would have listened to me. None of this would be possible." He pauses, something in his gaze twinkling before he says, "You'll be a brilliant queen."

At that title again, my flush returns twofold. We've never discussed exactly what our relationship will be after this. I promised to come back, we share a mark, but there haven't been any agreements beyond that. Queen is... It's a lot. Not just a promise to be together but sharing of power. The thought of it alone almost makes me want to run—or it would, if not for the fae holding my hand right now and looking at me like I'm a treasure. Like he didn't almost die today and actually won his prize instead of having things interrupted.

Sigurd draws me closer, and I let him, scooting further onto the bed.

"Was it truly foreseen?" he asks.

Unlike him, I can lie. Maybe it would be best to now, to tell him I made it up, but somehow, I can't manage that. He deserves better, a future without lies and deceit. "It's what Lysandir called me on the night of the ball, just before he left."

Sigurd tsks. "That boy, ruining the surprise of asking you." I gasp, but he continues, "Though I suppose I am grateful in this case."

"You want me as your queen?" I gape, staring at him wide eyed. Surely, this has to be some kind of a joke. It would be a lie to say I don't want it exactly, but it's just so much so soon.

"Of course I do. I love you, Wren."

Those words do something to me, drawing me further into his embrace until my legs nearly touch his where I recline on the bed next to him.

He loves me. Yes, even without his penchant for truth, the steady look in his eyes as he gazes at me says it too. This fierce and tricky man, this king, loves me. Not the woman he thought I was or that I look like, but me.

"I want you at my side but only when you're ready." Soft laughter slips from his lips. "I can be quite patient when there's something I really want."

I snuggle close to his side, laying my head on the pillow next to his. He turns to face me, lying just how we did the other night after we had sex and became a mated pair. I stroke his face, savoring the feel of his skin under my fingers—now clear of the blood and grime of battle.

"You love me?" I need to hear it again. Once would never be enough.

He curls an arm around my side, tucking me close. "I love you, Wren."

"I love you too, Sigurd," I admit.

And then my lips are on his, savoring the taste of him that I feared might be gone forever. He's peaches and cream. Rain on a summer day. An autumn breeze through my hair. Everything that I love and crave and could never get enough of, no matter how long we're together.

Gently, I pull away, despite his protest and his hand holding tight to my side, urging me closer. His eyes glow that intoxicating bright blue, showing just how much I've affected him.

"Only when I'm ready, right?" I say in the narrow space between us.

He groans, as if I've caused him worse agony than the duel, but releases me, rolling onto his back once more, his eyes tightly shut. When he opens them again, the glow has dimmed somewhat.

"You need to rest," I say. "Isn't that what the healer said?"

Sigurd grumbles but doesn't argue.

It'd be so much easier to do more, to give in to the desire coursing through my body and likely his, but that wouldn't help him recover. Right now, the thing I need more is for him to heal, to live, to be the fierce king I fell in love with. I won't hamper his recovery by stealing pleasure that can be found another day.

"You'll have plenty of time with me," I say. "Just not today."

He sighs. "That's right." A sad smile touches his face as he turns his head toward me. "You must want to return to the human world."

"I do. Tomorrow." I nestle closer to him, lacing my fingers through his again and earning a grateful squeeze in return. "Once you're through the worst of it. And this time, I won't be leaving your side in the night."

Mischief twinkles in his eyes. "Really?"

"As long as you behave yourself." I swat at him playfully.

"You know I'm not always good at that." He waggles his brows at me.

I bite my lip and fight the urge to give in to his teasing. "We're trying many new things today."

Sigurd sighs. "If you insist."

"I do."

CHAPTER 45

IT'S MIDMORNING THE DAY after the almost war and the striking of peace—one that's hopefully long-lasting—between the Court of Air and the Court of the Forest. Sigurd, Mark, and Hawke accompanied me to the door between worlds, along with a number of guards. After my abduction, Sigurd isn't taking any chances with my safety and making sure that I get back to my world as planned.

I don't mind today, but he's going to have to relax a bit when I return.

"So, I just walk through this space?" I say, gesturing to the circle of large stones surrounding an otherwise grassy stretch of land amid a pine forest.

"And you must wish to be in your world." Sigurd extends a hand to me. "Come. We'll go with you."

"Is that safe?" I ask, placing my hand in his.

"We can linger there a short time. Besides, I don't want you to have to go alone." The smile he grants me stirs up a mess of butterflies in my stomach. It's ridiculous how much something so small, so simple, can affect me.

Together, we cross through the stones, Mark, Hawke, and the guards following after us.

The shift from one world to the next is both subtle and stark. One moment, we're in Faery and the next, back in my world with the loud hum of cicadas and thick humidity already forming, despite that it's not even noon. The forest itself isn't all that different here, probably why I missed the change so completely when I ran into Faery. I must have wished to be somewhere else at just the right moment, almost like fate.

I glance up at Sigurd, fighting my amusement at the scrunched look on his face as he takes in my world.

Maybe we were meant to find one another at just that moment.

I look back at the forest, taking in the slope of the hillside stretching out before us. I ran down that, I think. Jolene's would be up ahead somewhere, through the trees. Nothing like a little trek alone through the woods to figure out what the heck I'm going to tell people or how I'll get home without my car. I'm guessing they didn't just leave it behind the bar. Not to mention that Derrick won't be in to open the place for several hours yet.

"Well, I guess I should get going." I give a nervous laugh. I've never been one for hiking. Just peachy, this will be.

"Wait," Hawke says.

I twist around at the unexpected request.

"I'll take you," he says. "Let me shift you there."

"You can do that?"

He folds his hands in front of him. "I went with Mark that day he tried to visit your grandmother. I remember the house. My memory is quite good." That, I fully believe. "Shifting is much harder for us here. I'm not sure I could go much farther, but it will be faster and easier for you that way."

"Are you sure?" I look between him and Mark.

I understand the full extent of what he's offering. It's risky for them to enter our world at all. If they got stuck here, it would mean death for them. Using magic, exerting oneself, and traveling away from the door only increases that risk. It's a big thing to offer, even if it makes things so much easier for me. Jolene's isn't open this time of day, and showing up there out of the blue... I can't even picture it. What would I say to Derrick or anyone else? Somehow, seeing Gran first sounds so much easier. At least she won't think me crazy. Hopefully.

"I am," Hawke replies.

"Let him take you, Wren," Sigurd urges. "I trust that Hawke will keep you safe." He glances toward his cousin, who nods in return.

"As do I," Mark says. "There's no one I would trust more with my niece. And..." The words die unspoken as he looks away.

He wants to ask about his kids. I can almost feel it.

"I'll ask after Matt and Tabitha. Maybe see them too?" I glance at Hawke. I have no idea if he plans to just drop me there or linger.

"You can stay here a while if you'd like," Sigurd says, maybe sensing my question. "As long as you need. I can post guards near the door so that, if you approach, they can let me know immediately."

"And if I can't find the door?" I hadn't thought about that at all, but suddenly I can't unthink it. What if I never find my way back to him?

He leans in close to me, his lips barely hovering above the curve of my ear. "Touch our mark, Wren," he whispers. "It'll have a pull to me, just like our bond did. It may be faint in this world, but I trust you'll feel it."

That's what I felt when I was captive of the Unseelie. That slight tug in a direction I couldn't explain.

"Yes." I slide my fingers under the hem of my shirt, right over the mark on my skin. As he said, I can feel it, a pull right toward him. "Yes, I will always find you."

Mark clears his throat. When I look back at the others, the guards are carefully looking away, though no doubt with their fae hearing they probably heard much, if not all of our discussion.

"Would you like me to tell them anything for you?" I ask Mark.

He glances away again, his shoulders hunching. "I don't—"

"It's okay. I won't say anything," I say quickly. "Maybe another time."

Mark looks back at me. "Maybe so."

There will be plenty of time for him to decide to reveal him-self—hopefully.

"Shall we go?" Hawke asks.

Right. Because the more time they spend here, the worse it is for them. I swallow my nerves and take his outstretched hand. Whatever I find at home, I can't change it now.

But I hope, I pray, it's something good.

The shift is slow and jerky, much like when I traveled with the Unseelie, though the distance is not far. That alone twists my stomach inside out, but it's not what nearly brings me to my knees when the world stops moving.

Gran's house—my home—sits in its little clearing like it always has, our little vegetable garden in the back and the forest circling around. The tin roof, the rocking chairs on the front porch, and even the one missing shutter I keep meaning to replace are all the same as when I left.

The only difference I can spot is the strange car sitting in the driveway next to Gran's old truck and my Mazda—I guess someone retrieved her.

"I'll wait here for a few minutes," Hawke says, snapping me out of my reverie. "Let me know if you want to stay or return."

"I will." I just need to see what awaits me inside.

As hard as it was to be trapped away from home, coming back is somehow just as hard. I don't know what I'm going to find when I walk through that door. In my head, I pictured Gran as being fine—shaken and upset, I'm sure—but okay. But that's what I had to believe to keep going. If I had let myself think the worst, I would've been a mess. I certainly wouldn't have been able to win the competition and release myself from Sigurd's bond.

That pretty illusion only lasts until I knock on the door though. Once I do that, I have to face whatever comes after, including trying to explain where I was in a way that doesn't make Gran want to lock me up in an asylum. Not that I think she ever would, but I have no idea how she'll react to what I have to say.

One step after another, I force myself to cross the yard. The stairs leading up to the front porch are harder, each one requiring a deep steadying breath.

I'm saved from knocking and the endless wait for someone to open the door when it swings open on its squeaky hinges.

"Wren?"

"Matt?"

My cousin stands in the doorway, as wide eyed and shocked as I am. Tabitha had said he was coming home soon, but I never got the date.

He's here though. Really here.

All at once, my fear and hesitation are gone. I leap the remaining step and rush into his waiting arms. His embrace is crushing but comforting all the same as pent-up emotion bubbles out of me in sobbing tears. He's just like I remember with his close-cropped hair and sturdy build—strong, reliable, a pillar of support if ever there was one.

"Is that my Wren?" The sound of Gran's voice breaks me anew.

I let out another sob before pulling away from Matt and rubbing at my tear-streaked face. I peer past him into the house, blinking as my eyes adjust to the dimmer light.

It wasn't my imagination. Gran sits in her favorite chair, looking as well as ever with her glasses propped in her short, white perm and wearing her favorite violet outfit. Tabitha stands next to her chair, one hand over her gaping mouth. A tumbler of water falls from her other hand to flood the carpets, but I barely notice the mess.

They're here too. They're alive.

I detach from Matt and rush to Gran, falling to my knees in front of her chair and wrapping her in a careful but fierce hug. The sobbing comes even harder, all the emotion I bottled up in Faery springing free at the sight of my family.

"Wren. We thought—" Tabitha sniffles. "I worried you—" Another sharp inhale cuts off her words.

The front door squeaks closed as Matt joins us inside.

"I knew you were alive," Gran says. She pets my hair like she did when I was a child, smoothing her wrinkled hand down its length.

"I just knew it. My Wren is a fighter, I told people. She'll come back to me."

"I did," I say through my tears, my face still buried against her. "I'm here."

"Where were you?" Matt asks. "All this time…"

They thought I was dead. I can hear it in his voice, in Tabitha's.

But not Gran. She believed, even when she probably shouldn't have.

Finally, I pull away from her and wipe at my face again, trying to bring my tears under control.

"The kids?" I ask Tabitha. If they were here, surely, I'd have seen or heard them by now.

"With Robbie," she says, still staring at me like I'm a ghost. He must have come home too.

"You're all right, dear?" Gran asks.

I nod. "Yes. Better than now that I know you're all safe."

"It's you we were worried about." Tabitha wipes under her eyes, trying to hide the tears slipping free. "Scared us all half to death. I really thought…" She shakes her head again, leaving the thought unspoken. "What on earth happened?"

"You might want to sit down," I say. "This might be a little hard to believe."

And so, I tell them my story—the simple version of it anyway. I leave out the war, the battles, much of the magic, anything that might complicate what happened. I leave out Uncle Mark too. That's a whole can of worms I can't quite spill yet. Tabitha is close to breaking down as it is, and bringing up her lost dad? She'd probably faint on me.

I hadn't planned to tell them the truth. I thought I might tell them some recluse in the woods took me in and nursed me back to health.

But they're my family. I love them.

They deserve the truth, no matter how difficult or strange it may be.

They listen. There are plenty of shocked looks, curious glances, and questions, but not one of them calls me crazy or thinks I've lost it, as I feared. Actually, they seem rather openminded to the whole idea of Faery, all things considered.

"A whole different world," Matt says. It's one of the first comments he's made. At some point, he got up from his chair and started to pace. Now he leans against the wall by the window, occasionally glancing out as if the world might have changed completely during the time I told them my tale. I guess, in a way, it has.

"It sounds thrilling," Gran says, leaning back in her recliner, a satisfied look on her face. "And that handsome gentleman of yours. Sounds like you found quite the man."

"Gran," I groan. Somehow, it never gets easier to talk to her about guys, no matter how old I get.

"I might have stayed and enjoyed that some more," she adds.

Suddenly, I want to melt into the carpets like the glass of water Tabitha dropped that no one has bothered to wipe up yet. I didn't even give them the details of exactly the type of relationship Sigurd and I developed, but leave it to Gran to make the right assumptions.

"It's all so much," Tabitha says. Of us all, she's been the most surprised and had by far the most questions, ones I tried to answer as simply as I could. "I'm never letting my kids near those woods."

Probably a good idea, at least until they're old enough to understand. That's if she ever tells them.

"You know," Matt says, gazing out into the yard again. "Your description of that king from your stories sounds a lot like the man standing in the drive right now."

"What!" I squeak, leaping to my feet. I rush to the window, my jaw dropping open at the sight beyond. There, halfway up my grandmother's drive is Sigurd. A fae king just strolling up to a human house. The risk of it, the stupidity to—

My heart skips another beat. He's not alone. Matt goes rigid beside me, and all at once, I know he recognizes the other man with Sigurd.

His dad, Uncle Mark.

Matt can see him. He can see fae.

I don't have the chance to speak before Matt races to the door, flings it open, and rushes out toward the approaching fae.

"What on earth?" Tabitha exclaims. She moves toward the door and then freezes. Color flees her face, and she sways on her feet. For a moment, I fear she might faint.

And then it strikes me. She can see them too.

"Daddy," she whispers. And then she's running out the door and racing across the yard to Matt, where he's already pulled Uncle Mark into a hug as fierce as the one he gave me.

"My Mark has finally come home too."

I turn to look at Gran, who seems happy but completely calm, almost as if she expected this, but there's no way she could have. I didn't even know he was going to show up here of all places, especially not after how we left things at the door between worlds.

"You're worried but not surprised." Gran gives me a quizzical look and adjusts her glasses. She always sees way more than the rest of us and puts the pieces together with ease. "You saw him in that place you were in. In Faery?"

"I did," I confess. "I'm sorry I didn't mention it—him. I..." I glance back out the door to where Uncle Mark sits on the ground holding a weeping Tabitha. Matt sits next to them, clasping Uncle Mark's hand in his.

"It's best he came himself," Gran says when words fail me.

I suppose it is. He can tell them all his story, if Tabitha is able to pull herself together enough to hear it. Maybe today this is all they need. Sometimes, words can wait. "But you," I say. "You truly believed he was alive all this time. You're not surprised?"

Of all things, she laughs. "I am, but I'll give them all a few minutes together. It's not the first time he's showed up here since he left all those years ago."

"What?" I stare at her askance.

She rocks in her chair, looking thoughtful. "A couple years ago, he showed up in the yard. But he was quiet, almost like he didn't want me to see him. I didn't have my glasses on, so I couldn't be quite sure. I went in to get them, and by the time I returned, he was almost all the way across the yard and disappearing into the woods. But I knew it was him. I felt it in my bones, and these old bones know a thing or two."

I gape at her. "You saw him that day."

Gran could see the fae too. All this time, she'd have been able to see him, to talk to him, but he didn't know. He thought she couldn't. Uncle Mark feared none of them could.

"I did." She nods as if we're talking about something as simple as the weather. "But he wasn't ready to talk to me then. Not really. I know my son. I knew he'd come back when he was ready."

"He's been happy," I say, still dumbstruck by the fact that a miscommunication caused me so much grief.

All that time I was in Faery, Uncle Mark could have just explained things to Gran if he'd known she could see him or had the courage to try once more. But then, things might not have turned out how they have, and I'm not sure I'd risk changing this outcome, given the chance.

"He has a great life," I continue. "He found a new love, a true one this time."

She nods, thoughtful. "As I always hoped he would."

Through the edge of the open door, I can see Sigurd's arm where he sits in Gran's rocking chair, of all things. The brief sight is so odd I have to blink a few times to make sure I'm not imagining things. A fae king on Gran's porch, just hanging out in a rocker like he has all the time in the world and this place isn't toxic to him. I shake my head and glance back at Gran.

She's still smiling, somehow seeing so much and taking it all in her stride.

"He's waiting for you." She nods toward Sigurd. From her place in the chair, she can probably see even more than me.

"I can't leave you. I just got back." I return to her chair, kneeling by the side, my arms propped over the armrest.

"You kids, always fussing over me." She clucks her tongue. "I'm stronger than I look."

"I know, but I..."

Gran cups my cheek in her hand, and I savor the moment. "I'm so glad you're back, Wren. I love you so much, and I'm so happy you're as well as I believed. Truly. But you don't have to stay here on account of me if you'd rather be somewhere else."

I shake my head. "But then who?"

She pulls her hand back into her lap. "Matt and I talked about him staying with me for a while."

"Matt has work. His deployment."

Gran just smiles. "He's honorably discharged. He wrote to me about it, asking to stay. Said he wants a civilian life, a quiet life, at least for a while. But, Wren, I think he also wants to give you a break. Let you stretch your wings for a while, like he did. Matt knows how much you wanted to travel, as do I."

The tears come back again, one slipping down my cheek before I can stop it.

"I started to tell you before you left for work that day," she continues, "but it didn't seem right to spoil his surprise. Matt wanted to tell you all about it himself when he got here. Plus, I knew you might fuss, and I didn't want to make you late."

That was what she wanted to tell me. And here I thought it was another lecture about college or something. In the end, it was about me getting out of our small town, but more than that. If Matt truly wants to stay here for a while, live with Gran, then I can go. Maybe split my time between the two worlds for a while.

Gran pats my hand. "Spread your wings, Wren. Go have your adventure."

A huff of laughter slips from my lips. "I already did that."

"A new one then," she says. Something sparkles in her eyes. But she blinks, and it's gone. "Maybe with that handsome gentleman of yours."

My cheeks warm at the comment. Even if Sigurd didn't have fae hearing, he'd have heard that one. Another tear slides free, and I hastily wipe it away.

"Would you like to meet him?" I ask.

Gran smacks my hand. "About time you asked."

I laugh at her antics and help her up. As I lead Gran out onto the porch to meet Sigurd, who now stands by the railing, looking resplendent and smiling at us, my heart has never been so full. The people I love most are safe. They're all together. And the future has never looked quite so bright.

Thank you for reading *Bound to the Fae King*!

Curious what happened to Galen?

Check out his continuing story in *Forgiving a Fae Warrior*!

Reviews are so important for authors, so I hope you'll take a moment to share your thoughts on this book.
Stay in the loop on all news related to this series and others by signing up for my newsletter at: www.authormeganvandyke.com/newsletter/

ALSO BY MEGAN VAN DYKE

The Castamar Duology

The Musician and the Monster (Beauty and the Beast)
The Artist and the Dragon (Sleeping Beauty)

Reimagined Fairy Tales Collection

Second Star to the Left (Peter Pan)
The Ugly Stepsister (Cinderella & Snow White)
The Alice Curse (Alice in Wonderland)

The Courts of Faery

A Gift for a Fae Warrior (Optional Prequel)
A Bargain with the Fae King (Book 1)
Bound to the Fae King (Book 2)
Forgiving a Fae Warrior (Book 2.5 - Optional Novella)
Destined for the Fae King (Book 3)
Marked by the Fae King (Book 4)

Stolen Empire

Captive of the Stolen Empire (Book 1)

About the Author

Megan Van Dyke is a fantasy romance author with a love for all things that include magic and romance, especially fairy tales and anything with a happily ever after. Many of her stories include themes of family (whether born into or found) and a sense of home and belonging, which are important aspects of her life as well. When not writing, Megan loves to cook, play video games, explore the great outdoors, and spend time with her family. A southerner by birth and at heart, Megan currently lives with her family in Florida.

Connect with Megan
www.authormeganvandyke.com
www.authormeganvandyke.com/newsletter/
facebook.com/AuthorMeganVanDyke
instagram.com/authormeganvandyke
tiktok.com/@authormeganvandyke
bookbub.com/authors/megan-van-dyke